THE RED SON

Mark Anzalone

WildBlue Press.com

THE RED SON published by:
WILDBLUE PRESS
P.O. Box 102440
Denver, Colorado 80250

WILDBLUE PRESS is registered at the U.S. Patent and Trademark Offices.

ISBN 978-1-948239-42-4   Trade Paperback
ISBN 978-1-948239-41-7   eBook

Interior Formatting by Elijah Toten
www.totencreative.com

THE RED SON

DEDICATION

For Stephanie and Max, my Sea and Sky.

ACKNOWLEDGEMENTS

This book would not exist but for the unstinting efforts of Steven J. Anzalone, my brother and keeper; Walker Kornfeld, my editor and literary surgeon; and Craig Carda, enabler to us all.

PROLOGUE

The retreat of the Great Darkness made a funeral of the sky, a bittersweet separation of past and present, fading memories filling the spaces between. I was more aware of the sky than myself. I never would have guessed it had been an entire year since my last waking recollection. It would take me some time to learn that the rest of the world shared my amnesia—what remained of the world, anyway.

I was already on my feet as the night lifted in earnest, tumbling upward, clutching tightly the time it had stolen from the world. A wailing moved in tandem with the vanishing dark, a collective caterwaul signaling the end of something familiar, if not altogether dear.

I was pleased when I realized my sisters were already in my hands, their curving metal smiles balancing the gathering dawn. Even stained with so much blood, they retained their cold beauty, rivaling the iciest brook that ever babbled through the apex of Autumn. Their pommels were calm and steady, and their laughter at my awakening sparkled through the air. My smile was automatic. They were my darlings.

I did not wonder if my father still slept upon my back. I could feel his seething dreams surging through me as surely as my own blood. The newborn light laid his shadow upon the forest, his massive axe-head showing monstrous and lethal, looming over me as ever he had. I was careful not to rouse him without the promise of killing. His anger demanded an awful price.

With my family accounted for, I examined my surroundings. The Darkness had all but evaporated, and the woods lay awash in the morning rays, scrubbing away the shadows with sunlight. But for all its polish, the world could no longer glitter.

I remember quite clearly my first look at what learned men would later term an *Obscurra*—a relic of the Great Darkness, some bizarre industry performed by madmen or monsters, for purposes unknown, if not entirely unknowable. I had awoken in its shadow—a rambling mansion made from uncountable human bones. The rough calcium of its construction all but ignored the strongest beams of direct light, begrudging the day only its sallow eastern face—a glaring prominence of squinting windows pinched dark and narrow by overhanging gables made from interlocking ribs. Its Victorian and Gothic flourishes summoned the image of a cemetery city of smoldering ivory, the dead wandering its cold lanes in a blind stupor. The structure's collective bearing of close-packed bones spoke to a preoccupation with performing the additional work of skin, closing off its innards to sun and strangers, barring entrance to the hallowed halls of its bleached body. I could not repress my want to glimpse beyond the nearest window. Skins—likely the wrappers for all the smartly placed bones—lined its interior. It was a bio-architectural inversion of the human body.

I was fixated by the place, its apparent violation of common sense a vulgar confirmation of a dream's ability to overcome waking, to stand defiant and solid beneath the sun. Yet, I would learn soon enough, I was wrong to think the manse of bones an exception to a conventional world. Such desecrations of the commonplace, though varying wildly in scale and scope and theme, had invaded the Earth like an army of alien eidolons marched out from the mists of the missing year, elbowing their way into cities, streets, caves, ballrooms, bedrooms—anywhere space and madness would allow.

I walked awestruck for days afterward, through cities broken by raw, violent revelation. Diffusing like smoke, the dead, dying, sick, and insane choked streets and alleyways, filled skyscrapers repurposed to madhouses, and tumbled into graves as deep and wide as canyons. I wandered for weeks through the fallout of the global nightmare, my family and I marveling at the new-world absurdities, living beneath a sky that had indeed proven capable of falling. I only watched—approvingly, I confess—as mankind, on a scale never known, collapsed beneath the combined weight of truth and mystery.

Religions burned to the ground almost overnight, as neither gods nor their books could ever again be trusted. Science fell to the gutters, wasted to bones, starved thin and wan for lack of sustaining facts and figures. Collective man was naked beneath the moon once more. To be sure, it was many years before mankind recovered some measure of its former contrivances and doldrums, but even then it walked a doubtful path between the tombstones of that lost year, the year of the Great Darkness.

There is darkness in everything, I have since concluded. The explicit variety that falls from the sky at night may be perhaps a sort of externalized counterpart of the more metaphysical brand that lurks the other side of our skin. I believe it was the joining of these two types, indeed their fusion, which led to the Great Darkness of 1999. This union resulted in nothing less than the construction of a Dream—where mind and matter conspire to supplant reality. And while no one remembers precisely what happened during our year-long blackout (forgetfulness has always been the bane of dreams), its echo still plays out across the world, tolling a dissonance of broken faiths—in solid worlds, and even the prospect of certain spiritual enterprises.

It was this metaphysical darkness—the kind slinking just out of sight, more wondrous than its traditional counterpart— that I'd always shared a special kinship. Along with its equally useful cousin, silence, they'd long accompanied me on many an excursion. At my beck and call, they provided me with certain advantages that made me especially good at my work.

But now, I could sense that they too had emerged from the Great Darkness altered. Whereas mankind was now broken, a mad fraction of its former self, darkness and silence were decidedly . . . more robust. Still hidden from the waking world, still forces beyond the understanding of the average person, but more prominent, more alive—more comfortable in this brand new world.

On balance, the Darkness should have made things better. But the world persisted as a graveyard, a landscape where dreams festered for want of realization. Despite the lakes of bile, the towers of teeth, the underground theatres, and countless other *Obscurra*, there was still an incompleteness to our existence—*we woke up,* and our lives were made worse by the fact that we now had some idea of what we were missing.

CHAPTER ONE

I am often misconstrued as a monster. One that has gruesomely repurposed the corpses of his family into killing instruments. While that description is somewhat faithful in a purely material sense, it misses the forest for the trees. Most conspicuously absent is that I am, first and foremost, an artist. The murders are but provision.

As for my family—another entirely misinterpreted subject—they persist as my best works to date. Together, we have created some splendid pieces, which have warranted no small amount of attention, albeit for all the wrong reasons. The proper study of the nature of my work, apart from its necessary departures from societal norms, would reveal a specific meditation concerning both the nature of my canvas and the secret dream I attempt to sculpt from its death. Flesh and blood may be the clays and paints of my medium, but dreams are the purpose for their contribution.

Despite my countless attempts, I have yet to achieve a true masterwork. I have always failed to properly conjure my true subject—the dream. While each of my pieces is its own truth, its own attempt at dream, they are all ultimately dead, stillborn. The fact is, nothing can live here, and nothing ever will. Sadly, this may be the only aspect of my work that is indeed properly understood.

This gets to the current futility of my undertaking, to what my skills can only, truly reveal. Despite all I've accomplished, despite the many galleries and exhibits of shadows and skin, I know only one truth best of all—art is merely the corpse of a dream.

Art attempts to change the world, enlarge its lonely box of living and dying. Nothing new can happen here, not yet. The Deadworld—the solid, banal, and ultimately inferior world of which we must all take part—would have it no other way. It is the obligation of every artist—every true artist, that is—to improve the universe, but because our canvases and brushes and paints are all dead, we can only outline life in ashes—never reveal it. My art, even for its vast departures from convention, is no different. For the first time, however, I may have stumbled across something that can change all that.

Not long ago, in the bowels of an abandoned chemical factory lost to the woods, during a particularly rambling art tour, my sisters and I were busy unpacking an individual who had momentarily focused my artistic senses. I was in the process of coaxing my subject's bowels to the floor to make room for the waxen statue that would replace them. The name of the piece—*A View of The Soul, The Curtains Parted*. I'd just pulled the body into the air, using a makeshift complex of rope and pulley, and was eager to begin molding the wax figure, a deliberately vague thing intended to demonstrate the soul's volatility. But to my surprise, something other than the traditional fillings of a riven body drifted out, caught upon a thermal of dead air. It was a piece of yellowed paper, old and covered in dried blood.

The paper was unremarkable but for five names written upon it, all of them stacked neatly atop one another—a list. Strangely, it wasn't even wet for its placement within the recently disemboweled body. Apart from its resistance to blood, there was nothing explicitly unusual about it, yet I think my life changed the moment I held it, felt the heft of its mystery. Beneath the list was a promise, as there is beneath all things—but this one was close to the surface, in no need of knives to be revealed. All it required was sleep. And so, without another thought, I slept, naked upon the steaming floor, a smile snatched from hope lining my lips.

***

I dreamed I was one of countless wolves, breathing fog into a cold, black sky. We were ravenous. Something else came among us, in us. It entered through the gates of our hunger, drawing us together, building a single ravening void out of individual starving spaces, until all shared the same endless hunger. Its memories raced through us like lightning, its mind emerging from our collective bottomless guts. Composing our thoughts, it wove them together into a single and terrible awareness. All but lost within the crush of this new, coalescing existence, I glimpsed, if only for a moment, the thing I was becoming. I was old as reflection, taller than fear, colder than death. My voice a sudden interrupted breath, my name the silence of conscience. I rose from the earth as the sum of wolves, and the world trembled beneath my gaze.

***

When I awoke, I had the distinct impression something vast and monstrous had moved over me while I slept, the portentous echo of its passage still shrinking into the distance. Compelled to scan my surroundings, I detected nothing amiss. But I couldn't deny the change now daring to be discovered. The matter took only a moment to resolve—the world had become lighter, slight but appreciable, alleviated perhaps only by the removal of a layer of finest dust. What it signified I was unsure. But one thing was indeed certain— the dream of wolves was the cause. There was something else as well, confided to me through sleep's last breath—a whispered promise of changes yet to come. The intimation was vast despite the smallness of its conveyance—the potential to change the world wrapped in a moment's Red Dream.

I left the factory at nightfall, during the coldest rainstorm of the season. My senses prickled, agitated by the ceaseless touch of icy rain. This was by design. I wanted every nuance of my journey fortified against forgetting. This was a special time—the beginning. Of life's phases, it was most powerful, mystical. It was the seed from which all things emerged, the point against which they would be measured. All my ironies, truths, failures, and victories would be balanced against the moment it all began—during the coldest September rain I could remember.

My father was asleep upon my back, his ever-present rage a soothing warmth. Only the loudest shocks of thunder moved his spirit, sounding so much like his own terrible laughter. Night owls to the last, my sisters were tucked into their beds, but not asleep. I could hear them giggling as they caught the lightning when it flashed, balancing its blaze across their serrated smiles. It was fall, and we were all together, at the beginning of something special. I smiled at the thought of having received autumn's orange blessing. Whatever inscrutable thing moves behind the amber fires of summer's death, I do not know. But if not a god, what then?

The calling behind the list seemed obvious to me, even without the blood and its insertion within a corpse. The names must be stricken from the list, and by that action, instigate some wider, perhaps cosmic process. The world seemed lifted from my shoulders as I walked the darkness. It revealed, possibly for the first time, a combination of elements that not often occupied the same space, their natures incompatible—will and wonder.

I wanted to set aside the practical considerations of my craft, to be exclusively guided by the weightless drift of dreams. But such practicalities are unfortunately required. This world is no fan of my work, and it makes every effort to see my art struck entirely from existence, if not just the headlines. Disguises and stealth and all the other maneuverings of common murder must occasionally intrude upon my artistic reverie. These distractions, in direct proportion to their exercise, diminishes the quality of my final creation. Or, in sum, too much applied reality can damage—weigh-down—a would-be work of transcendent art. Given this, I was thrilled the calling behind the list required a significant departure from my usual catalogue of considerations. Some measure of self-awareness and strategy would be required, but I was largely flying blind, only a sheaf of paper for a rudder in uncertain skies.

I floated through thickets and meadows, the shadows of dead trees falling across me, their appreciably colder shadows making gooseflesh of my exposed skin. The further into the woods I pushed, the more treetops and brambles converged, exuding the shelter of gigantic, enclosed places. Like a carrot strung before a goat, I chased the specter of the Red Dream, the wolves, and the thing that became them.

After weeks, something finally stirred within the mystery I walked, something coming into focus, if not clarity. It was dusk, so I could still see through the growing darkness, even as the shadows quickly gnawed at the periphery of my vision. While the night was closing off the world, the pull of an invisible force kept me one step ahead of the advancing blackness. Soon, the night was all around me, framing me within a single blot of dying amber. The dim light drifted beyond me, letting the darkness crawl across my body, soft and silent. The shrinking twilight managed to survive only a few seconds longer before melting around a small wooden cabin, leaving behind a ghost of warmth the cold breeze quickly exorcised. The tugging became the slightest cobweb, persuading me in the direction of the crumbling shack. I entered through a hole that had once been a door and strode into its blackened innards.

The first room was meticulously arranged with all manner of bones and stolen funerary fetishes, ranging from gravestones to whittled bones. A black carpet stitched from funeral attire lay unfurled across the floor, flowing patchwork and dust-covered beyond an archway fashioned from sculpted human jawbones. Throughout was scattered and heaped the dried remains of lilies.

This was clearly an echo of the Great Darkness of 1999. It was pleasing to imagine the madness that once filled the space I now occupied. Of course, imagination was all anyone could use to envision that lost year. Even I, a man who was no stranger to the bizarre, was left with no memory, nothing but the aftermath. I assume that fact also owes to the reach of the Deadworld, plucking out the precious memories of the only true freedom mankind has ever enjoyed—in this life, at least. But the wonderful aftermath, when the world woke from nightmare . . . Towers made from teeth, lakes of glowing bile, underground theatres of strange intent, houses built to the scale of monsters, and on and on. By the gods, what a fallout!

The shack, like the rest of the world, had been visited by the secret dream of the human condition—expressed for exactly one year and then wiped clean from memory, if not matter. For all I knew, the room could have been the product of my very own Darkness-fueled hijinks. Though, to be honest, while the theme and its respective execution were fine enough, it was hardly the caliber of my own works—those created outside of the Darkness.

The chamber beyond the archway was an improvement, however. It sported a throne made from tumbledown tombstones, and it was crowded with dozens of modeled skeletons. Every one of them stood frozen in various postures, but all pleaded with a visibly aloof Funeral King—a skeleton attired in purple robes made from dyed rags, crowned with a bone circlet joined by gold and silver-flecked teeth, seated upon a throne of cemetery stones.

It was not an entirely uncommon tableau, as Post-Darkness images of the Funeral King were found across much of the Northern states, as well as scattered around parts of rural Great Britain. Even so, it was an impressive piece.

The Funeral King, it turned out, was not the most rewarding find within the cabin. Heaped in a corner was a stack of newspaper clippings. The very first article I perused concerned none other than me. "The Family Man killer turns artist into living canvas." I believe it was the first time I'd been called by the name—*the Family Man*. I had once let slip to the artist mentioned in the clipping a small particle of my history. He was a kinetic bit of art—still breathing, in awe of what he had become—and supplied my admirers with insights I'd shared with him about myself. As he was an artist, I chose to share a bit more than was my custom. Thus, my new name was born. Clearly, I am more than the mere sum of my family's bones, but I do rather enjoy the name.

The next article I selected concerned a church built in the city of Suttercraft, three years ago, by the given date. One of the carpenters who contributed to the effort was also named in the piece—Hayden Trill. I generally don't do things in any kind of order, but it was nice to see that his was the very first name on my list.

CHAPTER TWO

When the town of Suttercraft came into view, I could see that it was in the process of being fed upon. Trees rose like stalks of towering fungus erupting from its spoiling flesh, and green waves of hungry woods had eaten away most of its roads and parking lots. Houses and businesses were hollow and broken. This place was merely a rotting trunk, and the people inhabiting it were no more than tomb-worms. I quickly determined that the place would pose little threat to me—it was already dead.

The city was not at all unknown to me. I'd heard of its penchant for producing strange black coffins from the churned earth of its planting fields, basements, and other deep places. I was also aware of the dreadful bodies that were removed from those coffins, looking much larger and fiercer in death than they ever had in life. However, beneath all the chatter about caskets and corpses, there lurked an even more fantastic tale—according to certain dreamers, the souls of the deceased citizens of Suttercraft were systematically reborn into those inhuman husks, and once returned to life, they rose to take their place within some vast and wicked enterprise beneath the earth. Such stories, if at all true, give me hope that one day, dreams won't be forced to hide behind sleep, but might find their way upon the earth to do the good work of abolishing this Deadworld.

I made my way through crooked streets, pinch-tight alleyways and sluggish fog, all of which lent the city an odd appearance of being either scribbled out or partially erased from the paper of time and space. I stopped momentarily, listening to church bells sound out the hour. They cushioned my thoughts with their overstuffed notes, lifting my mind from the sonic monotony of an ordinary day.

As I voyaged through the corpse-town, my fascination with Hayden Trill began to swell. What weird and wonderful things might result from killing him? I wouldn't normally work on a subject lest the outcome was—in that spectacular but fleeting moment—the embodiment of a forgotten dream, but my feeling was that I'd been invited to work on a much grander piece, in which Mr. Trill was merely a single, masterful brushstroke.

Pausing within the rippling shadows of a weeping willow, I reexamined the mystery of Suttercraft. Suddenly, I was quite curious as to the number of times I might be required to put down this mysterious Mr. Trill—and whether I should acquire a shovel to expedite the process.

I found Mr. Trill's residence easily enough, as it was listed in a phone book I found in an empty library. The subject of my next piece lived in an apartment building strangled by thick ivies, which no doubt conducted the last of its metropolitan juices through its hungry green tubers. The overall result was nothing less than a house half-eaten. A wide, cracked balcony sat high within the concrete crown of the dwelling, waving its massive arms above it, a living canopy of shifting green. A single lantern dangled from an overhanging branch, whispering amber light at the pooling shadows. I knew the balcony coupled to the room of my quarry—why else would it be there?

I kept well out of sight, moving behind the town's beautiful curtain of decay, allowing the germinating emptiness to erase all traces of my passage. The shadows barely reckoned my presence until I was well past the building's foyer. A warm breeze wandered the overlarge room, gently disturbing the billowing curtains that fell like filthy fabric waterfalls from the tops of the tall windows, splashing in ragged waves across the unclean floor. The spacious lobby held a singular note of choking desolation, playing to the void that frolicked its hollows. I moved to the stairwell, drifting upward like a whispered prayer, silent and secret. There were persons, after a fashion, ambling through the dim hallways, living and moving for reasons no one cared to know. The dust in the air was thick, playing like clouds of lethargic gnats idling between the fading bars of light projecting across the floor from soiled windows. I felt like a ghost, haunting the spaces of a tumbledown house, just a forgotten echo of the living, eternally condemned to chase the dust through endless halls of stumbling shadows.

I entered the room neighboring the apartment that connected to the balcony. The place was like a photograph after a flood, colorless and faint. An old man slept within, dried and crumbling beneath the bitter weight of too much time. He was perfectly pointless—hardly suitable for my purposes. Still, I was feeling charitable. Finally, I allowed him to express the power the flesh of his washed-out existence might have enclosed, had only it been fashioned by the songs of fallen angels, or the bright nightmares of lost children. In his last moments, the man seemed to appreciate what he was becoming, after I had thrown off the tomb of his flesh, allowing him to gaze at the dream beneath. There was so little of the man remaining I was not long at my work. I cleaned myself off in the tiny cove of a bathroom and proceeded out the window onto the thick tendrils of ivy.

I gained the balcony above in but a few moments, inching around the flickering sheet of light from its lantern. Unlocking its door barely broke my stride as I secreted myself inside. The room was drab, sparsely decorated, and hadn't been cleaned for some time. Everywhere was sprinkled the simple, stupid details that spoke to nothing save an occupant of the least imaginative variety. After a thorough investigation, all I discovered was that for some reason, a power beyond the bid of nature desired the death of a man who, for all intents and purposes, was only alive in the most basic of definitions. Doubting this conclusion enough to inspect the room a second time, I searched through its every detail, interrogating each pore of pointlessness. Mercifully, something stood out during my second look. It wasn't a detail I found, but a generality—the room was too eager to convince. It was all wrong, betraying a confidence born of skill. The furniture, the decorations, everything. Like a smiling corpse, the room was an expression without emotion. The interior appeared exactly as it should, but there was a precision and restraint to it all—a deliberate calculus of dullness. The room was a mask.

I searched with new eyes, looking for the edges of the disguise, wishing to pull it back. Of course, I felt like a fool when I realized what distinguished the apartment from all the other wan spaces of the fading building. It was the balcony—or more accurately, its view. The lofty vantage delivered a fine look at a small church leaning into the woods, where saprophytic legions searched its cracked skin, seeking nourishment.

No sooner had I turned to make for the church than I detected something strange, the implications of which were entirely fascinating. Through some means I assumed directly linked to the ominous Red Dream and the list that supplied it, I somehow perceived an echo of *someone else's dream*. The fading vision haunted the spaces of the balcony, faintly traced by the silence of lantern light and coiling shadows of ivy. I could see it as plainly as the moon looking down upon me. It maintained an etherealness, declaring its connection to the other side. The fragment was only slightly alive, like smoldering ashes after a fire. I could barely make out the dim shape of a singular purpose, timeless and thankless in its pursuit. That, and a prominence of sorrow nearly hardened to complete hatred. Before I could contemplate the wayward dream any longer, it died into a commanding silence, as though by the authority of dead kings.

The now vanished dream undoubtedly belonged to Mister Trill, of that I was largely certain. It was simply logical to assume the supernaturalism surrounding the list and the persons named within it were connected. But that was only logic, just mindless, meandering connections. There was also an unscientific connection, thankfully, one that I could feel in my bones, granting me knowledge through mystery rather than matter. This deeper intimation scored the name of the dreamer into the dream, and I was now wiser for it.

I went back inside, deciding to sleep in the residence hosting my most recent work, before heading to the church. I hoped to chase down my quarry's dream before it disappeared too deeply into sleep. Settling on the small bed, I proudly looked upon the congealing piece I'd created earlier—out of a man who lived only to supply misery its living equivalents. But now, wonder—as much as I could coax from so sorry a subject—reclaimed the spaces once filled by so much loitering debris. Had the glistening piece still possessed them, I'm confident its eyes would have shined with an abundance of gratitude. With that vision in mind, I drifted into slumber.

***

Unfortunately, I wasn't brought any closer to the desired dream, but I did manage to glimpse something sleeping beneath Suttercraft. I saw strange coffins nestled in deep earth, waiting like monsters under a child's bed. Far deeper into the black soil, within a stratum of earth so old it was little more than liquid darkness, I spied a casket the size of the entire city. The dream conducted me beyond the petrified wood of its construction, allowing me to peer at the thing within. Rotting and waiting within that damp, titanic box was an entity as ancient to the world as it was utterly alien to it. The sound of the creature's patience was bottomless and beckoning. I could only guess at the quality—or quantity—of death required to transmit life to something so far beyond all this blowing dust. I immediately understood why the White Gaia had pressed the thing so closely to her bosom, for if life were to reach such a thing . . . .

As I drifted away from the timeless sleeper, a familiar gaze burned into my dream, looking at me with equally bottomless and beckoning impatience. I could feel the scorching red hunger of countless wolves wash across me like searing wind. My dream was melting from the mounting heat, gazes and hungers collapsing into a single surging stare. The dream was no longer my own. The new dreamer crushed me into the shape of a wolf, and a cosmic starvation overfilled my guts. I couldn't contain the emptiness.

***

I sprang awake in a slick of sweat, my stomach gusting red and bottomless. The dream still lingered the room, fogging windows and mirrors with its hot breath. My mind turned instantly to killing Mister Trill—not dressing him in finest dream. I was lost to a vision that was little more than a gaping maw. Instinctively, I collected my family—they were aglow, nearly blinding, with the same blazing hunger. They were particularly suspectable to such cravings, as even in life they were never subtle creatures, always too eager and willing when blood needed spilling.

The Red Dream was no longer new to me, but now it had escaped from sleep, taking refuge within us all. My family's collective frenzy nearly threw me from the window and down upon the twisting ivies that searched all sides of the undead house. Once down the walls and across the courtyards of unkept vegetation, I found my feet placed firmly upon the path to the church. It seemed my quarry would not be allowed to survive the night.

I forced myself to slacken my pace and absorb the sights. From the moon-frosted meadows, I could clearly see the corpse of the town splayed out across the encroaching forest. Suttercraft looked like some dead-brown and drying serpent's husk, its crooked gambrel spines occasionally breeching the tops of the trees, revealing the places where it had fallen so long ago. I tried to focus on Mr. Trill—and the fresh changes his death might furnish the world—but my father would tolerate no more delays, and I quickly found myself thrust into the shadows surrounding the church. Instantly, and almost by my family's will alone, my hunter's silence spread out all around me, and my thoughts disappeared into my sisters' famished smiles.

The church was deserted—long since abandoned by the Lord and his flock. I entered through the front door and beheld the silence. It was old and unbroken, blossoming from the desert of dust that lay across the altar and pews. I moved to the rear of the church, leaving the silence as I'd found it. The rooms in the back contained nothing of interest save for the pleasant comfort of forgotten places, having slipped quietly the boundaries of memory, tumbling into oblivion. I moved to the cellar door, the cold of the underground lapping at my feet. Strangely, it was nailed shut from the opposite side. I wondered if Mister Trill had some idea of my coming, having been warned from something that walked the other side of the world—an opposing force to that which had invited me to transform him. However, if nailed-up doors were all he could offer in defense . . .

I returned to the exterior of the church, looking for a way into the cellar. It took me some time to discover the entrance, cleverly concealed beneath the ruins of an old shed. Opening the door, a new silence overtook me. The sound of waiting— the sound of a hunter—permeated everything. The darkness and silence belonged to someone who had cultivated it, trained it, cared for it.

I had carelessly allowed a white blade of moonlight to slice past me when I opened the door. The cold light cut into the subterranean depths, stabbing deep into the cellar. Quickly and quietly, I closed the door, repairing the dark, but the master of those deep places would now be alerted to my intrusion. I pressed on.

It was clear what I stalked was no mere human, but a man-of-prey. Whether he was a true artist, however, remained to be seen. I joined my silence with the hunter's, and I moved through the gloom to the bottom of the stairs. Deep in the underground, a weak light flickered—candlelight. This was either a distraction or a signpost. The smell of burning wax hung thick. The candles had been lit long before my arrival. I moved closer to the dancing radiance, wary of surprise. Somewhere, wrapped in obedient shadows, was the other. He would be waiting for me to make a mistake. I would make none. The darkness was not my own, but it would serve me nonetheless.

I slipped behind the flitting shadows of the candlelit room, touring as much as stalking. Even in such circumstances, I would spare nothing my wonder. The next chamber I entered was large and crowded with the forgotten ornaments of faith, and as I rounded a stack of boxes, barely touched by the trembling light, I was confronted by the bodies of over a dozen crucified men. They were arranged in no discernible order, most little more than crumpled paper dolls. All of them rotting upon crosses beneath the dimmest light, arms wide—welcoming the flies that wreathed them. Hayden Trill was indeed an artist.

Death had frozen horrified and pleading expressions to their faces, save one. The most recent victim, a corpse less than a week old, wore a death mask of an entirely different disposition—rage and indignation. This man was fierce even in death, his sunken eyes still holding echoes of a terrible and interrupted purpose—my hidden host had killed one of his own.

The crucifixions looked like giant crumbling flowers emerging from the lightless earthen floor, and the dusky basement seemed the perfect greenhouse to foster them. The slain hunter—its darkest flower by far—loomed above me, a cutting stare for thorns, bearing a heady fragrance of withered rage and broken purpose. As its shadow fell across me, I could feel the void of its dream, still and sterile.

The garden was pruned and pampered, carefully arranged and maintained with the diligence of a doting mother. I wondered what manner of thing should want me to destroy such an artist. The moment contained a hint of whispered purpose, suggesting perhaps that the beauty of the man's work required my intervention, to allow it to spread and take root.

Books and journals lay scattered across a nearby table. A slave to my overdeveloped curiosity, I began to read from them, remorseful for my rudeness. The books were all so very pious, bordering on pretentious. His journals, however, were not difficult to tolerate. They were the reflections of a man who lived inside a cold obligation, a mechanical penance that unfolded with small emphasis upon its material effects. The reward for his labors was intangible and withheld, merely the hope of reward. His deathly garden was not an end, but a pleasantly necessary side effect of his means. He was an unconscious artist—perhaps the most powerful kind—one who forgets themselves entirely within their work.

I didn't need to read the journals long to realize the identity of the man I hunted. He was known as The Crucifier. It was a much less subtle title than my own, and I'm fairly certain it missed the point of his undertaking entirely—as much as my own moniker missed the point of my work, subtlety or no. According to one of his journals, he saw himself as the reincarnated fifth prefect of Judea—Pontius Pilate. He professed nothing less than the destruction of all false prophets, which from the number of his works, were more numerous than I expected.

Initially, I continued with the journals, hoping to convince the killer I was off my guard, too distracted to afford a proper vigilance. But as I descended further into a particular journal, something did in fact surprise me—a drawing of a pack of daemonic, hungry wolves. It was as if the Crucifier had transferred the image directly from my own dream. However, unlike my dream, his picture included an additional presence—a solitary creature standing amid the sea of wolves, hooded and gripping a red crook. The words scrawled above the figure read, "The Shepherd of Wolves."

Unfortunately, my preoccupation did indeed cost me my vigilance. The Crucifier was already upon me, cloaked in hunter's silence. As he charged from beyond the light, my sister leapt into my hand, grinning through the shadows, whispering a warning from betwixt her metal teeth. I took several steps backward, placing Mr. Trill in front of the candles, silhouetting him.

A large, ornate hammer was swung at me in a blur, and I seized the arm holding it. I tossed Mr. Trill into the darkness that obeyed him, cowing the shadows rising against me at his behest. Across the chamber, I heard his hammer clang to the floor, far behind the candlelight. I closed the distance and the hunter bent low, avoiding my sister's flashing teeth. Stepping back and lowering his shoulder, he lunged at me with the force of a bull. Anchoring myself in the shadows that would have denied me, forcing them into service, I stood immovable. His momentum crashed across me like a wave tossed against a mountain. He stumbled backward, stunned. I delivered him to the ground with a fist, readying both sisters for the kill.

Immediately, Mr. Trill was thrown from the floor as if by unseen hands, brandishing a small silver blade. Hissing like a snake, it struck out all around me, arcs of blood tracing its rapid movements. My sisters greeted polished fangs with steel smiles, filling the air with their glittering laughter and the blood of my opponent. His strength was conditioned well beyond ordinary limits, born from the inspired repetitions his chosen calling exerted upon both his mind and body. More importantly, our respective might was an extension of our dreams—and mine was the night terror to his nightmare.

Realizing this as well, he attempted a formidable retreat, at one point drawing a bladed arc in his wake that nearly opened my retina. I would have happily allowed him escape—call it a courtesy between predators—but he was on my list. Just as he all but escaped into the darkness I'd stolen from him, my sister left my hand, flying across the room and finding his spine. His body fell at the feet of its own shadow, stretching long and twisted by the dancing candlelight. I stood over him in my new darkness, looming. His eyes glowed with fury, raging at his unresponsive body, a broken vessel no longer capable of killing or crucifying. I let him watch the shadows he no longer commanded fill my eyes. No words were exchanged, for what was there to say?

Suddenly, from upon my back I could feel a terrible unrest. My father was awake—his time had come. I lifted my great forebear from his resting place, swinging him high above my head, his edged face gleaming with the amber glow of candlelight. The massive axe passed through the crippled hunter so smoothly, I thought I'd missed him entirely.

CHAPTER THREE

When the candlelight began to die down, the shadows grew wide and indistinct as they joined with the larger body of darkness that flooded the under-church, and still I sat upon the stone floor, wondering. After the first night, the light completely passed away, leaving only my memory of candlelit spaces to illuminate the basement. Though the blackness had become absolute, I still felt the cold shadows of over a dozen crosses pushing softly against the currents of flowing darkness, refusing to melt back into oblivion. When the second night came and went, I was still sitting upon the floor, losing myself in the cool stream of silence pouring from corpses and cold candle wax, from old books and dried blood.

Interpreting silence was one of the first lessons my mother taught me, when I was but a child. In the middle of the night, during one of the fiercest thunderstorms I can remember, I was huddled in the corner of a room, wincing at the thunder. My mother knelt down beside me, placed her lips almost upon my ear, and whispered, "It's not the thunder you should be listening to, but the silence it leaves behind. Before there was anything, there was silence, and after everything is gone, silence will remain. All that ever was, or could be, whispers its soul into the sound of silence—and the only thing you will ever need to do, to know anything at all, is listen to it."

Within the piling dust I imagined the thing that held me in its sight, driving me onward. I conjured images of the Shepherd with the red crook, standing tall and solemn upon cresting, frothing waves of hungry wolves. I fantasized the thing in service to a secreted queen of murder, deep in her hive far below the earth. She wore a bloodied crown and held an ornate rusted knife in each of her many crimson-dripping hands. She was surrounded by her retinue of worker-killers, orchestrating the red business of murder. I smiled when I thought of her looking like my mother. But beyond my imaginings, I couldn't help but feel shameful—I had brought an untimely end to a wonderful dreamer, who had waged as fierce a war against the Mother of the Dead as myself. Still, as before, I could feel purpose behind my actions—a grand scheme that moved within and without me, gathering strength beyond death, preparing. Whatever the reason behind my new calling, it grew all the more forceful and terrible when I found a familiar list of names in the pockets of both the Crucifier and the hunter he had slain. Most important and perplexing of all—my own name appeared on one of the lists. Something familiar drifted down beside me, put its lips almost upon my ear and whispered, "The wolves are coming, son."

Before I left the church to the slinking death of its dying city, I nailed the Crucifier to one of his own crosses, merging artist with art, preserving his legacy. I hoped he would be taken for one of his own victims, and while his lethal dream would cease, he would remain an unnamed monster, forever. As for the new kill lists I discovered, I transferred the names that hadn't been crossed off to my own list—all save my own, of course. I noticed that the Crucifier's list included names from the murdered hunter's list, none of which were crossed off on the latter. I assumed I'd unconsciously followed some kind of unspoken protocol.

I wasn't one to devolve mystery into fact, but the game I was engaged in threatened my life in ways I'd never imagined—as embarrassing as that is to admit—and I needed a fuller understanding than what was provided by intermittent dreams and murdered men. Thus, my next stop was a place I had only called upon once before—New Victoria.

The city had been erected from the broken corpse of fallen Boston, its name and aesthetic lifted from the only part of the Cradle of Liberty to survive the mysterious storm that killed her—the South End. In short order, it would serve as the surest counterexample to solid reality, prior to the Darkness, that is. The New Victorian Dream Plague was almost twenty years older than the Great Darkness. And while it might have been more circumscribed in its range, it was no less portentous for the lesser reach. It was only after the military proved insufficient at halting the spread of contagious nightmare that it was determined the city would be evacuated and quarantined. Despite the plague and razor wire and walls, and given its association with dreams, I had once found it a suitable place to visit. But I was quickly and thoroughly disillusioned of any relationship my art and the city might have shared.

Perhaps foolishly, I fear very few things. What I encountered in New Victoria inspired a feeling that surpassed any of the best formulations of fear I know. While my memories only carry back a hazy recollection of my time in the City that Never Wakes, they're more than enough to convince me that sometimes, sleep is not worth the risk of dreaming.

Unfortunately, New Victoria was the only place my recent—and apparently, shared—dreams might be given some useful interpretation. I knew of certain persons who dwelt there, somewhere between this world and some much darker place, who interacted with dreams as intimately and completely as sculptors work clay. Given my insight into the wicked city, I hoped to safely and ever-so-briefly revisit it. I only needed to stay awake within its borders, or I might find myself eternally trapped within the alien sleep of wakeless, unspeakable things.

***

Soon, I was traveling the haunted countryside, wandering the dust of forsaken places, where artifacts of the Great Darkness still stood, heaving with mystery. In the distance, rising up from the mists of dawn and the green tresses of the wandering woods, I saw one of my favorite monuments, The Tower of Teeth. How many mouths were plundered to make the monolith, a thing taller than any man-made structure in the world? Here was a piece of art holding dream like a dam, threatening at any moment to drown the world in unreformed revelation. Most intriguing was that not all the mouths harvested for their teeth had belonged to earthly bodies. But the tower was as much a monument to banality as dream, for even in the face of such proof of paradox, there persists a belief in a solid world, a desire for the deadness of dreams, a want for nothing but nothingness. And the tower was but one of countless artifacts of the Darkness, a fact that through its denial outlined the enormity of man's addiction to dullness. But it rode high in the grey sky, blatant, if not altogether vulgar, tempting those who might believe in it to question the fitness of their pragmatism. I wouldn't let man's collective tediousness darken my spirits. Not today.

Around noon, I saw dust tumbling across the thickets and heard the asthmatic wheezing of an engine in need of repair. I emerged from the woods to see a rusted-out shell of a bus heading toward me. It was crawling along a narrow stretch of dirt road that seemed to move randomly about the woodland, as though it were looking for something. The man behind the filth-splattered windshield smiled at me and brought his groaning vehicle to a halt.

The door to the bus opened and a corpulent man with small, dark eyes called out to me. "Excuse me, pal, but I was wondering if you knew where I could find a decent garage? My jalopy's on its last legs, wouldn't you know. This is a new route to me and I'm not quite up on the lay of the land." The man's eyes studied me, an intense calculus burning between his ears, fast and lethal. He tried too hard not to stare at my father, who protruded from my back, sealed away in rags.

I withheld a response until my stare entered his blood and coursed through his body. My voice came out low and full of gravel—it'd been ages since I'd cause to use it. I placed my gaze within him, severing his concentration. "I can take a look if you'd be willing to bring me closer to my destination. I'm heading north."

He tried to match my stare, but my eyes only devoured him whole. He winced and pretended to shield his eyes from the sun. After he regained himself, he accepted my offer. "You got yerself a deal, mister. While you're working on the engine, I can stretch my legs a bit. I've been wandering these back roads forever. I could use a walk and a cigarette. By the way, the name's Grimes."

Mr. Grimes committed to his ruse, which was perfectly fine. Should he attempt my murder, the innards of the dying bus would make a fine gallery. The area I traveled was a notorious feeding ground for bandits and killers. The law was thin where the shadows of the Great Darkness were thick. The shunned locale was pleasant enough, and the murderer was a pleasant if predictable distraction.

The bus had nothing specifically wrong with it—just a few plugs and wires that needed adjusting. It was simply a part of the man's story to lure in victims—though I could tell it wasn't an altogether normal piece of machinery either, which was a delightful surprise. But as for its more mundane, mechanical aspect, it was rather sound. It had certainly seen better days, but the gurgle and roar of its straining engine were to be expected, given its age. I played along with the charade, adding some oil and checking the spark plugs while he wandered the area. Before long, I slammed the hood shut and joined killer-in-driver's-clothing, who was patiently waiting by the folding doors of the bus. The man gestured to the stairs leading inside, grinning. "Be my guest, big guy." I nodded, and we both walked up the steps, the vehicle groaning beneath our combined weight.

We were soon back on the road, traveling through a forest darkness so dense, it seemed to offer resistance to the big vehicle's movement. A thin rain began falling, and the distant flashes of lightning promised a far grander show to come. For the most part, the driver kept his eyes on me via the sizable rearview mirror, only periodically glancing back at the road for direction. A painfully poor liar, he was clearly no newcomer to this route.

"So, tell me, how far north am I taking you?" He asked with a smile.

"Until I tell you to stop," I replied. As much as the killer amused me, I was far more interested in the gathering storm.

"C'mon, I appreciate the fix and all, but I'm not drivin' ya too far off my route." His insistence at pretending to be a bus driver was comical, but the noise of his ridiculously transparent effort caused me to refuse him an answer. He finally reciprocated my silence, but I could sense dark thoughts orbiting his mind like flies circling a corpse. A few minutes later and he made his killing move. I didn't hold it against him— he was, after all, a killer.

"Well, I guess I do owe ya, so I should probably give ya something fer yer troubles, right?" His massive, hairy hand left its perch upon the steering wheel and moved to a small set of buttons beneath the steering column. Suddenly, his eyes widened, flooded with fear. It was the first time I could make out the whites of his beady eyes. After a few moments, the man cleared his throat and spoke again. "So, what's north?" His words were accompanied by an increase in his quite noticeable body odor. Mr. Grimes clearly had no head for operating at even the slightest disadvantage.

"My destination." Again, I hoped for the smallest possible exchange. If the man had indeed abandoned his bid to kill me, I wanted to be able to enjoy the coming thunderstorm in peace. Unfortunately, my brevity didn't deter him.

"Well, only thing I know of that's a-ways up north is New Victoria, and I know you can't be wanting to go there." After he realized I had no intention of responding, he added, "But what do I know, eh?"

I decided to do away with pretense in order to achieve the silence I required. "You know that I am dangerous," I growled. "You know that I've disabled your traps. You know that I might kill you. However, on the last count, should you take me where I desire to go, you will have nothing to fear—provided you remain quiet for the rest of the journey."

Again, he transgressed the silence. "So, what? You got a gun, or something? That some kinda weapon on yer back?" He was testing waters best left untried. "Look, yer a big guy and all, but do you really think yer gonna just stare me into doin' what you say? What's to stop me from just comin' back there?"

As I directed my gaze at him through the mirror, I knew his memory conducted my earlier glare to the other side of his eyes. A well-deserved fear of me now lived within Mr. Grimes, and he understood. After some quiet deliberation, he sloughed down into his dirty seat and took out a cigarette.

"Mind if I smoke along the way?" he finally managed.

"Roll down the window, please," I said, feeling accommodating.

"You got it, chief."

Thunder soon filled the killer's bus, and lightning made terrible things of the shadows, possibly illuminating ghosts of Grime's victims still in the process of digestion, deep within the rusted bowels of his demon-machine. My would-be killer was oblivious to it all, preferring to divide his attention between watching me and emptying his pack of cigarettes. Truly, he had nothing to fear from me—short of appearing on my list, there was no way I would take him from the world. Mr. Grimes cast a truly beautiful shadow, in his own depraved way.

With the storm directly overhead and the dirt road quickly becoming a swamp, our route became nearly impassable. Mr. Grimes had no choice but to pull onto a small patch of gravel sheltering beneath an overhang of tree branches, like a giant green claw reaching up for the storm. "We're gonna have to hold up here for a bit until the storm blows over," Mr. Grimes announced as he produced a fresh pack of cigarettes.

"Fine," I said, distracted, still watching dreams trying to break through the places where storm and death intersected.

"You ever gonna tell me where we're goin'?" As he spoke, and as the dashboard lights slowly sank away into the darkness, the killer blended into the unfolding nightmare, becoming a monstrous, smoking silhouette possessed of a single, burning eye. At that point, I had no difficulty engaging the monstrous man. He was now part of the nightmare whirling with the storm.

"You're bringing me to the outskirts of New Victoria," I said.

"You gotta be kiddin' me," Grimes said, exhaling smoke into the shadows. "What the hell ya gotta go there for?"

The sound of rain and rolling thunder filling the long pause between his question and my response. "I need answers that cannot be glimpsed by mortal dreams," I informed him.

"Ya don't say? Well, that's mortal dreams for you, I guess." Mr. Grimes' sarcasm was as thick as the smoke that filled the bus, but his crude wit was almost entertaining. "Ya know, a while back, I knew this guy, Jackie I think was his name, and he had a brother that got caught sleepin' just inside New Victoria. It was sometime just before the military put up all them barriers an' razor-wire.

"The two of them were drivin' through the city on their way to somewhere or other. I guess Jackie's younger brother had been asleep awhile, and didn't even know they was goin' through the place. But just when the car left the city, the sleeping brother starts screamin' like some kinda maniac. I still remember exactly how Jackie described it. Said it was like the screams was gettin' further and further away, like they was fallin' way down into some big bottomless hole— but the whole time, his brother hadn't moved an inch from where he was sleepin' in the passenger's seat. But that ain't even the scariest bit. Ya see, when the screamin' disappeared, like it finally fell too far away ta be heard anymore, Jackie's brother sits up, smiles, opens the door and jumps out into the street.

"'Course, Jackie slams the brakes and gets out to look for his brother. At first, he doesn't notice anything, just some noise in the tree branches over his head, like somethin' was moving higher into the tree. So then Jackie walks a bit further down the road, lookin' high and low for any sign of his brother, when he sees what looks like a floatin' man breakin' through the top of the woods, bobbing along in the air, sound asleep. Well, Jackie realizes it's his brother and starts yellin' at him to come back. Don't ya know, his floatin' brother just smiles and gives a little wave goodbye, and then off he goes, up into the clouds over New Vic."

It was stories like that one that had sent me to New Victoria the first time. However, I'm one of the few men to have slept in that dreadful city and awakened in the comfort of their own body. Despite it all, I could not repress a growing desire to revisit the place, and the living nightmares that stood under the deathly light of darkest sleep, casting their molten shadows.

The din of the storm had only grown since Mr. Grimes and I had begun to speak, so I had almost failed to notice the mechanical rumbling that was slowly growing beneath the thunder, drawing closer. When the noise finally dawned on

Mr. Grimes, and the headlamps of multiple vehicles pushed through the darkness of the bus, a long snaking grin slithered across his face. A once-banished confidence returned to his tiny eyes. "Looks like you might not be goin' to New Vic after all, big guy."

His speed greatly belied his size, as he nearly disappeared from the driver's seat of the bus only to reappear amid the brutish crowd lumbering out from behind the obnoxiously bright headlights. Clearly, Mr. Grimes wasn't the only predator using the back roads for hunting grounds, and it appeared that he had cultivated alliances among his fellow monsters.

As they milled around my former driver, I heard the signature sound of firearms—the small metallic clicking that spoke of tiny steel gun parts moving against one another, like the chitinous mandibles of a hungry insect. Eventually, the unsavory group surrounded the bus, hurling threats and challenges from behind the storm of wind, rain, and electric light. One of them fired a round into the air, and I almost laughed when a clap of thunder annihilated the weapon's report.

With the grace of a blind crowd, a detachment of gun-wielders entered the bus. Of course, I was no longer in it. I heard Mr. Grimes instructing them to take care, as I was a "big fucker, with some huge weapon on his back." One of the intruders started up the engine, hoping the internal lights might reveal my hiding place. I was glad that Mr. Grimes had chosen to stay outside while his allies invaded the vehicle, otherwise I might not have done what I did.

I could hear the high-pitched whine of Mr. Grimes's secret machinery coming to life as I reconnected certain wires. The noise was soon replaced by the sounds of flesh tearing, bones snapping, screams being chopped into small bits of groans and gasps, and finally the wet sounds of inanimate flesh being worked by busy, mindless steel. I wasn't sure what to think when I saw all the whirring blades and strange devices rushing in and out of my would-be killers. While Mr. Grimes was a monster, his wasn't a pedigree worthy of such machinations. I had to assume the bus some relic of the Darkness, something he'd found in forgotten woods, waiting for a master who matched its evil, if not its engineering. Whatever its origins, the men who remained outside seemed frozen by the antics of the bus-turned-devourer. Within seconds, the silence took me from beneath the bus and placed me behind Mr. Grimes' few remaining allies. One of my sisters awoke into my hand, giggling.

I made sure Mr. Grimes was a safe distance from me when my sister softly sorted through the thoughts of one of my harassers, reaching deeply into the convolutions of his brain. The man at my left swung a heavy chain at me, but his attack was so slow, I wondered if he intended for me to grab the inbound weapon. If so, I obliged, seizing it and pulling its wielder from the ground. My sister entered the hidden places of his body, dancing like a happy child from one red room to the next. After she had exhausted her enthusiasm, I hurled her ruined playmate at the last of Mister Grimes' associates. The flying body struck the man full in the chest, blasting him backwards into the side of the bus.

My sister was about to play with the stunned man when the thunderous voice of my father commanded her to stop. He wished for Mr. Grimes to see him and the wonderful work for which he was infamous. In an instant, he was revealed, awake and aglow with a fury to match the storm overhead. The man shuddered beneath my patron's terrible gaze, pleading for mercy, but my father had none to give. I was pleasantly surprised when the shadow decided to attack rather than die quietly. Like a cornered beast, he howled his last breath, launching from the ground, knives out like bared fangs. While his feral madness may have served him well against other foes, it failed him in the face of my father. The thunder roared as the axe collided with the man. My great benefactor seemed to channel the fury of the tempest, creating a second storm of blood, brains, and bone. My father turned toward Mr. Grimes, dripping what was left of the last interloper. The killer bus driver promptly collapsed to the wet earth.

"Holy shit!" he shouted, beady eyes wide. "I know who you are!"

"Then we understand each other," I said. With my father spent, I returned him to his sleep. I extended my hand to help the trembling killer to his feet.

"W-what are you gonna do to me?" Mr. Grimes stammered. "You gonna make me into some fucked up art exhibit?"

"Nothing has changed, Mr. Grimes," I assured him. "We are simply back where we began—you are taking me to New Victoria."

"And then what?" he asked.

"I will release you back into your natural habitat," I said. Mr. Grimes seemed relieved, exhaling what he surely thought was his final breath. Behind us, the vehicles of the dead still cast their yellowed light into the darkness, revealing my work, if not my art. The killer bus driver surveyed his losses.

"I can't believe you killed my guys!" he said, running thick fingers through his dripping hair. "I was friends with some of 'em, and they wasn't no pushovers, neither!"

"Friends, Mr. Grimes, are no substitute for family."

CHAPTER FOUR

The Deadworld is a prison. However, people tend to misunderstand those moments when it seems to defy its most hideous, despicable features. Forests, by way of example, are often romanticized for their beauty—but they are merely cracks in the dirty prison walls that keep us from the dream we came from, and exist as nothing more than fleeting reminders—symbols—for our freedoms lost beyond all this dying flesh. Granted, a dark forest is one of the thinner barriers separating us from whence we came—and thus why some confuse it for the beauty it imprisons—but a barrier nonetheless. Obviously, the same can be said for basements filled with the moldering dead, attics containing chests of burned toys and faded photographs, forgotten graveyards steeped in twilight, and all other places where the darkness endures beyond the day.

Undoubtedly, all these prisons contain boundless wonders vigorously testing the locks to their cells, but to my knowledge, none have ever escaped—though I can't remember a single thing that happened during the Great Darkness, so I could be wrong on this point. This isn't to suggest that the Deadworld is without limits. Its prison walls can be scaled, even demolished, as was demonstrated by the rise of New Victoria. However, the relevant distinction between New Victoria and the dreams that strain behind even this world's darkest environs is that the nightmare city was never a prisoner. It came here from deepest sleep, from an entirely different dream of existence. As strange as it sounds, the malefic metropolis actually chose to invade this wretched world.

As we approached the city, its ruined flesh was already peeling back, exposing overturned military vehicles filled with old bones and crusted blood, mass graveyards, sour winds stitched together from countless last breaths, and wandering patches of strange, sweet-smelling twilight—the Deadworld was hemorrhaging nightmare. Here was no symbol for dream, only dream itself, open and free. However, New Victoria held no hope for mankind. Its dreams were its own.

"I can't fuckin' believe you really want to be here," Mr. Grimes said.

"I have need to be here," I replied, "and despite everything I know—I want to be here. These things are clearly not our dreams, and must be nothing but the predatory nightmares of things that dwell beyond the shallows of human sleep. However, regardless of their malevolence, beauty is beauty." Strangely, I found myself enjoying my conversation with Mr. Grimes. Words are so often nothing more than thoughts hidden behind masks of noise, but when speaking with the killer, I found my words pleasingly free of disguise.

"Uh, yeah," Mr. Grimes said, "Well, I'm only here cuz I hafta be. You gotta be crazy to think there's anything beautiful about this freak-zone."

I hadn't considered it before, but I wondered if that invisible force—the one that draws people to abandoned places and gifts them with dreams pressed into yellowed paper—was still aiding in my journey. Surely, those things that dwelt in the City Beyond Sleep wouldn't see me coming—the deathly bus, now festooned with the ornaments of a butcher's red holiday, couldn't be taken for anything less than a conveyance for pilgrims of nightmare. Perhaps Mr. Grimes was sent to assist me.

"By the way," Mr. Grimes said, "I know you got some weird thing about beauty and art. The newspapers is always sayin' somethin' about you thinkin' of yerself as an artist. But do you really think those fucked up corpses you leave behind is some kinda artwork?"

I wasn't sure if Mr. Grimes was supposed to understand my work. Should a dream know it's a dream? Might that have been what caused us to wake up in the first place? I imagine a true dream, free and wandering, should know precisely nothing about itself—should it be so greedy as to possess a self. Humanity's true calling is to exchange all of its pointless knowledge for wonder, and Mr. Grimes followed his dark curiosity wherever it lead him—even when it caused him to be temporarily hijacked for a higher purpose. No, the daemon bus driver was far too busy chasing his darkest visions to grasp the purpose behind my work. He could only see its spectacle.

"Pearls before swine, Mr. Grimes," I said, not wanting my host to think me unaware of his jabs.

"Actually," Mr. Grimes added, "I got a kick out of those guys you made into the big snake swallowin' itself. That was some funny—" he stopped, straining his small eyes at something close to the road.

Moving through the nearby trees, sketched in fog, were four wisps of women. They were clad only in nightclothes, loping through rough thickets, helping one another along, exuding a despair that seemed to roil the fog outlining them. Their collective gaze fixed upon the nearby wakeless city, and I could hear secrets whispering them onward. Soon they were gone, swallowed by the forest. It was clear where they were headed.

"What do ya think they're up to?" Mr. Grimes retracted his gaze, bringing something warm and wicked back with it. I could feel his hunger burning deep within the secret killing machines of the bus. Whatever the killer's dark curiosity would have done to the women, I was certain it would've been a pleasure compared to what was waiting for them in New Victoria. I knew something of the endless horrors that preyed upon sleeping men, but I'd heard only rumors of the hell awaiting women foolish enough to rest their heads within the nightmare-fashioned city. Now my own dark curiosity was beginning to take hold.

"I'm not entirely certain," I replied. "But it would be a terrible waste of mystery not to find out."

"Yeah, well, I'm willing to skip the mystery, if ya don't mind. Y'know, on account of the whole dying in a nightmare city thing."

I simply nodded at Grimes, feeling no need to contribute more to the topic. For the next few minutes, we both sat silently in the bus, watching the dread city materialize from the fog of distance and dust. Finally, the military barricades and piles of soaring wreckage all but blocked our forward passage, and I could feel the vehicle's momentum drain away.

"So, yer really goin' in there, huh?" Mr. Grimes asked, throwing the bus in park and flinging open the swinging doors. We disembarked, looking clearly for the first time on the Victorian reimagining of bygone Boston, darkened by dreams blacker than pitch.

"Indeed I am," I said.

"Before ya take off, I gotta know," Mr. Grimes said. "Why didn't you kill me? You coulda just driven the bus on yer own. You didn't need me."

I wasn't quite sure how to answer him, as the question required a galaxy of nuance. "I dislike driving standard transmissions," I offered.

"Huh," Mr. Grimes said with a smile, not believing a word. "Fair enough, I guess. One more thing—those weapons really made of yer own family?"

"Of course," I replied.

"Yeah, kinda figured they were," he said, eyeing the protruding head of my father warily. "Well, I doubt yer gonna get outta there alive, but good luck tryin' . . . Family Man."

With that, we took our leave of each other. I watched as the hunter of dark roads disappeared into the dust that had first unveiled him—a corpulent killer who feasted through the terrible machines lurking his corroded shadow.

I stood upon a street severed by a portion of the massive steel and concrete wall that surrounded the entire city—a futile effort to contain what sleep would only free. Its length was punctuated by gaping holes, torn open by a storm that blew out from beneath beds and beyond sleep. I entered through one of these massive breaches, lined with an amalgam of encrusted human remains, warped together into a frustration of biology and nightmare.

The city rose before me, denuded of all earthly obstruction and covered in the blood of twilight, defiling the cold reality that lay in shambles at its feet. New Victoria was almost beyond 0at, the city seemed dead, at first. Its skyscrapers and minarets looked no less than the crooked, chitinous limbs of toppled insects, all of them frozen in an architectural rictus of death. The Victorian skin of the place had rotted away in places, revealing a nightmare of warped and fused innards beneath, the thin veneer merely paper wrapped around a fire. No single structure rose wholesomely to form the city's skyline, but only bent and skittered and crawled into and across the sky. And despite its stillness, the metropolis exuded a sense of movement—the unclean motion of a corpse being eaten from the inside.

It took no time for the preliminary powers of the city to test me, emerging without the corrupted ether, eager to infest a fresh mind with endless nightmare, their alien outlines manifest on this side of sleep as common shadows.

When they finally converged upon me, I could feel the gossamer touch of unseen hands playing across my mind, eager to find a door. Meanwhile, the invisible intrusion into my thoughts caused one of my sisters to rise from her warm dreams, deep within my own darkness. So long as she dwelt in that city of living nightmares, her words carried beyond her radiant smile, and I was pleased to hear them slice through the open air.

So many greedy hands and old hungers. What wonderful gifts have you brought me, sweet brother? I could feel the heat of her delight. Her blazing smile burned the darkness around me, searing shadows too foolish to run from fire.

Oh, you silly shades! Shouldn't you know what grinning terrors can await you behind closed doors? My dearest brother's mind has shadows of its own, and we'll suffer none besides. Now, now, there'll be time enough for playing, and I'll be more than thrilled to savor your screams as they pass betwixt my glittering metal teeth. But now is the time for hiding, I'm afraid. At my sister's prompting, my hunter's silence poured forth, drowning what remained of the alien whispers calling out from undead dreams. I slipped from beneath the scattering pack of shades to find shelter beyond the gaze of the wicked city.

I quickly found the darkness of an abandoned hospital and blended into its isolation. Careful not to linger in any one shadow for too long, I made my way toward the oldest calm. I could feel the currents of quiet rushing out a stairwell that descended deep into the innards of the structure. As I moved to the top of the stairs, I noticed four sets of small, delicate footprints descending the dust. Clearly, they belonged to the quartet of women I'd glimpsed earlier.

As I followed the prints, I realized they seemed to progressively sink further into the dust and grime that lay heavy and thick upon the steps—as if they had suddenly become burdened by something heavy. I waded into the densest currents of gloom, discovering the footprints had been joined by four sets of handprints. The women had crawled down the last few steps into the darkness, and then seemingly disappeared altogether.

I stopped to examine the anomaly, and while the dust and filth betrayed nothing useful, the silence showed signs of having been broken. Moving beyond the stairs, I encountered a set of wide double doors. The word above them plainly stated: *Morgue.*

An old darkness can be the deadliest of poisons— soaking up shadows unbroken by purifying daylight, mixing with the ghosts of unseeing eyes, and filling up with fears that cannot abide the light. It was just such a darkness that spilled from behind the morgue door, proving my sisters correct for the second time. After the molten void had thoroughly flooded the room, creating the ideal habitat for nightmares, I began to hear the toothsome glide of horrible things—deep-diving horrors called up from the sunless depths of sleep.

Somewhere in front of me, I heard a voice. "You've left nightmares behind from your last visit, little artist. They've grown enormous and terrible in your absence. They would just love to see you again." Something immediately began pushing into my mind. At the same time, a physical presence drew close to me, reaching out. Before the invading forces had a chance to unveil themselves, my father stepped in front of me. Bellowing, the axe fell, cleaving into flesh, bone, and noxious spirit. His rage elicited some of the most exquisite shrieks I've ever heard. My father's jeering laughter chased the inhuman screams to where they seemed to tumble and die away, deep into the unwaking spaces beyond or merely behind the material world. *What a wonderful place, this city of yours!* He exclaimed in a voice of steel and thunder. *So full of dreams that bleed and scream and die!*

With the gloom parted, I could see clearly the most conspicuous contents of the room—the riven body of one of the quartet of women. She had the expressionless eyes of a bird. Her mouth outlined only her last cracked breath. She had been dead for hours, unceremoniously stuffed into a body bag. It was not her that had absorbed my father's fury, but that which she carried—the woman's womb was filled with something gigantic and inhuman. Her lower torso was so incredibly bloated that it had burst the thick plastic confines of the body bag. The corpse of the unborn thing was a labor of hideous departures from human anatomy, pushing so tightly against the woman's skin that the details of the creature could be seen quite clearly.

The unborn nightmare was easily the size of a bear. One of its claws extended out toward me, stretching flesh far beyond its natural limits. Most noteworthy was the creature's massive jaws, a cavernous maw filled with serrated, dimly glowing hooks. The monster had been severed almost in two by my father, and its mouth, like its mother's, was frozen around its last otherworldly sound—a scream no human vocal chords could produce. Within seconds, the thing pent behind dead, striated flesh disappeared, leaving behind what looked like an empty sack made of flaccid skin and splattered blood. In the ether, I thought I could hear an invisible descent of something plunging into eternity, its limp body occasionally clapping against the walls encapsulating its journey.

It seemed the rumors I'd heard were correct—when caught sleeping in New Victoria, men were stolen away by their nightmares, while women gave physical birth to them. I grew annoyed at my father's impatience, denying me the sight of a nightmare breeching sleep. Yet such was my father's way, always overzealous where killing is required. Still, just before my father had broken the grip of the nightmare, I glimpsed something in the gutted spaces of my mind, through the hole made by the burrowing vision—a lost memory of my childhood.

I'm sure I spied lines of small cages filled with children, all of them pale and staring. As I looked over the hazy fragment, I could feel my family's collective disapproval burning me, so I gently set the memory down and watched it sink into oblivion. But before the memory had all but disappeared, a voice managed to slip free. It was no more than a sound, really, too weak to intimate words or meanings. I was surprised when it resonated with something deep within me, eliciting a reaction I thought all but conquered—fear. I quickly turned my attention back to the outside world, replacing the unwanted emotion to its place within the fading memory.

The rest of the room was unspectacular, decorated with an assortment of squirming mildew, whirling dust, and creeping shadow—nothing one wouldn't expect to find in a haunted morgue. With nothing else to command my attention, I reversed my course. Wrapping the newly liberated shadows tightly around myself and stepping into a dense fog of silence, I withdrew up the stairs, possessed of more wisdom than when I had descended.

The solitude of the first floor had come alive with a tangible vigilance, and I could hear the breathing of countless sleeping victims of the dream plague, all of them tucked away into the strangest places—heating vents, under floorboards, and all the smallest places one would never think to find a body. The massive collection of sleeping minds likely merged their dreams to form a great passage projecting beyond the strained limits of human sleep, emptying into lands where the oldest earthy darkness constitutes only the freshest topsoil.

Having satisfied my curiosity—as much as was healthy—I put aside my search for the impregnated women and renewed my quest for insight into my wolf-haunted dreams. I decided to move by rooftop, and so made my way to the top of the hospital.

Along the way, I snatched small glimpses into the hospital rooms on either side of the hallway. Each space succored the pain of its former occupants as a mother nurses her child, and nowhere was there an inch of wall, floor, or ceiling that had not known fluids better kept within the human body. As I neared the top of the building, I foolishly loosed a smile, causing my sisters to erupt into terrifying laughter. They had always found my face, when broken by a crooked smile, a most amusing sight. No doubt inspired by my sisters' insistent laughter, a pounding rhythm of heavy feet began to shake the floor beneath me as something closed from behind. I tried to quicken my pace, but my sisters' laughter was contagious. Soon I was so heavy with mirth that I tumbled to the floor. The joy of running through a solid nightmare raised from the depths of alien dreams was simply too much for me.

My father, however, was not amused. *This is no monster born of nightmares, but a patient wolf come to cross your name off its list! Rise up and kill, idiot boy!* My father was right. The footsteps quickly vanished into silence as flashing blades began hissing through the shallows of my body. Still, I couldn't stop laughing.

Given my rather foolish, if not entirely ridiculous condition, hiding and stalking were certainly out of the question, so I decided to simply meet the wolf head-on. The decision was apparently mutual, as the Wolf took no care at all in his approach, but only launched himself at me the moment he appeared. Whoever he was, he was on the larger side of the spectrum, wore all black, and brandished ornate daggers. He was upon me in a second.

My fist exploded across lips and teeth, ruining all, sending their owner soaring into a nearby wall. My family enjoyed testing my mettle from time to time, and so were content to stand back and watch as the wolf and I joined battle.

I rather admired this killer, following me as he had into a city far deadlier than his quarry. I almost thanked him, but my name blazed across his kill list, and he would only stop after my death or his own. Unfortunately for him, my death wasn't a feat he could manage—not even in a city where dreams have the preternatural tendency to come true.

I caught the killer by his forearms and squeezed. The bones of his arms snapped like dry twigs, and his knives fell from his vanquished hands. The wolf was unfazed however, somehow breaking free and thrusting his heavily-booted foot squarely into my face. But my body was chiseled from unfiltered purpose, and blows from even the greatest beast would not immediately prevail against it. Suddenly, the wolf wrapped his shattered arms around my midsection, and in a display of exhilarating desperation and strength, lifted me into the air and smashed us both through a nearby window. The cool wind, the bottomless night, the weightless blood and glass that caught the moonlight, the raging wolf himself—gifts, all. Our descent ended violently atop a large rooftop. Debris and blood rained down around us, the fallout from a beautiful dream. I rose to my feet, but the poor wolf would never rise again. The sight cut me deeper than his knives. Finally, I stopped laughing.

The din of battle melted away, and I inherited the remaining names from the dead hunter's list. I looked into the night—it was thinly pierced by the tiny amber lights of distant glowing windows. What power or device illuminated the rooms behind those windows, I couldn't say. They shined like gentle stars made from the calm of autumn. And the moon, while visible, seemed restrained by the city's presence—only the dimmest light drifted down to the world below. As I took in these exquisite sights, the wind grappled with my coat, snatching at my hair and beard. I took a deep breath, wondering if I inhaled air or darkness.

A slightly elevated rooftop hovered nearby, well within range of a spirited leap, so I climbed into the night, soon reaching the apex of my ascent. My destination was visible at this vantage—a distant and nearly collapsed apartment high-rise. Traveling the open streets was too risky an alternative, so I decided to find another way across to the next building.

After I quietly laid my shoulder into it, the rooftop door opened gently enough. The muted sound flitted down the narrow stairwell and would have gained the hallways below, had it not been for my expanding silence. I descended to the first stairwell door, entering the hallway of the fourteenth floor. The passage was dark and cobwebbed, so I crept along like a spider, plucking at the shadows and silence, testing the way ahead. Suddenly, the sound of a cracking whip exploded into the hallway. A few seconds later, a pulsating amber light made its way into the corridor, emerging from an open doorway several apartments away.

Something advanced beneath the silence, displacing shadows as it moved. Sidestepping into an adjacent apartment, I disappeared into the null of forgotten places. Music of some sort began to melt out of the air, blowing softly across the hallway and into my hiding place. The lights in the hall turned on, dimming to the weakest orange glimmer, soon followed by the lights inside the apartment I occupied. Eager to see what would come next, and with my silence wrapped securely around me, I took the most comfortable seat in the room and waited.

The music became almost tangible, forming a kind of transparent membrane that settled across the room, enveloping everything. The light itself blended into the mysterious composition as the wax and wane of the tender illumination transitioned into floating, glowing notes. The cadence of my breathing merged with developing harmony, and the movement of my very thoughts dissolved into nothing more than an accompanying rhythm. I was being consumed by the music, digested into a string of notes within its trilling bowels.

I tried to think past the horde of deadly sounds, but my every thought became a note within the widening theatre of melodies. My only hope was silence. I could feel the hungry music trying to master and devour it, but it was unyielding. That area of the contest became the focus of my attention. I listened as never before, to a soundless song only I could hear. Suddenly, the rapacious sounds vanished from the room, moving past me down the hall, still eating away at the world by means of the music and melody.

With the nightmare music gone, I slipped from the room and reentered the hallway, approaching the apartment where the unearthly music seemed to have originated. I took to the deepest shadows, minding my every movement, yet I couldn't resist peering as far into the room as I could. The apartment was filled with rusted musical instruments, suspended from the walls by large hooks, strung with glistening webs of what seemed to be saliva. Sitting in the middle of the room was a man sharply dressed in the dusty apparel of an orchestra conductor. Instead of a conductor's baton, his right hand held what appeared to be a lion tamer's whip. He was apparently sound asleep, bearing the signature features of a man afflicted with the advanced stages of the infamous sleeping sickness. His eyes were completely sealed shut, so much so that there was no distinguishing the fact that eyes had ever occupied the unbroken expanse of smooth skin that now lay placid and pale above his cheeks. He sat disturbingly still, only occasionally whimpering in his sleep. The pathetic sound seemed to come from an impossible distance buried somewhere deep within the man—as if he were crying out from the yawning depths of a deep pit.

After squeezing myself carefully through a large window and onto the fire escape, I paused to survey the night air and the dank alley below. I pondered my chances of getting out of the city alive—or more accurately, awake. My eyelids had already gathered more weight than was normal, and exhaustion closed upon me like a vice. But to sleep was to die, at the very least.

A seperate fire escape clung to the building across the alley. The distance was outside my comfort zone, but not my ability. Another determined leap saw me to the other side, my movements precise and unsounding. I climbed to the roof, ever aware of things eager to catch me off guard. Yet I also felt my family's vigilance surrounding me like smoke, seeking to feast upon the screams of whatever would take me for prey. Having reached the top of the building, I caught sight of a glassed-in penthouse, replete with a spacious veranda. A large telescope sat affixed to its outermost rim.

The worlds that wheeled overhead were pale alternatives to the sights I hoped to glimpse by aiming my magnified gaze at the concrete forest around me. With any luck, lighted windows might grant me further insight into the delightful nightmares pretending to be an abandoned city. A lingering curiosity concerning the quartet of women caused me to turn the glass toward the east, the direction from which they'd entered the city. Their original number diminished, I sought out the remaining three, curious as to their contents.

As if chance had answered my unspoken wish, I caught sight of something moving through the hallways of the hospital I had previously visited. It was indeed one of the women. She was strapped to a hospital gurney being conducted down a poorly lit corridor. The gurney was propelled by a creature that was largely imperceptible, as I could only discern its presence by the effects it exercised upon the shadows it touched—they seemed to adhere to the invisible thing, clinging to it like tar, supplying only a minimal suggestion of shape and size. From what I could make out, it was a thing of nonsensical construction—an organism that begrudged nothing to the traditional symmetries of earthen biology, partaking its shape solely from purest chaos. The unorthodox creature continued to push the gurney down the hallway, occasionally plucking the clinging shadows from the amorphous swelling that rose high and hideous from the woman's abdomen. From under her distended flesh, the dim outline of a germinating nightmare was scarcely visible as a mass of shifting shapes, twisting and flipping as if trying to assemble itself, one inhuman limb at a time. Suddenly, the head of the thing obtained a terrible definition as it pressed hard against its cage of flesh. It seemed to turn its attention toward the captured woman, leering into her panicked face. The unborn creature projected its hungry glare beyond its gilding of human skin, laying a cold glow across the dull and sightless eyes of its mother, eyes long since lost to the world beyond and behind them.

The woman was finally delivered into a large room lit only by a small collection of thin candles. After placing the woman in the middle of the room, her guide waddled back down the hallway by which it came, leaving wet shadows in its tracks. The woman struggled against the bonds that secured her head, arms, and feet to the gurney. However, after careful observation, I realized the movements were not her own, but the actions of the thing inside her. Her body—nothing but a pulsing gestational sac—began to rapidly swell beyond the scope of the gurney, her bulging mass spilling to the floor and rolling across the dirty tile like thick tides of mud. All the while, the woman's terrified expression never changed. Her mind and body were nothing but debris, broken dolls in an abandoned house—but she was aware.

The thing that was once a woman suddenly burst apart from the inside, releasing a septic spray of inhuman fluids that drowned all the candles, save one. By the solitary glow, the infant nightmare stripped off its mother like wet clothing, dropping what was left of her in a steaming heap of molted flesh. As the light played over the thing, trembling as it described what should not be, I beheld what seemed a demonic toddler dressed in the vintage garments of a mortician. The breathing dream waved its dainty inhuman hand before its eyes, inspecting the solidity of its new world, wondering perhaps if it might vanish back into the nightmare from which it came. Evidently quite satisfied with its new accommodations, it smiled with a thousand tiny teeth and walked off into the fade of the outer hallway, vanishing like a secret.

"They're our brides, called home from the distant cities we've secretly visited, if only in dreams. Our reach is only growing, despite the paltry fences your kind have put up to constrain us," the mysterious voice said behind me. "Our breeders of fittest nightmare, those women. Men like you—

why, you're our beasts of burden, naturally." I spun around to find a man floating above the floor, a ridiculous stovepipe hat on his head, eyes like hidden moons. A thin covering of flesh marked the space for normal eyes, yet behind that seal of skin glowed alien-blue lights, bright enough to backlight the tiny organic networks of the intervening tissues. The radiant blue of his eyes-behind-flesh was the color of sleep, and it washed over me like gentle water, sweeping me out to strange seas. It was one of the Wakeless—the true denizens of the City that Never Wakes, wearing whatever hapless dreamer it snatched from sleep—and I knew I had to escape its light. They possessed a depth far deeper and more dangerous than the distance from the balcony to the ground—so I leapt from the building.

I tumbled far longer than necessary to complete my descent, and the further I plummeted, the lighter my body felt. By the time I reached the streets below, I was nearly weightless. When my feet finally touched the ground, I looked up at the city—it had changed considerably. It was the dread face of New Victoria I had witnessed only once before. I suddenly realized my mistake. I hadn't actually fallen from the building, but had suffered a far worse fate—I had fallen asleep.

CHAPTER FIVE

Emerging on the *other side* of New Victoria, I confirmed everything I had suspected from my first visit—fear is the temperature at which dread solidifies, and conversely, the point at which stolid reality dissolves. A scream can become the glass of a window, frozen into place like a wicked memory, conducting blood-dimmed light through its invisible body. Sleep is a place where worlds spin atop the heads of pins and oceans gather into nutshells, and New Victoria is only the most visible part of a nightmare prowling the unclean depths of humanity's collective unconscious.

This nightmare-under-a-nightmare was a primal mockery of the sane and solid world, where a goblin-night—a shrewder, more enduring incarnation of our waking version—lived without cycle, light, or limit. It provided wakeless things a sky, oceans, shadows, everything they needed to survive and thrive. Whereas its waking incarnation wore the guise of death and desolation, New Victoria's unwaking counterpart was entirely vital, forged with feelings as much as whatever substituted for matter. Accordingly, every object and place possessed no fixed appearance, but only reflected a wild mutability born of darkest whimsy, free of the laws that prevailed over lesser, solid worlds. All this, and still it was not the world I wanted. While it was a dream in every sense, complete with all the wonder and uncertainty a mind could chase, it was only another iteration of failure—albeit a more attractive failure than the one I'd grown familiar with.

Regrettably, its every miracle and marvel were subordinated (weaponized) to the trite business of tyrants—conquering.

I sought shelter from the dizzying sights with equal parts caution and wonder—a difficult act to balance, surely. I entered a building stacked entirely from smoldering coal, and was instantly swept down a narrow arterial corridor, into a colossal chamber. The room was densely crowded with tall, worm-eaten bookcases, some spiraling beyond the shadows that spread wide and empty across the ceiling. Meeting at ungainly angles, the corners of what appeared a library stirred with tiny bits of activity—perhaps mice, but not likely. Light was contained within the room, but it hung in the air without source or consistency, tumbling and dimming wherever and whenever it willed. The rambling illumination maintained a largely subdued presence, yet more than adequate to read by. A nearby shelf heaved with books, and my curiosity grew so strong, I feared it would give me away. When I was sure there was no immediate threat, I took up one of the tomes and started reading

It was a dream journal—as were all the books, I somehow knew. Penned in exquisite cursive was recorded a young girl's nightly journeys into an exceptionally peculiar nightmare. She dreamed of a giant machine called the Spirit Grinder, a contraption that could distill, via a protracted and quite noisy process, the color of a person's soul. For reasons she could never deduce, she was obliged to remove the tied-up, squirming bodies of persons—always someone she knew—that dropped from a long, rusty chute and pass them through the strange machine. Once a particular soul's color had been rendered, she would use it to paint irises on the blank eyeballs passing by upon a shabby conveyer belt. All of this took place in a crumbling barn residing somewhere in the middle of a vast, dark forest.

I was about to withdraw another journal when I heard footsteps. Other than coming from somewhere below me, I was unable to discern their specific trajectory, but they seemed to be drawing closer. I slipped through an open window leading back onto the street. Quickly afterward, I ascended a rickety expanse of stairs wrapped around a gigantic apartment complex. Interestingly, the building seemed to be breathing. The observation only momentarily focused my attention as I opened the door at the top of the stairs and entered with little hesitation—the darkness initially seemed quite welcoming. I found myself in a bedroom with a massive four-poster bed, only slightly discernible from the flowing webs draped across it. The footsteps were getting louder, now emanating from under the huge bed itself. Suddenly, I remembered—I needed to wake up. I was so immersed in the darkling beauty of the city—not to mention the memory-dimming fog of dream—I had forgotten the danger I was in. Something was coming for me, to replace my waking eyes with dull expanses of featureless flesh.

I searched for a door out of the room but found nothing, not even the door I'd initially entered through. I was trapped. The footsteps acquired company as they moved along. But most important to me were the sounds I couldn't hear—the sweet laughter of my sisters and the terrible rage of my father. My family was gone. I was alone.

The surrounding darkness intensified, forcing me to stand out to whatever ascended the stairs beneath the bed. Fortunately, I sensed weakness in the trailing shadows that limped along with the stronger packs of darkness, turning from my gaze whenever I looked upon them. With supreme effort, I seized these stragglers with barbed thoughts and glaring eyes. I wrapped them tightly around my fists and poured them across my body until they soaked into my blood, conjuring depthless voids from what used to be my eyes. I ripped the alien silence from its hiding places, bending and breaking its body across my will, and when nothing of it remained save for loyalty to me, I draped its carcass over myself—until I was every inch the nightmare that was coming for me.

Wanting to deny my stalker the benefit of a dramatic entrance, I seized the ghastly bed and sent it crashing into the wall. Beneath lay a trap door, leaking cold air and laughter. Again, I would spare the nightmare none of its props and fetishes. I tore the door from its moorings and sent it to join the ruins of the bed. The stink of graveyard rot and old death drifted from the gaping hole, attempting to engulf me. Within moments, my killing thoughts crushed them of their ambitions and their corpses joined the dead silence that dripped from my shadow-haunted body. I stood at the edge of the hole, smiling as I spoke into the darkness. "Soon, I will wear your flowing skin, my dreadful friend. I will smile from the dark hollows that once held your face."

The footsteps were close now. I could hear only the coldest quiet where once there was laughter. A voice the size of the room exploded through the hole, sending me flying backward into the pile of debris I had created. "Oh, what bravado! What teeth! What spirit! I shall fill you with visions so fat and foul you will weep fire! But first, your soul will travel with me, under all the beds in the world, through every closet, and down where the whispers crawl upon you like spiders, where the darkness tastes you with a thousand terrible tongues!"

The near-solid words broke off, filling the room with an equally palpable stillness. Finally, and with a sort of comedic stumbling, rose a great shape. The thing was massive and ridiculous, like some infant devil's plaything. It was candy-striped and bug-eyed. A grinning hatch filled with mismatched teeth served as its mouth, and each of its movements were dramatically over-emphasized. It smiled at me with so much sweetness, my mouth filled with the taste of sugar.

Though difficult, I suppressed the impulse to laugh. "I think I will miss your whimsical smile the most, creature. I will think of it from time to time, long after you're dead."

The distance between myself and the grinning demon-doll began to shrink, but before we met, the wall beside me exploded, scattering nightmare like shrapnel. Something huge had broken into the room—it was my father, in all his former living glory. Froth and fire leaked from the corners of his mouth, and his eyes blazed like blast-craters. With his bloodless hands burned onto his axe, he intercepted the creature, throwing his massive shoulder into the stumbling toy from hell. The creature was lifted from the floor and sent crashing into the darkness. My father lifted his axe to the roar of his own laughter. Though glorious, the intrusion irritated me—this was the second time he had come between me and a nightmare.

Somehow, my sisters were behind me, their curving knives up in front of their grinning mouths. I wouldn't have guessed their next move for the life of me—they gleefully punctuated the length of my body with their happy knives, laughing all the while.

As I approached a waking awareness, still caught somewhere between dream and a slightly sturdier reality, I heard the sugary squeals of something inhuman, followed by the sounds of something wet falling down a long flight of stairs—perhaps in many small pieces. Then came the laughter of my entire family, fading into abandoned sleep. I sat up and looked around, finding myself prone upon a bed within the glass penthouse. A cold breeze lifted the edges of the oversized sheet that had been draped over me. My family lay carelessly scattered next to the bed, on the floor. The thought of someone else touching them stoked a rage almost beyond my control.

I retrieved my family and sought out the man with the ridiculous hat and blue-glowing eyes. He was easy enough to find—I could see him through the glass walls, where he lay upon a strange demonic bed, only a room away. The black bed was slathered in a membranous substance, which did not react to the breeze's touch, despite its apparently delicate construction. While he retained his hat, his otherworldly eyes were lightless and inactive, apparently sleeping beneath thin sheets of pale flesh. He appeared to be resting, but if I understood these creatures at all, the possessing entity was merely away somewhere, tending the wicked business of harrowing.

I waited for the creature to revisit its vehicle of flesh and bone, hoping my vengeance could reach beyond its stolen body. More specifically, I hoped my sisters were able to bleed a nightmare. I waited with the patience of stone until finally a glow began seeping from behind the barriers of flesh and blood. I hunched down behind the bed, not wanting the eyes of the thing to gaze fully upon me, lest I return to the deeper nightmare throbbing under the city. The creature began to stir, rising from the bed and into the air, borne aloft upon strange winds that never left the creature's side. I followed the light of its eyes to where it discolored the bed upon which I'd been reposed, to be filled with others of its kind. I lunged, my arms rushing beneath the creature's delicate neck, squeezing with all my strength. My sister slid into the nightmare's back, only whispering distance from its heart.

In a singsong voice of scarcely restrained laughter, my sister's words glided into the open air. "I wonder what color you will turn my radiant teeth, my light-eyed friend, after I've chewed you down to the echoes of your last scream!"

The thing spasmed as if electrocuted, its eyes becoming twin suns of cold blue light. Anything they shone upon became liquescent in appearance, indefinite. I could still hear my sister's laughter, dimmed somewhat by layers of intervening tissue. Ever-so-slowly, she moved closer to a killing depth. Somewhere on the other side of the creature's flesh, I could detect a living nightmare frantically attempting to flee its sinking ship. It raced toward an exit, hoping to attain the freedom lurking just beyond sleeping skin before its stolen host became its tomb. My sister corkscrewed into the creature's heart, freeing the death that lived within, ultimately denying the miserable creature its much-sought freedom. Instantly, the monster's dream-light became as confused as the matter it fell upon, becoming both illumination and sound—a glowing scream that shattered the glass of the penthouse. My father was absolutely right—the Wakeless screamed magnificently well.

Within the fading glow and dying echoes of the light-sound, there appeared a hideous shape straining the limits of its arms, like some desperate bird trying to gather the winds of a vacuum beneath its wings. Finding the solid world disagreeable to whatever life-sustaining systems it possessed, the creature slowly died, disappearing into a mist of drifting, freezing light.

My art had always been intended as a gift—an attempt at liberation, reunion, and completion. Certainly, these attempts have failed at their ultimate purpose, but while the Deadworld has yet to be invigorated by a single reincarnate dream—of the human variety—I have crossed many souls over into revelation. Perhaps when they are again renewed in fashions of skin and stupidity, they will be one life closer to the dream they left behind. However, at that moment, standing before the body of my family's defiler, I chose a new, if only temporary purpose for my art. I would craft a warning, simple and sincere—trifle with me, and you shall learn precisely how my art makes corpses of dreams.

Quite adept at the speedy reorganization of the human body, I fashioned my effigy of warning in short order—a dreamcatcher made from the emptied shell of the living nightmare. My wonderful work was held together by a damp geometry of broken bones, strung with red webs of vein and artery, feathered with a dripping scalp of flowing hair. The webbing I embellished with the thing's stolen teeth. Unfortunately, I could locate only two burned-out cavities where the thing's alien eyes should have been, otherwise the brilliant spheres would have made for excellent decoration.

With my warning complete, I walked to the edge of the rooftop and tossed the creature's foolish hat into the dark.

Shortly after, I stood upon yet another rooftop, watching as a twisting bank of angry clouds descended on the city risen from sleep. The drifting storm settled between the winking belfries and crooked spires, presenting a rolling field of muttering thunder. Merging from without the storm came the clamor of pointed activity, from nearly every quarter of the city. New Victoria was slowly coming alive. I could hear the rustling of unearthly things congregating into unwholesome crowds. Sighing, I wondered if my cobbled warning had been a bad idea.

Recessed deeply into the night, moving within the tumbling grey, I could see small shivering points of blue light. I knew very well what they were—the Wakeless had taken to the skies to find me. I looked down from the edge of the rooftop to where the windows beneath me turned the bright color of sleep. I watched the cold blue move ever upward, searching, room by room. The sounds of a second storm began howling from the streets below—inhuman gangs of nightmares born from living women trampled the earth upon countless hateful limbs, creeping, crawling, flying, leaping.

I couldn't afford the laughter that mounted as surely as the storm. I swallowed my amusement, wrapped myself in silence, and leapt to the roof of an adjacent building. I waded into the thick cloud cover swirling in front of me as a nearby rooftop door exploded outward. A gang of evil things landed around me like a downpour from hell.

The storm obeyed me as well as any shadow, and I disappeared into its coiling mists. There were a great many of the caterwauling things, so both of my sisters stood eagerly at the ready. The fiends flooded into the storm, heedless of the danger within. Within seconds, several of the things had been effectively multiplied—or divided, depending on how you wished to perform the math—before the rest of the horde became even faintly aware of the death moving within their ranks.

As I killed under cover of storm cloud, I could only make out the slightest details of my adversaries. When an arc of blinding light poured into the bloodied spaces around me, my eyes deferred to my ears for instruction. And when the crashing thunder robbed my ears of the world, I moved by the silence —beneath the thunder, between the night, from within the shadows that danced and frolicked to the music of the storm. The collective confidence granted them by the force of their numbers diminished by the second, and I could detect more than a few scrambling feet making for escape. The devils were certainly powerful enough, yet they were new to the world of stable things and could not fathom the strategies of a solid opponent, much less one who was unafraid. They came at me with claws, fangs, tentacles, and hooves, and I conducted each to my sisters' reddening smiles. One nightmare—likely an older iteration— proved wiser than the rest, waiting for my fury to abate. When the last of the creatures had been slaughtered or driven off, and I had returned my sisters to their sleep, it struck.

The creature secured itself to my back with flashing talons—organic hooks with searing, chitinous barbs. It tried to tear me in two with a passion rivaled only by my sisters' bottomless depravity. As I struggled to rid myself of the creature, it hissed sulfurous words into my ear, its breath the carcass of a dream. "What wonderful teeth and claws your kind's dreams have given me. Am I not a splendid thing, ripping the flesh from your bones? I swear to cherish your screams for as long as I care to remember them."

The creature was an undeniably exceptional member of its kind, deserving of my compliments. "You are indeed splendid, creature. But I'm afraid I have no screams for you today. Perhaps my sister's laughter will suffice." Already in hand, she shined a jagged grin into the creature's cavernous mouth. I could feel my enemy's teeth scrape my knuckles as my sister dragged my hand behind her, down what seemed an endless, convulsing hole.

I drew close to the monster's ear and whispered, "Is she not splendid as well, creature? Tell me, will you scream for her?" The thing had apparently lost its taste for conversation, which was forgivable, as its mouth was suddenly without tongue. It seized my arm with incredible strength, tearing my hand from the sucking wound of its face.

I felt my other sister slide into my free hand, her laughter infectious. She tore across the claw that held me, springing a honeyed howl from the bleeding trench of a mouth. "I knew you would find your singing voice, eventually!" she squealed. The thing reeled backward of my shoulders, screeching and bleeding from my sisters' joint assault.

Before I knew it, my sisters had been replaced by my father. "And your last scream shall belong to me!" my great benefactor roared. My father fell with such power that the very air around him warped and crackled. Unbelievably, the inhuman thing absorbed the blow, refusing to fall. Never had I witnessed a creature capable of weathering such direct exposure to my father's power. Regardless, the creature had been sorely wounded, its claws busy trying to stem the flow of strange fluids that sprayed from its broken body. It backpedaled until it found a wall and turned its furnace-eyes upon me, silently promising a death beyond comprehension.

My father's rage had grown beyond steel and bone, sending waves of purest hatred rolling through me. He roared toward the glaring monster with a fury that nearly burned through my hands. I should have been impressed by the speed and monstrous strength demonstrated by the creature when it leapt sideways onto a distant rooftop, but my attention was stolen away by the unearthly collision between the wall and my father. Where once there was concrete, steel, and monster, there was now only debris and a dreadful echo. My raging father suddenly went quiet and fell into fitful sleep, my sisters' laughter unwinding into the night. The mixing of dream and reality had certainly bent the physics of the physical towards the metaphysical, but my father's recent display of power was beyond any demonstration I'd seen before, in or out of New Victoria. Yet it was definitely a dream I suspected of enlarging the fury of my father, save that this one was red, and filled with wolves.

With their infantry momentarily diffused into the night, the generals of the nightmare army closed in. I could sense the cold fires of their blue eyes reaching out to me, eager to snuff my solidity. I wasted no time acquiring the dwelling of the man I had come to consult. Strangely, the floating creatures withdrew to the farthest darkness, their blue eyes dying like stars at dawn. I wondered if I'd crossed into a space beyond their power. Whatever the reason for their retreat, I had reached my destination. I sat down for a time to regain my strength, drifting into gentle memories of standing in the rain with my mother.

CHAPTER SIX

Reverence is an interesting word, often applied more discriminately than others of its caliber. So, when the young man I had come to see used it to describe his feelings toward his dreams, I felt inclined to listen a bit more carefully.

"There is wisdom within my dreams," the Sleep Sage said, "beyond the pull of standard reason and logic. It is crafted from experiences that have not been filtered through the waking senses, and so persists as a knowing without conventional form or substance." The man barely moved, lying on his bed, looking at the moths orbiting a naked bulb. Where the electricity came from to supply the light, I had no idea. The city was in ruins, but I was sure it wasn't suffering from a paucity of energy resources, no matter how gruesome or unearthly.

"Moths," he continued. "They are so much different than butterflies. They recall the difference between waking and dreaming. You see, the butterfly is a beautiful creature, but only and ultimately explicit, wearing its colors upon the dust of its wings. Such a creature can only decorate the world, just a living bow tied whimsically around a gust of wind, fluttering beautifully, pointlessly. Like most things, the butterfly is really just a dried-up dream that has lost its connection to the other side, and so has become an exhibition without substance or source.

"The moth, however, is a great adventurer, a night-thing—it is the custodian of uncommon desires. Not content with only its wings and the open air, it yearns for more, and so drowns itself in the night, every night, looking for something. What it seeks no one knows, not even the moth. It simply knows that what is, is all wrong—and there must be something greater hiding behind the night's darkness, something more wonderful than even tireless wings and an infinity of night could ever provide.

"It is as if the moth's entire life were designed for a singular purpose—escape. Or perhaps it was merely designed to believe that it exists in a place that needs escaping from, and that its nightly passions are somehow sufficient to locate a way out. A dream, you understand, takes wing into the unknown as well, traveling and never arriving, always searching for an exit and rarely finding one."

Obviously, I disagreed with his characterization of the Deadworld, as it could never be decorated—it can only ingest beauty, leaving behind the dry bones of devoured dreams. Yet the man's expertise lay in dreams and not the waking world, so I forgave the mistake—although his characterization of the butterfly was indeed correct.

He looked away from the whirling moths and stared straight at me, smiling slightly. "But you did not come here to talk about butterflies, did you? No, you want to know about the moths—about those strange dreams you're having." I nodded, and his eyes took on a strange energy, as if they were aglow in some other spectrum of light, or darkness. He directed his undetectably radiant gaze beyond the gaping hole in his ceiling, freeing his vision into the wet black sky. The rain was light, its soft patter blending easily with the gentle breeze.

"This place," he continued, "the entire city, has rested upon the precipice of some hazy and forgotten dreamworld ever since the daemon-sleep arrived from beyond our furthest nightmares. I've been dreaming myself closer and closer to that world every day and night, stealing into its pallid, high-walled lanes, eating of its food, spending my living years on dream after dream of a world that is precisely not this one.

"Do you think I leave this bed to eat? Of course not. I sustain myself there—within the grey drifting fields broken only by spindly trees and the ruins of visions long since passed. I partake of the whispering fruit and drink the weird smoldering waters tumbling across the endless sky like herds of rushing ghosts. And what about this body of mine, this youthful weight that lies before you? It is only a point of reference. My mind has spent so little time here that my body has barely aged. But I am far from young, farther still from truly old. I say this only to inform you of the paths that I have walked to learn what I know—and I know what I know quite well." I said nothing, only waited for him to continue. His eyes returned to the room and back to the wheeling moths.

With no small amount of concentration, he began a new tale. "Quite a few dreams ago, I was wandering a damp passageway constructed from interlocking basements, each one opening into the next by way of a different type of subterranean entrance. I encountered an entity who referred to himself as the King of Cellars. He was an affable old fellow, so I visited with him beneath the weak illumination of old and crusty light bulbs. We were having quite a pleasant time, talking and philosophizing as we drank from our chipped cups of softly sweetened tea, when from deep below we heard the savage bluster of numerous and clearly enormous wolves.

"The Lord of Basements remarked on the sounds only when he saw how frightened I'd become, saying 'Mine is not the deepest kingdom, for far below us lurks a pit deeper than any traditional spaces—and most non-traditional spaces, for that matter—could ever hope to admit. Those inhabiting that great depression are nearly as old as the machines that gave emptiness its color and numbered the dust. The great company of the pit are generally a quiet lot, but recently, one of them has become quite busy. I can hear the strange sounds of its dark enterprise, occasionally.'

"When I asked about the demonic wolves, he said only, 'The industrious one that I mentioned is lean and voracious, and the wolves are its voice. It speaks stolen breaths into hungry sentences made from packs of frothing wolves, wherein each ravening word can hunt and kill. It is speaking now, but to whom, I cannot say.'

"My host would say no more, and I was relieved to move past the topic at the time, as the deep sounds nearly startled me awake. However, after I departed the Kingdom of Cellars and its charming ruler, I resolved to learn more about this creature, the thing with a voice filled with wolves. Eventually, this entity became a point of some fascination for me, and so I dreamed as deeply as I was able, trying to find some trace of this pit of which the Cellar King made mention.

"After many dreams of unsuccessful questing, I finally located an ancient nightmare drifting alone in a sea of muted screams, replaying its bloody history over and over again. The apparent dreamers of this nightmare had been many and monstrous, but long dead. Strangely, as I explored the contents of the abandoned vision, it seemed that the dreamers had not only shared the same dream, but had actually killed one another within it, their battles still echoing in blood and memory. I returned to the dream often, and every time I sank beyond its cold membrane of shiftless sleep, setting foot upon the shores of its old death, I would feel eyes upon me, amused it seemed at my revulsion for the many evils it once contained. The sum of my many stolen glimpses would suggest that the dream is not the property of what I first took to be its dreamers, but rather a creation of another being entirely, likely the Unbegotten entity the Cellar King and I had overheard, so many dreams prior.

"It seems to me to be a construct, forged from powers that partake from no earthly source, functioning much like a dream—it joins with sleeping minds, granting such souls passage into its secreted spaces. And still it is not a dream for true—it holds the potential to be much more, something else entirely. You see, the thing starts out quite empty, just the potential for a dream, but as it blends with a sleeping mind, it begins to fill up, taking the shape of its contents. Yet even these attributes wouldn't visibly set it apart from any garden-variety dream. No, it's magic rests with the thing's ability to grow beyond sleep, to master the inferior world of waking. Further texturing its composition is that it is highly selective, choosing only the ripest, reddest dreams—those whose bloody vision might be sufficient to fuel its capacity to overcome reality.

"It is this last point that explains why the monstrous dreamers had been assembled—to claim the honor of embodying the Red Dream.

But this also reveals the cruelty of the thing, for the dream is not fitted to merely a single dreamer, but to many—monsters all dreaming the same dream. And it is through that red facility the dreamers will come to know one another, find one another, and finally, kill one another.

"However, on the last occasion I visited the dream, all was not quiet but for the baying of dead beasts. The nightmare was filling up with the voices of fresh wolves, growing hot with hunger and blood. These new creatures began falling upon one another, rending flesh from bone, and the dream had been removed from the depths of forgotten silence, lifted into red pools of terrible sleep. As I departed, familiar eyes watched me go, something whose age was nearly as deep as the pit itself. When its sight had fallen entirely upon me, I felt my dream-self nearly explode from the heat. I awoke that night to blankets of fire."

The man threw his gaze at a hump of burned sheets piled crudely in one corner of the shabby room. "But before I awoke, I caught a passing glance at the thing that could cast fire from slumber. It wore the likeness of a darkened shepherd, and it bore in its hand a bleeding crook."

I recalled the Crucifier's yellowed journal. "You speak of the Shepherd of Wolves, do you not?"

The man looked a bit irritated, as if I'd disrupted the rhythm of his carefully planned sermon. "Of course. He is the thing that calls to you—and all the rest of your kind." He waited for the words he knew I would speak.

"I have no 'kind,' dreamer. I am no wolf. I am a repairer of dreams, an artist. Everything else is merely parenthetical—nothing more, nothing less."

"Are you an artist, indeed?" the man said. "I will say this for you—you are different. But you have no idea what you are, do you?" Some of his words were like the distant notes of a weakly remembered song. His latest words were offensive, but his was the knowledge of things that walked the distant shores of dream, not of matters concerning the business of firmer worlds. He was again forgiven, or at the least ignored.

His smile returned to light up invisible worlds. He was quite pleased with himself. "You have no choice but to play the Shepherd's Game, and you have every reason to play it well, my giant friend. You see, the Shepherd is one of the Unbegotten. His will, even from down within so deep a hole, is simply inevitable. He cannot be denied his sport. He wrote you an invitation in blood and twilight, and he means for you to join him and all the others in a game that can displace stars and conjure worlds from whispers."

"And should I win, the Red Dream is mine for the wielding?" I asked, my curiosity rising.

"Who is to say? The Shepherd is as mysterious as the nightmare that dismembered Boston and raised New Victoria from its riven corpse. The wills and ways of such things are not for us to know. We simply symbolize their power, in the same way ink symbolizes our thoughts on paper—though we are not the ones holding the pen."

I took a moment to consider the man's words, imposing them atop the Game and its players, sifting for a theory, if not the facts. Might the Red Dream itself be the prize? A thing made whole in the winning, a power for the taking by the last wolf? It was an appealing thought, one worth further exploration—and killing. Which led me to my next question.

"I have one final query for you, dreamer," I said, sensing the answer stirring within him. "What do you know of the dreams of Sara Kane?"

The man's grin spread wide. "You mean, of course, Black Molly Patience. She is a poisonous one, a cannibal who walks under the world, serving her darkest appetites. Her underground tunnels, sweet venoms, and secret trapdoors are the very stuff of children's nightmares. She has stalked the underbelly of humanity since the close of the Great Darkness, chewing the courage of an entire generation down to its rubbery gristle."

The information transformed another name on my kill list into a wickedly wonderful thing. The thought of finding her darkness and making it my own was exhilarating, though I couldn't help but imagine the toll such an act would exercise upon my conscience. How could I forgive myself for such a thing? And why would this "Shepherd" want me to do the Mother of the Deadworld the favor of removing one of her greatest enemies?

"You are like a feral angel—powerful, pure, and deadly. But you are likewise ultimately beholden to greater powers," the Sage said. "I envy you, though—I must sleep to find my dreams, yet here you are in the middle of the solid world, hunting and hunted by them. But my envy goes only so far before it is replaced by pity. While you have the good fortune of being wrapped in wildest visions, day and night, I have walked between the headstones of that crimson nightmare, and I know—it does not end well."

"Graveyards can be gardens, dreamer," I replied, "and death can be as fertile as the blackest soil. Perhaps you wandered a garden that had been poorly planted, one only waiting to be sown with better seed." My insight indulged my best hopes. I knew that dreams were tricky beasts, and even the most seasoned dreamer is likely to misinterpret them. As any good dreamer knows, dreams make promises carved in smoke and speak in the hissing sibilance of snakes. "While we're lingering upon this issue of grim inevitability, I would very much like to know how you've come to be ignored by the things that inhabit this city."

"That is a particularly interesting topic, given your previous mention of gardens," the dreamer said. "You see, I too am being cultivated. This very bed I sleep upon is invaluable to the creatures that dwell here. Every time I return from dream, a little bit of my journey is left behind within its sheets, its rusted frame and creaking headboard. These creatures possess a kind of technology that harvests it for their own strange purposes. I learned all of this upon the close of the first day I entered New Victoria, just weeks after the plague began. After making my way through the silent crowds of shambling sleepwalkers, past screeching birth knells of infant nightmares, I finally took shelter in the spacious rooms of a derelict house, set gently afloat in the untended hands of a small meadow.

"At that point, I had become far too familiar with the unearthly sounds of nightmares risen from sleep, and so failed to immediately investigate the metallic droning that vibrated the ceiling. Eventually, the sounds of something creeping toward my bed renewed my exhausted curiosity. When I gazed into a small patch of moonlight falling from the bed to the floor, I could see the creeping machinations of a curious industry—throbbing, semi-organic tubers slithering across the floor and crawling up from beneath my bed.

"Of course, I was quick to leap from the bed, and just in time—a ganglionic tangle of smaller tubers descended the unseen corners of the dark room and seized my pillow within a death-grip of extruded hooks and needles. Shortly after the creeping lengths of flesh and steel had all but cocooned my previous sleeping arrangements, the collective apparatus of varied organics began to pulsate with a kind of sickening rhythm, composed of an orderly exchange between slurping and chewing sounds. It took no great amount of thought for me to deduce the strange technologies were extracting dreams from the materials of the bed. In fact, anything in routine contact with dreams was susceptible to the power of the alien devices.

"As perhaps you are uniquely positioned to understand, any dream that can survive waking—even in the minutest amounts—is a quantifiable victory over all of this intractable waking foolishness. So, these things have smartly devised a means by which no amount of residual dream is suffered to waste. Since that night, the things have left me to my own devices—so long as I dream in the right direction and do not distract them from their work.

"And with that, I can offer you no further insights. Eyes are upon me, and I am only tolerated here as long as I remain a quietly ripening fruit, not a vulgar flower that gathers stinging pests."

As a parting gift, the dreamer granted me one last bit of insight—a secret route allowing me safe passage beneath the city. I walked through the damp blackness of a long hallway toward the elevator. The dimmest of lights shone from above the vintage conveyance, its illumination little more than a glowing darkness indicating the direction of its travel.

As I boarded the lift, and just before its doors slid shut, I heard the piercing screams of the man I'd left to his demanding sleep. Apparently, the Wakeless had made a calculated decision concerning their pursuit of me, its execution boding poorly for my insightful friend, waxing resource or not. I knew there was nothing to be done for the man, so I hoped the better part of his mind somehow managed to escape into the weightless and rushing waters of his precious dreams. Sadly, the colder, more rational part of my mind knew better.

The doors opened into a basement, and I took a moment to look for entities who might preside over it in some official capacity. Yet, as much as the city partook in dreams, it seemed not to include the pleasant company of Cellar Kings and their subterranean sovereignties. This was not to say that some echo of the Kingdom of Cellars was entirely absent—a wonderfully wide hole occupied a wall, opening into a labyrinth of earthen tunnels. I quickly moved beyond the opening into the meandering maze of widely hewn stone.

Behind me, I heard the singular tone of an elevator reaching its destination. I chuckled a bit too loudly at the image of such brilliantly vile creatures as the Wakeless loading into an elevator like so many office workers, tapping their clawed feet to "The Girl From Ipanema" as they awaited the proper floor. Despite the amusement the chase provided, I grew tired of being rushed. I summoned my father to my grip, and with deafening force he brought down the stone ceiling—I believed he was still upset about his previous failure to finalize matters between himself and a certain tongueless nightmare. Massive chunks of earth crashed to the floor in thick clouds of dust and debris, blocking the way behind. My father was not pleased at having been awoken for so pedestrian a task, but the freedom he afforded me made the weight of his silent reproach bearable.

Wandering the cave system, I imagined myself as Black Molly Patience—listening intently, gliding the hollows of the earth, waiting to strike. With victim in hand, I send my venom coursing through its bloodstream and steal it into the subterranean rooms of my home. The bones of prior meals worry at my naked feet as I devour my paralyzed prey. I was so absorbed in daydream, I'd failed entirely to notice the gathering light. Before I knew it, I was exiting a densely overgrown cave in the middle of the woods. Not long after, I drew to the top of a nearby hill and observed the distant spires of New Victoria. They seemed to pierce the sky, the blood of twilight everywhere. I gave the city one final look, wondering if I would ever tempt its power a third time. I certainly hoped so.

Once out from beneath its shadow, I moved back onto the main road beyond the broken barricades. I wasn't ten feet before I sensed a presence, resentful for my leaving. Were it not for the smell, I might have thought it the residuum of sour grapes—one of the Wakeless bemoaning my escape. But it was nothing less than the White Gaia herself. She stood on the far side of the pavement, her sickly yellow light pouring atop the cracked blacktop, emphasizing each pebble of artificially blackened stone. I could feel her gangrenous thoughts pulling at the shadows around me, trying to weed her garden of stinking blacktop. Her stench—a horrible mixture of tar and heat—swept back and forth across the air, causing even the light to recoil. It was the pattern of cracks in a nearby concrete wall that betrayed her shape, a corpulence of swollen rot piled into the crude likeness of a woman. Her head was buried in the sun—just a sickly bloom of yellowed light spread wide and warm across my upturned face. This was a powerful omen, indeed. She wanted me dead in that city, so that I might not continue the Game. She was threatened by me. Before she vanished into the reeking air, I managed the Dead Queen a thin smile—a mere sample of smiles to come.

CHAPTER SEVEN

After many days of travel, I found myself in a small village, its sole redeeming feature a large stone statue carved sometime during the Great Darkness. With the blackest of anthracite wings framing a largely skeletal frame, the clam of death settled like dust across the expertly engraved nuances of pores and frown-marks. The creature seemed more breathing flesh than cold stone. Inscribed upon its base was *Mother of the Stillborn*. While lacking any Pre-Darkness existence, the statue was only a graven dream, a form without substance. But this fact had not stopped cabals and cults from gathering in its—her—honor.

Where there is mystery, there is religion, so they say, and the Darkness has been the source of many a new faith, often to the destruction of an older one. Here was just such a case—the dark woman seemed to demand a past, a mythology all her own. It might have been her exquisite construction, or perhaps her darksome, unending stare that compelled the specific folklore that was draped across her delicate frame. Or, more likely, and the reason I much prefer—the lady herself commanded such supplications, as she partook of a genuine existence that black stone and story had only recently caught up with.

Whatever the reason for her rise to prominence, her given mythology was fairly uniform. She was believed a spirit, or dour angel, who caught the tiny souls of the stillborn, replacing them to her own cold, dead womb, to later be reborn—or perhaps unborn. Supplementary concepts to this wishful interpretation included a rather whimsical function to the faded lady's soul-catching. Specifically, that after enough stillborn souls were collected, she would give birth to the Ancient Child—a tiny, wizened heir to the boneyards of the world, who would preside over the courts of the dead atop a throne of tombstones. It was a lovely Post-Darkness religion, one that I wished all the best.

The approach to the towering statue was crowded with small humps of piled dirt, each one marked with the browned blossoms of baby's breath. The meadow had become the burying place of tiny hopes, where grief-stricken mothers came to offer their departed children one last chance at life. The contemplative statue had become the sole gravestone for throngs of the tiny dead, a lonely anchor for a last and darkest hope.

I once considered a relationship between this mother and the White Gaia, supposing one for the cultural appropriation of the other, as Jupiter was of Zeus. But as I stood before Black Helen, as she was often called, I knew I was completely wrong. There was no lasting death among the tiny, nameless graves, only a desire to overcome at any price. Alternately, it was the elegance of her worked stone, the sublime coherence of purpose, which recalled my own mother. The resemblance stirred a memory—my mother's face, twilit and doubtful. Yet it was her eyes I remembered best, the gentle pull of purest darkness. When I touched the hand of the statue, I might have spoken a name, a sound haunting two worlds, lost to both.

I slept at the foot of the statue, where dreams might cluster thickest. I remember the touch of a hand against my cheek. It gently drew me to my feet. A composite mother made from my own memories and the one whose feet I laid at examined my face, turning it within her grasp. Two voices joined by their words came to me. "You might have been one of my own." Then, from behind me, I heard the baying of wolves. I turned toward the sound, but there was nothing. When I turned back to face the mother, I was met by a wave of them, monstrous and starving. As I sank into their numbers, I spied the woman made of two mothers. She only smiled as the beasts tore the flesh of my mind from the bones of an old dream.

When I awoke, it was night. It pleased me to imagine the black statue's shadow having swallowed up all the light. The goddess above me had exchanged her smile for a faraway stare that likely settled upon invisible worlds filled with the laughter of lost children, thrilling to games only the dead may play. As I rose to my feet, a third woman entered my thoughts—Black Molly Patience. I had no idea where to find her. She roamed under the night with the flow and freedom of a whisper, devouring whomever her appetite adored. However, like the deathly woman carved from coal, she was not without a following of faithful. I would start with them.

The next town was hardly in need of a name, untroubled as it was by any meaningful distinction. I roamed muted streets coiled lazily around staggered lines of nearly identical houses—if it weren't for the numbers engraved upon them, there would have been no telling them apart. The few people I observed were as iterative as the buildings, and I wondered if numbers hadn't been carved into them as well.

Coldchester—it did have a name, for whatever reason— was either remarkably brave, or so foolish it considered its fine view of the nearby mountains an acceptable reason to risk its close proximity to New Victoria. Although, oddly enough, the place did appear untouched by the sleeping metropolis. And I detected none of the characteristic screaming and moaning that generally accompanies an outbreak of the sleeping sickness.

Before long, I'd broken into the city's Museum of Darkness, which was significantly smaller than others of its kind. This was likely owing to the want for all evidence of the Darkness to be destroyed—despite the law decreeing its preservation—along with a burgeoning black market for Darkness artifacts, known as *Obscuruum*. A hopeless project to be sure, the official preservation effort had been abandoned years ago. Yet most of the structures still remained, though they were largely shunned by all but the biggest cities and universities.

I happily sorted through hundreds of bizarre baubles before finding my signpost. In a box marked *monsters*, I recovered yellowed newspaper clippings tracking the antics of persons referred to by certain medical professionals as *Noctu-psychotics,* or *Noctupaths*—individuals possessed of such Post-Darkness insanity that they proved capable of inhuman feats. It was speculated that they evolved a mental equilibrium with the Darkness, tapping into vast storehouses of human potential. Unfortunately, when the Darkness concluded, so too did the functional nature of the strange adaptations, abandoning affected persons to a world no longer capable of making sense of them, or to them. Her near-impossible feats of murder placed Black Molly on a short list of killers suspected of being Noctupaths. The articles detailing her exploits were many and varied, not to mention enthralling. But one stood out above all others—the tale and location of her fist recorded kill. She would have abandoned much of herself to such a place, clues she's since learned not to leave behind. And many of her doting well-wishers would likely flock to such a place—beginnings often overflowed with power, and few were stronger or more compelling than that of Black Molly Patience.

Likely due to its proximity to New Victoria, Coldchester housed a train station—though it was so run down I could scarcely believe any trains still called upon it at all. And the complete lack of travelers did little to bolster that belief. So when a train did indeed make its scheduled stop, I was happily surprised. The interior seemed oddly lean, as if the small number of commuters had caused its belly to narrow from malnutrition. I took a seat in a dark corner, the surrounding dirty windows pleasantly resistant to the setting sun's rays. All too often, the light overemphasized the world, eradicating shadows and denying mystery its purchase upon the unseen.

According to my travel guide, the train had been repurposed back to its initial use, having been used previously for the transportation of the dead. Corpses were as abundant as flies directly after the Darkness, and many fixtures of the old world were converted for the clean-up effort. Though smartly redecorated, the train failed to conceal its history, feeling more like a physical memory of darker times.

My car was empty save for one other man. He carried a vintage camera apparatus, the kind that sat atop a tripod of wooden legs. It appeared carved entirely from the darkest wood and the most lusterless of metals. He occasionally looked over at me, smiling like a mortician after a disaster, his teeth so large they seemed almost cartoonish. He disembarked at the next stop, somewhere in the middle of the woods, atop a platform even more abandoned than the Coldchester station. The darkness seemed to mourn his absence. I tried to imagine what the photographer wished to photograph, so far out in the middle of the woods, and so late in the evening.

The train pushed on for some time, its rhythm calming. The passing sights, frozen into view by the cold light of the moon, were hypnotic. Reclining my seat, I nearly merged with the aged leather, sinking into sleep as deeply as I did the seat. I wondered why dreaming wasn't listed as one of the train's enumerated attractions.

As soon as my mind drifted beyond the gentle specter of the moon, I reached out for a dream. Yet where my dream should have been, there was something else entirely—a changeling of sorts, as if my own dream had been stolen and somehow replaced with someone else's. I am a dreamer of no small skill, and I know my own dreams. This was not one of them.

***

I dreamed of a house—ample, outfitted with a sort of expensive, faux rusticism. I was looking out a window, watching a bird take its meal from a tray feeder. A sound spread across the sky. It wasn't so much loud as it was alien, and it was becoming everything. The bird vanished. In the span of a thought, the world changed. I ran through the streets wearing only the skin on my feet. All around me, the world was breaking apart, giving birth. The sound was as big as the world, and I felt incredibly small, caught underfoot, without place or purpose. Finding a hole in the earth, I plunged into darkness. There were other things in there like me, abandoned by the world, by nature.

The dream changed sharply. While I remained the same, I was also different—better. The time had changed, but my place underground had not. I was moving at a brisk but decidedly measured pace, despite the utter lack of light. There were other things surrounding me in the darkness. Whatever they were, they belonged to me, body and soul. Up into the moonlight we went, all clicking claws and licking lips. Looking upon the moon, I beheld weird shapes stretched dark and massive across its face. The intervening sky was alive somehow, alien, but not hurtful to look upon. I'd long made peace with the new world. I was right with it, prepared—designed for it.

My pack and I made our way through corpse-piled gutters and lanes carved clean and straight by rivers of gushing gore. We moved upon roads paved by living tars, crept the thickets of rambling, rusted, barbed wires. We ignored the pleading, ensnared shapes—prey to unseen things haunting the webs of bloody, serrated steel.

Finally, we came upon our destination—a gigantic factory. I lifted my gaze to leer at a massive smokestack throwing black plumes at the sky. We entered by way of a ragged hole, and something monstrous rose against us as we poured inside. We fell upon the faceless thing, devouring it. We were almost a single entity as we crossed the lower floors of the building, seeking the rooftop. More outrageous shapes attempted to block our path, but we were a biblical flood that couldn't be stopped or slowed. Every living thing we washed over became a pile of picked bones. The last door fell to us, and we surged across the roof.

There, squatting atop a throne of smokestacks, was a terrible creature—an unapologetic existence of violated logic and common sense. Snarling, it lifted itself from the toxic smoke. I answered in equally guttural fashion, the collective chortle of my monsters embellishing my voice. I had become no less a violation of nature than the thing standing before me, and I was pleased for the opportunity to demonstrate the fact.

***

The excitement from the impending clash woke me from my displaced dream, and I immediately wondered—if I was dreaming someone else's dream, who was dreaming mine? The answer was obvious. I hoped Miss Patience enjoyed the exchange as much as I did.

The swapping of dreams was a new development to the Red Dream—a power that seemed to visit itself upon those joined in the Shepherd's Game. The Sage was correct, though I never truly doubted the general shape of his knowledge. The players of the game—the Wolves—were indeed caught up in the same dream. More specifically, our dreams were now accessible to one another. Even more precisely, it seemed the specific dreams we shared were determined by the next names upon our lists. Black Molly was next upon mine, and so her dreams had come to me, enlightening me to the wonders of my opponent, and perhaps even the wider game now afoot.

With the dream concluded, I was immediately sad for the hope I had gained. But this was only a rote response, loath though I am to admit such occurrences. My entire life had been filled with moments of possibility, scattered between art pieces and dreams, affording me the wherewithal to continue my work, but only enough to persevere. Hope had become a predictable, even necessary staple to my life, at least as much as eating and drinking. But like food and drink, hope is consumed in short order, to fuel the mind if not the body. And so, the sight of hope was merely the expectation of its passing, a recognition of futility.

But if what I dreamed was true, and I was reasonably sure I was, I'd glimpsed a sleeping sliver of the Great Darkness—Black Molly's share in it, at least. Here was something precious and singular—a preserved fragment of a banished history. I saw what the world had become, and could perhaps become again. I witnessed the overthrow of the Dead Queen, her corpulent dullness scattered like ashes across a world of resurrected dreams. Was this the purpose of the vision—to advertise a possible reward for a game well played? Or was it only a parenthetical slideshow of the next name on my kill list?

Whatever the case, the dream had appreciably lightened my desire to eliminate the subterranean cannibal, for she was pure monster—forged from primal forces, mistress to dark hordes, and hunter of fiends. Alternatively, I was anxious to meet her monstrous legions and stand before her bleeding smile, which could easily pass for one of my sisters'. I would have liked to believe that I had some choice in the matter, but in truth, I had none. I was in love with the drift of inscrutable purpose and the power of endless possibility. As an artist, to see your work actually affect the world was too wondrous a reward to pass up.

A line of mountains meandered into view as the train slowed, clouds tumbling down their eastern face like a phantom avalanche. The next stop was listed as "Orphan." As the train came to a halt and opened its doors, I peered out the windows intently, hoping to glimpse the species of creature affording the city its strange name. While the train lingered at the boarding platform, a tinny voice announced a two-hour layover before resuming. I happily disembarked, eager to explore.

Few passengers departed the other cars. Exactly twelve people, all told, not a stitch of the remarkable about them. I took to the shadows of the path we all followed into town, not giving the small crowd a second thought. The town itself was trivial and quiet, but the echoes of horrors past still sounded within its neglected spaces, always reminding those sensitive to such reverberations that past is prologue. Yet beyond its connection to plague and death, it was a quaint, only slightly haunted little hamlet.

There were sights in and around any city, if you knew where and how to look for them. For instance, after following a trail of old death into the woods surrounding Orphan, I located a wonderful and well-hidden mass grave. It had nourished a collection of the most monstrous trees I'd seen since traveling the back roads around Autumn City, near the infamous September Woods. A short while later, I discovered a small smokehouse converted into an art gallery. Something left over from the past must have found a willing supplicant somewhere in the city, calling upon them to recount their darkest visions in pig's blood, and to paint those images across the dried skins of deer and bear. The gallery was fresh, as some of the paintings had dried only recently. One piece caught my eye—a tall, gaunt man had been painted against a background composed of many hundreds of knotted serpents. He wore a dainty crown fashioned of small snake bones. Above his head was written, *The Prince of Snakes*. Despite the one mature work, the remaining pieces were only fledglings. The animal materials satisfied an embryonic art that would soon call for more blood and skin, of a species requiring a gallery less easily stumbled upon by persons wandering the woods.

After returning to the station, I found that the small crowd had grown by one member. The new addition seemed out of place, trying too hard to blend into the gathering. Entering the passenger car, I took a seat behind the man who wished to move unnoticed. I watched him for some time before realizing he was looking back at me through the reflective chrome that wrapped around a handrail.

"I have no head for this sort of game," the man said, our eyes locking upon the reflection of the other. "I'm far too impatient. It's the chaos I'm chasing. The faster and faster I go . . . I just love it. You?" I said nothing. My sister was already near to hand, and I couldn't deny how badly I wanted to express the artistic inspiration gained via my sleeping glimpse into The Great Darkness.

The man—as if knowing that any untoward movements would lead to his death—slowly lifted a piece of water-stained paper from his front pocket. He unfolded it, briefly holding it within view. It was a kill list, replete with crossed-off names and numbered entries.

"See?" the man said. "I don't think you're on here. Or at least, you're not next on my list. I'm embarrassed to say that it took me some time to finally know the true face of my next playmate, and you certainly don't look anything like the Breath Taker. And from the fact that I'm still talking, I'm going to assume I'm not on your list, either. Are we permitted to kill out of order? If so, I suppose we may have a problem."

"You would have the problem, I'm afraid," I said, effortlessly sliding my sister through the fabrics and plastics of the seat between us, gently resting her deadly smile against his back. "But I've had no inclination to pursue the names out of order, thus far. However, there does seem to be an implicit formality to all of this. So for now, I'm willing to consider the order of the names as something of an unspoken rule."

"It's the damned linearity of this list that has me wanting to quit this awful game," the man replied. "As an artist, I'm sure you must feel the same, yes?" He knew who I was. That interested me.

"Why do you think you know who I am?" I asked.

"You're gigantic," the man said, "with what could easily be an enormous axe wrapped up and strapped across your back. To be honest, I'm not sure how you've lasted so long with such an appearance, and traveling via public transportation, no less." He still hadn't turned to face me. "Do I have you at a disadvantage, my friend? Have you no idea with whom you are speaking? I wonder how many faceless names you've already scratched off that list of yours, all the while having no idea as to the paths you've destroyed. Shame on you, if that's true. I mean, we're not, any of us, living inferior lives, are we? We've spared ourselves very little waste by way of lost opportunities. Again, as an artist, I assume you to understand the gist of what I'm saying. But the chance to see all the faces face the right way, follow all the lost paths . . . why, it's just too tempting to permit a little killing, even if ultimately misplaced, to give us pause. Killing to make the killing unnecessary, yes? That is what we're doing, isn't it? We're being made to thin our own ranks, in order for one of us to fill the world with their will. Or have you a grander explanation to share?"

The man was intriguing enough to warrant a response. "First, I knew something about the better majority of those I hunted, and those who hunted me. The others weren't permitted a proper introduction, I'm afraid. As to the nature of the game, I'll keep my opinions to myself. And while I admit to a temporary loss in our little naming game, your interest in lost opportunities and faces tells me more about you than the fact that you won't show me your face—or whoever's face that is. Even the moonlight falling from behind me can't reveal the unmoving portions of dead skin that make up that wonderful mask you've constructed. Although, as soon as you're on the move again, you'll turn it around, revealing a face on both sides of your head. Am I correct, Janus?"

The man laughed. "That's the reason you've proven so elusive! You're a clever fox, indeed! Yes, you've guessed correctly!" Still laughing, the masked killer finally turned to face me. I stared into eyes as lethal as the dagger that swiftly knocked aside my sister's gleaming smile.

CHAPTER EIGHT

It wasn't the moonlight that alerted me to the fact that the man wore another person's face over top of his own. The precision of the mask's fashioning was clearly exquisite, even superhuman—but the fit was too perfect. It was as if the victim had been genetically designed to blend into the features and nuances of the killer's face. But I knew the artist known as Janus the Two-Faced had been host to many faces, and the mask's fit was likely due to the skill of its designer, not some shared biological element.

The dagger that deflected my sister quietly tore through the headrest of the seat in front of me, stopping just beneath my chin. The dead skin of the mask smiled at me, somehow obeying the movements of the living skin beneath. The mask only slightly betrayed its inanimate nature via a small, solitary crease from the right corner of its pale lips to the right eye-hole. Visible only when the wearer smiled, I assumed his smile must have occurred in quantities sufficient to cause the crease in the first place.

"Cleverness is an admirable attribute," Janus said, "but speed is no less essential. Now tell me, Family Man, what do you know of all this monkey business?" His blade remained still as he peered at me over the headrest, cocking his head to one side. "Try as I might, I've only heard from this person or that of a weird little Shepherd who has an affection for herding wolves. The general thrust of the title suggests the Shepherd is some kind of master of murderers, and we're all his angry little hounds. Now, while I'm a big fan of wolves, I've never considered myself a suitable analogue for the hairy things. Besides, everything boiled down, we're all predators. And it should go without saying that any living thing could be, from the right rhetorical angle, analogized to wolves. It's really quite a lazy comparison, if I'm being honest."

He carried on in a relaxed and casual manner, as if we were old friends conversing over coffee. "Now, those that I must rescue from the path most trampled, they could be wolves—nearly programmed, from embryo to corpse, to wander the paths they walk. No, that's not quite right, is it? They don't even wander, those two-faced buffoons. Wandering would imply that they begrudged chance some teeny-weeny sway over their lives. But that's rarely the case. Never the case, actually. Well, until now.

"You know, Family Man, I never sorted out a life that faced the right way before—those with only one face, I mean to say. Take this one here, the one I'm wearing. It's the likeness of the Boiler Man. We met a short while ago. Wonderful fella, I have to say. He exhausted every last bit of his potential, practically wrung it out with his bare hands. He was a man who willed his way through the world— every curiosity satisfied, all chances taken. What the hell business do I have with his face? Sure, I'm wearing it. More as an apology than anything else. But he has no other face, nothing hidden. He is what he concealed. And I killed him—I destroyed what I've spent a lifetime promoting. And yet, here I am—*here we are*—chasing victory over top the bodies of our brethren. Still, I can feel the hidden face of the world, the right one—slowly turning around, with every "wolf" I topple. So, I suppose that makes it all just hunky-dory! But perhaps you feel differently? Speaking of different, I do sense a sort of incompleteness to you, a hidden face, something I could properly wear . . . .

In principal, the killer said nothing that I strongly disagreed with (except wearing my face). His reasoning was sound enough, save for matters that pertained directly to his worldview. However, I did take issue with the blade he'd placed under my chin, as that would certainly need to be remedied.

I used my free hand to wrench the seat in front of me sideways, jerking the knife away from both my neck and the killer's hand. As his knife fell to the floor, I plunged my hand through the hole in the intervening seat and grabbed the killer by the wrist. I pulled his arm through the hole, twisting it into an unnatural position, disallowing him access to any more surprises.

"Strength is also an admirable attribute," I said, revisiting his earlier comments. "When combined with cleverness and speed, you have a rather effective trifecta indeed. Also, I've no idea how you assume anything in this world complete, mask-maker. You don't strike me as a fool, so you must realize nothing in this world is as it should be. You don't have enough thread to sew up all the holes. Perhaps, should we live long enough to face one another in the truer spirit of the game, we can debate the issue more completely. But for now, tell me, Janus-of-the-Two-Faces, have you dreamt of him, this Shepherd?"

Janus laughed. "My, you are rather strong at that. My arm feels like it's trapped in a vise. But if you don't intend on killing me, I'd greatly appreciate it if you would loosen up a tad bit. Otherwise, you'll give my next scheduled opponent an unfair advantage, as I'll only have the effective use of one arm."

When it became clear that I wouldn't oblige his request, his mask somehow conveyed a withering look. "Well, I can't say for sure that I've had a mystical visitation in my sleep," he continued. "I'm pretty sure that's what you're getting at. But I have had a few unusual dreams. The first occurred just before I acquired my most recent appearance. I was looking over the face of a terribly perturbed sea when I quickly realized the whitecaps were completely unjustified. There was no storm to cause them, not even the slightest breeze. So, I bent close to the water, trying to sneak a peek beneath the foaming waves. That's when I saw the wolves under the water, thousands of them, biting, frothing, and killing. It was their battle that stirred the water, and let me tell you, it was quite the donnybrook.

"I was thoroughly enjoying the show when from the middle of the sea there emerged a figure. Now, I'm not all that knowledgeable when it comes to what a shepherd is supposed to look like, so who's to say what the being actually was? Although, he did have one of those lovely curving rods I know shepherds sometimes carry about. It was the color of freshest blood, and he lifted it from the water, up over his head. After a few seconds, he slammed the butt of the rod back down into the water, which seemed to have the effect of transferring the blood-red color of his staff to the sea. The waves rose and swept me into the depths, where I joined with the wolves in their war. Again, my arm, please. I'll be needing it all too soon."

I loosened my grip slightly, for which he thanked me. I had no desire to rid the world of—or even injure—yet another muse if I didn't have to. It was then, fully joined in conversation, that we noticed it—a cold blast of silence coming from the car in front of us. I released Janus from my grip, and we both slid into the shadows to investigate.

When we entered the next car, we discovered a space of emergent dreams—headless bodies, overstuffed with additional organs leaking like lolling tongues from their smiling stomachs, and tiny flames hopping and shivering from within an assortment of hanging, brightly grinning heads. The carved jack-o-lantern faces were just open windows to the small lights that burned within them, illustrating a fact beyond flesh—this was clearly the work of the artist known as Jack Lantern. He was in the passenger car beyond us. From that distant room, I could hear the methodic sighing of a busy blade, occasionally punctuated by the small ticking sounds that spoke to the fine adjustments of a knife working bone.

Jack Lantern was perhaps the most notorious living killer of all. Unlike so many of us, he hunted the same killing grounds, haunting Autumn City with his wonderful human jack-o-lanterns, evading capture and spreading nightmare. Not since our great forbearer, Dooley Hines—also known as Sleepy Head—who had nearly enveloped the entire city of New Victoria within his killing dream, had there been such an artist. For the first time, I found my chances of winning the Shepherd's Game lessened—if only slightly.

He stood at the very edge of the shadows, only slightly visible. Initially, I could barely tell he wore a mask—but as I strained my eyes to glimpse the face of the killer, I could just make out the dim orange of a smiling jack-o-lantern. As for Janus, he disappeared into darkness, prowling closer to the killer. Somehow, he'd managed to don his signature two-headed mask—a terrifying goblin-thing faced forward, while a monstrous goat glared from the back. He also wore a spectacular cloak made from the continuous, unbroken skin of one of his victims, giving the impression that the goat had a corresponding body.

Just as I was about to join Janus in his hunt, something delightfully unexpected brought the impending conflict to the very brink of bursting. The webs of silence I'd left in my wake had been lightly plucked by a careful predator—another newcomer was trying to blend his silence into my own. I whipped around and burned my gaze through the imposter-stillness, slowly approaching it as Jack Lantern's lilting voice filled the shadows. "Happy Halloween, Fredrick! And thank you for bringing me to this splendidly dark train! I absolutely love trains! Autumn City has some fantastic trains, but nothing so wonderfully claustrophobic."

The Carver of Souls, as he was also called, had come for Janus. I was somewhat disappointed the pumpkin-faced killer had not come for me. But when our eyes had met, I became certain that he was not averse to killing out of order, so there was no telling his intentions.

Janus snaked his response through the shifting arms of darkness between the weak beams of cold moonlight, careful to keep his words from giving away his location. "Oh, please! Spare me your pretentious yammering about Halloween, and let's just get on with it. And by the way, those masks of yours are the height of amateur hour. Such hack jobs could hardly manage to conserve more than a mere crumb of chaos. Just look at all the precious potential you've left to spoil, you blithering dimwit! It looks as if I'll have to show you how the make a proper mask, and how to do so without spilling so much as a single drop of distilled chance—though I'm afraid you won't long outlive my lesson."

Slowly, I made my way into the slightly inferior silence of the unknown killer. A gruff voice dragged against the quiet. "For such a big fella, you're plenty vigilant, aren't ya? As I speak, you're sneaking sideways inta the shadows, all quiet and lethal. Yer almost graceful—or just a bit more delicate than you look. I haven't decided which. Either way, a big dude like you squirreling around just doesn't seem right, ya know? I can picture you slipping behind a light post with nothing of yer giant body stickin' out, like some big dumb cartoon character. Now, that's your 'sister' you just put in yer hand, right? I can see why you like her smile so much, but ya really oughta think about gettin' her teeth looked at. They look a bit worn down."

I inched closer, testing my tendrils of silence, homing in on the newcomer's location as he continued. "By the way, I caught a dream of yers the other night. It was interesting. But it spilled some big fat secrets about some of yer favorite huntin' techniques and whatnot, so I came prepared. Oh, and that odorless gas you're not smelling? Well, it'll knock ya out soon enough. I didn't want to spoil the surprise, but I did want you to know that you'll wake up from it okay. And when you do—oh, boy!"

I wasn't completely sure with whom I was dealing, but I had some ideas. Regardless, it was quite plain the killer knew nothing of me, despite what my loose-lipped dream might have intimated. I decided to make him aware of the fact. "I've a fairly hearty constitution, friend, but I do appreciate the insight. Of course, I'm speaking of the insight into your whereabouts, not your undetectable mists. Also, if you did indeed learn anything about my particular methods from a dream, you apparently neglected to focus on my fondness for sounds, and how I determine from which direction they emanate. If you had attended to that fact, you would have realized I've long been able to detect you just fine. If you get another chance at this, which I seriously doubt, you may wish to consider looking into fixing your own teeth, and how you might learn to keep them from chattering on and on."

My sister flew like a grinning bullet, slamming into his chest a moment before my shoulder did the same. The man was wearing some kind of body armor, along with a gas mask, night vision goggles, and other combat accoutrements. His handguns clattered to the floor as my shoulder connected. He reached for the shotgun slung across his back as he tried to keep his footing, and I tore it from his grip. About to use it as a cudgel, an intense flash of light filled my vision. The slightest bouquet of ozone filled my nose as my body filled with pain. I fell to the floor, writhing and spasming—the shock from his homemade stun gun and the effects of the knock-out gas were wearing me down.

"Now," the killer said, "I know ya were awfully close with your mommy, big man. Where are *her* bones, I wonder? Did ya turn her into a switchblade, or maybe some kinda letter opener? Or did ya save her remains fer something a bit nastier?"

It was a base taunt, to be sure, but one that could not go unanswered. I rose from the floor and seized the man, lifting him into the air. I sent him soaring into the wall of the train car, but not before he managed to touch me once more with the stun gun. I stumbled backward from what felt like a kiss from a lightning bolt. I heard the rising din of blades dancing merrily behind me as Jack and Janus busily conducted their fatal affairs. Suddenly, Janus was sent staggering toward me. I grabbed him before he fell to the floor, allowing him to steady himself. Janus and I took our places in the middle of the orange-lit passenger car, back-to-back, our would-be killers closing in from opposite sides. I could feel laughter growing in my chest.

Janus's words almost seemed to come from the goat-faced mask strapped to the back of his head. "Alright, damn it, I admit it—this *is* a rather fun game!"

The four of us joined our silences together, and the resulting void was so fragile, a moth's shadow could have shattered it. The train seemed to vanish, leaving nothing but motion behind. The earth shrank to the size of blades, stun guns, and masks as eight cold eyes rose like killing moons above the surface of the diminished world. The shadows chose their champions and gathered around them, cheering.

I finally achieved a decent look at the killer who'd drawn my name. He was known as the Mad Merc. A killer of some repute, he was rumored to have been quite the accomplished mercenary. His last known act as a sane killer was the paid investigation of a residential block that had suddenly and quite mysteriously appeared in the middle of the city of Nailwood, compliments of the Darkness, naturally. No one knew precisely what had happened after he entered the mysterious location, but a good many persons are frightfully aware of what he did when he left it—he murdered and mutilated from one side of the country to the other, his services now free of charge.

I had once acquired a small bit of rumor that indicated many of his victims included popular proponents of the very unpopular Black Sun Theory—the tedious and vastly incorrect notion that a heretofore unseen phase of the sun caused the Great Darkness, its unusually high output of some type of radiation or another driving us all mad, and then saddling us with amnesia once the unique solar phase concluded. If the Mad Merc had indeed performed such a service, I would view his deeds as rather practical and not insane at all. Still, there was certainly some kind of madness upon him—in him—but it was frozen into a killing thing, disallowed from spilling out uncontrollably, channeled by skills that had been perfected over a lifetime of professional murder. Whatever his past, at that moment he was a large and volatile shadow, one with a heavily modified stun gun at his side and a smile painted across an otherwise ordinary gas mask.

Magnificently insane and incredibly crafty he may have been, but he wasn't particularly fast. My left hand crushed the gloved fingers around his weapon as my right denied his windpipe air, all before his eyes could do more than widen in shock. I slowly lifted him from the floor, my fingertips registering the intricate snapping sensations of his collapsing throat. Unbeknownst to me, his free hand had been busy clawing for the machete strapped to his leg. The weapon cleaved into my side, sending blood rushing down my leg and onto the floor. I was not amused by his willpower, or even his resourcefulness, so I kicked him unceremoniously down the aisle and into the sliding door at its end, hoping the resulting impact might take the fire out of him.

He tumbled past the rows of seats, catching himself with outstretched hands. However, my time with his throat in my hand had not been spent idly—I had successfully dislodged my sister from his chest armor. As he dropped into a crouch, my sister took him in the gut, just below his chest armor. I was unsure if she had managed to find a vital organ, but the scuffle had also compromised my secondary target—the breathing hose of his mask.

I rushed forward, my remaining sister laughing as his machete tried once more to taste my blood. She leapt into the oncoming blade, sliding merrily down its length, turning it away. Once deflected far enough, my sister reversed course and hissed across his fingers, sending at least one of them and the machete tumbling to the floor. In an effort to pull away from me, his bloodied hand thrust the stun gun to the wound in my side. But I was no longer in the mood for falling and writhing. Despite the truly exquisite explosion of pain, I crushed the stun gun and the hand holding it. His breathing was heavy beneath the mask as blood loss and his own knock-out gas sipped leisurely at his consciousness.

I tore the mask from his face and held him close to my ear. "What did you see in that place that should not have been? Tell me quickly, so that I might put the memory to good use after you are gone."

The mercenary wrapped his crushed hand around the back of my neck and pushed his lips close to my ear. "I saw a place that couldn't quit the Darkness. It . . . downright refused ta go. I wanted ta stay forever, but the things living there told me ta leave and never come back. They were so incredible." The memory seemed to renew him as he continued. "They were in love with the mystery of things. Some of 'em just sat at tables, all huddled together in the dark streets, sippin' cold drinks . . . watchin' and applaudin' the gigantic freakin' things that floated around the sky, blottin' out the colored stars that zipped around in all directions. Others were just lyin' in the trees, gazin' without eyelids at things that were never meant to be seen all at once. You would've loved it . . . I know you would've. I dreamed yer dream, remember? I needed ta get back there, but the only way back was ta win this freaking game. Ya see, they want me to help their little parcel of unreality spread—that's the only way they'll let me come back. But fer them ta stretch out, they need the world to loosen up, become a little less rigid, more bendable. So I been busy takin' out the load-bearing beams, ya know? The jerk's whose disbelief makes it hard for the roof to collapse, so's the whole thing can be torn down ta make room for a completely new place, a better place. That's overkill, I know, but I like to make sure a thing's done the right way. So here I am, with the rest'a you, tryin' ta be the last wolf standing. And I mean ta be. Cuz their aint no way yer gonna stop this house from comin' down, big man!"

The Mad Mercenary had been up to more than merely demonstrating his gymnastic ability when I'd thrown him from me—he'd been collecting one of his fallen handguns. Three bullets entered my belly. Not wishing to accommodate a fourth, I whipped my sister across his throat.

The killer's body fell to the floor, his head remaining firmly in my grasp. I turned, eagerly expecting to see Janus and Jack locked in their deadly contest. Jack was fully present, but Janus—his head and both his faces—hung pendulously from the Soul Carver's clenched fist. Jack, his pumpkin face aglow, raised his empty hand and waved furiously. "Happy Halloween, Family Man!"

"Happy Halloween, Jack," I responded with equal sincerity. Halloween is, after all, my favorite holiday.

We searched each other, sinking our gazes into the other's soul, seeking out even the smallest of insights. I had yet to determine if Jack intended to kill me, and so I used the moments leading up to that discovery to reach down and collect my fallen opponent's kill list. Upon standing, Jack's face seemed to grow inhumanly large and comical. I realized I was losing quite a bit of blood. I certainly couldn't blame Jack if he tried to take my life. I was clearly weakened, and removing one more player from the game—in the proper order or not—would certainly benefit him.

I was disappointed to learn that such a lean calculation could find a place in Jack's head—I'd hoped it was too full of candy corn and nonsense to do anything other than spread plump orange nightmares. He was airborne and above my head before I even realized he'd moved. He slashed down at my head with one of his reddened carving knives, laughing like a child. I simply bent low and allowed my father, asleep on my back, to intercept it. Jack dragged his blade across my father's face, calling up sparks that outlined the remainder of the Carver's leap to the far end of the passenger car.

I knew I was unfit for a second conflict. I flew to the opposite end of the car, gathering Janus's heads along the way, barreling through the sliding door at its end. I hopped to the connecting car and swung my father in a wide arc. His anger at being awoken for such a menial task produced a blinding shockwave that not only separated the cars, but tore through the immediate area with such ferocity that all became dust and wooden shrapnel—the Red Dream was surely upon us. I was launched through the door of the car behind me, the shriek of mangled metal and exploding wood close on my heels.

I groaned to my feet amid the whipping wind and swirling dust. Jack Lantern shrank into the distance, standing at the jagged edge of the disconnected train car. He was cheering, his hands clapping wildly above his head. "Bravo!" he called. I smiled and took a deep bow.

Despite the utter lack of a third of its construction, the train somehow still facilitated the expression of Jack's gallery, allowing it to remain intact. The decorated heads swayed smoothly to the car's motion, rocking gently to the rhythmic clacking of its travel. I replaced the mask of the Mad Mercenary, slipping it gently over his face—a thing that had no meaning beyond the gas mask that obscured it. I reached down and gathered the engraved remains of Janus's three now-grinning faces. I took the heads of the two monstrous killers and hung them from the ceiling, far from the other assortment of dangling, whittled heads of Jack's design. Wolves had no place among sheep, which was almost certainly true in life, and most definitely true in death. Perhaps Janus would have conceded at least that much, if not the larger analogy concerning killers and wolves. Although, if I'm being honest, I'm none too fond of the analogy myself, as no wolf was ever possessed of the powers of an artist, let alone the vision of a dreamer.

I nearly collapsed into a seat on the now tenantless, broken train, injuries pushing my mind further and further into blackness. I imagined my blood as the sole, dwindling weight anchoring me to the earth. As it leaked away, I feared drifting into the sun, where yellow gods peer from an infinite boredom, laying a sick-warm sight upon dead worlds long rusted into their orbits. I grasped the armrests to form an additional hold upon the world. Slowly, my mind started to inch back into focus. My eyes slowly moved across the combat theater turned art gallery that had formed almost organically from the day's events. *Poor Janus,* I thought, looking at his three faces, each spilling its collection of chaos across the floor. *What has the world lost with your passing?*

I hoped whatever was lost from Janus had been conserved within Jack. Of course, my hopes were the same regarding the Mad Merc and myself, but I felt only shame—nothing of the unique forces or insights that had made a monster out of a common killer-for-hire. I had hoped to learn at least something of the means by which one might enter the delightful place he mentioned, but I was no wiser for having held his head in my hands.

I wasn't sure if the blood loss had affected my vision, or if the previous dream had continued to swell like some contusion upon the skin of reality itself, but the passenger car in front of me seemed to house some remaining particles of life. As far as I knew, all the previous occupants were now the wet ornaments of Jack's grinning holiday. I could see dark shapes drifting through the aisles, moving away from me, apparently engaging some greater and more distant darkness closer to the front of the train. Having nothing better to do than bleed, I decided to follow them.

The second I moved from my seat, I knew I was dreaming. My body fell into a current of invisible movement that pushed me forward. As I glided, a group of strange young women standing on both sides of the aisle turned to look at me. Every one of them was raven-haired and possessed of the lightest blue eyes—glimmering beads of water that defied gravity through sheer force of beauty. The tallest of the group, whose height was only slightly less than my own, spoke to me. "Have you any idea who conducts this train? As many times as I've tried to ascertain that fact, I've never learned." Her eyes were rainstorms. I could hear the water of weeping skies falling across a world of tender young leaves. I almost forgot to respond.

"I have no idea," I said, "but I'm sure they're competent. Certainly, you have no cause for concern." My words seemed lost to the rain, and I was curious if I'd spoken at all. The woman smiled at me, as if I'd given precisely the answer she desired, and quickly withdrew behind the shadows of the train. Before I could begin to contemplate what had happened, invisible hands pushed me onward, far away from the women, where I felt compelled to refocus my attention upon a line of wandering shadows. In service to my new obligation, I observed that after each shadow crossed into the next car, the darkness beyond the threshold deepened, gaining the appearance of a massive hole that extended beyond the dream of the train. I drew up behind the last shadow in line and waited my turn to move into the next world.

The opening did not lead to some other dream, but into a supernal synthesis of darkness and silence which I theorized to be the product of the shadows merging together. The hybrid substance approximated the closest thing to a fully realized oblivion, and all of it stitched together from the rootless bodies of sacrificial shades. Within that near-nullity, I could detect the absence of memories and dreams, and most importantly, I could hear the sound of something about to begin. Swiftly, but with the caution of a mother lifting her child for the first time, the darkness enfolded me. It was at that moment when the calm broke upon a sweet and breathy whisper. It said, "The silence before the womb and beyond the grave—it's all for you, my son. Seek out the quiet of lonely places, and death may not hear you." It was my mother's voice. I determined the whispers must have come from some distant memory, sealed up within a void that required the death of several shadows to reacquire.

I thought I was about to exit the makeshift oblivion when another sound entered into the nothingness, unapologetically and sloppily scattering muffled voices as it blundered about. Again, I could feel the burning eyes of my family throwing fire, trying to force me to ignore some scorned thing that dwelt—hid—within sleep. Or was the sound coming from someone else's dream? With all the dream-swapping of late, the question had become a valid one. The sound became progressively distinct, gelling into the pathetic cries of a child. This was quickly accompanied by another sound, which seemed the inversion of the soft sadness.

What surprised me most about the second sound was that it frightened me, yet it was nothing more than a man's raised voice. "Stop whining and hold still! If you make me ruin another painting, I'll hang you in the room with the rest of them!" An image tried to connect with the voice, but it was blocked out by the high-pitched sound of a train whistle.

I woke up on the floor of the passenger car—it appeared that I hadn't even managed to make it to one of the seats. The train was in the process of exiting a tunnel. The shadows were stripped of their plump inky flesh, leaving behind only the boney silhouettes of solid earthly objects. I rose to my feet. There was no pain and no blood. I opened my coat, looking for what should have been an abundance of ruined tissue. There was nothing, not even a scratch.

The day was dying into twilight, the train bound for the source of all that wonderful crimson. The failing sun splashed bloody light across my skin, confirming my lack of injury. I walked deeper into the light, certain that once the dusk was more concentrated upon the areas where I had been shot and cleaved, there would be a mark. Still nothing. As I stared at my woundless body, something stood briefly in front of the red sun, throwing a rectangular darkness into the train. The shadow belonged to a large sign that read *Black River City*. I had arrived at the location of Miss Patience's first recorded kill, apparently no worse for the wear.

The doors of the train opened as I reached them, but before I departed, I looked back into the vehicle. As my sight moved into the dim passages and over the empty seats, I knew the train was far from vacant. The means by which it moved was not solely dependent upon the steel of its tracks or the fire of its engine. My eyes lingered upon the swinging faces of the two fallen Wolves.

As I followed the only road leading away from the station, I encountered a sign bearing the name of my destination, a small painted arrow indicating its general direction. I was surprised at its wholeness, as nothing along my path seemed entirely unscathed. I hoped it was due to the game I played— every death a blow against banality.

Closing on my destination, my mind was filled with mountains drifting like dandelion seeds, softly glowing rivers tugged along by the gravity of foxfire moons—I was more content than I believed possible. In retrospect, I should never have left the train.

CHAPTER NINE

Bared teeth, hungry mouths, and sightless eyes were all I saw as my blood complemented the already considerable red of the falling sun. They came from the tall grass, quiet and vicious. My sisters barely managed to fend them off, eliciting only a handful of shrieks for their troubles. They suddenly vanished, withdrawing behind the sinking day, spilled blood the only proof of their passage. I was sorely wounded again, but the renewed silence from the monsters' absence felt soothing against my ruined skin. My assailants might have been dogs, or even wolves, but I doubted it. They were too large, too fierce, too calculating. Preparing for another clash, I took to the deep grass and waited for chance or circumstance to deliver me a killing opportunity.

The very tops of the grass seemed aflame with the last touches of twilight, a calming breeze playing against the savagery of the previous moments. The creatures, whatever they were, seemed to be waiting for something. It wasn't long before that something approached through the field with a calm, two-legged gait. The steps paused to inspect—or admire—the joining of twilight and blood, creating an exquisitely deep crimson. The creature's movement was light and graceful—a woman, most likely.

I gathered the silence of the field, inhaling it while I listened. The night began trickling in as the sun grew colder. My sisters began to giggle softly, two impatient children eager for their turn at play. Clouds tumbled grey and ominous through the distant sky, mumbling. Having long since discovered where the great beasts crouched, I targeted their leader, an estimation based on the size and shape of its silence. But I wouldn't strike until I knew more about the woman.

Her voice slipped between the grass and the breeze without creating so much as a ripple within the calm. "You travel like a thoughtless bird, Family Man, straight and unwavering—and wholly predictable. I really didn't think you'd take such an obvious route, yet she assured me you would. I should know by now not to question her." Her voice was both soft and loud, and she made no effort to hide herself—confident, no doubt, in the beasts that served her. "Did you really believe she wouldn't know you were coming? Where did you think your dreams were going? After everything I've heard about you, you turn out to be nothing more than a simple-minded brute. You lack the cleverness of your art, monster. Now, I'm certain you must have at least learned enough about us from her dreams to know what comes next. Or were you foolish enough to believe you would have the honor of being devoured by our mother?"

With a heavy heart, I surprised the squatting beast from behind, having crept beneath the sound of the woman's monologue to get close to it. Its strength was fierce and feral as it tried to struggle free of my grip, but I proved the stronger. Its neck snapped loudly, summoning its minions to investigate. I took the intervening moments to study them. They were wolves from under the earth with white vestigial eyes, ash coats, and massive overhanging claws and teeth. My heart broke when they attacked.

My father met the first beast in the air. The creature became nothing more than a shriek wrapped in blood. Lunging at my knees, the second meant to steal my balance. The spiked counterweight of the great axe blade passed through the creature's brain, splitting its jaw and pinning it to the earth. Spinning around, I interrupted the beast stalking me from behind, passing the giant blade through the thing's neck. Its head dropping cleanly to the ground.

Wisely determining her beasts insufficient to her cause, the woman fled, her nimble retreat soundless. The last two monsters tried to cover her withdrawal, rearing up in front of me in a show of intimidation. My sister slashed their throats in a wide, sweeping arc before taking flight and plunging into the fleeing woman's back. She stumbled into the low-hanging limbs of a dead tree, just beyond the wood line. She tried desperately to hold herself up by the lifeless branches, even as they tangled within her hair and poked at her flesh. With a handful of broken twigs, she slowly collapsed to the ground.

I wanted badly to spare the remaining creatures, but I couldn't. Miss Patience already knew too much. They came at me almost passively, their fires cold and dead. With their task all but impossible, they simply wanted an end to things. It was a gentle affair, considering.

The woman was still breathing, as I'd intended. I looked upon her face—she was blind and terribly beautiful, her eyes a marriage of glass and spring rain. I immediately recognized her from my dream. "More like an eagle than a thoughtless bird," I said. "An eagle fears nothing, and it finds no critics among the littered bones of its prey." I had wanted to glean further insights from her, but I'd destroyed too much beauty to summon any lingering sense of purpose. I couldn't bear to look at her. As I turned away, I could hear the rain falling behind her beautiful, sightless eyes.

She gathered what breath remained and spoke. "I didn't know . . . eagles could cry." In the next moment, the blind woman and the sun were dead. The newborn darkness drifted across me, washing the remains of the daylight from my broken skin. I sank into the darkened field, defeated.

I had become a cannibal, subsisting on the flesh of dreamers and leaving their corpses to bake beneath the horrible sun. There was little rationalization left to me—I was clearly doing the Deadmother's work. I tried to tell myself it was all a fantastic and calculated gamble, the slain wolves a necessary sacrifice. Yet the barer truth had finally loomed too large to ignore—I was killing my own, and it wasn't at all clear how that was a good thing. Of course, whether I found the game to my liking or not, I would be forced to play along, lest I become merely another name scratched off a list.

For days, I lingered the field and the forest, sleeping away the sun and haunting the thickets by night, using the cover of darkness to raise a great and terrible monument. I hoped my newest piece would somehow exonerate my crimes, allowing the spirits comprising its wicked teeth and mournful eyes to spread a dream as wild and hungry as fire. My project took me a little over a week to complete, and with the exception of my family, she was my best piece.

Standing over thirty feet tall, she scraped her head against the ceiling of the forest, dominating the shadows. She wore many ferocious heads, each one grinning through staggered lines of eager teeth. Her central face beamed with beautiful, blind eyes filled with the soft patter of spring rain, staring into places where sight failed the visions dreams alone could bear. Upon her head, a crown fashioned from the bones of hunting birds. Her dress I made from feathers and flesh. Many and canine were her legs, each foot tipped with large claws projecting red and wicked beneath an ample, flowing gown. Covered entirely by her dress, her torso was a temple made of wolves, where interlocking ribcages sheltered the phantom rhythms of seven dead hearts. Like her many heads, they were arranged to honor the woman who had destroyed me. I placed her at the rim of the forest, where her sightless eyes could stare down the sun without wincing.

When I crept into Black River City, I found it sparsely populated, and only by persons who seemed glad for the relative isolation. Many of the citizens moved about by night and sang to themselves as they went down dark curving roads into the surrounding woods. The sound of strange industry and muted conversations could be overheard from the basements and attics of no small number of houses. It also appeared the people had renamed their township for some reason, as I found the name *Lastrygone* written upon a large sign set out by the only road connecting the city with the rest of the world. Overall, I found the little hamlet quite likable.

At last, just before dawn, I arrived at the abandoned residence of Martin Crook, the first recorded victim of Miss Patience. There were few occupied buildings near it, as if the structure had been ostracized. I entered the decaying Dutch Colonial—which looked untended since the murder, some ten or fifteen years ago—immediately touched by the cold echo of past atrocity. The gloom tangibly thickened as I neared the cellar door, and the basement stairs held surprisingly firm as I descended them. The flesh of the house may have all but rotted away, yet the bones of its dead body remained strong—no doubt reinforced by the wicked deed's refusal to abandon its home, preferring to keep the light of that wickedness alive and burning.

The basement was small and earthen, which of course was why Miss Patience had chosen it. Surprisingly, the large hole in the floor leading to her underground tunnels was meager by way of adornments, despite its historical significance— unless you counted stolen dreams, in which case this was far from her first documented kill. I looked more closely at the edges of the pit, and I noticed a small collection of teeth protruding from the inside rim, as if the opening were indeed designed to resemble a kind of mouth. I'm sure it was only the first of many mouths that ended up swallowing Mr. Crook that fateful night. The collection was comprised of mostly human and animal, though a smaller assortment were beyond my ability to identify. Nevertheless, I was fairly certain I was gazing upon fragments of the Tower of Teeth. I wasn't sure what they signified, if anything. They could've been nothing but an embellishment for art's sake—the many and varied followers of Miss Patience were known to be a creative lot.

Despite the lackluster features of the location, I was still thrilled to be in such a historic place, not to mention one step closer to my inevitable meeting with the renowned cannibal. But the sun was almost up, and I hated the idea of ruining the somber atmosphere of the house with daylight, so I retired to a corner of the basement and slept the day away. My dreams were hollow, filled only with the drone of common silence—nothing of the stolen dreams that had so often haunted my sleep.

I awoke to a dissonance of raised voices from without, like some rowdy crowd slipped from hell. The night was fresh, likely no more than a few moments old, and the noise almost masked the sound of something prowling the upper portions of the house. The excitement was excruciating. My sisters could barely contain themselves as they tried, again and again, to leap into my hands. I looked to the opposite side of the cellar, where a miniature window peeked above the rim of the unkempt side yard. I could clearly make out shadows pressed hard against the dirty glass, as they were nearly pinned by an obnoxiously bright light. I carefully made my way across the room to the window, ever mindful of the prowling creature, now silent, that lurked somewhere above me.

The tiny view revealed a mob of townspeople. They were all gathered around my latest work, screaming and waving their arms. How they had managed to transport it from the edge of the wood, I couldn't imagine. From the top of what looked to be a water tower, a powerful spotlight illuminated my creation. I was so absorbed by the exquisite vision of my art being exalted—or cursed, I wasn't sure which—I almost forgot about the silence of the thing upstairs. And how the cellar steps did not creak when walked upon.

I slipped between the clamor of the mob and the whispers of nearby movement. My silence wrapped around me like loving arms, and my hands filled with saw-toothed laughter. The rank smell of fruiting corpses traveled upon the breath of the thing that entered the shadows at the bottom of the stairs. Its movement vacillated between a shuffle and a purposeful gait, outlining a struggle between primal and prudent dispositions. It inhaled deeply, combing the air for signs of prey. A beam of light shot through the cellar window and brushed its face.

The thing's countenance was as conflicted as its movements, expressing the extremes of a barely human condition. Its white eyes were sunken into its face like heavy, lusterless stones thrown atop a filthy pillow, and they peered no deeper into the world than was necessary to locate sustenance. This most certainly concerned the swollen meats of the dead—more specifically, human corpses. A septic pit of rough-hewn teeth comprised the thing's mouth, which it kept slightly agape, as if to reduce the distance its jaws would have to open to admit its next meal. The longer I looked upon the thing, the more I detested it.

Ultimately, there were two principal attitudes concerning art. The first seeks to capture reality, faithfully reproducing its every mundane detail, admitting little to nothing of the imagination. The second type flies the world, chasing dreams, foolishly hoping to catch them. It goes without saying which art I practice, and this creature was clearly the work of a practitioner of the first type. The grotesquery was nothing but a portrait of a single basic urge, embellished slightly by the coarse appetite of a nightmare. The creature was, however, undeniably well-made, the attention to detail impressive. But I much disliked the trite theme it was obviously designed to reflect.

A second noise emanated from the upstairs as something else entered the house. The peripheral glow of a flashlight frosted the cellar stairs as the second intruder investigated.

The first creature immediately recoiled from the invading illumination, shielding its eyes and hissing. Surprisingly, it spoke. "Keep the light to yourssself, you blind idiot!"

The creature from above ignored the insult and croaked back in only slightly less inhuman tones. "Isss he down there?" I was being sought out, and I was sure it wasn't to congratulate me on my latest work.

"He'sss down here," said the first, "I'm sure of it. I can sssmell the death clinging to him. Come to me, Family Man. Hiding is for prey." The taunt was absurd on its face, but required a retort nonetheless. I decided I would savor my time with the thing in the basement, so I departed for the creature above me, as silent stairs go both ways. I had retired to the kitchen, clumsily roaming through the cupboards, of all places. The windows of the room were without curtains, and when the creature finally shined the light near the glass, my reflection betrayed my presence directly behind it.

The reflection also granted me a brief look at the creature, allowing me to measure the difference between itself and its companion in the basement. It was essentially the same kind of being, differing only by way of its greater share of human features, which were likely diminishing over time. This was typically the case with Post-Darkness afflictions, I had come to learn. The thing quickly spun around and I seized it by the throat, crushing its windpipe before it could marshal any kind of alarm. I didn't want to spill its blood, as I desired to remain as traceless as possible.

I had just finished packing the creature's body into the small fireplace when I heard more of them, this time entering through both the front and back of the house. A nearby window showed me the restless crowd of townsfolk, composed of creatures much like the ones I'd encountered, except for one. A massive figure passed through the crowd like a praying mantis strolling among tangles of swarming ants. However, these ants seemed to bow to the mantis, as opposed to attacking it. They gathered behind this new creature and fell silent. The thing was little more than a shadow standing before the great beam of light that shone down upon my work. It paused to gaze upon the piece, but again I wasn't sure if my artistic effort was being admired or admonished. I wanted to linger near the window to observe the moment's conclusion, but the creatures were closing on me.

I decided to exit through the back. On my way out, I encountered another creature and dispatched it as I had the first, except this one's body I stuffed into a nearby burn barrel. As I disappeared into the backyard, I detected the presence of other things moving through the night, far from the crowd and its light. I froze, waiting for the invisible things to make the first move. Within moments, a howl from something both alien and wolf broke through the quiet, issuing from the house I'd abandoned. They'd found the body I left in the chimney. I was simultaneously impressed and disappointed with the speed of the discovery—these creatures seemed to excel at locating the dead. It was little wonder why.

I was already inside another dwelling when a second spotlight burst to life from somewhere on the opposite side of town. The lights began falling across houses and trees and yards, hoping to find me blundering about in plain view—as if the one who had made art of their alien hunters, secretly infiltrated their town, and silently killed a number of their kind would be foolish enough to fumble about in the open. No, these creatures were not the smartest of adversaries, though I knew they were only the vanguard of a much deadlier foe—and I would be meeting her soon enough.

After several hours of fruitless searching, the creatures finally decided to relax their guard, thinning their patrols and once again renewing their apathy toward the occasional flitting shadow. I was far from idle during this time, taking great care to better understand my pursuers, stealing into their guarded chambers and slipping away with increasingly weighty insights. One of my more profound discoveries concerned the caverns beneath the town filled with the industry of cannibals. They were busily sectioning hundreds of preserved corpses into isolated and type-specific parts, which they proceeded to package in a variety of ways, ranging from the ornate to the industrial. Finally, and perhaps most interestingly, the flesh eaters passed their bundles into the hands of strange beings apparently called up from the very guts of the earth. It seemed the cannibals had transformed their rancid hunger into trade, distributing human meats to creatures hidden away beneath the ground. I was immediately curious as to the specific remuneration such inhuman things might use to compensate the cannibals— besides human flesh, what could such creatures want? Of course, my principal curiosity regarded the flesh trade's relationship with Miss Patience. She seemed a considerably less purposeful creature than was suggested by all the frenetic and subterranean commerce.

Another discovery concerned my dreams, or lack thereof. Strangely, my many attempts to conjure them from sleep had failed. Each effort summoned only the stinging absence of memories, of this or any other world. I began to interpret the void as a possible indicator of my quarry's proximity, as no further nocturnal hints were needed to bring the two of us together. If my theory was correct, she was certainly nearby, likely abiding in the darkness living beneath the city.

As for my latest piece of art, it had been hoisted upon a large flatbed truck and taken to an open field just outside the city limit, where it was left to float amidst the golden breakers of rolling, unkempt grain. I'm certain it was placed there to lure me into some kind of trap, which of course did more to cement my low opinion of the creatures' intellect rather than stimulate my curiosity. Naturally, I decided to reprimand the beings for assuming me so foolish, and ultimately to avenge my fallen tears—they had been wasted on creatures barely worth the flies that played at their slack, stinking mouths. Still, there was something behind the soft, blind eyes of a particular and bygone woman, perhaps an echo of something that forgot how beautiful it once was.

When the night sank into its deepest darkness, I proceeded to follow a specific cannibal—who had once thought to stalk and insult me—to a diner that sat lightless yet heavily attended near the center of the town. After I had entered the building through the back door, I was delivered the unwholesome sight of a man-eater's kitchen. Corpses wrapped in plastic bags filled with sweet-smelling marinades swung from stained hooks, and piled atop stained trays were the raw tubers and organs of the human body, sliced into cold cuts. Now, there did seem to be some lingering conventions of the human condition still clinging to the degenerates, as there were several recently used ovens and stovetop burners where meat had actually been cooked, though to what degree remained a mystery.

However, one area seemed out of place—a pile of decaying bodies lay in the corner, all showing enormous bite marks. Initially I believed the cannibals to be ghoulish creatures, preferring their food rotted and fly-covered. Later insights, however, showed it was only their breath, and not their appetites, that concerned the spoiling dead. Further, none of the creatures I had so far witnessed possessed jaws large enough to leave such enormous and ragged marks. It was at that moment the answer to my previously posited question concerning the compensation of certain underground customers was made apparent. A massive creature hauled itself into view, emerging from a distant hole in the floor I had failed to notice. It was something far afield the beings occupying the town—it formed no visible relationship with even the darker features the citizens shared in varying proportions and extents. The beast was an alien among monsters, most likely one of the remunerations I had earlier wondered about, gifted to the cannibals for services rendered. It seemed little more than a large roiling sack of greyish muscle surmounted with a wide, featureless head—

save for its mouth, which was overfilled with crooked, flattened teeth and several flailing, quasi-translucent tongues.

I had no idea how, but the creature found me almost immediately, wrapping its titan arms around me even as my sister buried herself in its thick, stinking flesh. Before I could brace myself, it hurled me through the saloon-style doors of the kitchen. After nearly colliding with the ceiling, I crashed down into the middle of the dining room filled with feasting cannibals. For the briefest moment, all was silent. Hungry eyes looked up from plates piled high with human meat. The next moment was a frenzy of hissing monsters and talons. Teeth made for man-eating entered my arms, legs, and back. Fists smashed into my face and ribs. A new type of alien behemoth leapt upon my back, its razor-sharp claws sinking into my flesh as it attempted to wrap its jaws around the back of my head. I rose to my feet, bearing the weight of the toothy mob. Inopportunely, one of the cannibals produced a large chair and smashed it into my chest, causing me to topple to the ground. The mob was crushing me beneath its collective fury. My bones would soon fail me, and my blood would be nothing more than spoil and stink stained across so many mouths.

I would not fall to these degenerates. They weren't even proper monsters, after all, but only puppets of meat and bone stuffed with the souls of pigs. I had to get to my feet. I had to kill them all. I managed to roll to my back, flinging a number of the hungry patrons into the wall. The larger beast descended upon me again. I locked my hands over the creature's monstrous fore-claws, stopping the serrated things just short of my eyes. Dirty boots slammed into my temples, and greasy hands wrapped around my arms, trying to derail my strength and allow the beast to fall upon me completely. I could feel the bones of the creature's paws slowly beginning to crack beneath my strength. The monstrosity tried to end our contest by tearing the flesh from my face with its wide maw.

I pushed the creature upward, fully extending my arms, disallowing it access to my face. Tucking my legs beneath its torso, I launched the beast into the ceiling fan. My sister flashed her deadly smile, grinning in all directions, opening arteries and exposing innards, sending a number of my attackers screaming. One of the cannibals leapt at me with reddened steak knives clenched in both hands. My fist removed its lower jaw and my sister freed its bowels. I began to rise up a second time. The gigantic creature was upon me again. I seized its jaws, prying them open. This time, something heavier than a chair smashed across my back. I reeled as they piled atop me once again, sinking down.

"Take his weapons!" one of them screeched. The alien creature occupied both my hands as I felt my father clawed from my back. My anger cracked the monster's jaw as I threw it into the mob, and a subsequent blow cracked a cannibal's skull like an egg. I saw more rushing in, brandishing guns and machetes. A bullet tore through my shoulder. My sister retraced the path of the projectile. A stray silence amplified the sound the gunman made when she entered his eye. Something like a club struck my head and neck, over and over again. I felt hands and claws pulling me down. The world was becoming blood and outrage. The man-eater I had followed to the restaurant was holding the great axe above his head, as if to bring my own father down upon me.

When my father was raised into the air—and just as my final and greatest rage brought me from the floor—I watched the cannibal's shadow swell monstrous and gigantic. Its face twisted into a knotted mask of engorged arteries and inhuman wrath. Its mouth exploded open, sending rotten teeth spinning through the air. My father's booming laughter exploded from the thing's ruined throat. The cannibal who now cast my father's shadow swung the great axe into the huge beast, opening its brains to the darkness. My father's gaze burned from beyond the possessed creature's eyes, searing my face with a fury beyond calculation. While the flesh-eater's mouth was little more than a portal to endless, monstrous laughter, I could hear my father's words clearly. "To your feet, whelp! Kill with me! Kiiiilll!"

For the first time since his death—and outside of a dream—my father killed by my side. Together, we conjured blood and scream as surely as sorcerers. Death became the air we breathed, and we were father and son once again—unstoppable.

The calm that replaced the killing was deep and satisfying, framing the moment and washing the cries of the dying from the air. An unusually warm breeze made its way into the red rooms of the restaurant, where bodies lay in piles, and the distribution of spoiling blood and flesh made for a confusing portrait of the moments preceding the gathered ruin. I drew a deep breath and readied myself for reprisal as I opened the front door and stepped outside. The city was almost fused to the silence, as nothing remarked on the presence of a population, much less one waiting to avenge its fallen citizens. The breeze continued to play within the calm, invisibly dancing across severed bodies and rolling in the scent of the dead. It also carried with it the smell of smoke. I looked to the north—a smoldering cyclone of smoke and fire rose up in the distance. They had set my art aflame.

My father stood beside me, wearing the dead flesh-eater. He directed his gaze to the distant fire and laughed like wet thunder, further destroying the face through which he spoke. "She's calling to you, boy! Don't make her wait!" He placed himself into my outstretched hand, the corpse of the long-dead cannibal collapsing to the ground. My forbearer's laughter still traveled the night, rattling the windows of the silent city, no doubt rattling the courage of the things that hid behind them. I would give them more than fear. Much more.

My art had always been dismantled, redistributed, cremated, buried—but its meaning had always drawn fear, if not respect. Never had it been burned in spite. My hands turned white as they gripped my father, and for the first time I felt him retreat from the rage growing within me. I would give these wretched things to oblivion, beyond the whispers of myth—where even memory would never touch them again.

I would not be baited like some dumb animal, so I bypassed the field leading to the barn and disappeared into the darkness—far beneath the silence, where the scurry of a draft can sound like a blast from hell—and I made my way into the caverns beneath the city. There were many entrances into the great hollows scattered all around me, beneath broken statues, secreted away in basements. I chose a yawning hole that opened up from the bottom of a dry creek bed. As I descended into the earth, I found the darkness to be old and untroubled by the sun, but it was stained by an unfathomable degeneration that caused it to flow sick and slow. It had become a corpse of its former self, having sheltered too much debauchery than was healthy. Its shortcomings were to my advantage, as the slothful pitch was slave to no one, and felt no obligation to alert the under-creatures to my presence.

As I traveled the spaces beneath the world, I encountered entire caverns filled with machines designed for the preservation of dead bodies. Thick electrical cables unraveled from the devices, moving up the walls and disappearing into the many cracks of the ceiling. Other rooms were occupied by a more completely degenerated form of cannibal, a type which apparently had no place even among the filthy comforts of a ruined town spilling over with mold and rot. They were ungainly things, mouth-heavy and blind, as nature had perfected for them a body that was meant only for hunting and gorging. Like plump vermin, overstuffed by a limitless banquet, they squirmed and croaked from the cave floors where they lay belly-up, slick with gore. They wore only the blood of many meals upon their bodies, and were too full from their eating to feel the heat of my gaze as I looked upon them from hidden places. Their mindless indulgence was painfully offensive, but I did not wish to spill so much as a drop of my rage upon the unwholesome things, preferring to conserve my indignation for more deserving causes.

As I suspected, many of the caverns were not natural at all, but were the products of carefully placed explosives. I could see piles of blackened stone distributed liberally around the mouths of freshly created caves. The new hollows seemed to travel in directions that would eventually bring them beneath nearby cities, one almost paralleling the route taken by the train. It had become clear that not all of Miss Patience's victims were killed by her own hand, though they were almost certainly collected on her behalf. Many times, as I skulked around and within Lastrygone, I had heard the creatures refer to their "great and hungry mother under the earth." I wondered at how long Miss Patience had been expanding her industry of cannibalism.

The caverns were every inch a maze, and it took no small amount of time to navigate to my destination. At one point, I encountered something that nearly stole the breath from me—a gigantic stone archway covered with beautiful reliefs and carvings, all of which depicted what I could only imagine were some kind of titanic alien beings, all of them thick with rot and filled with strange worms that wore crowns. The cavern beyond the archway was large enough to admit a city, and the darkness rushing from the mouth of that terrible entrance was of a type that had never known light. The structure was clearly not the work of cannibals, as they were neither creative enough nor sufficiently ancient to have wrought such magnificence. In direct proportion to the painful beauty of the archway spilled a nauseous odor, as if all the earth's dead had been collected within to fester and rot. If not for my strong constitution, I would have been most assuredly forced, retching, from the cliff where I stood. Undoubtedly, this was the passage whereby the inhuman clients of the cannibals came and went, and from the smell of things, they were repeat customers.

After I forced myself from the sight of the monstrous archway, I made my way through another collection of rambling tunnels, past crowds of lumbering dead-eaters and the mounds of corpses they ate from. I didn't know if it was day or night when I finally came upon my quarry—I was just happy to see that the cannibals were in fact thoughtless enough to store their explosives in one central location.

When my work was done, I made my way to the field on the edge of town, where I'd first been set upon by the beasts. I smiled beneath the glow of reddest twilight, waiting. The city seemed to shrink down, as if coiling hidden muscles, preparing to leap into the air. And leap it did.

Lastrygone was lifted upon shoulders of flame. The ground shook wildly as fire chased the darkness from every secreted cave entrance, sending geysers of flame high above the buildings. The earth rolled like an angry sea as the sunset winked out, the air thick with towering black smoke and giant clouds of choking dust. The explosives certainly made for a fine cake, but the ruptured gas lines beneath the town made for a satisfyingly decadent icing.

I quickly made my way back into the city, as the second series of explosives was timed to detonate shortly after the first. I needed time to reveal myself to the creatures, so they would know who destroyed them. I walked in plain view, basking in the heat of raging fires, breathing clouds of thick smoke. But a dream was upon me, and I knew I would endure. I could see the wretches trying to flee into the underground, only to find their fiery deaths. Screams— louder by far than any that had escaped their underground slaughterhouses—battled the smoke for dominance of the air, and the burning debris of flesh-eaters lay everywhere, crackling. My laughter rose above the sounds of fire and dying as I waded into thick crowds of fleeing flesh-eaters, wielding my father, extinguishing the light of fools. Houses tumbled to the earth beneath the heat of shooting flames, cannibals became tinder, and the shapes of forgotten gods moved within the smoke—my art engulfed it all.

I stood amongst the fires and bodies and shrieks, calling out to the Mother of Cannibals. My voice rose with the smoke and fire, crashing down upon the burning city, cracking aged timbers and worrying the red-hot flames. Suddenly, emerging from without the smoldering mouth of a giant crater, they came—baying and hungry, blind and monstrous. This was the great company of Black Molly Patience, atrocious creatures from the underground, all of them sculpted by the dusky hands of a blind god under the earth. There was a white bear, without hair or eyes, equipped with claws so overgrown as to seem almost comical. Alien wolves with their frosted eyes of lightest blue. And a lean, hungry cougar with a mouth that occupied nearly every inch of its head, evicting even its ears and nose in favor of jaws that could open wide enough to admit a whole person. My sisters moved to my sides, our laughter growing with the fire.

The wolves were the first to fall to us. They attacked as a single force, hoping to drown me in their numbers. My sisters were like whirlwinds, twisting and turning with maniacal precision, entering and exiting the beasts like wind blowing through tall grass. When the wolves fell to the earth, they did so in pieces that quivered and whined.

The gigantic bear-thing came next, its unearthly roar a challenge to my father. I returned my sisters to their sleep, and he entered the fray, striking the fool creature's head with such force that it exploded into a starburst of blood and brains, the finale of a fireworks display made of gore rather than gunpowder.

It was the great cat that managed to momentarily break my stride. It attacked from behind, seizing my neck in its enormous mouth. I reached behind my head and spread apart its jaws until I heard the wet cracking of bones deep beneath flesh. When the creature reared backward to escape my grip, my sister glided across its exposed belly, releasing a crimson tangle of gleaming entrails. The beast collapsed upon the street and was quickly set upon by ravenous flames. The fire seemed to join my side, surging and roaring across streets, engulfing or routing the crowding cannibals that tried to stand in my way. Then, she appeared from the darkness and smoke.

I had no idea the Deadworld could encompass such a dream. She was a wicked song of teeth and claws, set to the awful melody of burning, sightless eyes. Though she was a living horror, an echo of dethroned beauty reverberated throughout her features, suggesting the distance she had fallen from grace and dream. Blind though she may have been, some invisible force from her whited eyes plunged beneath my flesh, searching and summing. I could feel her conjuring alien hungers from the emptiness of my stomach, trying to fill me with forbidden appetites. Something about her eyes held an actual power, not some abstract force, but a tangible violation of nature, and it was trying to change me. She took a step from the smoking ruin of a tunnel entrance, as if looking more fully upon me would better allow her to focus her strange power. But my body kept its own secrets and would admit no mysteries beside its own. I felt the searing gaze of my family meet the sightless eyes of Black Molly Patience, and I could smell her fear.

I was airborne, my sisters laughing out in front of me, their metal teeth glittering with the lights of a thousand fires. Molly snatched me from the air in a cage of claws. Though my body ceased its advance, my sisters' journey was far from over. Their laughter dimmed as they sank into filthy layers of cannibal flesh, severing the vital tubers of Molly's neck. Pitching me with surprising might, Molly sent me crashing through the wall of a nearby barn slathered in hungry flame. I toppled to a dirt floor covered with burning hay and corpses. Quickly leaping to my feet, I prepared to receive the monster as she came charging after me, through wall and fire. She lowered her horned head and rammed into my chest, lifting me from the floor and pinning me upon her lethal antlers. She hurtled onward, smashing me through anything in her path. Finding nothing else, she finally crushed me against the undercarriage of an overturned truck.

Somehow, I still lived. I think the Red Dream had been born between us, and within its extents, she and I were true monsters, beyond the call of conventional pain and fragility. I tore myself free of her evil headdress, snapping off spines like branches from a tree, calling up screams from her hellish, gaping mouth. I seized hold of her remaining horns and attempted to twist her head from her body. Shortly after her vertebrae began to crackle, she stood to her full height, well above my own, denying me the leverage of the burning earth, dangling me before her forest of teeth.

I reached to my back, raising my father into the air. Miss Patience lunged forward with her terrible mouth yawning impossibly wide, revealing the path so many had traveled. Before either of our blows could land, the world became thunder and fire, and the ground opened beneath us. The second batch of explosives had detonated, and Miss Patience and I tumbled into the stygian depths.

We led a tumbling parade of fire and stone into the smoking pits of the earth, intertwined like two serpents, each trying to swallow the other. Comprising the tail of our downward procession toppled the cannibals and flaming structures and smoking earth that comprised the corrupted town of Lastrygone. I found it ironic that the detestable creatures suddenly found themselves swallowed by the fiery maw of the earth, dinner to the greatest cannibal of all. Though the earth had ever been the eater of its own children, it was also shelter to the oldest darkness—and I had just betrayed it to a dead, burning star.

Even as we plummeted, Miss Patience was busy trying to work her enormous jaws around me. All the while, I was doing my best to wrest her head from her thorny shoulders. We splashed beneath the waves of near-liquescent darkness, the depth we achieved containing shadows sufficiently old enough to turn away the glare of the sun. Once the light had vanished, the quiet of buried secrets rose and stole the sounds of thunder and death from the air, plunging them beneath the unceasing knell of nothingness. We were alone in a void, and for a moment, it seemed we were no less than gods, floating within a primal void, battling each other for the right to fill creation with our singular and inscrutable designs. The fact that we survived the impact of our fall proved further that a Red Dream had been joined by our meeting—the Deadworld was denied the full measure of its power over our flesh and blood, allowing wonder to undo the work of wisdom. Burning debris rained down seconds after we crashed to the shrouded earth, yet the darkness fought back the fire's light, begrudging it an impossibly small dispersion.

Miss Patience rose from beneath a mounting pile of burning wood and fallen rock, throwing it aside with little effort. Her dead eyes, while incapable of affecting me with their hunger-inducing glare, bore into me with a hatred that almost set me aflame. Just before launching into another uncalculated rage, she paused—an expression formed, for the first time reflecting her human origins.

Black Molly's teeth scraped together violently as she spoke through a mouth no longer designed for speech, her tongue bleeding as she struggled through her words. "You've made a fine revenge of things, little killer. You've destroyed all that I've worked for, and now you're trying to add me to your collection of artwork. I am carved from a darkness you can't even remember, much less imagine. I'm a collage of grimmest truths, assembled by grinning poets that watch and laugh from behind this game of light and darkness. And like some angry child, you would break me apart and leave me in ruin? Destruction is the cheapest form of art, little killer. I wouldn't hold my head too high, if I were you."

I became Goya laughing at Pollock. "What do you know of art, Sara? You simply eat your own. You really think that warrants my admiration? You took a fragile darkness and filled it with petty evils, nothing more. What would your cult of well-wishers think if they could see you now? Would they see a great and dark mother of the underworld, or merely the breeder of freaks and fools? They worship a blind mother who gathers them into filthy holes and sets them about the task of appeasing the crawling worms of the earth with offerings of stolen, rotten meat. I'm going to do you the kindness of opening you up to the elder darkness, releasing your stolen shadows to the bowels of the deep earth. Perhaps if your offering proves precious enough, I'll even redeem myself to the shades I've wronged this day. In either case, Miss Patience, I will hold your head high for all to see."

My father was already in my hands as I flew at her. The scream she issued was almost as much a violation of natural law as her alien sight. His killing edge sank beyond her flesh and into bone, splitting her sternum and unrolling the sallow lengths of fat that curled beneath her unclean flesh. A vile fluid that must have been blood washed over me, and I resisted the urge to retch from the smell. The Queen of Cannibals backhanded me into the air, dashing me against the unrelenting limestone. I slid from the wall and fell back to my feet, bleeding and doubled over. She lifted a giant length of burning lumber and brought it down upon my head. I crashed to the stone floor as she casually kicked me into a large debris fire. I lay in a heap, burning, and she paused to enjoy the sight. I certainly couldn't begrudge her a last look at me—a fallen artist beneath the prehistoric earth, crumpled body steaming and bloodied flesh sizzling beneath angry flames. I would have loved to see what it all looked like, myself.

Miss Patience laughed, ignoring the sucking wound in her chest. "You remind me of your last work, little wick, full of fire and failure!"

She wasn't the only one capable of ignoring wounds. I charged the queen once again, colliding with her. She moved only slightly, laughing hard and horrible at my apparent failure. I wrapped my arms as far as they would reach around her bulk and sank my sisters into her many layers of wan flesh, using them to hoist the giant cannibal over my head.

While resting within the flames, I had spied the engulfed ruin of a church steeple across the cavern, the splintered wooden cross at its peak somehow still intact. I raced across the uneven stone, holding Miss Patience high, and slammed her into the jagged tip of the cross. I ducked my head as the spire exploded from her left breast and shot past my shoulder, splashing her foul liquids everywhere. Miss Patience fell quiet, grasping at a stake thicker than my leg. Its length was ablaze, slick with boiling blood, its wicked tip well beyond her reach. I shed my burning coat and threw it to the ground, watching as Sara Kain tried in vain to pull herself free from fire and death. She was beyond even the significant shelter our dream provided.

She looked upon me with pleading eyes and held out her clawed hand. "I don't want to pass without telling someone. I'll tell you . . . and then I can fade away. Please!" I waited until her flesh had crisped and blackened, sloughing off in places, sizzling as it slid down between glowing embers. Finally pulling her seared body from the pyre, I laid her head upon the smoking remains of my coat.

"Tell your final tale, Miss Patience," I said in frozen tones. "And should your story please me, I will spare it from the hungriest monster of all—oblivion."

"Very well," She said. Her teeth sounded out a terrible rhythm as they scraped and gnashed. Her words fell from her mouth like stillborn babes plummeting to the cold earth, naked and hopeless.

CHAPTER TEN

"It was a splendid morning. At least, that's what I thought at the time. The birds were singing, I was taking some muffins out of the oven, and my family was waking to the smell of my masterful breakfast. My little ones were the last to drag themselves down to eat. I honestly don't even remember what their names might have been. I think the tall one with the blue eyes wore glasses that didn't fit quite right—her vision must've been poor. She would have been easy to sneak up on, I imagine. My husband was a nice man, thin with rangy arms, but wide muscular calves. I believe he might have been named after someone famous, someone tall. After the table had been decorated with baked goods and fried delights, my family and I began our meal. I can only remember where everyone's eyes were looking, and how far their hands were from the butter knives and expensive forks, and I could easily imagine how the little girl might have tasted. I should probably feel awful for thinking that, but it's true.

"The little boy—I think it was a little boy—said something about having a nightmare. It's always the children who know first. His hand was adorably tiny as he wrapped it around his fork and clumsily delivered food into his messy little mouth. I think I might have loved him, then. I might still, but I'm not sure. I suppose it doesn't matter anymore, does it? My husband was talking to the little girl with the crooked glasses. His hands seemed so weak-looking as they gestured alongside his words. As I picture them, they kind of remind me of a couple of dead, featherless birds. Yet there we all were, with our pointless words scattering the breakfast table as we shared our morning meal. At some point, as hard as it is to believe, I think I actually declined a plate of bacon that was passed to me, instead reaching for a grapefruit! Can you even imagine such a thing!

"I do recall there being a steady breeze. The wind chimes never let up for a second. I was trying to hear something behind the noise of the tiny chimes, something that seemed out of place on such a beautiful day. I remember that I needed to look out the window, and thinking how odd an impulse that was, and how I had never in all my life felt something so strange. It were as if something from a dream had taken over my free will. Right there in the kitchen at breakfast, surrounded by greasy dishes and sunshine—the most unusual moment of my life (of that life, anyway).

"No one at the table had any idea how terrified I was at that moment. They just kept eating and talking and laughing. Beneath my clothing, I began to tremble. I couldn't speak. I just turned my head toward the window and looked out into the yard. There wasn't a thing amiss. Everything was accounted for—trees swayed in the breeze, sunshine dappled patio, and a big blue sky hung overhead. But then I realized, in the very second I turned away from the window, something had indeed changed. The sound I couldn't hear for the chimes had entered the room. It had to have come in through the window, naturally. I was still paralyzed. No one even noticed the invading thing. They were still carrying on as if the whole world wasn't about to change. The little boy looked at me, and he tried to speak. (Yes, I'm sure now that it was a little boy.) His words, along with his entire body, just sank away into the sound of the soft breeze, gently, finally. Then there was darkness everywhere. I still held a grapefruit in my hand.

"I think everyone imagines the Darkness as an event that was visible at a distance, like some kind of apocalyptic tidal wave, rolling slowly towards land. When everyone sees the wave rise up above the clouds, they run screaming, falling over each other as they go. But it really wasn't like that at all, at least not for me. Of course, it could have been different for everyone, so who can say?

"The world seemed so much smaller, more personal, like everything had been locked into a closet, but the darkness gave the impression that the closet might go on forever. I looked out the window again. I can clearly remember staring at a tree that was all lit up by a stray beam of light falling from somewhere above. Its branches were bizarre, wrapping around one another like eels in a bucket, and they were filled with the strangest, blackest fruits, each one the size of a cantaloupe. They looked absolutely delicious, but they were squirming every which way, like something might've been trying to get out of them, or like the fruit itself was breathing. I really didn't know which. But neither reason would've made me want to eat them any less, not even when some of the fruit fell off the tree and rolled into the darkness, where I swear I heard them scurry away on little feet. I couldn't take my eyes off the tree until I saw my little girl walk up to one of the branches and sink her teeth into a low-hanging fruit. Her glasses were gone, and she was looking around as if her eyes were working just fine. I think she looked at me briefly before she backpedaled into darkness, her smile all sweet and black from the fruit. I wanted to chase after her almost as much as I wanted a piece of that peculiar fruit, but somehow I knew I wouldn't catch her. I was quite a mess, then. Just a thing that cried and cried. When I finally turned away from the window, I saw my husband, dressed for work and walking out the door with his briefcase. All he said to me was, "Don't wait up, honey."

"I wandered around the house for quite a while, looking at familiar things. While I sat on my bed, staring at the cream-colored walls, I thought I heard someone knock at the door. I hid under the bed at the sound of the front door opening and what could only have been the footsteps of a large crowd of people entering my home. Whoever they were, they came right up the stairs and into my room. I could see quite the collection of footwear from where I lay—dirt-encrusted boots, well-worn slippers, sneakers, even some expensive-looking high heels. There might have been twenty or so people in there with me, and besides the sound of them walking around on the wood floors, I couldn't hear a single one of them so much as breathe. They just kept walking around, moving close to one another and then away, like a gang of socializing mutes.

"After a while, little drops of blood started falling to the floor. They didn't react to it at all, they seemed far too busy scuffing up my polished floors with their nonstop mingling. Severed fingers littered the floor next, then all kinds of body parts. The blood started to pool around me, but I hadn't even the tiniest inclination to pop up from beneath the bed. This went on for several minutes, with whole limbs and heads and whatnot thudding wetly to the floor. Long after it became obvious that there were far more body parts than could have been provided by twenty people, the strangers left the room—at least, their feet and ankles did. I can't vouch for the rest of their bodies—trudging through blood and carnage as they went.

"Once they were all in the hallway and moving down the stairs, I could hear them talking incoherently. I suppose they were just your everyday, ordinary crowd of partygoers. They just stopped by to wander wordlessly around my bedroom and shed hundreds of pounds of mutilated body parts. Of course, the blood and meat has a completely different effect on me now, but I'm sure I don't need to tell you that. After I heard the front door close and the voices move out into the streets, I decided there was no safety to be had inside the house. It took me some time to gather enough courage to leave, but finally I put down the grapefruit and made my way into the darkness of the streets.

"The outside was dark, terribly so, yet I could see far and clearly. There was a sense of enclosure to the darkness, as if it were a structure built up around the world, providing shade. My feet were still tucked into my blood-soaked wool slippers, and they made a comical squelching sound as I tiptoed around. Whenever they creased from my movement, little red bubbles appeared. I remember at one point as I wandered around, I noticed the branches above my head were creaking from the constant breeze. But when I looked closer at all the pretty autumn colors, I realized they were moving all on their own—they were waving against the wind, probably trying to shoo away the gigantic moths that were playing about their branches.

"There also seemed to be a kind of melodic absence tolling somewhere in the background of the world. It was tiny and fragile, and the slightest thought could block it out. I think it was just a fancier form of quiet—it reminded me of cursive writing made from silence. The air was incredibly soft and forgiving, and I moved about as though I were in a dream, never worrying about tripping or falling. Lesser technical issues were completely resolved during the Darkness—you never had to worry about splinters, tripping, swallowing wrong, stubbing your toes, frog-in-the-throat. It were as if all the jagged edges of the previous reality had been blunted, if not entirely removed. That's not to say the Darkness lacked subtlety. The nuances were exquisite, I assure you. I could feel the shadows trickle over my skin, tickling like cobwebs against gooseflesh. And whispers could become various kinds of insects. I once whispered the story of *Little Red Riding Hood* to a pet of mine, and suddenly all these little red crickets were hopping out from the corners of the room. Nasty-tasting things, crickets.

"Anyway, enough of all that. This is my last story, and I'll hear it finished before you cobble me into some kind of bone-gilded music box, or whatever you plan to do with me after I'm dead.

"Where was I? Oh yes, I remember. I was walking down the sidewalk. As I snuck around the neighborhood, I could see a line of people twisting out from behind the brambles of what I remembered to be an abandoned house. The house was peeling paint and the lawn was wildly overgrown, and it had been the source of endless complaints by the neighbors. All the people were silent and apparently happy, as everyone was smiling. I hoped that it was a crowd of neighbors waiting to receive rations or the like from some form of emergency services group. I walked up to the back of the line, somewhat in shock from all that had already happened. I suppose I played up my fright a bit, as I was in desperate need for some good old-fashioned pity.

"I wandered, sobbing and shivering, over to the people at the end of the line. They didn't even look at me. They were all too busy staring at what looked like movie tickets. They cradled the little things in their cupped hands as if they were too precious to hold one-handed. In a somewhat breathless, exaggerated tone, I questioned the woman at the end of the line about all the darkness and insanity and what have you. She placed an index finger to her lips and shushed me. That's when I noticed her footwear. I'll never forget that pair of red sneakers as long as I live—which, in view of my current situation, won't be that long. She was one of the mutes that had wandered around my bedroom, flinging bloody body parts all around!

"My little epiphany seemed to be the woman's cue to activate her next level of weirdness, because just as I figured things out, she curved her face into a dreadfully vapid smile—the sort you'd see stretched across a sugar-drunk child's face. I quickly exchanged my indulged expression of horror for the real thing and ran as fast as I could in the opposite direction. Those stupid, blood-squishing slippers made a fine joke of my exit, by the way.

"I ended up squeezing myself into a small gardening hut in some random backyard. I just sat in there, scared like you wouldn't believe, wondering how long I could stay hidden before some horrible thing or another prompted me to leave. Do you know that I stayed in there for two weeks? Well, at least it seemed like a couple weeks. Time was a tricky thing during The Darkness. I never got hungry, and I never had to powder my nose, so to speak. The Darkness was a wonderfully immaculate enterprise, at least as far as the more unpleasant requirements of the human body were concerned—another one of those dampened technicalities I mentioned before. I should also mention that sleeping was all but impossible, so all I could do to pass the time was hum old show tunes and talk to myself. At one point, I began to sing a funny little song. It was a really odd ditty, full of all kinds of cut-up and pasted-together rhymes and songs I'd heard. I don't know where it came from, but the more I sang it, the braver I became. Just when I had worked up the courage to leave, a small piece of paper was slid through the crack in the wooden door. All it said was *Louder, please.* I decided that it might be wise to wait a bit before leaving, song or not.

"When I finally felt safe again, I crept slowly from the shack and skulked around the edge of the yard, on the lookout for people wearing familiar footwear or smiling like psychopaths. I could see that the line of people had stretched into nearby streets, all of them clutching their tickets and grinning. I have to admit that I was pretty curious about the movie showing inside the abandoned house. I eventually decided that I needed a change of scenery, so I carefully made my way through side streets and parking lots until I was closer to the downtown area, where I hoped to encounter sane individuals. I had no idea what a tall order that was.

"When I arrived at the center of the city, I encountered a throng of people carrying around metal fittings and various other mechanical odds and ends. This time, I was a bit more careful about how I approached people, so I watched and waited. I soon discovered they were building a rollercoaster inside a skyscraper. It wound down from the top of the inside of the building, twisting into hallways, offices, up and down elevator shafts and stairwells, and presumably into the basement and maybe even the sewers. I could see the cars zoom past some of the windows, and I could faintly hear the joyful cries of the passengers. Soon, a ridiculous little absurdity began to wiggle around inside me—I desperately wanted to take a turn on the ride. But a derailed car filled with screaming riders came crashing out of a thirty-story window, so I decided to move along. At least, until the roller coaster was repaired.

"It didn't take me much longer to figure out that the whole world had pretty much gone off the deep end, so I decided to find a quiet place to relax. I was about to sit down behind a dumpster and read from a damp fashion magazine I'd fished out of it when I heard something behind me. It was sneaker-woman, smiling so hard she made my face hurt. She just stood there like some kind of demented doll. After I don't know how long, she put her hand out like she was checking to see if it was raining. Suddenly, across the entire city, it started raining bloody body parts.

"Twitching arms, blinking eyes, quivering livers—you name the body part, it fell all around me as I ran. The sharp slapping sounds of flesh meeting concrete punctuated the dull wet thump of bodiless heads hitting the ground. Blood splashed everywhere from the constant rain of limbs, and I was soon covered from head to toe in gore. I would have loved to ditch those damn slippers if I hadn't needed them to run across the bloody pavement. *Squish-squash, squish-squash, squish-squash!*

"I looked back over my shoulder. She was still there, smiling, not so much as a drop of blood on her. I had no idea what she would do if she caught me. She was all of my height, which wasn't saying much, and about the same build—again, not saying much. She didn't have anything in her hands, no visible weapon at all, just a great big smile full of smoldering madness.

"As I ran, the bones of my mind were beginning to snap and rub together. Little bits of pain began to pop and crunch inside my head. The insanity that had taken hold of the world was trying to get to me, smashing its shoulder against the door of my mind, but something wouldn't budge. Some piece of stubborn sanity had propped itself against the door, firmly holding it shut, forcing me into the role of a lost sunbeam wandering a night that wouldn't end. I knew the woman had been sent for me.

"She was going to put me with all the other newly outdated relics—sunshine, morning strolls, coffee dates, and all the other staples of the previously ordinary world. I prayed for a breakdown, for my mind to split open and start spilling hordes of flying, headless clowns into the sky, but it just wouldn't happen. That's when I discovered one small sliver of notable change—I was hungry. I hadn't been for weeks. I knew I wasn't supposed to be. It wasn't part of my script. I'm sure I was intended to busily pile dung beetles into mile-high pyramids or something crazy like that, but all I really wanted to do was eat.

"A falling foot hit me directly on the head, and I had to slow down. I stumbled into the doorway of a laundromat. The crashing of blood-soaked limbs beat a wicked rhythm on the roof. It was like God was using the top of the city as a gigantic bongo drum. I moved away from the large windows at the front of the place, giving me a far better view of the chaos outside than I was comfortable with. Namely, Sneaker Lady came strolling through the downpour.

"She just calmly walked toward the laundromat, smiling her nuttiness into a world already clogged with the stuff, staring at me through the gore and glass. The 'rain' still avoided her like the plague. As she moved closer to the windows, blood started dripping from the ceiling tiles, and the crashing of body parts onto the roof seemed to multiply. She didn't even try to open the door, she just stopped in front of it and stuck her hand out again. It seemed like her smile was becoming brighter, more real. I know that's a hard one to wrap your head around, but it was like her smile had been muted all along, barely visible from behind the thin plastic curtain of our cheap little reality. It was somehow burning its way through the divider, showing its true colors.

"Like a thunderbolt, a severed elephant's head smashed through the roof, taking out the door, granting Sneakers access to the building. The woman stepped around the head, the arc of blood spraying from its still-flailing trunk always seeming to miss her. I screamed and ran out the back door.

"I ran until I crossed beyond the city and into the woods. The body parts were still coming down. The only real change was the sound. The loud smashing was replaced by the cracking and rustling of parts falling through the forest canopy—limbs falling through limbs, I guess you could say—and the softer thuds as they landed in thickets and underbrush.

"It wasn't long before I found my salvation—a cave. I practically dove into the thing. I didn't care who or what might've been in it, I just wanted to shut out the sounds of the rain. It was a huge cavern, going far deeper than I expected. I squish-squashed my way inside, hoping I would just dissolve into the darkness and be done with everything, once and for all.

"Well, I didn't dissolve, but I did eventually collapse into a sobbing heap of blood-soaked ruin. And no, I wasn't crying over my lost family, or the insanity that had replaced the world. I was crying because I had become so very hungry. It was like a blazing, ravenous fire growing inside my belly. To my surprise, I had almost unconsciously begun to stuff my mouth with whatever crawled across the dank floor. Spiders, salamanders, it didn't matter—in they went. I did this for hours, until I was full. Soon after I was done gorging myself,

I realized I wasn't alone. There were other things down there with me.

"Animals of every stripe haunted the darkness around me. The poor things were horribly sad. The world had betrayed them. It had become unnatural, and so there existed no place for them. No place, that is, other than at the bottom of a cave, sharing their misery with a bug-eating human whose feet squelched when she walked. They just milled about or slumped against the rocks. I was perfectly safe, mind you, as even the biggest bears and cougars were in too much shock to consider eating me. We all sat down there for quite a while—I'd long given up trying to keep track of time—resting against one another, depressed. Eventually, it occurred to me to do the only thing I could think of to raise our spirits—I sang my little song.

"Now, I wasn't much of a singer, but the words were easy to find, and my throat felt better, having eaten. The song just sprang out of me, and my new friends sang along with me. We sang louder and louder, harder and harder, longer and longer, until we were all screaming the words in the languages of both man and beast. What else could God sound like, if not the combined voices of his greatest creations?

"My Lord, did we ever dance and roar and spin! We were making such a ruckus, but we all thought, *To hell with the end of the world! We'll just sing until there's nothing left of us!*

"Now, who do you suppose showed up to try and spoil the party? Yup, Sneakers. I could see her by the light of our lovely song, still smiling, still crazy. Suddenly, I could feel the fire in my belly burning through my meal of worms and lizards. I smiled back at her, and I could feel my lips and teeth playing at the limit of my own newer, greater reality. We were still singing when we rushed her. Oh my, were we excited! We were just insane, I tell you! The foolish little thing had no idea what kind of a family we had become, what kind of song we were singing. We buried the woman under our combined weight.

"I was still singing when I ripped and tore at her with my thin painted fingernails. Yet there was something missing from my song, something that my new family had long understood, that my stomach had been burning for. Then it came to me—I plunged my teeth into the woman's chest and ate out her heart.

"You should have heard us howl! I was laughing and gorging at the same time, hugging and kissing my new family. The blood was everywhere, all over my clothes and hands, drizzling down the back of my throat. It was glorious! I was happy, and I was safe. I was home.

"I wasn't scared anymore. I didn't even miss the old world. In fact, I wanted nothing more to do with it. It's surprising how quickly you can change when you have to. And that was just the beginning. We would change so much more by the time the rest of the world woke up. Speaking of change, I finally got rid of those lousy slippers. The red sneakers were a perfect fit.

"I found the world much more to my liking back then, when everything was simply meat and darkness. Even though I was built from Sunday shoes and daytime television, it was the absence of all those things that really cleared me up and put a good sharp edge on me. The Darkness made me aware of what I could be, showed me my calling, I guess you could say. But all that was just a big pile of dry kindling for the fire in my belly, a fire that was just as gigantic as was the world's supply of thick, delicious meat. The fire burned so bright, I could actually see by it, for God's sake. It was like the sun was all nestled up deep inside my guts, shining across the world through my hunger, letting me see through a spectrum of gluttony.

"My appetite proved contagious, too. Soon, it spread to my new family. It burnt away everything that wasn't needed—eyes, fur, memories, and all other useless organs and systems. We were reborn in hunger, and we loved it. You know that feeling you get when you're starving and finally take that first bite of your favorite food? Now imagine never being full, and sitting down to an infinite buffet table filled with all of your favorites, and just eating and eating and eating. That first glorious bite lasts forever, and we were like roaming voids, forever gnawing away at the world. Hell, I'd have swallowed the whole damn planet if only I could've opened my mouth wide enough.

"Eventually, I learned to detect all the empty mouths of the world, glowing like fires burning on faraway shores. I could see them below the earth, across the oceans, even hiding behind dull, lifeless eyes, salivating from salty tear ducts. I knew it was my job to fill them all up. Just by aiming my hunger, I could transform their desires into a single burning appetite for the soft whisper of sharp teeth gliding through tender meat, and the sweet streams of blood that slide along the tongue.

"I aimed my hunger at you. Sure, you tamped it down, but it's still there, smoldering. I can see it plain as day. It's never too late, you know. Go ahead and try me. I'm sure I'm delicious. You know what they say—the only thing better than raw is still screaming.

"No? Suit yourself, then.

"I'm surprised you haven't gotten it by now. It's hardly my fault. I've been forthright with you all along. But my life is only as long as my story, so I'm certainly not going to spell it out for you.

"Now, I couldn't make everyone hungry, mind you, but you'd be surprised at just how many I converted to dedicated carnivores. Funny thing, hunger. Everything being equal, that's all we really are—a collection of small, hungry mouths. I have a knack at consolidating them, is all. It feels like I'm making things right—putting all the teeth in a row, so to speak, where they all belonged from the very beginning.

"On second thought, I guess I shouldn't be so judgmental of you. I didn't get it right away either. And I suppose that brings my story right up to the close of the Darkness—when I realized what I was. It's not that the epiphany meant much to me. I was too busy being what I was to really care about what I was, if that makes any sense.

"Anyway, my family and I were hunting the hollows of an old paper mill, where I knew lurked a thing made from meat and metal and paper and old ink. I'd seen it cross the black sky, one night. It flew on membranous paper wings, written all over with black pen. Besides being made from paper and black script, it was apparently also a creature of habit, making the same trip every time I spied it. After I watched it for the umpteenth time, I followed it as it sailed the skies on its written wings, dripping the sweetest-tasting ink you can possibly imagine.

"We were quite practiced at hunting by that time, but by no means had we grown so accustomed to hunting and killing and eating that we were bored with it. If anything, our song had become stronger, louder, and fiercer. We were all smiles and saliva when we crept up the elevator shaft. I remember our claws sinking into the steel walls, sounding like an army of madly-ticking clocks. When we reached the top of the building, where the roof had been smashed open to reveal the sky, all we found was this little frightened man. He lay face down, all tied up with rubber bands, inside what looked like a gigantic paper nest. His skin was covered in tiny messages, all of which were written in ballpoint. One of them written around his neck read, *Twist counterclockwise and lift up.*

"For some reason, he was barely visible to me. I'd known far more bizarre things by that time, so it was no cause for alarm. There was a hunger in him, but it was different, somehow. I didn't think much on it. After all, meat was meat. As it turned out, I was wrong. The instant my teeth pierced his skin, I nearly threw up.

"I demanded the little man tell me what he was. Begging not to be eaten, he told me he had been a banker, but now he was just scared. In fact, he was terrified—he still didn't understand what had happened to the world.

"That was all I needed—it just clicked. I understood, finally. I knew why I hadn't gone insane like everyone else, and why I was able to eat—I was a leftover from the old world. I was designed to indulge myself and grow fat, complacent, and stupid. I was the need to devour the Darkness—to guzzle molten potential like it was animal grease. My life—my ordinary, rote little life—was too filled with ordinariness, you see?

"I was proof against the Darkness.

"And like anything one can't understand, I wanted to destroy the Darkness—chew on it, swallow it into my guts and feel it scream and squirm and die. That's why I became blind—the Darkness meant nothing to me.

"I let the little man go. He was useless, after all. He apparently wasn't quite ordinary enough to grow an appetite like mine, and he wasn't quite imaginative enough to work within the indoor rollercoaster industry, or even secure himself a job as an usher within one of the popular underground movie theaters. Most importantly, when I bit into him, he tasted awful. He tasted like he would have if I'd bitten into him before the Darkness. So, off he went.

"The Paperman never did come back to his nest of piled newspapers, but that hardly bothered me. I was too busy thinking about what I'd figured out. That's not to say my realization shook me at all. Like I said before, it was all just so much kindling.

"Do you finally see, Family Man? It couldn't be more obvious—all things glittering are not always gold. And to think, you had a mind to admire me. Me!

"I dreamed your dream, little killer. I saw how you pictured me and my kind. Do you still feel that our dead eyes are filled with oceans of precious spring rain? And that concoction you made out of one of my slaves—what a joke! It was just a bunch of bones and weeds tied around a dead woman. Did you know that the woman you decorated once got herself pregnant, only so she could experience what it was like to eat her own child as she was giving birth to it? She only stopped gorging long enough to belch and laugh. And here's another bit of trivia about your muse—she regularly slept where I so often squatted-out the remains of my many meals! And you think you made some kind of deep, meaningful art out of her? You really should quit the art business, Family Man. Your future lies in comedy.

"Oh, and one more thing I forgot to tell you—one last bit before I conclude my tale. I heal incredibly fast."

Miss Patience's claws quickly became unwelcome tenants within the various rooms of my body, calling forth no small amount of blood. The cavern wall I flew into was particularly uncomfortable. I could feel a number of my weaker bones crack and snap, which is to be expected when bones pick a fight with stone.

I wasn't stunned by the impact, but my inaction seemed to convince my opponent I was a bit more injured than I really was. In actuality, I was still processing all the queen had said to me. Could she even be trusted with the contents of her own story? Did she really know what had actually happened to her? Or might she be so pure and beautiful a monster that she lacked even a fiber of reality woven into her fabric?

For the most part, her beauty lived in her appearance, if not her appetite—at least not the philosophy behind her appetite, as she presented it. I speculated that her strict diet of Darkness-infected meals was the means by which she acquired her most conspicuous and attractive features, as the Darkness must have progressively seasoned her soul with its protean flavors of nightmare and wonder. If my thesis was correct—and I had no reason to doubt that it was—then Miss Patience would be better classified as a shadow, rather than the exclusive product of the Great Darkness or the Deadworld. This effectively rendered her the offspring of both. Granted, all of us contain shares of death and darkness, but with much less impressive potency.

I was sure of it—Molly Patience was a hybrid of the Great Darkness and the Deadworld. This fact nullified the cannibal's previous contention that the Darkness meant nothing to her, thus causing her blindness. Having untied the philosophical knots Miss Patience proffered, it was finally time for me to kill her.

The giant cannibal lumbered after me with far less energy than she had previously demonstrated. She may have healed quickly, but not completely. It wasn't terribly difficult for me to evade her clumsy lunge and leap atop her back. My sisters weren't long at their task of removing her eyes, and it took them only a few additional seconds to slide into the bleeding pits that remained. However, the size of the monster's head made it difficult for them to complete their job, as her brain was tucked away quite deeply within her enormous skull. Her awful claws were upon me again, raking across my back and shoulders, tearing me from my perch.

The queen spat the blood pouring down her face as she spoke, her voice betraying the pain she suffered. "My eyes are baubles, I'm better off without them. I'd rather be rid of the foolish things, anyway. They give the wrong impression. I can still see you, little killer. Your fires are still burning plenty bright. If you'd do me the enormous kindness of holding still, I'd like to eat you now. It's a long climb back to the surface, and I'm going to need all the protein I can get!"

The claws of her left hand barely missed my face, instead sinking into the boulder beside my head—so much for my theory on bones losing fights with stone. She retrieved her claws with remarkable ease and wrapped them around my neck. Lifting me from the ground, she held me at arm's length, hoping to disembowel me with her other hand. My sisters flashed their steel smiles, and I dropped to the ground as they severed her claw at the wrist. "Was your hand a mere bauble, as well?" I asked, using both hands to peel the giant claws from around my throat.

"It'll grow back," she returned. "That's not the first hand I've lost to a knife."

The queen was fond of charging at me when a more nuanced battle strategy eluded her, so she came at me again, shrieking. Despite her lack of finesse, she succeeded at crushing me against the boulder with her enormous bulk, pinning me between herself and the unwavering stone. Sisters back in hand, I thrust them into her distended belly. Using the boulder to brace myself, I pushed them forward with all my might, plunging them deeper into the heavy folds of the queen's gut. She shrieked as my arms delved elbow-deep inside her, my sisters making a playground of her vital organs. The queen shot back reflexively, holding her gushing midsection with her one good hand as she stumbled away, finally collapsing to the ground.

My father's blackening shadow fell across the prone monstrosity, adding a substantial measure of weight to the queen's efforts to shrug off gravity. I strode behind Miss Patience as she crawled through piles of glowing embers and sizzling bits of flesh, finally collapsing against a cavern wall. "Born of nightmares and fresh apple pies. You are surely a perplexing creature, Black Molly Patience. I must admit, I've come to both loathe and admire you, simultaneously and in nearly equal measure. While you may have once been an artifact of the Deadworld, your hunger has made you a tar pit of sorts, filled with the fossils of the bygone Darkness. You are, after all, what you eat."

Miss Patience laughed, little more than a gurgle. "I . . . suppose you might be right, at that. I hope you win this thing, little killer. You'll find my kill list in my sleeping chambers . . . provided you haven't blown that to smithereens as well." She paused for a moment, grasping ragged breaths. "I really thought I was going to take the prize. That dream of starving wolves—who better than I to appreciate that? My poor . . . poor beasts. I suppose it's better that you killed them all. I'd rather not have them outlive me. They'd have no hope of surviving without me."

Sightless eyes or not, it was hard to gauge her face in their absence, but her voice took on a resigned tone. "I'm . . . flattered you held me in such high regard. I just wish the Darkness had sunk a little deeper into my old, wretched bones. Every time I sat down to a meal of madness, I could feel such wonder fill me. But then I'd swallow . . . and it would all disappear. After the Darkness receded, it became more and more difficult to find meals like the ones I'd enjoyed. Eating became so horribly empty. Worst of all, I forgot the words to my song. Perhaps— "

My father was quick. I doubt she sensed him coming.

Her corpse was brilliant, and I would take no credit for it. I left it where it lay, sprawled out and in mid-thought.

I made my way through the injured underground, spying the furtive movements of ancient things as they picked through the ruin for the ripening corpses of cannibals. Apparently, the rot-eaters beneath the earth held no grudge against me for ruining their supply line of meat, which suited me fine. I was eager to be done with cannibals and ghouls and mutants.

A short time later, a slight breeze had found its way into the cave. I saw the queen's kill list drift across my boot, its names clearly displayed. I picked it up, sat down upon a pile of old bones, and transferred the names to my own list. I crossed off Miss Patience's original, less inspired name and moved my eyes to the next.

Tom Hush. I couldn't wait to meet him.

CHAPTER ELEVEN

The funny thing about the next name on the list was that I already knew it, as did most people. Tom Hush lurked the labyrinthine hallways of darkest folklore, having done so for as long as I could recall. My first inclination was to assume copycat had taken the name for himself, spreading nightmares behind a lushly antlered mask. Yet, of the many killers I knew to be roaming the countryside, I could think of none brazen enough to take up the name. Of course, the title could simply belong to a man with a wonderfully folkloric name, having nothing in common with the infamous daemon at all. But the chorus of whispers that purred behind my thoughts said differently.

I shrugged off the hungry shadows and smoldering ruins of Lastrygone, leaving it to the oblivion I'd fashioned for it. I made my way westward for several days, hoping to learn more about the myth of Tom Hush, as my dreams had been disappointingly absent of any meaningful signposts—of late, they had been concerned only with the wonderfully dark subjects that typically populated them.

As I passed town after town, deliberately avoiding large cities and their inherent loathsomeness, I analyzed the arrangement I had—perhaps rashly—entered. I was now killing on a mystery's behalf, hoping dreams would flood from the wounds I inflicted upon the Deadworld. But after the many deaths fashioned by my own two hands, I could only feel the world congeal, ever-hardening for its absence of liquefying dream.

The Crucifier, The Mad Mercenary, a nameless Wolf, untold numbers of living nightmares, an entire village of degenerate cannibals and their loping beasts, and the near-legendary Black Molly Patience herself. All of them, my beautiful bouquet of dead flowers, handpicked.

And now the Shepherd of Wolves would have me slay what appeared to be the living embodiment of one of the happiest, darkest myths known to me. Through it all, I had only the reddest dreams to assure me of the righteousness of my path. And while dreams have never misled me—despite what the Queen of Cannibals may have suggested to the contrary—I was growing more and more leery of nightmares dripping with the skin of wolves.

After many more days of wandering, I finally came upon a circle of trees, bent in stature and sallow of color, completely denuded of their fall coats. Immediately, I realized nightmares had routinely traveled through this small, leafless space, and that some of the visions may have become entangled within the grasping limbs, awaiting picking like dark ephemeral fruits. It was plain to see that if I was to receive a proper dream, it would be in this place, though I had to be careful not to allow my excitement to offset my fatigue.

As I entered the crooked circle, I could feel their cold shadows playing across my skin, trying to find a handhold upon my soul, to lift it from my flesh and use it to cover their naked, emaciated frames. But my soul was anchored by shadows far darker than theirs, and the mad grasping proved futile. I was dreaming before I knew it.

I walked through a dimly lit hallway, passing creatures whose shapes were too wild to describe even by their own shadows. The darkness abandoned any attempt to represent them—only confusion resided where should have fallen some semblance of obstructed light. When I reached the end of the hallway, I found a giant window far larger than should have been permitted by the trim dimensions of the corridor. It looked upon the entrance to a massive and feral woodland—it was one of the most spectacular forests I'd ever laid eyes on, inside or outside a dream. The trees were like an army of leafy monsters that had paused mid-march.

I gazed through the window for some time, searching the dense tree line, following a wide beam of moonlight that moved among the treetops like a spotlight. After a time, something began to draw close to the edge of the forest—it was gigantic and terrible, older than the light that tried in vain to penetrate the thick canopy of trees. The lesser creatures of the woods fled its approach, followed by the lean and ferocious barons of the forest. Even the moon seemed to retreat from it. The forest inhaled and held its breath, waiting. Something stepped from behind the curtain of silence, and—

I awoke violently to the sounds of gnashing teeth and throaty growls as something ripped the dream out of me. I jumped up from where I lay, the hot light of the blazing sun pouring through the circle of trees. Not a single merciful shadow fell across me. I was in full view and covered in the sick warmth of unfettered daylight. I had been left like the debris of a wolf-kill—scattered, ravaged, exposed. Far beyond the pain thundering behind my temples, I could hear the wet sounds of my dream being devoured.

I had yet to completely grasp the logic behind the game of dream-swapping, but it was clear something had eaten the dream right out of my skull. I was equally sure the event was nothing less than another killer who had come to that point on his list where appeared my name. But this was no average killer—it was a true Wolf. And from the impression I got, it was a big one. I smiled at the thought.

I moved on, walking ponderously for some time, rolling over this new dream-eater in my mind. When I next looked up, the sight I beheld brought a warm memory to mind—one harkening back to the conclusion of the Great Darkness.

The entire world stood balanced on the very lip of complete madness back then, secured by only a single strand of spittle. But the madness was not of the purest variety, only the reactionary insanity ignited by commonplace minds crushed into the spaces of merciless revelation, without the slightest application of imagination for proper lubrication.

This particular memory concerned the March of the Scaremen. I remember precisely where I was when I heard the story come over the radio. The rain had been lightly falling on the rooftop of a house I had entered, and I was enjoying the fresh food I'd discovered stuffed inside a refrigerator in the basement.

The voice on the radio described them as "unholy deformations of the human condition, congeries of twisted anatomies assuming the most horrific shapes and positions one most likely couldn't imagine, all of them posed via the assistance of sharp implements and other stabilizing materials, like wooden stakes and barbed wire." The voice went on to report that the sculpted bodies had been created "for reasons that seem to relate to the scaring-off of people, like some variety of macabre scarecrow." I sat in the shadows, chewing slowly, listening intently. "Reports are still coming in, but preliminary investigation puts the numbers in the thousands. From everything we're hearing, it sounds as though a nightmare has taken up residence in the hills surrounding the city of Paleton."

That very evening, after the occupants of the house had returned, I used their bodies to create an homage to the Scaremen of Paleton, who had marched wicked and solemn from nightmare into waking.

That same sense of wonder I'd felt back then came upon me now, as a large, foggy cornfield filled with ordinary scarecrows opened up before me. I could imagine their artificial bodies overfilled with ripening human meats, surmounted by heads that partook from a multitude of unrelated species. As I moved closer, the fog retreated from me, giving the illusion that the fabricated monsters were on the march, shambling toward me through the cornstalks.

I was somewhere in the middle of the massive field when I heard a well-aimed whisper from the rolling fog. "Hi," said the sad little whisper.

"Hello," I responded.

"Come here," the whisper said, eagerly.

"Certainly," I assured it, moving further into the mist and corn.

"Hurry," the voice continued. "You're almost there. We're waiting for you."

Gradually, the fog mixed with blood and the corn turned crimson. Hordes of dead cattle were strewn about, their insides scattered everywhere. "Don't pay them any mind," the whisper said. "He did all this, but he doesn't want you yet. So don't worry, okay?" The whisper inflected genuine concern.

"I rarely worry, little whisper," I responded, matching the whisper's concern with genuine honesty. Eventually, the corn hallways fell away and revealed an unobstructed view of a stable. The doors to the structure had been ripped from their metal hinges and repainted in blood.

"He did that, too," the whisper indicated.

"I assumed as much," I said. "I will also assume that all the animals in the stable are dead, along with whomever owned this farm."

"Oh, yes," the whisper confirmed. "Quite dead. That's what he's like. Not much I can do about it, anymore." Its tone grew mournful. "He killed me."

"That's too bad," I offered.

The whisper led me into the farmhouse. The bodies inside were almost unrecognizable as human—they had been mindlessly disorganized. As I continued to follow the whisper through the house, I noticed that all the intervening doors had been blasted open, as if some gigantic creature had rampaged through the structure. There were signs that the corpses and damaged objects had been gnawed upon.

"Just a little further, now," said the sad, dead whisper. "We're almost there."

"Very well," I said.

As I ascended the stairs to the upper levels of the farmhouse, I was passed by a small pack of red-mouthed coy dogs, apparently tempted into the house by a free meal. We moved to the third story, my journey occasionally punctuated with more ruined bodies and wild, hungry dogs.

The darkness clung to the hallway of the third floor as if it had dried upon its walls. I could barely see the ladder that led up into the attic. Whispers drifted down from above. "Here we are," the little whisper said. "Come on up. Its ok, you're safe. We promise."

As I climbed the ladder, I was certain that the smile stretching across my face glowed. I emerged into the attic, and the darkness transformed into crows. They took wing through a large hole in the ceiling. The pecked remains of more corpses lay heaped into corners.

"Up here," said the whisper from somewhere beyond the hole in the ceiling.

"As you wish, little whisper." I climbed up, making my way to the rooftop. The sky was a vault of deepest gray.

"Now, look," my host instructed, hissing out from somewhere deep within the chimney to my left. I gazed across the countryside, my vision pushing the haze from its path, and I spied all the glorious death. Spread all around the distant fields, glens, and meadows were the corpses of untold numbers of persons and animals. Fires burned in the distance, lines of distant houses bleeding smoke into the blackening sky. Cars and trucks stood motionless in the middle of the one road that cut across the countryside, their operators crumpled beside them, red and wrecked.

"He wanted you to see, to appreciate what was coming for you," the whisper informed me. "He said that he'll be coming for you soon, but not quite yet. He wants you to have time to run. He really likes a good chase. I'm very sorry about all this, but he drew your name."

"No apologies necessary, little whisper," I replied. "I completely understand. But may I trouble you to send a message to the creature that killed you?"

"Yes, of course," the whisper said. "What would you like him to know?"

"He drew the wrong name."

The whisper, which was quite likely the killer himself—split personalities were as common as colds after the Darkness—had already silently departed when I heard the first sirens. I was surprised to see the throngs of police cars and other emergency vehicles. I had traveled the wilds between cities for so long, I'd almost forgotten about the formal consequences of murder.

As for the whisper, he was no one I recalled, but the sheer scope of his work spoke to a thoroughly practiced monster, well versed in the ways of killing and vanishing. And I must admit that at first, his brushstrokes seemed hopelessly uninspired, merely the feral craft of a common thrill-killer. But when I looked out from that high vantage, beyond the crows and corpses, it all came together into a finely woven tapestry of death and solidified purpose.

The killer had deliberately recreated a scene from one of my memories. No doubt the image had been somehow preserved within the dream the killer had stolen from me. The memory seemed to be a selection from some portion of my dimly remembered past, as it possessed no context, just texture—bodies and ruins and fire. It was a distant and time-yellowed recollection, and carried with it the smell of burning flowers.

All that I recalled beyond the image and the fragrance was that my mother was present in the memory. I could clearly see her standing atop a distant flowered hill, surrounded by fire and death. Her lips were glistening like wet sunsets, and her eyes swallowed the sunlight into bottomless oceans of blackest ink. Flower petals, burning and delicate, blew across my view of her. The rest of my family was there, standing at the top of the killing hill, the sun burning behind them all, turning their silhouettes into the blackest shadows light can conjure.

The Wolf had proven his reach, and it extended all the way into my past—there was nowhere I could hide from him. Or at least, that's what he'd have me believe. In truth, I was grateful for the artistic recreation of my memory. And the method of its execution did high honors to my family, as I was certain they were as impressed by the feat as I was.

In addition to stealing a glimpse at my memories, the killer had also deprived me of a clear view of my own prey—though it was strange to think of a mythological figure as prey. I could see that the mechanics of the Game were ever changing, tightening, better enabling the separation of wheat from chaff. However, the dream that I had presumably taken from Tom Hush had not been entirely stolen, as I had awoken with a small portion of it still intact. The dream seemed less like the nocturnal art of a legendary horned demon and more like a dream merely inclusive of its imagery. So I returned to my original thesis—the Tom Hush on my list was merely a pretender to the otherworld, not the supernatural entity itself. If true, then I was seeking out a man, which of course was a tremendously disappointing hypothesis.

Despite my analysis, the partial dream did contain something pleasing—and importantly, it was beyond the simple imagination of the killer, regardless of his pedigree. There was something terribly vital about the thing that drew near the edge of the forest, and I couldn't deny the possibility that the actual daemon had indeed tread the fleeting soils of the wooded dream. Where exactly that thought left me, I didn't know. I would need a more complete view of my adversary, and for that I would need to pry my dream from the jaws of a particular and toothy whisper.

As the only man to have ever trespassed into the nightmared lanes of New Victoria—both its waking and wakeless incarnations—and lived to contemplate the experience, I had good reason to believe I could shield my dreams from the predations of a fellow monster. My sisters stretched out in my hands as I laid upon the ground, their laugher lulling me into sleep. Soon after, the baleful eyes of my father led the way into contested nightmare.

I set foot into a room filled with cages hanging from a water-damaged ceiling. In each rusted space huddled a pale child studying me from behind the bars. One of them started to speak. "You know our names— "

My father's giant hands seized me by the shoulders and thrust me beyond the words of the small boy, aiming me toward a gigantic wooden door.

I did know their names.

The door was nothing to me, and I tore it away with ease. The darkness that replaced it was pierced by a single tawny light. With my family walking by my side, I realized the light was a window looking down upon a familiar fantastical forest.

My sisters were fogging the glass with their breath and drawing strange shapes upon the misted panes. The hot light from my father's awful gaze fought with the moonlight atop the canopy of the forest. Finally, his illuminated glare settled upon something I'd missed the last time—a small straightjacketed man seated upon the ground near the entrance to the wood. Before I had a chance to inspect the person more thoroughly, the forest began to hemorrhage woodland animals. I needed to know who the man was. My father's axe was almost to the glass when we heard something from behind.

A door had opened from the shadowy depths of another hallway that also converged upon the window. I initially failed to notice these details, as is the way of dreams. Something was strolling boldly toward us, soaking up the darkness.

"Hi," said the whisper.

"Hello, little whisper," I said. "Have you come to again deny me what is mine?"

"I'm afraid he has," the whisper replied. "You really should have run. This can only go badly for you."

"So you've intimated, through memory and fire and death," I said. "Thank you for that, by the way. It was quite lovely. I'd like—"

"Enough of this stupid banter!" my father bellowed. "Let this first death be a taste of the death to come, whispering fool!" His hateful eye-light fell upon the whisper, revealing a corpulent and unusual man. He was covered in stiches, straps, ropes, and staples. Even his eyes, nose, mouth, and ears were painfully sealed off from the outside world, leading me to wonder how the whisper managed to whisper at all.

"Oh, no," said the shivering, sealed-up man. The sound of straps stretching and stitches ripping began to fill the corridor. "Now you've gone and done it. He's coming,"

"Who—or what—is coming, whisper?" I asked.

"I call him The End of the World," the whisper said, sadly. "I've tried to keep him locked away, but I'm afraid he gets out from time to time. You should see the awful things he's done, before I'm able to coax him back inside. But ever since he killed me, he's proven much more difficult to put back. Goodness, is he ever a foul, foul thing. I'd wake up if I were you. He's all the more terrible inside a nightmare."

A bleeding seam tore the man's abdomen open, revealing eyes the color of blood. They ignited, pushing back against my father's burning gaze. A terrible voice blasted into the room, washing the lingering echoes of my father's rage from the air. "What a fantastic nightmare you've brought me, Marvin! And you've even managed to corner my next victims! How delightfully thoughtful of you!" The tearing and snapping sounds intensified as "Marvin" began to swell and split, firing blood and flesh and staples and stitching into the shadows of the nightmare. Something was stepping from beyond the ruined curtains of Marvin's dreamed flesh. The End of the World was as monstrous as it was marvelous.

Heedless of the unearthly transformation and the doom and pain it foretold, my sisters and I advanced. But before we could engage Marvin's lovely counterpart, my father's massive arm swept us aside, clearing the way for himself. He roared with laughter, stepping before the monster Marvin had become. "I didn't expect the end of the world to be so puny, whelp!"

"Come, then, you fool!" Marvin raged back. "Do you really expect to defeat the end of all things with an axe?"

"With this axe," my father bellowed, holding up the giant weapon in front of his burning eyes, "I do, indeed!" My father charged, only to crash headfirst through the gigantic window from a blow that, should it have been delivered outside of a dream, would have beheaded a man. But it was a dream, and my father was no ordinary man. My dread forbear immediately recovered from his flight, firing thunderous laughter up through the twinkling rain of glass shards. The End of the World leapt through the shattered window after him, following the stream of burning laughter.

My attention lay elsewhere, however. After my turn through the window, I approached the shivering man in the straitjacket. The forest was on its last breath, the fleeing wind having shrunken to murmurs. The quiet of forgotten, ancient things swelled monstrous.

I looked back into the broken sky of the nightmare, where glass tumbled like broken teeth from the gaping window. Two devils wrestled across the worlds of three minds, all of it held together by the unseen hands of a dark Shepherd. My father continued to laugh in the face of The End of the

World, who continued avoiding the axe that hung upon his every move as if it were his own hateful, serrated shadow.

The tethered man's eyes fixed upon a small path that disappeared into the forest as a storm of shadows took shape just beyond the brambles. The man's fear was drawing the thing from the forest as surely as corpses catch flies.

When I reached the man, he was pleading at the encroaching presence to be spared. "Who are you?" I asked, looking down upon the trembling man. But my words were pulled into the woods, absorbed into the silence of prehistoric secrets. I seized the man by the leather straps so tightly binding him, drawing him close, so that my words might reach him. The enemy silence was nearly upon me, and the entire world—molded from dream though it might have been—began to fade into whispers as the night paled into the quiet of forgotten places and half-remembered names. I began to feel my own persona washing away, leaving behind only the uncovered bones of my wonder. The man was screaming now, trying desperately to convey something to me. I could almost hear what he said, but before I could make out his screams, the world died into the raging silence of unguessed secrets—and something stepped from the woods.

Standing atop cloven hooves, casting a horned and hateful shadow that caused the grass it fell upon to twist and curl like spasming insects, stood the inimitable Tom Hush.

The creature was dressed in the finery of a child's unfettered imagination—claws, antlers, and a death-mask of palest bone displaying a grin colder than winter. And when his shadow crawled across my body, I could feel the claustrophobia of buried bodies and the rhythm of countless dead hearts soaking into my skin.

"So, the Shepherd has sent another of his 'Wolves' to the slaughter, eh?" The dreamworld had become the creature's voice—the singular and fearsome sound of deepest secrets.

"Yes," was all I could utter. I was compelled to say aught else.

"You had better cry quits, man-child, lest your little life end in shrieks. I'm off to do my good business, and I'll not suffer the bother of sparks who think themselves stars."

My voice was dead. I could not speak. The creature was beyond my expectations, extensive though they were. My purpose had melted into wonder, my confidence merely awe. Distilled from all the macabre spectacle was one simple realization, although its simplicity made its implication no less monstrous—I had indeed been called upon to kill the actual Tom Hush, the Eater of Secrets—not some hollow prop molded from human dream. Despite the intoxicating mystery of the creature, I'd been tasked by the Shepherd to meet his challenge, and I meant to demonstrate my prowess.

Having no words in reserve, I roused my sisters from their resting places, their teeth sinking into the flesh of a god. Tom Hush broke his own silence with a roar that rivaled my father's, and I turned to the man wearing the straitjacket. "Give me your name! Now!" I shouted into the broken storm.

"Josh Link!" the man shouted. "I'm Doctor Joshua Link! Please find me—and kill me!"

Tom Hush's outrage melted the dream of forest and night into a ghastly scene of red-stained stone alters, where the rotting husks of numberless men, women, and children uncoiled in gruesome displays of ritualistic death. Looming above it all was a somber and sinister antlered idol, whose barely concealed smile spoke to an endless fascination with humanity's ridiculous attempts to satisfy what they could never hope to appease.

"You dare?" howled the daemon as my sisters laughed, cutting and dancing.

"Yes," was all I could utter. I was compelled to say aught else.

The dream shook and convulsed, tossing the bodies and blood and stone idols like toys. All the while, the sky darkened with shadows that spread like fire, burning the world back to primal pitch. My sisters continued their onslaught, but to a nearly negligible effect—the monster's explosive reaction seemed largely due to indignation rather than laceration.

The creature was cocooned in secrecy, disallowing any clear view. Though Tom's antlers were visible where they tumbled skyward and beyond, his eyes became suns. As for me, I was but a mote of dust caught momentarily in the eye of a storm—and I was enjoying every second of it.

I don't know whether Tom Hush had struck me with his hand, or if the force of his burning red glare sent me crashing into the margins of the dream. Either way, I was nearly destroyed. Everything began to tremble as Tom began forcibly detaching his dream where it was joined with the others. Like a supertanker pulling away from a dock it was still moored to, everything began tearing away, pulled along in the wake of Tom's withdrawal. I was caught in the middle of the tug-of-war, my mind trying to occupy all dreams at once. I could feel my physical body, stretched out and sleeping beneath the cold shadows of dead trees, begin to convulse, outlining my mind's destruction as it outlined the death of the collective dream. My muscles tensed around my frame with such strength, they threatened to snap my every bone. My teeth ground my tongue to a flap of raw, red meat.

It was not a gentle hand that seized me from oblivion, snatching me from death and throwing me down upon the ground of what was left of the shared dream. My father stood wreathed in rage, his aspect darkened by the blood of The End of the World. "Weakling!" was all he said to me as he returned to his battle with Marvin's monster.

Tom Hush had vanished, his ancient dream fading into distant sleep, Doctor Link in toe. As I returned to my feet, a stray fragment of the god's nightmare settled across my mind—it was a message from the antlered lord himself. *'Twas merely a breath that defeated you, child. Imagine if I had chosen to enunciate, or if I had reached out to you. Now, away with you. And tell the rest of the Shepherd's dogs of the calamity that is my displeasure.*

I looked to the molten spaces that once held Tom's dream—or more likely, Joshua Link's dream. Ancient things like Tom Hush have no need for such things. They exist entirely at the pleasure of their own will. No, the Eater of Secrets was likely amusing himself using the body and soul of the poor man. The nightmare of the primal woodland and brooding idols were just a medium for Tom to work through. Finally, the spaces where once thundered a god went still— the red wake of a killer shark—as if the monster had never been.

Marvin and my father were buried in rage and bloodlust, having nearly smashed the remaining dreams to splinters, allowing me to make my way into Marvin's dream unhindered. When I drew upon the hallway door by which Marvin had entered, I heard the most pathetic wailing imaginable—it was the cry of a child. I opened the door into what appeared to be a tiny, squalid apartment. Trash and debris lay heaped as high as the corpses. The bodies were in varying states of decomposition, the people seemingly killed in a variety of unrelated yet horrific ways. The dream was mostly memory, containing only the slightest specks of fantasy. Thin layers of cardboard had been crudely taped over the windows to prevent sunlight and unwanted attention. Occasionally, the shapes of monstrous things pressed their silhouettes against the covered windows, and a bit of rain fell from the shadows that stained the ceiling.

I followed the cries that now vacillated between the voice of a child and an adult, sometimes transitioning within the middle of a spoken, if indecipherable, word. While the words themselves were indistinct, they were intelligible in the broader terms of pain and suffering. As I closed on the voice, a single word broke through the static of sobbing—"mother."

One memory overtook another as the hallway I walked distended and became the muddy tunnel of an underground maze. The rain had stopped, and the monstrous shadows were replaced by the sounds of titanic things digging just beyond the hewn dirt walls of the burrow. The tunnel eventually concluded with another small, untidy room, replete with another menagerie of corpses—except these bodies had been far more brutalized than the ones prior. Still, the vacillating voice was beyond my reach.

The next door opened into an even smaller space—the bloodstained and corpse-strewn innards of a ruined RV. Through a filthy, cracked window, I could see the figure of a man on his knees, crying, pleading to someone. Clearly, this was Marvin, minus his monster, covered in his now signature stitches and staples. I could see a woman's slender, delicate shadow falling across him. He was begging the woman—who I took to be his mother—not to abandon him. I bent lower to get a better look at the woman through the window. My breath vanished. The woman was my own mother.

If I'd only seen her smile, I would have known her. I would have remembered how it lived beyond her lips, and how the sweetness of its red glow always put the taste of honey in my mouth. She began to recede slowly into the shadows of the forest behind the RV. Marvin chased after her, collapsing to his knees in the mud.

As she merged into the darkness of the woods, I heard her speak to him. "The end is yours to keep, now. Cherish him, my son." She called him *son*, but I knew this man to be no brother of mine. He was something else, though I had no idea what.

Her eyes blossomed at the touch of the shadows, as if like the moon, they were meant to be viewed exclusively from a position of darkness. Without thinking, I plunged deeper into Marvin's memory, hoping to catch a final look at my vanishing mother. But she was gone, and my sadness knelt beside the sobbing memory of Marvin's misery.

I needed to know more. I had to find another memory somewhere in the dream. I entered the ruined RV, searching. I flung a cupboard door open and watched as the space beyond stretched out and became a dark hole, leading somewhere deeper. Tearing away the old dream to get to the newer one beneath, I clamored into the hole, struggling over the corpses I suddenly realized were all but choking the small space. I heard something crashing behind me. Desperately, I scrambled through the narrow, earthy passage.

Again, the tunnel yielded a room, this time a closet. I was looking down into it from a small heating vent, where I heard the whimpering of a child. It was Marvin again, and this time, he spoke to me. "You think she's your mother, don't you?" said the miniature Marvin, standing on his tiptoes, whispering into the vent. "In that case, I should tell you— "

Something exploded into the tunnel behind me.

Child-Marvin giggled at the monstrous interruption, whispering, "You're going to have to bleed for this one, I think."

A titan hand wrapped around my ankles and pulled me from the tunnel. The transition from crawling to dangling was almost instantaneous as the hand quickly moved from my ankle to my throat. The grip was unbelievably strong. Again, my father held me in his hand. "Where are you crawling away to, whelp?" He was a specter of blood and fire. The previous dream-memory had ignited beneath his rage, and only the closet door remained, smoldering, covered in scratches made by the tiniest of fingernails.

"Release me, Father," I said, despite the pressure applied to my neck. He held me up to the fires of his eyes. It had been some time since I had cause to look upon him for so long, and with such scrutiny. I searched his nearly indecipherable expression for some sign of an underlying motive. What was it I was not to know? My request was met with greater pressure. He left me no choice. My right fist collided with his jaw as my left moved to pry his immense hand from my neck.

He didn't move or speak, but only squeezed tighter. The fire from his eyes burned across my face as he held me closer. I could see my sisters standing behind him, their smiles gone. Now, both of my hands were trying his individual fingers. They were immovable, squeezing tighter still. My father's eyes poured fire into my mind, and I could feel certain memories crisping and curling within the inferno. I tried to open my eyes against his own, to dowse his fires in my silence, but all I could do was gasp. The Deadworld was opening, and I could feel waking sensations move into my fingertips as my father's grip began to crush me out of sleep.

Beyond the burning dream, within the smoldering ruins of so many deadened memories, I could see Marvin, his body renewed in stitches and staples, aiming a whisper in my direction. Before I heard my neck-within-a-dream snap like a twig, I heard the hushed words of the man-monster. "Serpents are far deadlier than wolves, my friend—and your bed is teeming with them."

When I awoke, the sun was burning into the retreating night, and my throat still vibrated with a phantom pressure that refused to submit to waking. I replaced my sisters to their sleeping places and made ready to depart, my itinerary ever-growing. Though I had my sights set on Tom Hush and Doctor Joshua Link, my mind was pinned to the dream of my mother, and only to a slightly lesser extent, the whispered words of Marvin the lunatic. His warning burned like a small fire in a dry field, an infant inferno. Even under the hot light of the sun, I could feel the burning gaze of my father, watching. I put down the dream-memory and walked away slowly, waiting for the sun to fall away. I had no intention of entering the next city in broad daylight.

The eastern entrance to the sprawling metropolis of Nighthead was littered with the lingering machinations of the

Great Darkness. Obscuruum here were treated with far more respect than other cities, and nowhere else was the history of the Great Darkness exploited with more enthusiasm, save perhaps Autumn City.

The glassed-in monuments to madness were legion and breathtaking. Some of the buildings located within the city's downtown area even incorporated various Obscuruum into their construction, allowing nightmares outlined in glass and concrete to stand beneath the sun and beyond the sleep of reason. To be honest, there were several other cities I could have traveled to for the information I sought, but it was the lure of grimmest history that brought me here.

I made my way through the cobblestoned streets, around nightmares frozen in municipal stone, and into the finest shelters for shadows available within city limits. At last, after I stepped out from an alleyway sideshow of black-clad clowns reenacting a scene from the Darkness, I found a newspaper left to the wind. The headline read: ANTLERED CORPSE FOUND MUTILATED UPON STONE ALTAR.

CHAPTER TWELVE

There's more to an artist than this world can ever satisfy. Thus, an artist is ultimately born inherently incomplete. I suppose it wouldn't be too much different than realizing—through a dream, more than likely—that one's eyes held the power to see in the dark, but regrettably, there was only sunlight. How terrible would it feel to know such sights existed but could never be glimpsed? This is the exquisite torment of the artist—to know something has been omitted from reality, or worse yet, never created in the first place. In either case, the artist finds the world wanting. The only reasonable resolution to this conundrum, of course, is to create—to change the universe.

It was my mother who taught me what an artist truly is. I refuse to believe that such lessons, and the time and energy required to properly impart them, would have been wasted on anyone less than her own son. But what I learned from the madman's dream couldn't be minimized, no matter how hard I tried to keep my mind upon the many wonders of Tom Hush. On that score, it had become altogether obvious to me that Tom Hush had successfully hidden himself away in a tidy cluster of what appeared to be random occult murders, all of which were most likely perpetrated by unwilling dupes. I didn't know if Joshua Link was one of many such enablers, or the sole vehicle through which Tom worked.

I was torn between tasks. On the one hand, I wanted desperately to speak with Marvin the monster, and on the other, I needed to seek out the latest pawn in Tom Hush's murderous undertakings, this Joshua Link. Marvin would come to me eventually, seeking to strike my name from his list, so it seemed a waste of time to reverse my course to find him. Therefore, I reasoned, Tom Hush must garner my strictest attention.

When I learned the occult slaying had taken place on the outskirts of Nighthead, I realized the delicate, imperceptible pull of the Shepherd's Game. It had blended itself into my very thoughts, masquerading as free will, causing me to believe I'd chosen to visit the City of Many Shadows of my own violation. Had it not been for the lure of unnamed possibility, I would have quit the game then and there. But I was an artist, and the chance to change the world was too great, both as an obligation and as a passion.

Tom Hush was a strange addition to the game, though. I had no doubt the demon was killing in accord with its own inscrutable designs and not at the behest of the Shepherd, so I failed to see the reason for his inclusion. That is, unless he functioned as a test to further demonstrate the mettle of those who had been chosen. Or perhaps he was a rival of the wolf-herder, and the Shepherd's Game served as an effective means to eliminate him—provided of course that Tom Hush didn't eliminate all the competition first. Regardless, he was on my list, and now that I knew Nighthead was predestination rather than a mere destination, there was only one place in the city fate would offer a straightjacketed lunatic.

Moving through the plentiful back alleys and sunken gutters, I drank heavily from the city's conviction to mystery, trying as best I could to collapse the distinction between the secrets within and without myself. I would need to be nearly invisible to have any real chance at surprising a secret-eating god. Yet I could not repress my desire to turn over certain memories, knowing full well the consequence of such attempts. Not only would their mystery give me away to Tom, but my father would sooner set me aflame than let me dwell upon them.

I loved my father. He taught me how to summon the fire of my body, how to own it and to kill with it. He showed me death, let me hold it in my hands, play with it, master it. I remember the heft of his shadow, the smell of his ruined skin, the thunder coiled in his voice. And now, after everything he was to me, he would deny me a part of myself? Though it pained me, I finally resolved that if he would not step aside, I would have no choice but to force him to recall the one lesson I'd taught him, the one he had failed to teach me—how to die.

The approach to Warfield Sanitarium was thick with trees, which only assisted me as I made my way to the main fence enclosing several small gardens and koi ponds. A single leap put me on the other side, and I stared up at the building, soaked to its steel and concrete bones with madness. I could hear its soul, a song no longer restricted to meter and tempo, fully free despite its body of walls. I slipped into and beyond a service entrance foolishly left ajar.

The interior was remarkable, every inch the face of a practiced sociopath—tender with flourishes of false empathy, and totally placid in places where one might expect a dash of compassion. A soft music played into the darkness of the hallways, almost a lullaby. Here was the comedy of lunatics, trying to pass off pigeons for doves, water for wine.

I entered the first room I came upon, encountering a man secured to his bed with strong leather straps. As I'd hoped, there was a button located on the bed that could be pressed to summon an orderly or nurse. The man awoke quietly, looking at me with no small amount of concern. He did not speak, but only eyed my father with fear. I'm sure I was an awful sight, with my coat of shadows and red-dimmed family eager to escape their resting places. I put a finger to my lips, and he nodded in understanding. He even smiled as

I moved to push the call button—there was seldom any love lost between the insane and their keepers.

As I awaited the arrival of a staff member, I chatted casually with the lunatic, who informed me they were rather slow to respond to summons. The man, Cecil Barnes, was pleasant enough, and even possessed a delicate sort of sanity, whereby a single thought out of place could send it crashing to the ground. I decided to inform Cecil's swaying mind with tales of my exploits. My goal was to fill his dreams with some measure of my own. Joined in the collective sleep of over a thousand lunatics, I could only wonder at the shapes they might make. *Would they do as fine a job with them as had the New Victorians?* I wondered.

The orderly was not pleased to see me, much less the stinging smiles of my sisters. I handled him a bit rougher than was necessary, for Cecil's sake. "Where is Joshua Link?" I asked.

The man swallowed deeply, his eyes bulging. "Room 349."

I rarely if ever actively deny myself the pleasure of my art, but I'd never set myself against a deity from antiquity—so, to pause for art's sake would not be helpful. I had little choice but to leave the orderly unconscious in the half-lunatic's bathroom. I also loosened Cecil's straps. I always rooted for art of some kind.

When I stepped into the hall, it became immediately apparent all was not well with the darkness—it seemed too rich, like the soil of a nightmare. It seemed as if the insanity of the patients was somehow being pumped into the darkness of the hallway, whipping it into a frenzy, shaping it. There could only be one reason for the disturbance—Tom Hush had discovered me.

What most failed to understand was that some lunatics are like artists—they court dreams just as surely. Regrettably, their refusal to accept defeat for their efforts leads them to become entirely absorbed in their work, and like art, they become only symbols for dreams, even if they don't realize it. Still, such a doomed enterprise is not necessarily without its worth. There is wisdom in madness, just not the kind belonging to this world. It was that alien insight that Tom Hush, the eater of darkest secrets, worked through.

While madness was busy endowing shadows with lungs, I couldn't help but laugh at the passing sights. The wardens were being overtaken by the manifest infirmities of their wards. A fairly stout man, who likely possessed an infinite happiness only when cruelly exercising his limited authority, was being filled with locusts, and no small representation of the species, either. The faces he made as they turned him into a human hive were beyond hysterical. When they came bursting out of his mouth, flying away with chunks of his organs, I nearly burst open myself. But it was to the madness-repurposed custodian with the handgun that I was forced to direct my strictest attention. He tried to say something—which his new foot-long tusks made quite difficult—as my sister passed through the pipes of his throat. Likely, it was something terribly menacing passed along from the mind of Mr. Hush, but I had little time for an exchange of threats, as unfortunate as that was.

My shoulder opened the way into an adjacent room, as the hallway before me had become complicated by a web of barbed and knotted flesh embellished with dripping spears and hooks fashioned from the bodies of once-wardens. Some of them were still trying to push screams out of their red, clogged mouths—those who still possessed that particular orifice, at any rate. The Red Dream was upon me again, engaged no doubt by my proximity to prey—my strength ignored the customs of its construction, allowing me to smash through the wall and circumnavigate the fleshy custodian-barrier with relative and enjoyable ease.

I couldn't help but chuckle as some of the remaining wardens and a small group of garden-variety mad-persons took me for their savior, following my path, hoping I might deliver them from wickedness incarnate. I had never been thought of as such, so I decided to indulge the fantasy, if only for the opportunity to be part of their nightmares to come.

I could feel a lingering animosity as I gripped my father. Yet it was not the time for griping, and so he yielded to my strength and allowed me to lift him into the air. But before I brought him down upon another wall, which would have likely freed my small bevy of well-wishers, I decided to grant him a boon, for reconciliation's sake. I handed my father to one of the custodians, and the uniformed man smiled as if I had done him a favor.

My father's strength was a poor fit for the man's body. The eager custodian's muscles began to rip and tear, for my benefactor exercised a willpower that ordinary flesh and blood could not contain—at least not without great and horrific expense. Unfortunately for my small gathering of followers, my father did not relish the role of savior and quickly annihilated them, howling and laughing all the while. Together, my father and I tore through the sanitarium, decimating the shapes that madness made, closing on room 349.

As quickly as I might have regained my father's approval, I just as quickly and foolishly decided to stoke fires best left to die. "Why won't you stand aside, Father? I must know." The hallway we walked was empty save for the echo of battle. My father, still wearing the wrecked body of the now-dead custodian, paused briefly. He did not speak, but only let his silent reproach attempt the extinction of my curiosity. At least that's what I believed he was doing.

He struck out, his axe destroying the wall behind me in an eruption of smoke and fire. I barely escaped—the attack was not a warning, it was a killing blow.

"And what, pray tell, do you want to know, exactly?" It wasn't my father's voice. At first, I didn't understand. Then I knew myself for a complete fool. "He may be your father, child, but his secret—that belongs to me. And now, so does he."

Tom Hush's antlered shadow replaced my father's, where it once fell from the body he occupied. The custodian turned to face me, but it was Tom who looked at me, eyes blazing a terrible curiosity. "In time, all things are reborn, in one form or another, to lope across the stage of life in an infinity of pointless returns—but not you. It pleases me more than you could ever know to rob you of your fate, to sup upon one of the blackest secrets I've ever had the pleasure of knowing."

Before I knew it, my father bore down upon me. My sisters rose against him, all of us wearing smiles worn countless times before, by gods and the fools who amused them.

My sisters were innocents in all of this. Carved from clearest purpose, they smiled out of the softest love for blood, spilled only for fun and family. I could not bring them before our father, not like this. As the Eater of Secrets hedged his bets by flooding the hallway with more maddened orderlies, I thrust my sisters into the metamorphosed flesh of two of the nearest abominations. Instantly, my sisters' sweet smiles transferred themselves from steel and bone to insanity-infected flesh, their new bodies dripping with the honeyed and horrible laughter of the Devil's children. They were beyond Tom's reach, as they were absent worldly complexity, having long since filled their minds only with the brightest, sharpest thoughts that children could kill with.

As for my father and I, our battle would commence in earnest, but first I would need to relieve him of his weapon, for its lightest touch promised death. The axe—now no longer the seat of my father's spirit—moved with prehistoric brutality, smashing about furiously, ceaselessly. Keeping the monstrous hordes at bay were my sisters, two slaughter-honed monsters whose wits were whetted upon the broken bones of countless victims. All the while, each swing of the giant weapon brought my death closer and closer.

The dream that unfurled around us translated my father's seething indignation into fire, which poured upward and spilled across the ceiling. Pent within the raging flames was visible the shape of my father's ruined face, filled with fury and stretched apart by the smile of a horned god.

I found a drifting patch of shadow and called it into my service, moving the itinerant darkness between myself and the deadly axe. Locating a surging vein of silence concentrated by the surrounding discord, I quickly put myself into its ghostly rhythms, disappearing.

My sisters sugarcoated the scene with wildest laughter and the squeals of dying monstrosities. My god, how beautiful the two of them were, free and feral, laughing and killing and dancing for the love of their dearest brother. They spun and leapt as they called out to our father. "Unburden yourself of your secret, Father, and join us! What good are secrets but to ruin those who keep them? Secrets want to be told! Look at what fun our sweet brother has given to us! Look at us, Father! Look at us killing and dancing and singing! Hurry and join us, before we've used them all up and there's nothing left for you!"

My father's burning eyes looked to his deadly daughters, where they played with death like two cats toying with wounded rodents. His envy ran thicker than the fire that poured from his dead flesh. I struck, springing from shadow and silence, seizing the handle of his axe and tearing it from his momentarily distracted grip. But it was sent crashing to the floor when my father's fist detonated across my skull like thunder. His strength was monstrous. My own fist answered his bone-cracking attack by smashing open his dead, flaming mouth. Despite his hatred at being used as a puppet, I could see him thrilling at the prospect of a good fistfight.

Tom Hush rudely violated the purity of our contest, smiling words into my father's burning, broken mouth. "What secrets your father could tell you, boy! My goodness, what a horrible and wonderful thing that mother of yours was. That is, of course, if she is indeed your mother." I could feel Tom's hand moving around inside my mind, seeking out a secret for the seizing. I felt his power washing through me. He found something. "What's this? Tell me, who are all those children in cages? Who put them in there, I wonder? Care to tell me?" His claim over me increased with each pass of his hand across the emerging face of the tarnished memory. Tom forced my arms down to my sides, allowing my father's blazing fist to crash into me, crushing my left eye into pulpy blindness. Tom bellowed through my father's fire-breathing mouth, "Who put them in the cages, Vincent?"

My name. He found it. He was running amok through my mind, carelessly flinging secrets to the wind like a child pillaging a toy box. Strangely, I found myself trying to mentally reinforce the barriers around the secreted memory, though I wanted nothing more than to know it.

My father carefully studied my face even as he went about destroying it, blow after bone-smashing blow. I could tell that the eyes which now looked upon me belonged only to him, and something powerful was stirring within them.

Another layer to the hidden memory was torn away beneath a storm of Tom's laughter, and a terrible knowledge began to trickle into my once abandoned recollection. I remembered that the cages were filled with little muses. There were also paintings, such beautiful paintings, filling the walls of a wine cellar. I remember looking out at it all from my own cage, which hung from the ceiling by a rusty chain. *He* put them in there.

Before the memory could reach its terminus, my father roared like never I'd heard, his stolen body freezing, disallowing even the slightest twitch. He was trying to fight back the Secret Eater's grip. Tom only laughed at my father's efforts, but perhaps sensing a change in the wind, chose to rip my memory free of its prison rather than entertain the slow process of recollection to conclude its awful course.

A forgotten memory emerged from the blacked-out spaces of my mind, and spoke. *Vincent, what a fine collection of cherubs you've led me to. That raw sugar of innocence! Oh, how I admire the sweet crudity of childhood, its vast potential mixed with little limbs and soft skin. They will do nicely, my boy. Very nicely, indeed. There's a showing next month, in a gallery not far from here, and my mind is already alive with the art from another world. Those lovely little ones will brighten my paints and bless my canvas, allowing dreams to flow like blood from the deepest wound, and all the world will love me for it!*

My body trembled as poison memories began to master my body. What had been done to me? What had I done? The man's voice belonged to no one I could clearly remember. Tom was laughing again, holding my secret in his hand and squeezing it over my head, allowing its terrible juices to fall over me, seasoning my soul for the eating. I knew that once I remembered completely, I would be over, just an unhappy tenant of Tom Hush's churning bowels.

"Poor little Vincent, all alone with your terrible truth. No mother to whisper to you. No fiery father to save you. Your sisters all but lost to their darkest passions. Where, oh, where has your family gone, Family Man?" Tom almost sang the words.

I looked to where my sisters whirled and laughed, splattered with death, having forgotten me within their wild red dance. I looked to my father, where he struggled against the power of his captor, apparently in vain. I was almost entirely the property of the antlered god. I was no longer a Wolf, but merely a caged animal—and perhaps, given my recent memory, quite ironically so.

I could feel the finale of my once-forgotten memory fast approaching as the maw of Tom Hush widened. I could feel myself falling across the bloodied alter of ancient stone, where man sacrificed to the horned god of darkest secrets.

All faded as the man's voice rose again into realization, this time bearing a forgotten lesson. *Children are merely the larval dead, Vincent, waiting to bloom into full-fledged corpses, dried and colorless. While in that larval phase, they are fat with the stolen nectars of lost dreams. They conserve it, I believe, for their long crawl across the face of a dead world, finally draining the last of that wonderful elixir to grow transparent wings and forever worry at the flaccid and rotted bosom of Mother Death.*

It's a rather sad and senseless journey, really, but it's that rote effort that supplies us, you and I, with the brittle bones of our frailest hope. We take their burden from them, you see, ending their painfully protracted and wholly pointless metamorphosis. And unlike them, we employ that potential to a purposeful end—we create wonder. Like the magician devil standing upon the shore of the burning lake, dipping his fiery hand into a bottomless black hat, we conjure flowers for the damned.

This is our art, Vincent—to spite the world by painting all the corpses the color of dreams, and defy death with the beauty from another world. Just you and me, my boy.

Am I ever going into the gallery? my younger self asked. *I can feel myself getting older. I don't want to go to waste.*

Oh yes, certainly, the man replied. *But not just yet. I still have need of you in this world, my little wolf in sheep's clothing. After all, I must have supplies if I'm to conjure miracles.*

Why do the other children hate me? Is it because I tricked them, like you taught me, to make art for the artless? I asked, my voice as small and fragile as the memory that contained it.

It's because they don't understand the importance of what we're doing. They are such little flies anyway, the lowest hanging fruit, really. You shouldn't pay them any mind. They'll thank you once they've gone into the gallery. I promise you.

I had a dream last night, Father. I dreamt that Mother was coming to visit us, but she looked different. Really different. She was dressed in fire, and when I hugged her, I didn't burn. She said she was coming to see you, and that she was going to give me a new father. Oh, and I had little sisters, too! You should have seen how they smiled at me! Can Mother even come back from the gallery?

I woke up, standing in the middle of a hallway choked with red debris. My father was in my right hand, covered in steaming blood. My sisters were asleep at my sides, exhausted. Every muscle in my body burned, and I could hear the echo of my father's terrible laughter disappearing into an inner darkness, where he waited to lay his giant hands upon the world. On the other side of my senses, the smell of burning flowers—my mother's perfume.

As I stood in stunned silence, mentally pushing away my incipient and desperate curiosity, I watched the pale hands of moonlight struggle through the gore-sprayed windows, sifting through the devastation, slightly reddened by the journey through blood. I could feel the killing-dream lingering over me. Tom Hush was still alive, and he was close.

I heard a vehicle start. I ran in the direction of the sound, toward a barred window. As I dashed across the corpse-littered floor, I heaped darkness and silence upon that raw reopened memory, hoping to drown it away, forever. The sound of my flesh overcoming steel bars and concrete did well to mute the shouting, caged children who cursed me. The ruin of the wall was swept up in my wake, following me out onto the rooftop, three stories above the ground. The reawakened memory was right behind me, burning and screaming.

Below, I could see a single pair of headlights piercing the night. I leapt into the darkness, my father stretched out before me. Forsaking silence, I roared through my parched throat, a sound like thunder falling down a mountain. I watched my shadow soar across the pavement beneath me, framed in moonlight, closing on what I quickly recognized as an ambulance.

My father and I crashed through the back of the speeding vehicle, my body raked by riven steel and glass. Bottoming out upon the road from the weight of my fall, the ambulance called up a shower of sparks. Glass and steel fragments were still turning through the air when I returned my father to his rest. Plunging my open hand beyond the small window into the driver's compartment, I closed my fingers over the intervening steel partition, tearing away the divider to reveal the driver—a hapless professor of folklore, overfilled with the unwholesome essence of the God of Secrets.

Producing a handgun, he emptied its contents in my direction, laughing hysterically above the din of screaming steel and shrieking rubber. "Do you feel their hatred, Vincent? Their righteous rage reaching out from your own broken mind, demanding retribution?" The god's aim was terrible. A shot struck something volatile behind me, causing it to explode, splashing fire and glass and debris into my back. I didn't care.

The ambulance careened out of control and skidded into a tight knot of traffic. The weight of the barreling vehicle prevailed over the smaller cars caught within its zigzagging path, smashing them into the moonlit darkness where they wheeled and corkscrewed. The impact hurled me through the windshield, but not before I caught hold of Tom. We tumbled through space, my fingers passing through the flesh of his shoulder and alighting upon bones that shattered beneath my grip.

My other hand punched through the hood of the flaming ambulance, allowing me to deny my momentum. The roar of the engine spoke to a stuck accelerator as we screamed through the wreckage and continued barreling through the streets. I drew him close to me and growled, "I will crush whatever lives you hide behind, creature, until there is only yours left to kill. But before I'm finished with you, you will know pain beyond skin and screams. This, I promise you."

Tom's stolen face twisted into a blistering expression of hatred that outstripped his host's ability to articulate. His coat of graying professor was shredded into gory flaps of hanging facial flesh, revealing the death mask the antlered god was far better known for wearing. When the meat of his face had all but retreated from his cleft, glistening skull, Tom's cracked teeth and bloody tongue came together around the words of his counter proposal "I will forget your name moments after you fail, little killer."

Before I could sink Tom's real face into the steel of the vehicle's hood, the ambulance struck a tractor trailer and flipped, rolling over and crashing through the glass façade of a rambling hotel, finally coming to rest within the glittering lobby.

Rising from the conflagration, I glared at the retreating figure of Tom Hush. I no longer cared about the Shepherd's Game or the approaching police sirens at my back. Not even the terrible memory that burned through my mind like poison fire gave me pause. All I desired was before me, backpedaling away in the ruined skin of a folklorist—no doubt wondering how a mortal could rise from a bloodstained alter, bearing fire and vengeance against the gods.

A storm broke behind me as a fresh gust of bullets blew across the already ruined lobby. Before the Darkness, the police exercised far more discretion as to where they pointed and fired their weapons. But now, with remainders of the Darkness seasoning an otherwise dead world, discretion was not a care they took very seriously.

Luckily, the Red Dream held fast, transforming most of the deadly injuries I should have suffered into only cuts and bruises. Yet the police and their gunfire were far from primary to my thinking—only the fleeing form of Tom Hush pinned my attention.

He raced up a nearby staircase, still laughing. I almost stepped on his shadow as I gave chase, nearly catching him in the grinning arc of my sister's shining teeth, but he managed to push the remains of his borrowed body just slightly beyond her reach.

As we rounded a corner I was surprised by a mob bearing knives, keys, canes, anything they could seize upon. I should have known that a luxurious hotel, little more than a hive of the rich and indulgent, would be thick with secrets for the antlered god to sup—and feast he did. I could hear the floors above me shaking under the wide trample of secret-keeping crowds. Mercifully, these new devotees were without the physical adjustments that madness could supply, so I was confronted only by crazed humans.

My father cleared a flowing red path amidst the teeming throngs, but my pace was sorely wounded. I lost sight of the bleeding god somewhere on the third floor. I slipped into a hallway that had been closed off for some kind of maintenance, hoping the god had taken the same route. Sure enough, he stood at the far end of the corridor, holding the slack darkness that tumbled all around him as if it were a pull string. "Where is your mother now, Vincent? Do you even remember what you did to her? What she did to you? Think hard, Vincent. You can do it, my boy. I'll even help you." I felt the god's psychic fist slam into my mind, crashing past memory and dream alike, searching and clawing for more secrets.

This time, though, my family was home, and they were admitting no visitors. I grinned at the terrible violence that greeted the god's efforts. After all the slashing, hacking, and smashing, Tom seemed to reel from the inner conflict, holding himself up via the grip he continued to exercise upon the flowing darkness of the corridor. After a few moments of satisfying quiet, Mister Hush seemed to regain his sense of humor, letting drip a small stream of oily laughter as he rose from his psychic defeat. "Oh, yes. I forgot about that awful family of yours. It's funny how they look nothing like you, hm?"

The taunt found its mark, and I raced forward, heedless of the god's cleverness. Tom yanked away the darkness as if it were a magician's curtain, revealing the trick beneath. His laughter sank beneath the sound of something large and mechanical, and the god's shadow stretched toward me, pushed by a large, blinding spotlight projecting from somewhere behind him. The shadow transformed as it fell over me, revealing the monstrous outline of the thing hidden within the dead, ever-crumbling folklorist.

The sight almost distracted me from the gunfire thundering through the window at the end of the hallway—a police helicopter fired both its mounted machine guns, chewing the world around me into so much smoking ruin.

I followed the curve of silence where it diverted into an adjoining hallway. More police vehicles massed around the building as the skies filled with additional spotlights. I needed to finish the god quickly if I was to have any chance of escaping. Tom would need to conserve and repair what was left of his vessel, I suspected. It seemed a worthy idea to make my way toward the hotel wedding chapel, should it have one. Secrets have no greater haven than beneath the shadow of religion.

Regrettably, according to the map of the hotel carved beautifully into a nearby wall, the chapel was located many floors above me, near the "rooftop lagoon," of all things. The most direct paths to my destination lay on the outside of the building or up the elevator shaft, and I was fairly certain my armor of dream would not long survive the vulgar reality of several police gunships' sustained showers of high caliber rounds. I pried open the elevator doors and scaled the shaft to the top of the building.

It was a predictable route to take, I confess, but I hadn't realized how predictable until large numbers of people began tumbling down at me from the floors above. I was growing more irritated by the antlered god, though I admit I was slightly taken with him. He was a crafty one, after all. It was a surreal scene—persons falling silently through the darkness at me, each one carefully aimed to knock me from the wall, to send me hurtling down. Tom smartly denied them their screams, so that I was given no warning as to the direction or angle they fell. When Tom finally ran out of people to drop, I continued my ascent.

Reaching the appropriate floor, I was confronted by a wall of armed and armored policeman eager to be done with their night's business. Pushing their obnoxious lights from my face with obedient shadow, I stood to my full height, my father's head nearly scraping the ceiling. One of them croaked into the radio, "We got 'em, alright. He's cornered and all out of tricks. Were gonna bring him down the easy way." I was amused by the bravado.

Without warning, the power went out, followed by explosions and screams. It seemed my sister had done her work well. I'd inserted her into one of the plummeting secret-keepers from the elevator shaft, hoping that she might help improve my situation from below. The bravado vanished from the men gathered before me. I remained amused, but no longer stationary.

I was quick, if not particularly gentle. I sensed no good reason to spare them the pain they would have gladly given to me. I heard the police radio squawk a second time. The voice on the other end called out to the dead policemen as chaos and death reigned in the background. Apparently, my sister had transferred herself to the operator of an armored communications vehicle on the scene, and was making quite merry. The voice ended in a single, wet shriek.

I hastened up the stairs to the rooftop, weeding my path of any lingering ill-wishers as I went. I saw a small bit of blood just outside the door to the chapel. Tom was inside. Somewhere in the darkness of my mind, I heard my father cracking his knuckles.

Closing the double doors behind me, I could feel the ample spaces around me piling with an elder time—a forgotten age of cold stone and burned offerings. Tom was setting up shop, his ancient props—idols and alters and antlers—materializing. Prehistoric shadows flooded the chapel, removing the contemporary darkness entirely, allowing lost epochs purchase upon the present. This was to be our last stand—we would finish things here.

My father shook with poorly contained anger as the leather of my gloves began to smolder. He was still quite upset over his mistreatment at the secret-seizing hands of the ancient god.

Tom's words came from across eons as much as from across the room. "I'm left wondering, Vincent, if I should take your secret with me. There's little flavor to be had in the eating of a secret that's not yet ripe. And while most secrets are tastiest just before the telling, yours seems like it would be spoiled if eaten a moment before it was told."

"You speak as though you've been given invitation to eat of my secret, whatever it might be, but I don't feel inclined to turn it over to you just yet," I said. "You may find my mysteries harder to acquire than those of a dusty folklorist. But of course, you know this already."

"Please!" The god shouted. "You face a timeless opponent, Vincent. Do you truly think my violence your inferior? Your hands have gripped weapons less than a lifetime. I've been eating secrets long before man had hands."

I recalled the god's aim with a gun and chuckled at the superiority of his violence. "I suppose I grasp some measure of your problem, Secret Eater, but I can see no resolution to it, save for the testing of your timeless violence." I hefted my father in both hands. "Which, as you can see, I've come prepared for."

Tom Hush smiled. "Oh, the violence is inevitable, certainly! I wouldn't dream of leaving without it! But it's the degree to which I should want to apply that violence that confounds me. I wouldn't want to ruin your ability to enjoy your . . . *my* secret, now would I? But unfortunately, I can see your father's anger has you far too inclined to put away the civility of a pleasant conversation. So, if you're ready?"

"I am."

The floor cracked at the thunder of the god's charge. He still maintained some semblance of the folklorist, stretching the dead man's body across his monstrous spirit, in the process outlining the wickedness that was his unwholesome essence. He may have been taking lives long before the advent of hands, but he certainly hadn't been doing it with his own. The monstrous creature swung his oversized claws with all the grace of a blindfolded bull, telegraphing each attack long before it was delivered. However, I may have underestimated his alternative resources, for the very moment he noticed me smiling at his combat prowess, he gave me a look that carried the weight of a hammer. I found myself on the receiving end of a psychic blow that shattered my nose and both my collar bones.

My father was all too glad to return the attack with one of his own, crashing into the twisted flesh of the god with such force, he brought Tom to a knee. Returning the blow with another glare from his eyes, the god blistered much of my skin and set my hair on fire. Again, my father returned rage with rage, the blade of the axe sizzling deeper into the Lord of Secrets, calling up flames from the wound. The god roared, from pain or outrage or both, and moved to tear the axe from where it sat wedged into his chest. I continued to push my luck, using the moment to bury my remaining sister into Tom's face. Unlike most organisms born upon the earth, he seemed largely unbothered by the cleaving of his brain. The monster glared from above my sister's smile, the heat nearly evaporating the flesh of my right arm, strands of muscle tissue peeling back across areas of exposed bone.

The dream preserved me somewhat from the flames, which seemed hotter than most I'd known. I decided to ignore the fire as long as I could and double down on my attack. I tightened my grip upon my two family members, using all the strength I could muster to lift Tom from the ground, hoping gravity might assist my relatives at achieving a killing depth. Again, Tom seemed less than impressed.

"You call these simple antics *coming prepared*?" The god seemed almost bored by my efforts. I realized that stopping Tom would not be a matter of finding his weakest point, but the unwrapping of his soul from the stolen flesh of the folklorist.

Changing my strategy, I tore my father free and sent him roaring down upon Tom's knee, nearly severing his leg. Tom deduced my new strategy easily enough and affected his own.

Lightning split the ceiling and lashed my arm, exploding skin from bone and evaporating blood into smoke. The pain was unexpectedly bearable, but my arm was largely useless. I fell to the floor beneath the thunder and smoke and smell of ozone. Tom laughed from his mangled maw. "You creatures are always so impressed by lightning. It's just a toy, really."

Another blazing lash from the sky licked my body as thunder shook the entire building. My chest bubbled beneath the blinding touch of the storm. Within seconds, the swelling erupted into smoke and charred skin. The Red Dream that enfolded me was buckling, and I could feel death waiting impatiently.

"Humans are merely domesticated birds flying beneath ceilinged skies," Tom said, "looking out dirty windows and declaring the spaces beyond themselves to be infinite. You have no idea. You couldn't, really. Why the Shepherd thought you and yours could interrupt me, I have no idea. If not for my amusement with your affairs, you would be nothing but smoke and a terrible echo by now." I tried to pull the darkness over me, to allow myself the luxury of a temporary withdrawal. But the shadows had already chosen a side, and it wasn't mine.

It was after the third lightning bolt that I noticed much of Tom's torso was missing, a growing number of large, smoking holes remarking upon its departure. The secret-eater's face deteriorated as well, including the glaring eyes that had caused me so much pain.

My second sister stood in the doorway of the chapel, feeding fire to the smoldering god through two automatic rifles. She had returned, wearing the body of a heavily armed officer. What a splendid thing, she was! Tom's folklorist rapidly flew apart, and the antlered god began to lose his grip upon the corpse of this world. Searching for a new handhold, I could feel Tom reaching into me again, hoping my secret might anchor him better than Joshua Link's rapidly deteriorating skin. As his power closed around me, something unexpected came loose in his grip—something that did not want to be touched.

Tom howled like never he had, tumbling backward into his own idols, the relics crashing down around him. "I had no idea!" He laughed as a new fire washed over him, consuming what was left of his folklorist. "I bet they don't even know! How could they! What a game this will be, indeed! And for all the bother they've caused me, I'll be keeping the secret to myself!"

I had no inkling what the god was carrying on about, but my chance would not wait long. Still aflame and bubbling, I rose and slowly made my way to the burning, bullet-ridden deity. Just before my father destroyed what remained of the god, Tom whispered through the smoke, hurting me more than his lightning ever could. "And as for you, child. She's your mother in the same way that I am a professor of folklore. She'll show you to hell before she's done. You're like the lightning, Vincent. Just a toy."

CHAPTER THIRTEEN

My past has always been like a dimly recalled dream. But to be perfectly honest, I've preferred it that way. I feel it's the way things ought to be—to have no solid starting point, no fixed center, no clear definition. This way, one is not beholden to pattern or circumstance, the trajectory of the mind is free to wander. Patterns over time lead us to become machines—action starved of thought, repetition deprived of meaning. As soon as the doldrums become automatic, we die into the process of living. Given this rationale, one would think I'd forget about my mysterious past and occupy myself only with the business of repairing dreams, as I always had. But secrets have power, as Tom Hush had well demonstrated. And this secret, whether I liked it or not, was affecting me. Specifically, it was causing me to doubt myself. Perhaps the greatest killer of art, besides cold reality, is doubt. Tom opened an artery in me, and I was bleeding out. I needed to close the wound.

The role my mother played in all of this seemed significant, as it appeared my actions were somehow scripted by her, intending more from me than I was aware. Whatever the case, the signpost to understanding my mother's agenda clearly pointed in a single apocalyptic direction—Marvin the man-monster.

After a few days of regaining my strength within the ample shadows of Nighthead, I began the task of finding him. As I traveled channels of forgotten darkness throughout the sprawling city, the echoes of painful light still rang within my ears and burned beneath my seared skin. The antlered god's half-finished meal of dark secrets still lay upon the floor of my mind, spoiling.

I confined my wanderings to those streets caught in the melting ocher of twilight. As one who had tasted some small flavor of my dreams, Marvin could reasonably expect to find me in such places. At one point, I found myself on a stretch of street that seemed impossibly narrow, capable of admitting only the slimmest cars and thinnest crowds. It seemed oddly comforting, however, like warm blankets pulled thick and close on a cold winter's night. I gazed upward, and the gestating night sky appeared pinched by the closely crowded rooftops, resembling a star-flecked creek pouring infinitely overhead.

There were others walking the street as well, barely perceptible beneath the ripening darkness. They conducted themselves like cold draughts of wind, drifting aloofly, slaves to their darkest selves. Nighthead had always been a darling of the dark, sheltering more shadows than sunset, and I was almost overwhelmed by my swelling curiosity to know even one of the stranger's stories.

It was sometime after midnight when I detected a familiar whisper, wandering lonely and soft across a thickly trash-lined lane. "Hello," came the little whisper, almost lost to the rustling wind and the crackle of urban decay.

"Hello, Marvin," I said. "I'm pleased to see you again. I was hoping we might suspend our obligations to the Game, if only for a moment, so that we might chat."

"Actually," said the whisper, "he's of no mind to hurt you, and we're happy to see you, too. We'd love to chat, but I'm afraid that we're both very, very hurt. Since there's no longer a chance for him to win the contest, he wanted me to find you and wish you luck. It seems likely that you and he share some history, or at least a relative. He knows what you saw in that dream from so many nights back."

"Who hurt you, Marvin?" I asked, finding myself strangely concerned for the poor man-monster's well-being. After my question evaporated, a thick, bloody finger issued forth from between the bars of a nearby sewer grate, conducting my view to somewhere above and behind me.

"He did," the whisper replied.

Stretching my vision up into the night, I detected someone standing amid the metal cables of a radio tower that roamed high above the surrounding buildings, waiting like a patient spider gazing at a crippled fly.

It was Jack Lantern, The Son of Halloween.

I absolutely needed to speak with Marvin. The only way I could do that was to keep him alive, which meant fending off the world's most notorious living serial killer. With a single effort, I tore away the sewer grate and slipped down into the rank darkness. Marvin was indeed sorely wounded, which impressed me much. Jack Lantern was not one to fail at killing.

"Run, Marvin!" I shouted. "I will find you once I've dealt with your attacker." My words made assertions I felt difficult to evidence. In my forbidden quest for a lost past, I had stupidly slipped myself into the path of proven death. Although I had recently defeated a god—if only a relatively minor one, and only his weakened vessel, at that—Jack Lantern was something far more challenging. He was the state of the art, the pinnacle of modern murdercraft. Clearly, I knew that winning the Shepherd's Game would have me facing off with him at some point—I knew of no other killer who could hope to defeat the Scourge of Autumn City—but I'd hoped for more time to heal and prepare. Despite my recuperative powers, I was far from peak capacity.

With my sisters glittering their deadly promises, I prepared for the pumpkin-masked killer. A fragrant wind blew past me, carrying the scent of fall. Staring into the spaces the wind had come, the filthy sewer seemed almost filled with the ever-dying trees of the September Woods, whose leaves forever burned orange, red, and yellow against the bleeding sky. I watched a single crimson leaf cartwheel across the surface of the murky water, leaving tiny expanding rings wherever it tumbled. I could hear something pushing through piles of fallen leaves, drawing closer.

Suddenly, Marvin's mad whispers filled my mind as he seized me from behind and pulled my ear to his bloodied lips. "She's the mother of many, Vincent. But you're her favorite child, by far. She came to us all, searching, but in the end, there was only you. I hate you for taking her away from us! But now, after I've seen something of your dreams, I understand why she left. She chose you! She chose you over the rest of us!" As he disappeared into the darkness, I heard him hiss, "Damn you, brother! But good luck!"

My last memory was of exploding light and the sound of leaves blowing across darkened fields. When I awoke, my sisters were still in my hands, apparently exhausted from the effort of conducting my unconscious body away from my would-be killer.

Sometime later, after limping through miles of sewer tunnel, I saw the glowing lights of a displaced Halloween. Marvin's carved head swung from a piece of red yarn tied around a steam pipe, its bloody hollows lit by several black candles placed within his skull. A chunk of concrete lay upon the headless body, the words *Happy Halloween* scribbled across it in colored chalk. A bag of dirty candy lay stuffed into Marvin's dead, knotted hand. I gazed into triangular holes that had once been partially stitched-up eyes, and offered one last whisper to the whisperer. "Good night, brother."

I made the sewers my home for a time, healing and ruminating. Eventually, and as is often the case, it was darkness that led me to my next step. The principle of darkness, if one can forgive the possible misappropriation of the word *principle*, is to reveal that which is hidden. Now, this may seem a bit ironic, but for the realization that light simply settles upon the surface of things, surrounding them, sealing them off. Thus, light offers only superficial insights, the outside of things. Or, put another way, light is only skin deep. By contrast, darkness is the absence of the apparent, it is the inner quality of things, the deepest truth. It is what's left after all obstacles to understanding are removed, what lies behind or under the light. From this, I realized, there was but one place to go for the answers I sought.

The door was hardly visible beneath the heaping desolation of the unclean alley, and seemed unlikely to lead to anything but the lowliest accommodations. Once beyond the door, I encountered a species of darkness I had come to expect from the forgotten corners of the metropolis, having some portion of its construction owing to an elder blackness that could, should it choose, stand firmly against even the brightest light. However, these shadows were not to be trusted, as they answered only to the lords of Nighthead.

The tunnel beyond the door was winding, remarking upon the basest kind of usage, sporting litter and dampness as a chameleon puts on the colors of its surroundings, tempting one to put aside curiosity and accept illusion. Only after I'd traveled further than any casual observer, did the passageway offer hints to its ultimate destination, and to those who might walk its lengths. Granted, normal eyes would never have seen past the alien dark—even with the assistance of artificial light, trespassers would only confront darkling illusion, tricking all but the most through inquiries. But I spoke some portion of the shadow's lexicon, and so was admitted a sliver of insight.

There were batteries filled with darkness at every turn— objects that had set for miniature eternities beyond even the weakest touch of light, filling with a pitch that defied the stars. Everything here had been infused with the oldest shades. The stone of the floor had been inlaid with grave-dust. Alien bones that had lain under the earth longer than mankind had walked upon it scattered the floor. The walls were lined with some of the oldest funerary idols ever offered to the grinding bowels of the world. These ancient artifacts magnified the common darkness into otherworldly bastions for the Walking Dark—the true high priests of the Order of Nox.

When I reached the end of the tunnel, I encountered a large cavern, the entire back wall of which was carved in the image of a great fanged maw. Before the wall sat a man upon a large seat hewn from a great protrusion of onyx. Initially, I assumed him part of the cavern itself—then his eyes opened. I could feel him looking upon me from every pore of gloom that haunted the chamber. His voice was the sound of nightfall and the spaces beneath beds and the unknown depths of the earth.

"Stand there," he said, gesturing to a small platform to his left. I said nothing and did as instructed. When I assumed a place upon the dais, the man rose from his seat and pulled a lever extending from the wall. Within seconds, I was descending deeper into the earth. How long I traveled or how deeply I descended, I cannot say precisely, save only that I was lowered to a depth that made the caverns beneath Lastrygone seem like divots in the soil.

At some point, the walls around me disappeared, giving way to a vastness that, like the titan ghost of some long-dead prehistoric sky, opened dark and primal, offering black heavens to the dead and damned. There was movement all around me—I was reminded of sharks gliding casually around their intended prey. Regardless of how much I strained, even my eyes failed to pluck shapes from the surging void. I was hesitant to summon my sisters, despite their pleading. I had been invited to this place, and a show of arms could be poorly received.

The platform settled atop something solid, the sound echoing within a great emptiness. I was unsure how to proceed, as there was only oblivion. Suddenly, cold words floated up to me from below. "I shouldn't be impressed that you chose to come, being who and what you are. But I am." The voice seemed inhuman, though not for a different arrangement of vocal mechanisms, but rather the odd modulations affected to the speaker's tone by way of what seemed an intervening mechanical filter. I could feel something drawing closer to me from somewhere below, and I could hear the careful and repeated contact of metal meeting stone.

"No," I said, "you certainly shouldn't be," I offered with a slight bow. "I thank you for meeting with me." I could still hear the metallic stride in the wide silence around me, suggesting the approach of something rather large. I muted my family's howls for blood and felt their soundless and searing reproach.

The speaker's words now drifted down from a height well above me. "I assume we both know, to some extent, who it is we're dealing with. This is to the good, I would wager. As far as your reason for coming to us—yes, we do know something of the entity you mentioned, this Shepherd of Wolves. Let us sit and talk." The darkness shifted into intelligible shapes and discernible distances. Not through the ordinary medium of light, but rather by some alien wavelength of darkness—it didn't expand on what could be seen, but only revealed what my mind was allowed to know.

The darkness showed me my host—a large mechanized thing that stood well over eight feet tall. Great lengths of black cable tumbled from its back and slithered down a great stone stairwell, both unravelling into oblivion. It looked something like a vintage deep-diving suit, complete with the round iron helmet.

The creature noticed my curiosity and offered an explanation of its attire. "The dark, even at this depth, is far too bright for the likes of my kind. We must channel what we require through the mechanical apparatus you now admire. But let us discuss the matter at hand, shall we?"

I hadn't at that point adequately absorbed my surroundings within the underground world. As I seated myself at a small nearby table, I realized we were situated atop a great sable skyscraper carved from the dullest anthracite. It was but a single structure amid an endless cityscape, stretching beyond the dark horizon in every direction. This place was made to the specific comforts of living shadows. I was at last in the darkly fabled city of *Unduur.*

The thing sitting across from me was known as a Darkling. Nourished by purest darkness, I could hear the kindle of shadows surging through the metal coils and tubers that adorned his armored exterior. For all of that, he was a perfectly pleasant host, even offering me a beverage. I declined, of course. I was all too familiar with the sweet blackberry wines derived from the dusky fruits of the deep woods, where the eldest Dark Hats are known to pray to strange gods. The inky beverages were likely to contain spirits of a decidedly non-alcoholic variety.

Without conversational nuance, my host began his exposition. "The Shepherd of Wolves is a type of being called, by my kind, an *Unbegotten.* These creatures are without beginning or end, and they seek nothing but the limits of their own pleasure. They have been known, from time to time, to put on a semblance of definition—merely a trifling whim on their part, we suspect. The Shepherd, in particular, enjoys the occasional solidity of shape and title, and has made great sport of his pet murderers, even fashioning games of death to further satisfy its fascination with killing and killers. Surely, this last bit is why you have sought us. You are a player in one of his games, are you not?"

"I am," I confirmed.

"I see. In the past, the Shepherd's contests were small, consisting only of a handful of participants, and taking place across a relatively minute killing field. But since the Darkness, all that has changed. The powers behind the night have been given substantially greater license to tarry beyond the threshold of our solid world, to more completely master their desires. The Shepherd has gathered together some of the greatest of your kind, and he means to see them dance and kill and die."

"I've gleaned most of this already," I interjected, "but what I seek is the precise meaning of the Game. What is the purpose of it all?" My words trailed into the silence, leaving small whispering motes of insecurity as they traveled over black peaks and graven anthracite.

"The last time a winner was declared," my host replied, "tens of thousands of people were found impaled upon the leafless winter branches of an entire forest. The jaws of every man, woman, and child overflowed with sparkling gold coins that littered the forest floor like yellow leaves at the height of autumn. At the time, there was a killer well known for this very treatment. That killer, it is believed, won the Shepherd's Game."

I shook my head. "Nearly every greedy child has at some time or other been forced to heed the cautionary tale of 'The Golden Leaves of Winter,' though the Shepherd of Wolves wasn't mentioned in any iteration I've ever heard." Despite my intrigue, this was far from the definitive answer I was hoping for. I was beginning to understand why the supplicants of the ancient darkness were willing to meet with me.

The being from the deep darkness continued. "But you understand what might come of such a Game, specifically one that reaches its conclusion after the Great Darkness?"

I could feel the gloom around me tighten, trying to hold me in the chair. I decided to answer the creature's question honestly. "Certainly. Entire populations of people could die, perhaps much more. I know the identities of only two living players—myself and Jack Lantern—and I can only imagine the dreams that might spring from our killing fields. I can see it now—a nearly endless Halloween, burning dim and orange across half the world, clean-carved smiles glowing from every window. Or perhaps it will be a global art gallery, its exhibits filled to bursting with lost dreams, spilling weird and wonderful from coast to coast, immortal and explicit." I fixed my gaze upon the creature. "But you don't care anything about that, do you? Your only concern is that Nighthead might come under the knife, yes? You don't need to say anything, I already know your answer. You wish to end the game by destroying its players, thereby sheltering your own wicked industries from the Shepherd's touch. It's the purely logical move for your kind to make, after all. I'm quite sure that somewhere upon your person, perhaps hidden in some strange metallic compartment, there rests the kill lists you've taken from the fallen Wolves, players your kind have hunted down and killed. And now you would have my list."

The being rose from the table and pushed a button on his armored forearm. With a tiny hiss of steam, a compartment opened on his belt. Out tumbled no less than three kill lists.

I decided to continue honestly. "I certainly don't hold any of this against you. And if it makes you feel better about attempting to impede this wonderful Game, I will tell you I had no intention of leaving here without first tasting the shadows swimming through your veins. This could very well be my last time in your magnificent city, should I fall to Jack Lantern or some other Wolf. I just couldn't leave without showing you my art, and basking in your unsurpassed darkness."

My vision of the under-city, the rooftop, and the creature clad in solid shadow winked from sight, but I had already memorized my surroundings. Immediately, I roused my father from red dreams, and while the alien dark was somewhat constrictive, it was not immovable. With a little effort, I rose and swung my father where I expected to find my host.

As I'd correctly assumed, the being wasn't the fastest of creatures and hadn't moved far from his seat. My father collided with the armored darkness, sinking deep beyond the layers of steel into a near-ethereal body of shadow. The being cried out, simultaneously loosing what sounded like gunfire. I had already shifted behind the creature when the worst of its weaponry discharged, and the vantage allowed my sister to sever the cables from the armored helmet. No longer fed its nourishing pitch, the Darkling collapsed.

I sought out the dead body within the armored suit, but found nothing—merely a silken darkness weighing slightly more than the surrounding silence. My aspirations for art dashed, I took up a new idea. Removing the severed nubs from the overlarge helmet, I replaced the cables and donned the armored suit, breathing in a darkness I could never have imagined. Then, like some deep-sea explorer, I began to probe the primordial depths of the dead-black city.

With each inhalation of darkness, my senses turned away from the solid world and addressed, with curiously little hesitation, only places where its truest form lived. As I passed into the narrow lanes of the sable city, its citizens looked upon me with the quiet detachment of philosophers. They nodded to me, smiles like funeral songs and soot. There was no malice here, only friends to a different dream, abiding with the quiet dignity of fallen kings, ruined and beautiful.

I strolled to the edge of a fountain of smoothest onyx and listened to the words of a sackcloth-clad poet. He extolled the virtues of dying into the night, and wondered loudly over "the dead eye of Luna, burned white and blind by the sun. Man thinks it the face of the moon, and all the while, your remaining eye, still turned to darkness, away from the world, spies the other side of his soul. When, good mother, will you look again upon the world?" I assumed he was referring to the Great Darkness—I had once heard a story claiming the dark side of the moon once faced the earth, and it was that very event which caused the Great Darkness. But I didn't dwell long upon that portion of his poem, instead fixating upon the word *mother*.

Almost lost to the endless train of questions that tumbled from the utterance, my focus was regained by the sight of others dressed as myself, though the newcomers stood far taller than even my height. They carved through the drifting black crowds with no small appearance of purpose. They were looking for me, naturally.

Here the darkness was law, and as such, the powers of the Deadworld were weak, which allowed me to move more quickly than I was accustomed to. After I discarded the apparatus obscuring my head, I raced beyond black gardens, between statues hewn from cold anthracite, past sanctuaries for creatures lost to the lighted world—until I finally drew upon the legendary Night's Orchard, whose trees spilled over with the ripest, darkest fruits I'd ever seen. Here was the real reason for my wanting to visit Unduur.

I quickly snatched a single fruit from the limb of a nearby tree. It was not entirely unlike an apple, save that it was dressed in the color of oblivion and possessed all the heft of a whisper. I placed the black fruit in my pocket and prepared to take my leave of the wonderful city.

Before I could make good my escape, dark shapes discovered me. They initially kept their distance, as they knew what I was capable of—or at the least, they knew what I had done to their kinsman. Above me, knotting and coiling their bodies into terrible shapes, were strange eel-like creatures, apparently obedient to the gathering shades that sought to end my role within the Shepherd's Game. Unlike the other creatures of Unduur, these beings were bone-white, expressing their fondness for the darkness by means of colorless flesh and eyeless faces.

After the Unduurians had gathered in sufficient numbers to quell their fear, they began to drift cautiously toward me. I made for a tactical retreat as our battle became a game of darkness, a test of our respective affiliations to pitch. While my body was comprised of only flesh and blood—whereas the Unduurians partook almost exclusively of shadow—my deeds courted a blackness that rivaled any shade that ever lived beneath the earth. My contest with Tom Hush had taught me something of the fickle nature of shadows—how they might betray one master for another.

I whispered to the surrounding darkness of the fire and light I had delivered unto the spaces beneath Lastrygone, how I had filled the hollow earth with the sun—and that I might choose to do so again, here. The darkness came to me like a lost dog, circling me, whispering its allegiance. At my command, the last breath of pitch was denied the Unduurians' heaving lungs. Within seconds, my pursuers began to fall away like the fading memories of childhood. Soon, I was left only with the drifting eel-things that haunted the high branches of the black orchard. But without masters to command them, they glided away.

I traveled far and for days into the darkness of caves, hoping to find my way back to the surface of the world, but I was confronted only by fresh gloom. Perhaps it was my ninth day under the earth when I encountered a thin stream of light draining down into a wide stone chamber, signaling for the first time my nearness to the lighted world. However, no sooner had I began my steep climb toward the source of the emaciated light when something gigantic detached itself from the titan shadows of the chamber.

Sane words were never meant to describe such a creature. Only the language of madness and nightmare could do justice to the thing. The cave walls behind me exploded into stone shrapnel as a bizarre extrusion struck out. The thing, appearing to be neither god nor animal, gathered darkness with each step, moving between visibility and oblivion. Its size, easily greater than any prosaic earthly creature of land or sea, failed to produce even the smallest sound—its movement was betrayed only by the overabundance of its silence.

My speed bested the creature's next swipe as I plunged into my own gathering of supplicant shadows. A split-second after my deep dive, my sisters blazed a wet and glittering path across a monstrous appendage, the fluids that followed as foreign as the creature itself. It wailed with such intensity, the stones of the ceiling awoke from their abiding sleep and rained down around me.

A world of teeth snapped shut inches from my face. Before the creature could raise its head beyond my reach, I sprang at its face, my sisters full of glee. The creature's flesh was an inconsistent tangle of competing textures, as if it were stitched together from dozens of different species. Its eyes were traditional enough, however, thankfully resting in relatively customary places. My sisters liberated them from their sockets. The weight of the giant orbs and the accompanying optic fluids sent me to the ground with a squishy thud.

It wasn't until it bellowed at me that I realized I was locked in mortal combat with a thinking, feeling creature. "Wretched little thing! I'll spin the flesh of your soul into a hatchery for flies! Their tiny white children will gnaw at you until your spirit has nourished a swarm to rival the sky!"

I saw no harm in engaging the creature in conversation. "As I have no intention of being sewn into a worm garden, perhaps I should introduce you to another member of my family. His bite may rival your own, creature." My father roared every bit as loudly as the nightmare, tracing an arc of fire and rage through the darkness so bright, it sent the shadows fleeing. The monstrosity's head burst in a spray of gore and bone, yet it didn't seem fazed. Unlike its eyes, its brain must have been more uniquely situated.

Surprisingly, without benefit of a head, the monster took its turn within our burgeoning dialogue. "You have a lovely little family, my plucky friend. I only wish I could work their metal as easily as I mold flesh. But I smell souls beneath their steely corpses, and while it's a bit trickier than skin, I've been known to spin a soul or two into the tapestry of my webs." Regrettably, the creature's words camouflaged the advance of its gigantic stinger.

I felt the monster's venom course through me as my heart pumped liquid fire to my every extremity. The stinger itself was more than adequate for tearing through my shoulder, almost severing my arm in the process. The force of the attack drove me from my place upon the creature's shoulders and into the grasp of a massive embroidery of spun skin. By no means as placid as the silken works of a spider, the web of flesh came to life at my touch, whispering its welcome through hundreds of sewn-in mouths. "Come and suffer with us," the web of skin whispered.

Within moments, I was trapped in its weave, snug and motionless. The lord of the tapestry, now taking no pains to remain hidden, gathered its labyrinthine body above me. It was a wonderfully horrible thing, made from a patchwork of organic nightmare. It began to lower itself upon me as a number of facial formations protruded from its giant body. At least this explained why my father's blow had proven insufficient to killing the horror.

I had the feeling the creature had no immediate plans for me, which would allow the deep silence of the underground to mend my wounds. After a quick assessment of the situation, I allowed the creature's wicked and tentacled extremities to seize me. It spun a fine casing of liquid skin all around me, twirling me in the manner of a spider applying its webbing. The strange liquescent pre-skin congealed upon every rotation, and I chuckled at the tickling touch of the trembling, lacey flesh. Finally, I was wrapped in a hearty veil of solidified skin, replete with strong interwoven layers of muscle tissue that flexed against my body, enhancing the already strong grip the enclosure exercised upon me.

As I expected, the creature allowed for my head to project out from the flesh cocoon, permitting me to hear it gloat—an activity of which the creature was eager to partake. It smiled with a half dozen mouths, first one and then another speaking, creating a singular, uninterrupted voice. "I see you have met my family, little morsel. They are a rather cozy bunch, to be sure, and they seldom if ever depart each other's company. Soon, you will be even closer to them than you are now. But for that level of intimacy to be properly achieved, you must first spend some time writhing and rendering within me— I'm afraid I will have to swallow you." Its many mouths illustrated their delight with smiles and smacking lips. "Before I do this, I will allow you the courtesy of pleading for your life, as I'm sure you will be inclined to make an argument for your continued survival. I will also tell you that I have, on rare occasion, been compelled to release a few potential meals on the basis of some rather compelling dissertations. Do you find this generous of me?"

I chose the last mouth to speak as the focus of my reply. "Firstly, you're a liar. You've never neglected yourself on something else's behalf, this much is clear to me. Secondly, I have no intention of begging. However, I'd be more than happy to ask some questions of you, if you'd be kind enough to answer."

Some of the mouths growled at the insult, others smiled at the appeal. "A strange yet harmless request, to be sure," the creature said, amused. "I'll entertain what you clearly think is some kind of trick that will allow you to escape from me. Ask your questions, my little web-to-be. I look forward to your attempt at freedom."

The web of flesh continued to constrict, trying to force the air from my lungs. "Well, you certainly have enough limbs to pat yourself on the back, but my intention to escape is hardly a deduction worthy of such self-congratulation. I could escape even now, if I so chose, but I'd like to gather your story, first. Where do you come from, creature?"

"I see," the creature mused. "You wish to stir me by having me recall the story of my life. Very well. It's been a while since I've even thought of my lost home, so it might do me well to remember it out loud." It lowered its massive ruin of a head level with my suspended body.

The silence hoarded within the creature's chamber lay heaped like gold in a dragon's lair. I seized it, pouring it across my cocooned, wounded body, attempting to heal it. All the while, the creature regaled me with tales of its home world and its exploits since being stranded upon the corpse of Earth. It had been marooned here sometime after the Darkness, and had abided ever since within the underworld, weaving tapestries of fleshy webs while it waited for the day it might return whence it came. I felt my shoulder reset just as the Flesh Weaver addressed me anew.

"And so, there you have it, little morsel, a brief recounting of all the lonely years I've spent away from my home, where webs and worlds are one and the same, where flesh looks to my kind's weaving for its place and purpose. Have you any further questions, my dear fellow?" The creature seemed eager for another question, and I realized that my captor was truly enjoying the opportunity to use its multiple mouths for a purpose other than eating and weaving.

"I do, indeed," I said. "What can you tell me about the beings known as the Unbegotton?" I hoped to gain a bit of insight into the species from which the Shepherd of Wolves hailed.

"A strange question," the creature said, its mouths frowning. "Why would you ask me such?"

"I happen to be playing a game hosted by such a creature," I explained, "and I was wondering what you, a being from the Outer Spheres, could tell me about them."

"Well, what's to truly know?" the Flesh Weaver said, seeming satisfied with my answer. "They are wholly unknowable, and well beyond attributes that can be caught within even the largest web of words. If you think the game you're playing with them has any outcome aside from death and madness, then you are sorely mistaken. You should thank me for saving you from their awful schemes. Being digested alive and woven into my web is a glorious end compared to the bottomless hell they'd have flung you into."

"Well, if it's all the same to you," I said, "I think I'll continue playing their game, shortly after I've done with you, of course. But please, anything you can tell me—anything at all—would be greatly appreciated."

The beast chuckled, its mouths upturned in various degrees of mirth. "You're an amusing morsel, indeed! But as much as I've enjoyed our time together, I must sleep and regrow the mess you've made of one of my heads, to say nothing of what those wicked blades of yours did to a number of my legs. I recommend that you sleep as well, little gnat. Dream wonderful dreams, for they will surely be your last taste of happiness before horror everlasting becomes you." With that, the creature withdrew into a great pit that plunged into darkness and stone.

I did exactly as the creature recommended. The silence—completely relieved of the creature's voice—combined with darkness and sleep, would do much to restore me. However, as I should have come to expect, sleep only brought new and more glorious horrors.

With all that had happened, I had neglected to examine the next name on my list—Garret House. The cocoon of darkness and silence held me closer than the web of flesh ever could, and within my slumber, I found myself inside the man's dream. As with my current waking reality, the dream was a wonderland of un-fleshed things—a gallery not of webs, but of carefully tailored skin-suits. I saw manikins made from polished bone, endless rows of the wonderful things, each one attired in a different fashion of stolen skin. On platforms that rose high above them were beasts dressed in the skins of men, and men clothed with the flesh of beasts. Lights carved through the darkness above the fantastic amalgamations, making them seem not unlike trophies within a display case. Garret House immediately transformed from a faceless name into a monstrous identity—Mister Hide.

My heart leapt so hard with unrestrained delight that I wondered if its frantic clapping had compromised my quiet. My fellow artist was a monster of a man who exchanged the skins of his victims with the hides of other creatures— creatures that he believed better suited the nature of his victims. He had once reupholstered an entire room of bankers with the pink leathers of swine.

It occurred to me to challenge the Flesh Weaver's assumptions concerning the Unbegotton's endgame—the world was becoming absorbed in dream, as it should be. Here I was, confronted by a killer who obsessed over the appropriate skinning of both man and beast, and in the waking world I had been met by a beast who was itself a fusion of untold numbers of reconstituted skins. The Deadworld had become merely a symbol for dreams to come, a signpost for wonders waiting to be dreamed into existence.

Unfortunately, I should have been a little less delighted by my surroundings and a bit more observant, as something had drawn close to me, undetected. "Another interloper, I see," sounded a voice made of rock and deep places. "What name has the waking world given you, my scripted opponent and future victim? Wait just a minute now, that impressive axe of yours has already given you away, I think. Why, you're the Family Man, aren't you?"

I turned around to see a massive man, every inch as large and powerfully built as myself, dressed in the skins of men. By his sides hung two great skinning knives, every inch the size and sharpness of my sisters. "Indeed, I am," I replied. "And you, my friend, must be the infamous Mister Hide. My compliments on such a wonderful dream. I've been hosted by many of my victims' nightmares, and I must admit, yours is by far the most splendid." My sisters emerged from their sleep, grinning at the massive knives that had moved into Hide's hands.

Behind the Mad Skinner, a small army of skin-swapped men and beasts gathered. I could feel their searing hunger collide with the burning stares of my family, who had risen from their sleeping places and materialized behind me, standing at the ready. I was again doing precisely what the Flesh Weaver had suggested—having a marvelous dream.

Of course, it was my father who began the festivities. Jumping high into the air with a roar, he brought the power of his weapon to bear directly into the center of the gathered man-beasts and beast-men. The result was a hellish detonation—his strength, augmented by the surrounding nightmare, was transformed into searing fire and death. During the cacophony of blood and flame, my sisters slipped silently into the shadows, smiling and killing and dancing. I can never stress enough just how wonderful a pair they truly are.

The Skinner and I were like two stubborn oaks, survivors of a tornado, standing solemn and straight amid the ruin of lesser flora. The clamor of ceaseless violence rang out everywhere, but Mister Hide chose to contrast the moment with some pleasant conversation. "This shared dreaming business is all very well and good, my friend, but the violence you've brought with you is entirely uncalled for. There's no need to rend my secrets from my sleep—I'll gladly tell you where I am. Beyond my location and my real name, I haven't any other secrets for you to take."

I can't say I wasn't a bit disappointed with my adversary's lack of enthusiasm for our first confrontation, but I supposed it was refreshing to see that he was an especially collected individual, even if his calm bordered on indifference. "So, you would have nothing from me, your future opponent, to afford you some potentially valuable insight into the violence and killing to come?" I asked, hoping to rouse the killer. "Am I supposed to be impressed by your disinterest?"

"You may be precisely whatever you choose, Family Man," the Skinner replied. "I've little use for mock battle, as I can't skin a dream, now can I?"

He made a good point. Regardless, if he chose not to seek my measure in dreamed combat, he would be ill prepared to fight me to the best of his ability within the waking world, and I would be given an unfair advantage. I did not enjoy victories that were only half-gained, and unfortunately, my art would reflect as much. I decided to press him. "I certainly understand your reticence. You may need some time to determine how you might wear my skin, given that I might hang a bit too large on you." A base taunt, to be sure, but the killer's physique was chiseled and polished—well beyond his needs, whereas my own was simply the byproduct of my craft. There was vanity in the man, and I would seek it out.

"You disgrace my body when you compare it to your own, little man," the killer retorted. "But I shan't fall for your jeers, as anyone with eyes can see you're the smaller of us. Besides, your pelt is so riddled with scars, I wouldn't wear it were I freezing to death. No, I see your skin better worn by a stray dog. A feral, three-legged mutt."

I smiled. "You're right, there's no sense in banter or battle, so I will have whatever you will surrender to me. I will take your one remaining secret and leave you to your much-needed sleep. Also, I shall not make any assumptions as to the strength of your mind, given that it can carry only two little secrets." From over the Skinner's shoulder, I saw my father bathed in battle, aglow with the heat of killing. He smiled his approval at my tactics.

"I'm losing my patience for you, Family Man," the giant growled.

"Is it because your patience grows too heavy for you to heft?" I asked, still grinning.

The beast dressed in human leathers was finally beginning to show its teeth. The Skinner fell silent, and I could see his movements take on precision, a well-oiled grace that could steal a man's skin in as little time as it took to bleed. "I'll not waste any further words on you, mongrel," he hissed, slowly stalking toward me with blades in both his hands. "I'll let my actions do the talking,"

"Indeed," I said, marching to meet him with my own blades at the ready. "Let's have a conversation."

Sparks danced as we came together in steel, muscle, and dream. We locked our blades together as anger poured from his bloodshot eyes. I could feel the raw power of the dream guiding him. His was a quest to perfect the collective body—a skin for everyone and everyone in their proper skin. He was a corrector of botched geometry—not some simple exchanger of skins. He was disgusted that the world had failed to be honest with itself, concealing vice under virtue, hiding ugliness beneath beauty, smuggling death behind the veil of life. He would strip the earth of its dishonesty and reupholster it with sewn-together skins cut from raw truth.

I felt as though I were pushing against a brick wall—as did Hide, no doubt. Perhaps it was just a figment of my own vanity, but I thought I began to feel his wall cracking. Inopportunely, before our contest could conclude, we were interrupted by a tumbling beast-head one of my sisters had delightedly liberated. The bloodied weight of it collided with our knot of blades. We stepped back from each other, evaluating.

The atmosphere had become fire and fierceness and screams. I felt as if we were standing within the very eye of a tempest, yet my opponent seemed as placid as a puddle after the rain. He was reassessing me, no doubt—just as I'd hoped he would. He would take no chances when next we met, for he would remember my strength and the willpower that funded its fire. He would remember my eyes, for they had shown him the darkness I concealed—and they dared him to cut it from me. For my part, I learned that I was wrong about the man. There was no vanity within him, just the desire to put the world right. He was built from the stone of his conviction, every muscle declared the strength of his truth, and their polish and preen spoke to the excellence of his purpose—he was in his proper skin.

Finally, after staring at me through the frenzy of monsters and killers that spilled all around us, he said, "You are no beast, my friend, and you are no man. I will have to think long and hard on what to do with your skin." As the world between us faded and the dream began to flee the dull crush of waking, I heard Mister Hide's parting words. "I will see you again in the town of Willard, where we will finish our conversation."

CHAPTER FOURTEEN

When I awoke from the dream of Mister Hide, I could smell the distinct aroma of burning flesh. Apparently, there were some lingering fibers of the killing dream still clinging to my father, indulging his penchant for distilling fire from fury. The flesh cocoon ignited from its mere proximity to my father's ill temperament. Not one to look a gift horse in the mouth, I decided to use my burning father to awaken my captor.

I emerged from my fleshy bonds, wrapped in fire and dream. The firelight moved into the deep hole to which the Flesh Weaver had retired. I could see him, an utter chaos of parts, hunkered down into itself. Like my father's deadly blade, my strength was still attached to the Red Dream. I cleared the intervening distance between myself and the Weaver in a single bound. My father seethed with dissatisfaction at the monster that slept when it should have been dying.

The narrower space of the Weaver's home focused the light of my father, and I could see the crouching horror that had recoiled into itself like some gigantic spider within its sanctum of web and shadow. I don't know how many sets of eyes opened upon me as I descended, bearing fire, blade, and lingering nightmare. And while the creature possessed a wealth of toothy maws, the scream that ripped loose from them was dreadfully uniform.

To the creature's credit, it was fast enough to move its mountainous body clear of the killing share of my father's blow. Still, it was sorely riven, as was the ancient stone upon which it slept.

It became a storm of glistening shadows and elongated stingers as it proceeded to fill the stone chamber with its lethal assortment of slaying limbs. It discharged a boiling stream of liquefied flesh into the darkness at me. The Red Dream had almost evaporated, and I tapped its last reality-defying reservoir as I leaped beyond the scorching fluid.

While airborne, I freed my sisters into the darkness, their laughter skipping across the webs of squirming flesh that filled the Weaver's lair. The alien abomination quickly recoiled from their glittering smiles, and they disappeared into distant darkness, their laughter following after. When an adequate amount of space had opened up between myself and the Flesh Weaver, it hauled itself up to an impressive height, presiding like an insectoid mountain over the range of its underworld. "'Twas no idle boast you made, was it, human? You really do have the power to kill me. But it seems your fires have died away, and your precious knives are lost to you. While I'm certain that axe of yours is death incarnate, I'll not again let it so close to me."

The beast extended two lengths of serrated bone pincers from sheaths of flesh that lined its swollen abdomen. Its speed again proved incredible—it crossed almost instantly the distance between us, stabbing one of its boney appendages into my leg. The monster lifted me from the ground by my wound and attempted to fling me into its throbbing webs, laughing as though it had already triumphed.

I wrenched free of the spiny weapon and launched my father into the darkness. The Weaver withdrew with a lopsided combination of fear and wisdom, but the creature was not my target. My father collided with the stalactite-dripping ceiling of the cavern, detonating like laughing thunder. For a moment, it seemed as if the earth itself had lowered a cleated boot upon the loathsome weaver of skins, crushing a mere bug beneath its gargantuan stone foot. All became a deafening cloud of dust as cavern ceiling met floor—still the creature lived.

The small mountain of fallen stone fell away as a badly mangled pincer broke through. Soon, the creature had entirely risen from its would-be crypt, shaking off the broken earth like a dog shedding rainwater. The ruined horror addressed me anew. "A fine swan song, if nothing else. But you will find my death harder to acquire than you might have originally calculated."

It pleased me no end when my timing was impeccable—or in this particular case, my sisters' timing. Just as the Weaver poured itself away from the sundered rock, my sisters made their move—but not before I countered my opponent's previous assertion. "Ah, but you have still to see the product of my calculations, monster."

From a pile of the creature's smoldering and disembodied parts—the result of my father's previous efforts— rose a severed, claw-tipped limb, which took little time plunging into the weaver's most conspicuous head. Before my opponent could employ its incredible speed to avoid further ravaging, a thick mass of squirming flesh from the Weaver's web engulfed its struggling form.

My sisters had found their mark. I took a moment to describe the scene to the clearly confounded Weaver. "Only now do you see, creature, that my sisters were never meant for you—at least, not those parts of you that were still attached." With that, I allowed my sisters to continue their good work. They took their time, laughing that sweet laughter of theirs, smiles like sugar.

The surviving mass of the creature, now little more than a towering heap of quivering flesh and crushed carapace, collapsed before me. I walked to the pile of my enemy, trying to find a functioning set of eyes to look into. After some considerable searching, a large eye blinked at me, assuring that consciousness still lingered. When I was certain the thing focused upon me, I spoke. "Unlike you, I won't pretend that I might spare you, should only your pleas for mercy properly entertain me. That would be rude. Instead, I will simply allow you to live. I have no quarrel with you, and you are already so much art. In time, when you have adequately regenerated from the lesson I have imparted, you will be a marvelous nightmare again. And nothing would please me more. Perhaps, should your ego allow, and if I'm still alive after my quest concludes, I would very much like to call upon you again. But I can see that you're in no condition to give your answer now. However, do please think it over, won't you?"

With that, I collected my family and departed the underground lair of the wretched Flesh Weaver. I was off to the town of Willard to finish a conversation.

The road out of Unduur's darkness and back to the surface was longer than I'd assumed. The gloom from the subterranean city still seemed to cling to me, lending my actions an additional heft that culminated in the early search for shelter, well before the formal conclusion of nighttime. I theorized that the killing dream that made my escape from the Weaver's web a tenable enterprise had also left my body nearly empty of any viable earthly energies. Or perhaps it was the residuum of the Weaver's venom, still skulking about my body in some dwindling measure, seeking my undoing. So, when I came upon the remains of a house stinking from the natural powers that worked against its manmade composition—the express purpose of bringing man's works back in line with the duller needs of the woods—I realized I had found my sanctuary from the sun.

Once inside, I made immediately for the attic. I had very much hoped to gain both a sufficient view of my surroundings and the luxury of reposing in a room with only one way in or out. I generally don't bother to take such pains, but I was exceptionally low on energy and alertness. The house and its rooms were unexceptional for a structure of its type and circumstances, except for the view I managed to acquire. The pleasing vantage allowed my vision to fall invisible and sharp upon any who might test my silence, weak and slack though its webs might have been.

I gathered myself into the thickest coils of both spider and cobweb, allowing gravity to settle me into the most natural resting position. Due to the possibility of falling into yet another Red Dream, I chose only to relax, rather than to sleep. The silence came to me like a twilit breeze, soft and glowing, passing through my body like a cleansing breath, gently whispering away the clogs of time and trouble, serenading my soul with the invisible songs of forgotten singers. But silence can be a tricky beast, as it is no respecter of time and space, nor does it distinguish between the real and unreal. Thus can it deliver you into the strangest hands, with whims as rootless as tumbleweeds.

From somewhere within the lower floors of the house, I heard a voice. It was a voice that once ruled over me and all my world. As familiar as it was, I did not know the name of the speaker. But the speaker knew mine. "Vincent, you impish little wretch! Come to me this very instant! Come to me now or I'll forget the fine plans I've laid for you, and you can join the rest of them to fester in undying colors and unflinching smiles. Is that what you want, boy? Come to your father right now!"

I found myself standing without so much as a stitch of hesitation. My family loomed before me, barring the way downstairs, but I marched forward, heedless of their burning stares and lethal smiles. I would have answers, even if they would destroy me. For once, I invoked the solidity of the Deadworld and banished the specters before me to the darkness whence they came. It pained me to treat my sisters with such coarseness, but I trusted they would forgive their big brother this one indiscretion. My father, however, would seek his vengeance against me when the opportunity allowed.

The interior of the house became a ghostly memory of my past, and I remembered with painful difficulty the features that greeted me as I lowered myself into the hateful din of a man's commanding voice—a man who called himself my father. As I went along, I heard strong winds roaring at the glass of the now unbroken windows. I could smell the acridity of fresh blood. With each step I took down the stairs, a feeling I had rarely known began to freeze every layer of my being. I was terrified.

The darkness at the bottom of the stairs began to drift away at the somber touch of candlelight, and the twitching shadows that remained were not my friends. There, framed by the clutch and titter of the gnarled branches moving against the windows behind him, stood the man who had stalked unnamed and unrealized behind the scenes of my every nightmare—my father.

There was a haze upon him borne of candle smoke, or my mind's mercy perhaps—I could not tell which. But I could see that he was average of height and quite lank, not at all like the thing his son would become, if indeed I was his son. He was dripping with blood, and his eyes played in tones of rage and hate. Yet there was a graceful repose to his glare, the whispered poise of a perfectly balanced weapon. And his hands were liquid in their movements, aglow with a quantity of natural talent rarely concentrated within such dainty things.

His voice came at me again, but this time his words carried the prettiness of a cleverly baited trap. "Ah, there you are, my very good boy. How the dim light loves you, Vincent. Not even the sun could better reveal the truth of you. I'm so lucky to be one of the few who can recognize your potential—what you truly are. Those better not be tears I see on your cheeks, my boy. If they are, they had better not be for that mother of yours, or your sniveling siblings."

He sighed. "Despite the weakness it betokens, I can't deny the beauty of your sorrow. It's sweeter than the dawn laid out across a fresh silken corpse on burial day. Whited death, all made up in bows of youngest light, soon to be lost to the catch and drowse of funeral memories. Do you want to see them now, son? Do you want to see what a wonderful, if completely undeserved, gift I've given to them? Shall we replace to the gallery?"

Before I could take a single step toward or away from my beckoning forebear, a knife slid across my neck, followed by a whisper at my ear. "Looks like I caught you unawares, man-giant. Your vaunted silence seems to have let you down. But fret not, for I shall raise your spirits, all the way into the sky and beyond. Or perhaps below, yes? Regardless, your affinity for silence and darkness holds no advantage over magic—mine in particular. And so, the time has come to make you disappear, from the world of the living and from my enchanted list of names. So, Presto— "

I thrust myself backward, attempting to deny the blade in my throat any additional depth. Firing my elbow behind me, I hoped to catch my attacker in some vital place. Nothing. I felt as if I were struggling with a wisp of smoke, with only the smiling wound in my throat as proof of a solid attacker. My elbow swept across what could have been the fabric of a long coat, which hung loose and flowing around its wearer, but nothing so firm as a killer who managed a blade as a poet wielded words.

The man continued to talk as if my actions had done nothing to disturb his perch near my ear. "Well done, my less-than-gentle giant, but I'll still see those guts of yours vanish, compliments of my very splendid and very serrated disappearing act, likely in the next second or so." I swung my sister behind me, her teeth hissing through air. I began to suspect the Red Dream worked altogether differently for this particular Wolf.

Desperate to find some use for my hands, I clawed the spaces around me. Finally, I seized the wide collar of a coat. I wasted no time in hoisting the killer above my head, hurling him into the darkness. Or at least I would have, had the man not disappeared entirely. All that commented upon the wolf I held was a magnificent cloak, its silken blackness tucked firmly into my grip.

The room—stage, perhaps—had become a void. I wiped the blood from my neck and released my sisters into the darkness around me, supposing my attacker nearby. Their smiles fell upon only dust and air. I moved to the doorway and peered over the tangles of creepers and moss-smothered cement blocks that had once formed a formidable courtyard.

From the moonlight and willows came the voice that once lingered at my ear. "What sport you've given me, big friend! I'd taken you for an oaf, given your size. But you've a smidge of magic about yourself, as well. Or is it those blades that smile like children at a magic show? Why, they very nearly touched me—a rarified miracle, if I don't say so myself. And of course, I do. But the show is far from over, Family Man, and you must be warned—not a single soul has lived through all of my acts. I somehow suspect you won't either. But, whatever the outcome, we'll give the audience quite the show, won't we?"

The voice faded into the night. I turned back toward the abandoned house and reexamined it. This was not a structure serving only as a provisional surface upon which a dream of a forgotten house had been projected. Rather, this was the forgotten house itself. I lived here once, as a child. Almost immediately, the thought of my recent attacker passed. I was filled with wonder at the house fallen at that very moment from dimmest recollection.

My sisters tried desperately to pull me into the forest, far from the house, but I refused their invitations to play. Likewise, my father burned me where he dwelt upon my back, demanding my withdrawal. But I ignored him as well, instead returning inside.

While I was apparently entering a material structure, I felt as if I were passing into the halls of my own mind, where a secret past barely lived, having nearly been crushed to death beneath so much time and neglect. One room above all others called to me, and I instantly knew why. It was a most curious art gallery—an ever-growing tribute to visions lurking the other side of the eye. It was a secret place hiding beyond a false wall. Its presence was so smartly concealed, not even the inhabitants of the house knew of it—save for the master of the gallery, my father.

My *real* father, through means of his artist's blood. The memory I'd chased round in a circle finally stood still, waiting for me to seize it. My real father was an artist from hell, whose paints were the stuff of the unraveled human body, the incomplete translation of a dream. He strived, perhaps quite in vain, to return flesh to its rightful place— in service to the dreams it tried so hard to forget. But like all those before him—and quite possibly after him—he had failed. I realized, sooner than I was prepared for, that I had always been my father's son. I unconsciously outlined his life's purpose, all while walking and waking as he had— lonely and inspired and lethal. I could remember nothing else about living in the house, save perhaps the still-glowing embers of a single horrible night.

***

My father took me gently by the arm and led me through a great hallway. The darkness of an unlit room fell over us, but his pace remained brisk. A door was opened somewhere, and I could feel a cold breeze kiss my cheeks. I breathed it in, tasting smoke and death. There were stairs leading gradually downward, gently glazed in the smolder of orange candlelight. My father cautioned me to mind my footing.

But I stepped upon the hem of my night-coat enough times to draw criticism. "Art should fill your feet as well as your hands, my boy. Grace is the grammar of art. Never forget that." When we reached the bottom of the stairs, I could see cold marble flooring, polished so completely it resembled grey glass. We stopped just short of a huge room, where a massive archway emerged from the sparkling sea of marble. It was like the chiseled mouth of a great whale, perpetually breathing orange light and threatening to swallow the world. "You still want to see your wretched mother and your worthless brother and sister, do you?" I must have nodded, for we proceeded beyond the yawning archway.

Quite suddenly, one memory cannibalized another. I could hear my mother's voice—my true mother, which should not be misinterpreted to mean my *real* mother. Truth and reality should never be confused for one another, as the two are often bitterest of enemies. I could hear her clearly, superimposed atop the memory of my father's gallery. "Flesh obligates us, doesn't it, Vincent? It can determine who and what our family will consist of, if you let it. It can force mothers and fathers and brothers and sisters upon us, solidifying our families as surely as a seating chart carved from prehistoric bone. In truth, we are not beholden to such conventions, as I'm sure your father has already explained to you. Skin can be severed, blood rechanneled, even bones can be broken into bridges that span worlds. We needn't be troubled by the whispers of the flesh, Vincent. They are the bearers of half-truths and complete lies. What is the skin when compared to the dreams they imprison? You and I have different skin, but we are closer than shadows at dusk. I am your true mother, Vincent. And I always will be, no matter what your skin may tell you."

My mother's words faded into the prior memory, where I stood before a large sculpture within my father's great gallery. The sculpture was molded from the preserved trappings of three dead dreams. His creation had been formed from gristle and guts, bones and plastic-coated brains, broken smiles and whispered pain. All of it had come from the hideously transformed bodies of my remaining—biological—family. My mother, brother, and sister had passed into art and beyond the world. Despite the deadness of her eyes, I could feel my real mother's gentle gaze upon me, whispering across my face, trying to wipe the tears from my eyes.

***

The lost memories slowly died into the darkness of the dead house. The skin on my back had practically melted from the heat of my father's anger, and my sisters danced across my palms, hoping to rouse a laugh from me. I stood silent for quite some time, burning and bleeding and crying.

The days when things could remain hidden from me were gone. The secret door to my father's gallery yielded to my strength. Cold air and unbidden memories rushed at me as the door crashed open, revealing a secret only slightly younger than myself. As I descended the crudely chiseled stone stairs, the shadows embraced me, welcoming me home. The marble floor was no longer glittering, as time and the advance of the earth had long since laid a thick tarnish across the meticulous stonework. However, the great archway was no less impressive for the passage of time, even if it no longer billowed with the glow of candlelight. Even now, its great jaws appeared ready to devour the world—my world, at least.

I lingered at the threshold, wary of the things that might lay beyond. My father continued to burn me, and my sisters still called upon me to play—but finally, I walked into the gallery. With my first steps into the antechamber, I was but a shivering child, cold and shaking, in awe of the unknown. With my next steps, memories became my master, and the darkness tumbled beyond time.

Small cages hung from the ceiling, each containing the tiny bones of children. Thankfully, the little skeletons had been deprived of their eyes—eyes that had once clawed and pinched at my tender flesh. This was the room where my father kept a good deal of his most prized art supplies. He insisted his paint be mixed with the blood of children, as it was "the protean stuff of dreams, worthy of only the finest artists."

My hands glided across the cages, at one point grazing a slender, white finger bone. It came away in my hand, light as a baby's breath, yet heaving with finality. To my father, the child was nothing—just an empty tube of paint. I cannot deny my father's methods, but I've always held children to be closer to dreams than any other creature. I have never felt impelled to use them in my own work.

All the days I'd spent in this room, the subject of many a hateful and panicked stare, started to overfill me. After all, it was I who delivered them here, into the hands of my father. He would lead me to such beautiful places, filled with love and laughter. I'd fly to them—to play, to laugh, and to lie. He taught me how to play like a cherub, to widen my eyes to reflect the blazing sun. To laugh as sweet as sugar, to smile like innocence. Of all the things he taught me, the lie was most important—my promise to take them somewhere secret and wonderful, beyond the sun, beyond all eyes. But all paths lead to the inside of the same black canvas bag. They'd just hang from the ceiling, encaged and gagged, staring at me. So many eyes, all of them screaming, *Betrayer, betrayer, betrayer!*

I just wanted to play with them. I always hoped it would end differently. It never did, except for the last time, of course—when the two little girls came to me, smiles like crescent moons. I dropped the finger bone to the floor and continued into the next room.

The walls of the galley were like curving glass, the frozen contour of a sea wave sweeping over and above the room, framing the art of hell in cleanest relief. As I looked out across the arcade of dead things, I realized my own works had yet to outnumber those of my father's. His life was spent almost entirely upon his art, and the grey that swam through his hair remarked on the length of his time upon the earth.

My eyes landed upon the centermost piece, showcased like a diamond upon a bed of silver. It was my father himself, just as I'd left him. The recollection fell upon me like a ravenous beast, ripping through layers of forced forgetting, sinking stained teeth into the flesh of my hidden, tender memory.

My father was my first piece of art. The realization drew me into a red memory.

***

When I entered the gallery, my father had already placed the bag filled with the two smiling twins upon the floor. He stood at his work area, a place covered in the stains of countless works, many still in their incipiency. As he sorted through a variety of his wicked "artist's tools," I noticed something was wrong—the occupants of the bag weren't crying out. In fact, they might have been giggling. Out of nowhere, the gleam of a knife pierced the big bag. I chose to say nothing—they say curiosity is the muse of any good artist.

The girls slipped silently from the bag, twin shadows brandishing bladed smiles. Within seconds, the candlelight was gone, replaced with dancing, glittering laughter. A voice from somewhere behind me spoke, filling me with unexpected glee. It whispered, "Hello again, Vincent. We can't wait to play some more. Our time together has only just begun." My father called out to me, but the tiny voice advised me to remain silent, shushing me softly. I didn't make a sound, only covered my mouth with my hands. I felt the smallest breeze and knew immediately the little girl was gone. My father continued to call for me, his voice growing louder and somewhat doubtful. The whispered slash of a knife transformed my father's words into screams. He pleaded with me to come to him, to help him. I did nothing.

From the sound of things, he had started searching clumsily through one of his cupboards. After a moment or two, there came the small click of a flashlight. The beam of light shot frantically about the room, searching, occasionally broken by the flitting shapes of the knife-wielding girls. After some additional probing, my father's light discovered me—squatting in a corner with my hands covering a grin that had likely slipped past the edges of my fingers. My father frowned as he put his free hand to the bleeding wound in his left leg. He'd taken the actions of the little girls to be mine.

"The time has come, boy, for you to take your place within the gallery. There is too much of me in you, now. Those eyes of yours, son—cast of perfect darkness. I've always known what you are, what you would become. This will be my one true sin, to take you from the world. You should have succeeded me, but this life is too much with me now. I can't leave before I've finished. I only hope that I can do you justice. You may be beyond even my skills."

As my father's words faded, there came a sound like wet thunder trudging through gravel. "You are correct about one thing, little man—he is beyond you, now." My father's light rose from me, ascending well over my head until it fell upon the face of a monster. Its face was an open wound frozen still with countless scars. The beam of light raced around the room chaotically, describing my father's frantic attempts at escape. Despite his best efforts, I heard my father's breath rush from his mouth, and I knew his neck had come into the hands of the monstrous thing. The flashlight fell to the ground, and a gigantic booted foot crushed it into darkness.

There was an enduring silence, and I began to wonder if I wasn't dreaming. Slowly, the smell of burning flowers filled the room. And then the sound of light footsteps slowly descended the stairs. For whatever reason, I decided to stand up within the pitch. I had known the burning perfume from a dream. Someone stood directly in front of me. They knelt, their soft breath murmuring at my cheeks. I could feel a gaze, even in the dark, falling across my face. I knew it was a woman, with eyes that could pluck out a child's worst fears, turn pain into laughter. It could only have been my mother, back from the dead. Tears rushed from my eyes. Thin arms embraced me, cool lips pressed to my forehead, and the softest hair played at my ears and cheeks. Only a single word escaped my lips. "Mother."

In a voice I didn't recognize, a woman spoke to me. "Indeed, my wonderful child. My Red Son. I am your mother. Your *true* mother."

The darkness of the room retreated from the woman's eyes, in which I could see my premonitory dream of her, all flowers and fire. Her embrace seemed doubtful, like the clutch of shadows. She whispered my name. As it passed her lips, processed through the darkness of her body, it seemed almost biblical.

From somewhere nearby, I could hear the strained breathing of my father, whose throat was still in the giant's hand. The twins were nowhere in sight, but I could feel their smiles at my back, burning like fallen angels.

A single candle was lit, no doubt held by one of the girls. The woman's hands drifted to my shoulders, slowly turning me to meet the bloodshot eyes of my father. The candlelight created a soft bridge between us, and I could see that my father's gaze, while afflicted with no small amount of pain and hopelessness, retained its glint of lethality and poise.

His eyes made me unsure of my saviors—even in the grip of such a monster, he was still a beast of many heads, each one possessed of skills sharper than stilettos.

My father was finally released, and he fell to the floor, gasping. I knew the sorest injury he'd suffered was to his pride. He carefully returned to his feet, even taking time to straighten his collar, unfazed by the monster at his back. He looked beyond me, returning the heated glower of the strange woman. "You just took your doom by the hand, woman. I'll die having at least that satisfaction." My father's words shot across the room like spears, but they were immediately deflected by the woman's smile, which shone like darkest night.

"What a shame," she said. "Here stands your greatest work, and you've grown all but dumb to the fact. Luckily, I don't share your foreshortened senses, artist. It seems to me you've been the one holding your doom by the hand, and for quite a few years, at that. It would only be in keeping with a sort of cosmic propriety that your son be your doom—here, in this gallery, tonight. There's still art to be had in that, isn't there, artist?"

My father's eyes didn't so much as twitch. "That would be an honor, of course. But don't look so smug, woman. It's not like you've tapped into the unseen world by seeing him for what he is. I've known this day would come. I've known since the first time I saw myself reflected in those coal-black eyes of his. And now you've seen them, too. You know, now. Pray you last as long as I did." I had no idea what my father was talking about, but something secret seemed to shift within me, somewhere deep in the pits of my stomach.

"Vincent, tonight you will become an artist," the woman said matter-of-factly, still locking eyes with my father. It didn't seem as if I would be given a choice. I simply smiled up at her, my new mother.

The giant reached out with a single hand and broke my father's neck. Yet somehow, he still lived. My father collapsed to the ground, never again to rise from it under his own power. The creature then bore my progenitor's limp body to one of the work benches and laid him on his back.

My new mother turned me again, this time to face the wall of my father's tools, all of them barely discernible from the twisted shadows they cast in the trembling light. "They all belong to you now, Vincent. You have the remainder of the night to make your father into that which he was always meant to be." I knew almost immediately what I would do.

When I heard the last of my saviors exit at the top of the stairs, I wasted no time drawing preliminary sketches for how I would transform my father. It took only a few hours for me to gather the materials I needed. Next, I began organizing my workspace. Through all of this, the gaze of my father never left me. I could see pride welling in his eyes as I prepared my utensils with the grace and speed of a seasoned master.

After I pinned the last of my sketches to the wooden wallboards that lined my work area, I stripped my father of his clothing and thoroughly washed his body. The only question remaining was—how should I kill him? Death was no mercy here, merely a requisite work condition. Any unwanted movements or mistimed rictuses could ruin the mood I was attempting to cultivate.

I had no idea how to feel regarding what I was about to do. My father was always a source of fear and wonder to me. But my affections always lived in the conjurations, never the conjurer. I brought him to a seated position, propping him up against my worktable, looking him in the eyes. He winced for the first time—and the last. His breath was weak, yet I could see he was trying to say something. I waited patiently for his rasping attempts at speech to cohere into intelligible words. Just before I could wait no longer, he spoke. "A graveyard with flowers . . . is far better . . . than one without." I nodded, and my blade passed through his right eye.

The most difficult part of the undertaking was the draining of all my father's blood. I finally accomplished this through the painstaking process of positioning his body such that pressure forced it from his veins. Replacing his vital liquids with paint proved a much easier task to achieve, and I was careful to use every color, every shade and intensity I could evoke. Next, I removed all his major organs, delicately replacing them with artist's tools. Each item was placed in corresponding importance to the organ it substituted. I used my father's skin to replace the hemp of my canvas—he was a traditionalist, of course—and then re-skinned him with the aforementioned hemp. Certainly, the eyes were essential to my piece. Natural eyes had a nasty habit of decomposing, so I procured a set of the most beautiful glass eyes I could find.

Finally, there was the staging of the piece. It took me some time to affect, but I arranged the entire gallery so my father was the black sun around which his dark worlds wheeled. I situated all the heads of his works such that they seemed to look upon him, perhaps thanking him for their transformation.

In the light of the few candles by which I worked, my father's true self was dimly exposed. He was art incarnate. He was the hand that held the brush, the paint that fell to the canvas, and the very canvas that held his dream. I had inextricably fused my father with his craft.

In the darkness of the extinguished candles, I whispered my father's new name, the name of my very first work of art. "Red Ouroboros."

Through the medium of my small hands, guided by dreams dimly guessed, I'd cultivated the truth buried beneath my father's flesh. I kept in mind, of course, one of my father's principal lessons—truth is merely the fleeting property of a dream, caught momentarily at the scale of the universe, not to be confused with permanency. Still, my tears came as never before. They had been well earned for the first time. My father's gaze joined my real mother's, both sweeping across my face, searching for my eyes. But as they no doubt hoped, my eyes had slipped the world to wander and wonder. And my hands, while still of the earth, would now repair the way back—from death into dream. My brother and sister also looked upon me, glad for their place in the gallery. Together, united in dream and slaves to nothing, my first family celebrated my second birth—between two worlds, artist to both. It were as if the universe shrunk to the size of my purpose, narrow but infinite, every shadow a signpost, leading to forever. There was song in me that night.

It was dusk when they returned to gaze upon my work. The twins were at my side before I knew it, their wild hair playing all around me as they held me in the quiet of my first piece. I knew they were pleased. Their laughter sparkled in the dark, twinkling and turning in the blackened air of the gallery. I held their admiration inside like a last breath, not wanting to exhale. Then came the giant. When he looked upon my work, his thunderous laughter filled my tiny body with everlasting strength. I knew, somehow, his strength would one day be my own. My smile grew wider.

Then she came to me, my new mother. Gliding from the darkness, endless with mystery. She stood revealed in the smoldering debris of day. Her eyes followed mine beyond the solidity of the world, joining them in the gallery beyond the gallery, where vision was the property of the mind. "Your work is the light the sun pretends at bearing," she whispered. "Your brilliance shines only to enlighten, never to expose. Your art is the voice of a dreaming god, Vincent. And you need never again want for a family. You could have all of this, in us. You have only to say yes, and we are all of us, yours forever."

"Yes," I whispered to her, choking back tears.

CHAPTER FIFTEEN

Finally, the recovered memory took its lasting place within my mind, even as it burned into murmuring ash. I placed my father and my grinning sisters onto the floor. Before I could speak my mind, a familiar presence invaded the place of my second birth, for a second time.

"We were gonna wait till you were napping again," the invader dressed in an all-concealing cloak said, "but then you laid down your weapons. This is quite the little freak show you've got down here, by the way. Who's the star of the show?" He pointed to the Red Ouroboros. "Is it a friend of yours, maybe?"

He said *we*. I scanned the darkness and found others lying beneath the shadows with malice aforethought and weapons aplenty. Before I could take up my sisters, a figure rose from the stairwell and kicked them away. Another shape leaked across the stones of the ceiling, raining bullets down upon me. I leaped behind a nearby worktable, disappointing the swarm of bullets chasing me.

"We're social animals, aren't we, big man?" the speaker continued. "So, how better to win this contest than to mobilize some help? And just in case you've got escape on the brain, don't bother. I've got guys all over this place. You're all done, big fella."

More shadows poured into the room, bearing blades, guns, and arrogance. Sparks leapt from the walls from additional bullets. Lights and shadows played all around me.

An explosion to my left, then fire and pain. More explosions and fire everywhere. My father's gallery—my gallery—began to burn. I heard laughter within the flames. "A life's work up in flames, eh, Family Man?"

I saw the eyes of my once forgotten family reflecting the flames within their perfect glass eyes. My father, clothed in fire, began to bow to the conflagration. I would see those eyes no more.

Something stepped in front of me. Knives and the eagerness to use them glowed in the orange light. My naked hands reached out and began parting ribs, lungs, and at last the spine. I covered myself in his cooling blood, threw his skin around me like a cloak, and challenged the ravening flames. The fire was cold to the touch as the rage within me humbled the heat without. My eyes returned to the world bearing killing dreams.

The murderous shadows fell upon me as I breached the inferno. Blades traveled the roads of my body, bullets sped into the house of my spirit. My hands became monsters, devouring and killing and crushing everything close to me. My teeth came together within throats, and I howled into the flames, blood, and death.

I was almost to the stairs, but my family, both, lay behind me in flames. I turned around. A firing squad opened up, washing me in lead. The stone pillar nearest me came away in my ruined hands, and I crushed the firing line beneath my crumbling weapon.

The speaker called out to his minions, this time no longer laughing. "Take him! He's only one fuckin' guy, fer Christ's sake!"

My eyes defied the smoke and blood that filled them as I peered through the flames, seeking the leader of the gang of shadows. I saw him wrapped in a peal of churning smoke, conducting the violence, doubt and disbelief filling him up. I stepped without the maw of the inferno and addressed the other shadows. "Bring him to me, and you can all live," I shouted above the roaring flames, pointing to the slim killer who once vanished like smoke. The army's loyalty began to crack. I could see gun barrels and knives begin to consider the emaciated killer. Yet before the revolution was complete, another explosion belched fire and force from behind, smashing me into the marble archway. Still I drew up, even as my broken bones ground against each other while others tried to flee through my skin. Before I could properly right myself, the mutiny collapsed, and they fell upon me with all their numbers.

As I slowly began to lift their combined mass from my body, the thin man walked through the flames toward me carrying the hammer my father would often use to drive his massive chisel. He rained blows down upon my skull. I caught a glimpse of my sisters strewn across the floor, all but buried in debris. I could hear them weeping. With one last blow from my father's hammer, I heard no more.

There was no dream, only nullity of time and space. Yet there was experience, if only the rawest and least imprinted type. It was an almost ephemeral means by which I could deduce the passage of events, the inexorable movement of cause and effect—dragging my body from the burning house of my youth, where my first family smiled through fire, long dead but forever vital.

My body had been reduced to a smoking ruin, yet it lived—as did my attackers' intent. Another fire, well-fed and ever-fattening, bellowed in my wrecked guts, waiting to burn the world for what had been done to my family— both of them. Still, there would come a time for burning, but it was not now. Now was the time for waiting, reveling, wondering.

In this minimally vital state of mind that clung to the dimmest of lights, there was a presence, coiled and lethal, previously unknown to me. I held out my mind to it as an offering. Nothing. Only the coldest sleep, taking in the ages with nary an upward glance, touched my damaged awareness. It dressed in the scales of a monstrous snake, each one smooth as polished glass, shaped for the purpose of killing. There was the slightest intimation of identity. The thing was old and sharp, like a knife left to rust in a hidden place, ever dreaming of ripe tender flesh for the cutting. There was a size to the thing, too. It unfurled to the very borders of my understanding, and likely beyond them. It was a leviathan asleep on the floor of my mind, waiting. With the curiosity of a child, I made to poke the thing. I wanted to see it move.

Before I could rouse the sleeping giant, the world broke in on me, and my eyes were made to open. I was immobile, cold, and confronted by a lean shadow. "And so it rises. Hello, Family Man. Welcome to your last stop on the journey of life. I hope you like it."

It was the voice of the thin man, filled with a familiar confidence—a confidence that I was growing rather accustomed at dispelling. Before I responded, I took a moment to absorb my surroundings, which were initially rather spectacular. From all appearances, I was in a monstrous, ancient castle. Yet when I looked more closely, my accommodations were revealed to be nothing more than a replica, horribly overdone with thick and clumsy flourishes of the medieval and gothic, making the place appear more caricature than castle.

I could see my captor growing impatient with my silence, so I spoke. "Thin Man, I have not enjoyed your disrespect for me and mine. This will not go well for you, but please tell me how you think things will end before I show you how they actually do."

"You're a mouthy cuss, aren't you?" replied the thin man. "Well, you're draped in about two hundred pounds of steel chain, and the Red Dream seems to have faded between us, so I'm fairly sure you're not going anywhere."

"That's your mistake, Thin Man," I said. "Whenever has a fact flouted a dream, let alone a nightmare? But I'll leave you to your folly, for now."

The thin man was then joined by a second, identical thin man. "I think we're gonna be just fine. We've fried bigger fish than you, big man."

I shifted my gaze to the newcomer. "Wrong on both counts, I'm afraid."

"You don't seem at all curious as to why you're still alive," said the first. "Doesn't that strike you as the least bit odd?" He was growing visibly annoyed by my indifference.

By the conclusion of our time together, he would be begging for my indifference. I made no outward show of my anger, but I was in immense pain from the rage that ate away at my innards. I could still hear the weeping of my sisters. Even now, they were alone, without their brother, buried in the smoking ashes of my past. And my father's rage and indignation—I could feel it, scorching and dreadful.

"You see," continued the first, "my brother's been studying all this supernatural hoodoo. And the way he figures it, if we keep you here, like bait you might say, we can pick off all the killers that come for you, one by one. You probably also noticed that we took out quite a bit of insurance in the form of some hired men. They're the best money could buy, my man. So, whoever comes lookin' for us is gonna have a small army to fuck with. We've already nixed about seven names from our list, so far. Unfortunately, the last fish swallowed our bait, so we had to find another worm. That would be you, in case you were wondering. Not a bad play, huh, big man?" He was desperate for me to feel desperate, but all I felt was the weakness of the chains I'd been wrapped in and the loss of my family.

A third thin man joined the previous two. "I see you've been speaking to my brothers. Please, don't let their crudity give you any confidence in the prospect of surviving us. You're here until the wheels fall off, I'm afraid." Clearly the leader, he stood there waiting for me to marvel at the fact that he was one of an identical triplet. These three were in the habit of surrounding themselves with admiration, so I gave them none—not that I truly had any to give.

The third continued. "You don't recognize us, do you? Pity. The glory of being three men sharing two singular identities is obviously lost on you. Or perhaps you've been lost to the wild too long to recognize the fabulous David Shadowes, the greatest living illusionist this side of the Great Darkness.

"Still nothing, eh? Well, maybe you might know us by our second name, The Prince of Smoke—the killer who vanishes with the night, leaving no trace of himself behind, who has been likened to a monstrous combination of Houdini and Jack the Ripper."

I squinted. "Yes, the last one, perhaps. I may have heard of you, once or twice. But even Jack the Ripper—or Houdini, for that matter—is no Jack Lantern or Dooley Hines. Or even, dare I say, the infamous Family Man." The trio's weakness was quite obvious, so I decided to toy with it.

The third sneered. "You think you're a match for us, you shambling pile of mindless muscle? Why then, pray tell, have you fallen victim to us? Clearly, you've been oversold by the press."

I shook my head, smiling. "I didn't say you were my match. I implied you were my inferior. It would seem that in this case, three minds are not better than one." The three men barely contained their rage. I had high hopes for how that anger might serve me.

The third clapped his hands, ushering in several mercenaries. "Well, I suppose at the end of the day, it makes little difference what a dead man thinks. Fortunately for me and my now frantic need to see you suffer, you needn't be entirely whole for my clever plan to work. You're going to wish you were nicer to us, you monstrous oaf."

Within moments, I was hoisted from the stone floor by burly hired hands and placed cruciform upon a stone wall. My captors were careful to see that more chains were added to better secure my outstretched arms, once they realized that I had already—quite unconsciously—deformed some of the links of my original trappings. My strength was in no need of the Red Dream to be formidable.

All manner of petty torture followed—whippings, the plying of many red-hot objects to my body, the pouring of scalding-hot liquids over my skin, and on and on. All of it was quite painful, but none of it was sufficient to warrant even the slightest reaction from me, save perhaps for the occasional glare. However, my eyes were only reflecting the pain I felt from internal fires, rather than those paltry flames that had been laid upon my flesh. Of course, my reluctance to yield so much as a whimper gave no satisfaction to the triplets. This in turn only inspired them to concoct more elaborate but equally fruitless attempts to elicit screams from me.

My torture lasted for weeks, and as was predicted by my captors, many Wolves came for me—as well as the brothers. All of them, each in their grizzly turns, fell to the small army of hired killers assembled by the triplets. While I continued to burn from within, the efforts of the miserable trio finally began to take a toll, as my body became less and less a discernible thing. I had become a confusion of sores, blood, and exposed muscle and bone. I would scarcely be able to fight even if I did manage to break through my bonds, which out of paranoia and fear, the triplets had considerably augmented. My heart had never been host to fear, yet I did begin to wonder if I had finally reached the end of my dream.

I took my silence wherever I could find it—in between my captors' words, even between their breaths. Between the brief spaces separating my thoughts, where reposed tiny sparks of quiet. Between the very din of shadows, as they glided close upon the heels of their casters. It was all that kept me together. The torments affected by my captors were growing less fanciful and more forceful—a typical and predictable escalation once the imagination fades. There wasn't much imagination between the triplets, perhaps less than what one might hope to find blowing about within the most average of heads. No, the engine that powered this Prince of Smoke was little more than the combined powers of greed and glory—two vices that were as correlated as flesh and bone. Of course, as the Deadworld loves its petty ironies, their vainglory would most certainly be their unseating. I would see to it, loath though I was to do the Deadworld's work.

There were always several of the hired guns milling about the room where I had been showcased. The triplets must have been wealthy, indeed. Given all the noise they made, I was left without a proper healing silence, so I made do with scraps. Unfortunately, whatever progress a night's efforts of sipping at silence gave me was immediately stripped away the following day, as lash and hammer and knife saw to the lessening—and then some—of my night's recovery.

On what night I cannot say, there came a quiet that stoked the coldest fire within me—I could no longer hear the lament of my poor sisters. Did they think their brother dead? Or worse, did they believe I had abandoned them? I would be free that very night, I swore it.

As had become routine for the closing of the evening, the thin men came to me, boasting of their most recent success at "cheating the Shepherd's Game," as they called it. I saw their technique as one of many perfectly valid strategies that could be used to win—I couldn't fathom how one cheats at a cosmic game of mass murder.

"After that last fish, I'd say our worm isn't long for the world, eh?" spoke the leader of the three. He was referencing the Wolf that had come for me the night prior. A killer known as the Baker's Man had killed the first round of hired hands and managed to spend a minute or so trying to cut me from my chains—limb by limb—so as to "prepare some meat for the heat," as the Wolf had put it. However, the killer's desire to whisper said phrase into my ear had put him in range of my teeth. I don't believe even a master chef could have prepared that man's flesh to taste any less rancid. He was largely a yellow supper of flab soaked in sweat, clearly far too indulgent of his appetite. Perhaps he was a better cook than he was a meal—it was certainly difficult to imagine otherwise. But I hadn't been allowed to eat since I'd arrived, and beggars undoubtedly cannot be choosers. By the time the second round of guards arrived, I had already dealt with my appetite. Normally, I would not stoop to cannibalism, but my sisters were at stake—I would need every bit of energy I could amass, however I could get it. I wondered what Black Molly Patience would have thought of me now.

The third thin man continued. "Tonight might be even messier, I think. This next killer dreamed some serious weirdness at us last night, and I'm pretty sure he's making a beeline straight for us. But who knows, maybe you'll last another night. I did after all double the guard. There might yet still be something wriggling on the hook come morning, but I seriously doubt it." The leader took a long look at me, perhaps expecting me to speak. I did not. He slapped me on the shoulder and said, "Good luck though, big man, I really mean that."

I was about to let them take their leave of me, but if a killer of unusually high caliber was coming for them and had even the slightest chance of prevailing, I would have my final words with them. "I sincerely hope you and your brothers survive this next killer, for I intend to hurt all of you quite badly before I kill you, for what you've done to my family. But whoever or whatever comes tonight, even if they prove to be the devil himself—if they should happen to kill you in the most horrible of ways, you should thank them on your way out of this world for saving you from my vengeance."

The third's face grew dark. "Well, thanks for that, then. I'll have to make sure the boys work you especially hard tonight. That way, even if you do somehow escape, you'll be in no shape to avenge yourself or anyone else." Despite the bravado, I knew my words had done their job. I could see fear in the triplets, which I hoped would prove a valuable ally later on.

My muscles were already proving stronger than the chains that coiled about me, but I had remitted my efforts at the approach of the thin men, disallowing the straining iron a voice. Soon, I would be free.

A short time later, seven mercenaries entered the airy room into which I had been painfully reposed. They drew up to me with their hammers and blades, their fire and laughter. I took the pain they inflicted and smiled until I had no more teeth with which to do so—a wise precaution on their part, given what I had done the night before. I timed my efforts against my bonds with the laughter of my tormenters.

Suddenly, I smelled a terrible sweetness in the air. It rose upon a plume of screams that blossomed into the contrived castle. The seven men turned to face the threat. The other killer had come, and I determined to send back my own greeting of screams.

My arms, filled with the coldest fire I'd ever cultivated, moved beyond their bonds. At that very moment, my chains exploded, a noise like thick ice shattering beneath the fury of a sledgehammer. I was free.

The seven men came at me, seeking the death I gave them. I crushed the screams from their throats, creating a song far sweeter than the fragrance of the newest Wolf. I supped upon the silence of the dead men, and I could feel my wounds knitting and the shattered studs of my teeth pushing up from my ruined gums.

I could hear the fiery munitions of the small army discharging wildly, desperately—sounds I had coaxed from the very same group only a short time ago. I kicked the tall medieval doors from my path and investigated the growing conflagration unfurling before me. There were only vague shapes, pent in so much smoke and fire, fleeing and fighting, but mostly just dying.

The thing rapidly shrinking the mercenary army appeared to be a monstrous undead child, dressed in powder blues and bright pinks and holding a giant lollipop—the sweetness I'd smelled earlier, no doubt. I believed the urban legends referred to the thing as the Missing Child—an elemental of murdered children. Regardless of the high pedigree of the interloper and my innate desire to seek it out, I would have the triplets as my first contest of the evening.

I descended the cracked stone stairs, revealing myself to the fleeing mercenaries, allowing them to see that certain death now surrounded them. I was curious to see who they would find more frightening—myself or the Missing Child. I felt quite insulted when the dying masses risked my fury by flooding past me, seeking the exit at my back. I resolved to meet the undead child whether he was on my list or not.

Yet I spied the Prince of Smoke—one version of him, at least—wrapped in thick darkness, standing high above the slaughter, grinning. He looked down from the ramparts of his fake castle, scoffing at both me and the murder-elemental.

The Missing Child made for the thin man and I stepped in front of the creature, signaling that on this day, we were going off-list. The thin men were mine. The shambling thing's dead eyes fell upon me, and I could sense he mistook me for easy prey.

I felt the cold hands of the undead creature close upon my arms as the thing thought to tear me into pieces as one might a piece of paper. I was growing quite tired of my most recent opponents attempting to rid me of my limbs. My arms had just shrugged off the coils of heavy iron, they had lifted monstrous cannibals into the hollows of the underworld, and they were routinely called upon to heft the incalculable weight of my father's rage—they would certainly endure beyond this creature's grip.

I threw off the monster's hold, and as it staggered backward, surprised no doubt that I had overcome it, I delivered my fist hard and fast across its perpetually grinning face. The thing tumbled to the floor, and the tides of fleeing killers reversed their course, realizing the elemental was clearly the lesser of the two presented threats. I was pleased, but the elemental and the army were peripheral to my course.

I could feel the Red Dream fill my body, thundering through the cracks of the mundane Deadworld, powering my efforts at negotiating the combat at hand. Now renewed and then some, I assumed the Prince of Smoke would be a fairly easy name to cross off my list. I was to learn otherwise.

Magic shares much in common with dreaming, in so much that it is an effect without explanation—a staple feature of any dream. And contrary to the more common assumptions about magic, it isn't merely the defiance of reality, but is more specifically the annihilation of causality. This realization ran to the forefront of my mind when I saw the Prince appear from the choking smokes of unchecked fires, moving towards me with a grace borne from practiced lethality—an attitude that had no place within the spoiled spaces of any one of the triplets. Here was magic, surely.

My amazement rapidly turned to pain. The Missing Child had already risen from my blow and was quick to put me into the stone and mortar of the false castle. Its attack was more than sufficient to send me flying through the wall and into the next room. Unsurprisingly, the creature failed to follow through with its bid to kill me, as it was clearly more focused on the Prince. I found it humorous to think of such an undead monstrosity as this carrying around a list of names, periodically perusing it for direction.

The fires from the initial meeting between the army and elemental continued to flood through the structure, spilling across wooden fixtures and climbing into the rafters. I certainly enjoyed the developing venue of this particular contest, even taking a few moments from my pursuit to approve of the seething ambience.

I was surprised when I saw the Missing Child draw up to the Prince—whited fist held high, exuding the howls of murdered children—and fail to land a decisive blow against his designated target. While the creature's cold fist seemed to connect with the Prince, who seemed more than willing to receive the attack, the very moment of impact revealed the magician to be nothing but a wall of mirrored glass. Through the sound of it shattering and the roar of the fire, I could hear the high-pitched laughter of the Prince of Smoke mocking the goliath from the grave. At that moment, I may have discovered a bit of respect for the killer magician. Yet where were the other two brothers? Surely, they were part of the show as well.

As I began scanning the spaces around me for his cohorts, the magician appeared behind The Missing Child, emerging again from the smoke as if he were truly a hierarch of flames. The Prince silently slapped an explosive device to the back of the elemental and shrank into cloud.

The undead giant disappeared into a storm of fire and fury. I was stunned by the cleverness and efficiency of my opponent. I never guessed the killer to be anything but a financier of murder—certainly not the demon of smoke and mirrors he now revealed himself to be. Where I had only discovered a bit of respect for the Prince of Smoke, I now found admiration.

The shockwave from the explosion rippled through the bones of the copycat castle, and the Prince's apparent victory over the Missing Child sent a fresh gust of courage surging into the sails of the remaining army. They cheered their employer as they trained their attention and weapons back on me.

The Red Dream was doing its job well enough, but the stark reality of so many bullets washing over me began to buckle my powers. My hands instinctively went to the space where once dwelt my father, finding only air. Having no apparent route to victory, I sought out the silence beneath the fire and guns and smoke. I felt the soft cold of the hidden quiet splash over my broken body, repairing me, if only slightly.

I breeched the darkness within a large cluster of soldiers. Disappointingly, the circumstances allowed little opportunity for art, so I dispatched the armed assemblage with little gusto, replacing flourish with brutal minimalism. It was a quick piece, but it had the desired effect upon my intended audience—a renewed fear.

Before I could exploit the fruits of my labor, the Prince was upon me. Where he came from I cannot say, but his blade turned crimson cartwheels in my guts. Had it not been for the timely intervention of a brick I'd pulled from the wall, I might have been emptied there on the spot. The magician reeled from the blast of my crude weapon, but did not fall—he seemed to melt into the piles of bodies that lay all around me, as if matter were no more restrictive to him than mist.

I speculated that the brothers were dressed alike, attacking at different times from different directions. After all, they had bragged to me about how they all shared a single identity. Publicly, they played at being the illusionist—David Shadowes. Privately, they assumed the mantle of the deadly Prince of Smoke. And while I could not speak to the persona of David Shadowes, the Prince of Smoke seemed more like a complete entity, replete with a cultivated skill for killing, and not simply a single trick played by three brothers. I had paid careful attention to the brothers over the course of my stay in their castle, and never did I detect anything that might have passed for even the slightest sign of a killing grace. Something wicked and truly wonderful was afoot with them.

I was about to submerge myself back into the darkness when I heard the sound of tiny gliding feet. It was an altogether different sound than the relentless clunking of the mercenaries, and it came from the spot where the Missing Child had been blown from the world. Within moments, I was treated to a wonderful sight.

Out of the still-lingering smoke of the murder elemental's demise, there spilled a multitude of pale children, all of whom moved swiftly despite appearing quite dead. At least fifty of the little things darted into the shadows as quickly as hummingbirds. When they had all been thoroughly absorbed into the smoke and fire and darkness, I could hear the screams of the troops rip through the smoky air. I was delighted to see that the Prince of Smoke wasn't the only creature capable of magic tricks—it seemed that the Missing Child was a master mystifier, on par with the best magic makers.

My amusement at the proceedings died quickly and horribly, when from behind me there came a chorus of familiar voices. I turned around to find a gang of dead children standing upon a pile of rubble, glaring at me. I knew each one of their names.

All save one fell silent. Her name was Lilly. "Look, it's little Vincent, all grown up! We all had such a good time playing that day in the park, didn't we, Vincent? That is, until you turned us over to that awful father of yours. He put us in cages for months. He used our blood to make his paints, Vincent. Did you know what he'd do to us? Did it make you happy to see us slowly killed? Why didn't you try to stop him? Why didn't you let us out of our cages, Vincent? Why did you let us die?"

Their questions sent me tumbling into yet another terrible memory.

CHAPTER SIXTEEN

Young Vincent: Why are you hurting them, father?

Father: Honestly son, what harm can really be done to the dead? Do you think those children alive? You've so much to learn, my little apprentice. There's no life in those little corpses. They're merely the freshest cadavers this Deadworld has to offer, nothing else. You see, my art is very much like blood magic, in so much that it draws its strength from the most vital sources that can be had. And here, where people are only plastic and dead, the youngest corpses are the most useful corpses, as they are the only things likely to furnish even a speck of vitality. The dust of their dreams is what gives my paints, clays, and canvases their true colors—not the dull, lifeless combinations of earthly constituents.

Young Vincent: But they cry for me to save them. How could they be dead?

Father: They have no idea they're dead, son. They woke up in the middle of their sweet dreams, spilling out cold and lifeless into this land of unloving, shuffling strangers. They—we—are all at best, only ghosts. At worst, corpses. I pray we are the former, for that means there's still a chance that life—and by *life*, I mean *dream*—can again dawn upon us all. But for that to happen, I must play god, which is the purpose of any artist worth a bucket of paint. I must reconstitute life from loam. The only thing those little creatures can try to save is their skin—the webbing that constricts their dreams, anchoring them to this alien graveyard. What you hear is the dead pleading to stay dead, nothing more. Do you want those poor children to stay dead forever, Vincent?

Young Vincent: No.

***

Lilly's face lacked even a shred of understanding—it merely hung dead and vengeful, long lost to the tides of pain that had stayed her soul from oblivion. Neither she nor the rest of the dead children understood what had been done to them, for them. And while I didn't share my father's particular views concerning the role of children in art, I was nonetheless sympathetic to his efforts, if not his methods. However, my sympathy was not shared by the deceased children standing before me.

"I did not allow you to die, little ones," I said gently. "I had been given to believe, incorrectly, that you were being made to truly live, as once we all did before all this death became us. I am so truly sorry that my father's efforts failed you. But, I am afraid I cannot be the inheritor of his sins. All I can do is hope that my efforts will be more successful than his. Perhaps you might assist me in my efforts, if you truly care to rid yourself of all that aforementioned death. I want nothing more than for you to learn to dream again, little ones."

I knelt down before Lilly, and the little corpse searched my eyes, finding only death, dream, and truth. I could feel the dead flower of her soul take strength from my conviction, blooming in the darkness of her tiny, beautiful sadness. She threw her arms around me and sobbed into the shadows. One after another, the dead children came to me. With each new embrace, my strength swelled, joining with the power of the Red Dream. Their fragile, wonderful hugs were so filled with hope, even after death. It was that rootless little hope, in amalgam, that powered the undead giant known as the Missing Child.

Lilly placed her blackened, twisted hand to my face. "You poor, poor monster. So broken, so beautiful. Go to them. We will tend to these fools for as long as we are able. Find your family, Vincent, and avenge us all for being so rudely awoken from such a beautiful dream." I kissed her upon her spoiling forehead and rose from the gathering of children, changed.

My tears held the smoke from my eyes as I strode through the fire, crushing the fools who rose against me. I now moved through the hordes of soldiers with a new conviction, a new burning dream—dead children lifted from grave to glory, thrilling through black skies, with bits of rolling thunder surging through their hopeful hearts.

I reached the last door—a fabricated drawbridge, barred shut by a length of red-hot iron. Standing before it was the Prince of Smoke, holding a dagger in each hand, laughing. However, the laughter was not the property of any one single triplet, but rather the conjoined cackling of the lot of them. "I see you are finally coming to understand things, Family Man—if only slightly. Yet secrecy is ever the magician's prerogative, is it not?"

I clenched my fists, every fiber of them aching from the absence of my sweet sisters. "I'm rather relieved to see you're not nearly so dull as I had been led to believe via our many conversations together. Regrettably, like the many interesting individuals before you, I must remove you from my kill list. And because of what you have done, you will be removed with great and painful prejudice."

The Prince twirled a dagger and smiled. "Out of respect for the Game—and no small amount of fear of consequence— I've not inspected your kill list. However, I'm certain it isn't nearly so extensive with crossed-out names as mine. Soon, you will discover why that is." I hoped his surprise was more than the realization that the Prince of Smoke was a composite entity, manifested from the joining of the three miserable brothers, as that rabbit was already out of the hat. Though, how they managed it remained an interesting secret. In the next moment, the men of one body vanished in a thick plume of smoke.

Wrapped in the Red Dream and the hope of lost children, I moved to the massive door and seized the glowing steel bar that held it shut, snapping it in half. My hands caught fire, allowing me to augment the blow I struck against the Prince as he appeared behind me, knives in hand.

The composite man was knocked into roaring flames, but I knew it would take more than fire to finish him, just as it would take more than a predictable sneak attack to finish me. "If the extent of your magical prowess is limited to performing such cheap tricks, you may have oversold yourself, Your Highness."

The magician fell silent, allowing his soldiers to answer my taunt, but the Prince of Smoke wasn't the only one who could vanish. The killers' gunfire failed to find me as I loosed myself into a strong current of shadow and silence, disappearing from sight. Within moments, I had gained the courtyard surrounding the false castle. I could hear my sisters' weeping like never before, the sound filling me with even more fire. I couldn't bear their cries. The Prince of Smoke would have to wait.

Just before I merged into the nearby woods, I cast my glance backwards. The Prince was standing in the sky, apparently held against gravity by only the plumes of smoke that rose out of the burning castle. His gaze pushed against the darkness by which I traveled, and I could feel his strange power reaching out for me. I threw out a cloud of quiet and disappeared anew.

As I crossed beyond the entrance to the nearby forest, I quietly asked the trees and the cool babbling brooks if they might keep my presence a secret. For incentive, I promised to unpeel them all from the solid world, should I manage to win my war against waking. Only seconds passed before the forest had completely embraced me, taking me into its confidence and revealing to me all of its secret paths. I quietly thanked the woodland as I rushed through its ancient darkness—a silken gloom that had been hidden and nurtured since time immemorial, passed between shady meadow and benighted thicket, to be preserved against the day forever. Yet despite the forest's best efforts, I could detect from somewhere within those undisclosed lanes a Wolf keeping pace with me, deciphering the confusion I left in my wake, avoiding my every trap and predicting my every feign. The Prince of Smoke was a formidable hunter, indeed.

A hollow in the woods yawned wide as the Prince, preempting the path I would take, rose from the mists directly in front of me. He showed me his hands, clad in black leather gloves, and began moving them with an awful celerity. He thrust them out in front of the darkness that held his face from sight, beneath a hood seemingly stitched from the gossamer of shadows. Instantly, a swarm of fat flies swept out from between his dancing fingers and splashed across my face, the entire cloud trying desperately to bury itself in my eyes. An enemy silence bloomed all around me, turning my vigilant senses aside and inviting a blade deep into the flesh of my back.

I followed the pain to the exact point at which my skin ended and the Prince's knife began, hoping to seize it. But my hands only clasped the tail of a mist that twisted in the moonlight. My renewed silence closed the wound as the blade vanished, and I called the shadows to reveal the void where hid my opponent.

My fist followed where the shadows led, and the magical murderer spat his broken teeth onto the twisting coils of ancient tree roots. The conjoined triplet backpedaled into his strange and magical smoke as I sunk into my obedient darkness. Not even the searching songs of crickets and frogs could find the silence through which we stalked, nor could the gloom of moonstruck swamps foreshadow the savagery we intended to impart to one another.

Cold whispers from the pursed lips of the Prince would drift across my path, searching me out. "Come and see what wonderful magic tricks I've yet to show you, my friend. They'll wrap you in wonder and allow you to see by the most wonderful and secret lights." I can't deny that I found the offer nearly irresistible, but my sisters were in dire need.

At last the sun began to stir at the horizon, and the sky began to pool at its most distant edges with drowsy light. I assumed the Prince, if he was any kind of a hunter or at all like myself, would likely postpone our dealings until nightfall. I found a cavern filled with wolves hidden deep within the woods, replete with the recent kill of a large deer. I slew the wolves and lined the earthy space with their soft bodies, providing myself with comfortable sleeping arrangements. After I had filled my belly with fresh deer meat, I slept.

I was finally allowed to sink into the depths of dream my previous earthly accommodations had made all but impossible. And as is usually the case, there was something waiting at the bottom.

"Shall I be forced to come find you, Family Man?" It was Mister Hide, calling out to me from our shared dream. "Given the dwindling number of contestants, I'd thought to get things done and over with. I've all but sent you a written invitation to my whereabouts, so I'm curious if you've reconsidered your chances of victory against me. Perhaps rather than face me, you've elected to hide in a hole somewhere."

I couldn't blame him for his impatience, or even his theory concerning my prolonged absence. It would certainly seem that I'd reconsidered my bid against him. "My most sincere apologies, Mister Hide. I have been somewhat detained as of late. Have you ever heard of this Prince of Smoke?" I wondered if my most recent opponent was as famous as he would have me believe.

"I have," replied Hide. "He's a bit of an escape artist, is he not? I believe he was responsible for the mass killing of several convicted murderers reposed within a maximum-security prison, a structure quite famous for its impregnability. Quite the feat—if the story is true, of course."

"From what I've seen, it seems likely," I said ruefully. "I have to admit my initial impression of the creature was a bit lackluster. However, that impression has since been revised, and considerably so."

"I can't say I'm not disappointed he hasn't killed you," Hide said. "I see our meeting going rather poorly for you, and with precious few stand-out moments to satisfy me long after your pelt has been treated and hung. When you get right down to the bones of the matter, you're little more than an inferior version of myself. Your chief attributes are all similar to my own, only less refined and powerful. It seems to me the Prince of Smoke could do you the favor of sparing you an awful lot of humiliation, while providing me with a more diversified and thus challenging opponent."

"Your obsession with your swollen muscles is disappointing," I countered, smiling. "I'd hoped you'd be a bit more refined by way of an operating philosophy, which is precisely why you and I are not very alike at all. You see, my primary attribute is my artistic sense, a particular quality that seems wholly lost on you, regrettably. And there's the fact that you're clearly the smaller and weaker creature between us." I desperately wanted to yield to at least one of the baser temptations I'd experienced that night—though truth be told, I was much more interested in the Prince's advertised magic show.

Up to this point, the dream was largely unformed, merely a dark place at the bottom of a murky ocean. After my poorly veiled insult, the waters began to churn with the blood and body parts of ferocious beasts. Each of the sundered creatures were entirely undressed of their skins. Moments after the water had been all but replaced with blood and bodies, the Skinner drew up to me, seeming much deflated, as if he'd lost a considerable amount of his vaunted mass.

When the once massive killer spoke, it was in a much different voice. "You've chosen a poor place to hide, Family Man. Magic within a dream is so much stronger than beneath the sun—or even the moon, for that matter." The Prince of Smoke stood before me, from the bottom of a Red Dream, from behind the poached dream-skin of a massive serial killer.

The Prince laughed as my body was overcome with a thousand points of pain. Suddenly I was awake, covered with the dead and drooling wolves I had slain earlier. I threw them from me, crushing out what life had been smuggled into them by the unclean magics of the Prince. I saw a familiar mist gathering at the mouth of the cavern, giddy from its most recent assault upon me.

"You are a fine opponent, Family Man," said the Prince, "and I now feel that if I'd continued to dangle you out as bait, I would have denied myself some of the grandest fun I've ever known. Most importantly, you seem to have a unique appreciation for my craft. I can tell by the way your eyes retreat from the world as you marvel at my tricks. And unlike so many, you never seek to look behind my apparent chicanery. You stare into my mystery with the wide eyes of a child, accepting everything and questioning nothing. As a magician, I can prize nothing so highly as your ceaseless wonder. For that, I must thank you."

It was a sincere gesture, and I received it in the intended spirit. But this would not stop me from tearing him limb from magical limb, trickster from triplet. I would not relent until all of them were so much indecipherable ruin, their true magic left to fend for itself in a world of two-way mirrors, false-bottomed boxes, and eyes that could never behold wonder. My sisters would have it no other way.

My fists could find no purchase for themselves—nothing, that is, save empty air and the filthy walls of the cavern. While the Prince of Smoke was nowhere, his laughter was everywhere. It came from the deepest recesses of the cave, the broken jaws of twice-dead wolves, it even seemed to tumble from my own mouth.

I thought perhaps the deeper darkness that slept within the very guts of the cave might deny my opponent the trick of attacking from anywhere—I hoped his eyes were not as keen as my own. After much calculation of the Princes' tactics, I managed to seize hold of him and cast him into the depths of the cave. Yet again there was no sound of flesh striking rock, only the laughter of a man who could apparently be everywhere and nowhere at once.

I splashed into the thick currents of darkness, brandishing a large stone I had wrenched free from the earth. I took pleasure at the thought of my enemy—as gaudy in his ways as a refined jewel sleeping upon a wrought bed of gold and silver—being dispatched by a crude and common rock.

The Prince revealed a side to his power I had not anticipated, a side that was as wonderful as it was wicked. I dropped through the world, ostensibly through a trap door that had been recessed into the irregular filth of the cavern floor. It would have been impossible for the magician to have the foresight to place it there. I realized the power of the man—men?—became greater the further he moved from the prying eyes of the world, where his magic could churn butter into butterflies and the world would never be the wiser. It became clear to me the banality of the trio was as fake as the floor, as deceptive as a mirage—as polished as a two-way mirror.

I fell into the thickest darkness that could be found within the steadier boundaries of the Deadworld. This was a place of uncertainty—perhaps tucked under a leaf or at the back of a lunatic's mind, it hummed with a potential that could only be coaxed into shape by the sharpest of wills or the strongest of magics—itself merely a dream given direction. Yet this was the Prince's mistake, as my will was equally potent even without the benefit of magic words and sleight of hand. I had no idea where I was specifically, which was to my advantage. Without knowledge aforethought, my will could place me wherever I wished "here" to be. Hence I was able to bend the darkness into a journey—back home.

As I rode the darkness linking one shadow to the next, I could feel the blackness parting behind me, pushed aside by the Prince as he gave chase. I emerged from a night sky, tumbling like a comet to the earth, through tree branches and brambles, till at last the world rose up to greet me. I splashed down into the murky waters of a cold forest pool.

Of the Prince, I heard nothing, but he was close, perhaps only slightly farther than the distance of his magician's blades. "I bet you didn't know this, but your opponent is the son of a witch," he said from nowhere in particular. "And his father was a thirteenth son. So you must see by now, you've really no chance, here. I've been charitable with you thus far, primarily because you're nearly the anomaly I am. But regrettably for you, nearly isn't quite good enough."

"Strange, but you sound more like a cliché to me," I jeered, "not at all the anomalous creature you make yourself out to be. You're so rote, in fact, that I'm now fairly certain your trio form is merely the predictable side effect of the Power of Threes, undoubtedly exercised by your mother at your birth. Why, I'm even beginning to wonder what a common Halloween costume such as yourself is even doing in this Game of Wolves."

It was clear the Prince would not be so easily rattled at the cusp of what he assumed were my final moments. "And what noble blood makes you a more qualified attendee to this sport of murderers, eh? It certainly couldn't be those awful 'works of art' you leave in your wake. I've known butchers with more artistic flourish than you. You're little more than a brute with a vocabulary."

Seconds after I exited the water, there descended upon me a flurry of throwing knives—the type blindfolded magicians throw at beautiful women tied with brilliantly colored rope. Except these blades hadn't found bright balloons or smoldering cigarettes, but the blood that surged beneath my skin. Yet I continued on my way, heading towards the smell of wet ashes and old wood. Upon seeing my family's home before me, the Prince conjured back into life the fires that had once consumed it, again setting the charred remains alight. I plunged through the mouth of the flames towards the sound of my sisters' weeping and the undeniable heat of my father's rage.

From somewhere within the billowing smoke behind me emerged the wizard, hands filled with cold steel. I felt his knife pass through my neck and exit out the front of my throat. I fell silently to the ground.

"If it makes you feel any better," the Prince of Smoke crooned, "I will certainly enjoy looking at your name, cut clean in half by a straight black line."

I felt something emerge from the smoking ruin of the house and fill my hand. It burned as my fingers closed around its handle, completing an embrace I had for too long been without. A wrath that had been building for weeks consumed me, blinded me, nearly destroyed me.

I was lifted to my feet, my father held high in the molten grip of my hand. I turned to meet the Prince, this time the one performing miracles and he but a dumbstruck onlooker.

"You'd be dead even within a Red Dream," the Prince sputtered, backpedaling away.

I fought past the rage to offer my opponent a wan smile. "I have an impressive mother and father as well, magician. And doing the impossible runs in the family."

My father blasted into the ground near the retreating magician. The world tumbled and separated as dirt and stone barely resisted his will. A familiar and monstrous laughter exploded from my throat, rattling my teeth. I could still see the flagging killer through the debris, and I found myself charging forward, my forbear's will filling me with the need to kill. Fire ignited around the Prince of Smoke as he attempted escape, but my father's fury proved greater. I felt the axe cleave the plume of otherworldly power in twain, stranding the triplet out in the open.

The Prince proved a spry creature, sliding inside my father's killing arc and slicing open my belly. Yet the rage that had become me had no time for bleeding, much less dying. My knee rose to greet the Prince's chin, shattering bone. As he reeled from the impact, the butt of the axe found the spellcaster's nose. Wet fireworks of teeth and blood pinwheeled from my enemy's face, coaxing a storm of renewed laughter from my aching jaws.

Finally, my father collided with the body of the killer, sundering it in an explosion of wooden shrapnel. A decoy of the Prince lay in pieces all around me as his laughter echoed from all directions. The rubble of the house suddenly disappeared as I fell, the solid earth beneath me transforming into a dark pit. Pain rivaled rage as a floor of sharpened stakes skewered me like a wild beast. I had brooked my last insult from the Prince.

The Red Dream seared the air around me as I leaped from the pit, landing upon solid shadow and plunging into my servitor silence. I watched the Prince from the hollows of the world, waiting for my next opportunity.

As the revived fires continued to burn, the Prince climbed the snaking smoke like a staircase into the night. Lifted beyond the ceiling of the forest, the magician traversed the smoke as it curled in upon itself and raced sideways across the treetops. I kept pace, following from within a brook of shadow that fell thick and quiet from an ancient stand of oak trees. The magician circled around the glowing wreckage of my ancestral home, riding the smoke like a steed.

He called out to me through broken teeth and a stream of blood that poured from his left eye. "You know why I turned my talent to the stage, both in front and beyond the eyes of the world, Family Man? Because I wanted to flaunt the power that had been derided and shamed into magic hats and storybooks and myths. I wanted to show my audience the world, the better one, they themselves had destroyed—the world they mocked when they told their snot-nosed kids that nothing but hollow imagination lurked the spaces beneath beds and behind closet doors. I wanted to see their faces when they realized too late it was not all a clever illusion. That is why I've let you live this long—because you know what I know. I can see it in your eyes."

Of course, he was right. I had an intimate awareness of the powers of which he spoke, and a nearly boundless wonder for what that awareness could never hope to comprehend. What little I might have understood only suggested an infinity of mysteries that lay beyond me, never to be resolved into solidity, and I was glad for that ignorance.

Yet I still desired to plunge deeper into the darkness of that wonder—by winning a game set by a god. And now, as so many times before, I would be forced to kill a kindred spirit. But unlike the majority of previous killings, this one I would enjoy.

"I've dedicated my life to that spectral world, Family Man," the Prince continued. "I've become its vengeance, I suppose you might say. And like any good avenger, I must show my victims the error of their ways before I dispatch them. Yet that justification can hardly contain my actions tonight, can it? Tonight, I kill to invite the lost world back into our midst, to realize my own Red Dream. On that count, you and I might be brothers, I feel. It is with this in mind that I offer my thanks—and my apologies for the dirty tricks that must take place."

"I accept," I said, appreciating the truth of his words. Another surprise rose from beneath the burning debris as I was about to strike. Two surprises, in fact.

My sisters broke through the remains of my old home, riding the art-forms of my first family, inside of which they had buried their glittering smiles. First came one sister in the wondrous piece my father had created from my mother and brother and sister, titled *My Family, Divided*. It was a beautiful sight, my sister joined with my first family in death and vengeance. Then, hands—sculpted from their original shape by my father, well beyond the design nature had reserved for them—reached up through the smoke that bore the Prince and tore him from the sky.

Then came my other sister, piloting the masterwork I had made from my own father—*The Red Ouroboros*. They rose as a single creature, terrible and new, like the black dawn that breaks upon the newborn monsters fresh from nightmare. They might as well have been father and daughter. *The Red Ouroboros* fell upon the struggling shape of my enemy. My sister's smile cut through the darkness, glowing with the darkened crimson of deep sunset.

I watched my beautiful sisters, now joined with my first family, throw the plump organs of The Prince of Smoke at the yawning black sky. Smiles like sickle moons played above the Prince's screams, bobbing in his shrieks like burning paper boats set upon rough red waters.

I walked to where my family, all of them, had gathered around the still dying magician of murder. His bleeding eyes met mine. I wrestled with my father's mounting laughter, trying to produce coherent speech. "My dear, dying prince. You should never have crossed us so coarsely. To employ a crude but appropriate phrase—you fucked with the wrong family."

CHAPTER SEVENTEEN

It was time that my first father be known to the world. I unearthed the rest of his works and placed them upon the burning stage of my former home. I took one last look at the family that could never have been, then replaced into sleep the family that had taken their place. Of the Prince of Smoke, there was nothing left save perhaps the stuff of his namesake. I had given him over to the fire, and his bones I had smashed to dust.

Throughout the Shepherd's Game, I'd endeavored to maintain the dignity and vision of those who had fallen to me. Never had I reveled in the death of a single artist or hunter or Wolf, and never had I the desire to do so. This competition did us all the kindness and decency of placing its boundaries beyond the world, and as such, I believed it was our obligation to strive to exhaust those boundaries—not to settle on keeping the ball, so to speak, in the mud of the physical realm. I resolved to show no consideration to those who played the Game for the sake of solidity and namesake, especially those who would disrespect and malign its players. Those sorts I would destroy, utterly. And so the Prince of Smoke's name was struck from my list and from the world, as completely as could be managed.

My mood improved once I recalled my next destination—Willard, where dwelt the skin-switcher, Mr. Hide. I was relieved to know that my next opponent had both feet firmly planted in wonder—even if he was a bit caught up with his own physical immensity—and was as excited as I to see our contest resolved in the corridors of a city carved from untamed madness. Wasting no time on one so undeserving, I took my leave of the Prince and quickly made my way to the City of Madmen.

As was my custom, I made my way across the most haunted environs as I could put between myself and my destination, wandering and wondering as I went, willingly lost in dreamy reflection. Soon finding myself in new surroundings, I drifted with even less direction, simply aiming myself at the cardinal points that would bring me, eventually, to my terminus.

My journeys were filled with all manner of wonderful weirdness, as I often encountered some scrap or other of Obscuruum. Either standing lordly and alien over the prosaic fields of the dead earth or squatting within the hidden margins of some grotesquely resolute slice of reality, such contrasting aesthetics always made for delightful dreams. They informed and imprinted my nocturnal visions with the works of artists beyond the world, their canvases nothing less than the stretched and dried skins of the Deadworld.

This particular journey was no different than any other, and in short order I stumbled upon a dream—or so I believed.

A pearl-white stream flowed through the woods, apparently killing any flora that neared its crumbling black banks. It reflected the moonlight in a way I had never seen, almost shattering the pale illumination wherever the moon sought to touch the albino rivulet, creating a kind of visual debris from the cold lunar light.

I moved to the edge of the water, careful to search for any untoward presence as I went. There was nothing save for the strange water itself. I looked for my reflection upon the surface of the flowing stream, yet found nothing—only endless, empty white. I became keenly aware of a certain familiar feeling, but could not put clear memories to it. There was also a tremendous artificiality to the scene—a deliberate and immutable falseness. I realized the stream held no relationship to the moon, the night, or even the forest through which it unfurled. It was an alien.

The darkness refused the stream its enshrouding touch, creating a thin film of light above the water where the night was left incomplete. The revenant light was sickly, holding a coldness that reached beyond the skin, a strain of radiance that failed to illuminate its surroundings. Instead, the light seemed only to solidify its immediacy in a way that removed the fear and wonder of unseen things, all while not visibly disclosing them. Within moments, I felt utterly alone, without dream—purposeless. I was as bleached and bottomless and indistinct as the whited brook. I sat down beside the water and stared into its infinite, pointless depths. It was then that I realized what was happening to me—*who* was happening to me.

I had encountered the White Gaia, the Queen of the Deadworld. I had only once before felt her presence as keenly.

I was but a child roaming the back roads of the world with my new family. One afternoon, as we lay in the darkness of hidden places, my mother woke me from sleep and requested that I walk with her into the nearby city. The place was horribly new and over-bright, a plastic corpse laid at the feet of the terrible yellow noon. We walked deep into the urban thickets of glass and steel. My mother whisked me into a ruined apartment building, up a flight of rotting stairs, and into the shabbiest apartment I'd ever seen. Before me, there was a double-pane window, its lowest pane filled by a sheet of white-stained glass. Gently, my mother brought me to kneel before the white aperture, and told me to gaze through it. As I peered, I could see outlined in the white fog of the window the undead mother of the world—The White Gaia. She spilled upwards, thousands of feet, upon the skinless ragged bones of her bent legs. Her body was corpulent and heaving, with breasts like rotting moons. Her arms were as naked as her legs, terminating in crooked, skeletal hands. Her head was deathly yellow and hollow, and her eyes shone like open graves.

"There stands the enemy of all enemies," my mother whispered. "You will come to know her and her works. She already knows you well."

As I recounted my first glimpse of the Dead Queen, I hadn't noticed the white waters rising above my waist. Unseen currents tugged at me, and I heard a summons spill from the rotting lips of my greatest enemy. "I would speak with you, artist."

After being pulled beneath the white waters and feeling that I had sunk to an impossible depth for such a small stream, my hands found the bank and I pulled myself back onto dry land. The world beyond the waters seemed too bright, yet the darkness of the benighted woods had not lifted, as per the hour's dictate. The trees seemed locked into their soils like saprophyte statues, the moon appeared rusted to the night, the darkness fell empty and dead from the open grave of the sky. Everything had changed, yet everything remained the same. I wasn't even wet. More than likely, I had been abducted into a deeper stratum of the Deadworld— its calcified spirit—where the pretense of a living breathing world was neither asked nor supplied.

Before me stood a nearly solid wall of dead trees, behind which lingered equally dead earth. The land was entirely denuded of thickets, and no animals stirred. The trees were uncommonly tall, standing stronger and fiercer than any dead thing had a right to. They were completely without blemish, apparently unbothered by both insect and beast during the entirety of their lives and deaths.

I approached the barrier without hesitation or caution. This was a special place to the Queen of the Deadworld, so I would not waste time thinking I could prepare for what was ahead. I could feel an unclean power leaking out from the line of trees, pooling around the weakest parts of me, seeking entrance. Of course, it found me an impenetrable fortress, dressed in silent armies and burning moats. I smiled openly and victoriously at the unseen places behind the corpse-trees. At last, the ground began to shudder beneath the ungainly shamble of the Dead Mother. She approached.

I held fast only a few feet from the barricade, waiting to be addressed. I was not made to wait. "How long we've know each other, artist, and yet only now will we exchange words. Strange, yes?" Her words were immense, filled with a poisonous, vaporous warmth—the kind of heat that rose from fever dreams born of plague. Although I could not see her for the trees between us, I sensed her size was beyond the reckoning of numbers. Her appearance, even further beyond conception.

"Strange indeed," I said, "as I feel we have spoken often, if only through our actions. Perhaps our conversations would be best characterized as an ongoing debate. Though I feel you've heretofore dominated the argument, I'm currently working on my greatest rejoinder yet." I thought to get to the bones of the matter, as it was the contest that concerned her, and we both knew it.

"Yes," the Queen replied, "about that rejoinder of yours— you haven't much of a chance with it, but I think you know that. As a being familiar with all its enemies, I know only too well which are most deadly. You are not the greatest player in the Shepherd's Game, artist. You are the tragedy of all contests—you are second best. I needn't say the name of the fated winner, as your fear spells it out for you, in words of coldest fire. Your death lives in Autumn City. It always has."

I smiled. "I have made a living—and a killing—from being underestimated, Queen Mother. I have no reason to expect that tendency to abate any time soon. I will defeat Jack Lantern, and then I will destroy you."

The Queen continued, unperturbed. "While I have quite the mind to laugh at your bravado, I will not. I've not come here to belittle you, but rather to help you. I am no admirer of the Shepherd's Game—this one, the countless ones before it, or the countless others yet to come. I would see them stopped. Forever. You might help me in that regard."

My laughter echoed through the dead trees. "I'm afraid I can't pay you the same respect, you foolish thing! What are fools for, after all, if not for laughing at? You think I would help you? I would sooner let Jack Lantern carve my head to resemble a jack-o'-lantern than to dream of helping you. You've wasted your precious props and omens to bring me here, creature. Although, despite the wretched feel of this place, I am rather fond of this immured forest of yours. It gives me hope that one day it will be filled with the appropriate darkness, replacing this inferior brand you employ." I turned away in disgust. "I take my leave of you, you hopeless, thoughtless thing."

A monstrous creature barred my way. It was terribly mouth-heavy, its many eyes gleaming with a singular hunger. I sensed I was not the creature's preferred food, yet its rapacious state would likely find my flesh an acceptable substitute.

"This is my son," the White Gaia informed me. "One of them, anyway. He is called the Eater of Idols, and he wishes very much to join you at the Shepherd's Game. One way or the other, he will do just that. It is my hope that we can strike a somewhat civil tone for the remainder of my offer. Shall we continue, or would you rather fight without even knowing why?" She had locked me in a cage of sparkling curiosity. I would hear the Queen out, so I turned to face the dead trees.

"Excellent," she continued. "You see, since you have no chance at winning the game—your ridiculous boasting aside—I thought to make you an offer that would benefit the both of us. My son and I would like to give you a chance at achieving more than just winning the Shepherd's prize. We can offer you the pleasure of killing a god. Imagine what marvelous art you might make from that kind of clay. But, even more importantly, you would be entitled to a share of the spoils—a share of that godhood. It would make you fat and drunk with power, power you could use however you decide. Why, you would be so much more of a threat to me with such potency. Of course, you would certainly be less of a threat to me than would be the Shepherd, if he should be left alive to continue with his wretched tournaments. Either way, it's a chance I'm willing to take for an immediate, appreciable result. How say you, artist?"

I turned to leave for the second time.

"The second of my plans," the Queen continued quickly, "the least preferable of them, in fact, is to force the issue and have my son join the Game at your expense. It's a little clumsier than my previously outlined scheme, but it should do the trick. I assure you, this latest plan will hurt, artist. Why not take the easy road for a change?"

Her proposals were absurd, and my sisters were eager to supply them with the raucous laughter they so richly deserved. The Eater of Idols began to stir, sensing my decision. The creature was of the most bizarre cocktail of mismatched limbs, eyes, maws, and horns. I was shocked to know that such a fantastic thing could have originated with the White Mother. Yet there was an ordinariness beneath its demonic extravagance, as if it had been made demonical for mostly superficial reasons. Though I must confess, I was at a loss to even guess at such motives.

The beast's ungainly form made me take its sloth as a given, and for the most part I was right to do so. However, at one point, as I dashed beyond a darting wave of barbed tentacles, the creature proved a bit faster than I had anticipated. A few of the graceless extrusions lashed my back, causing some of the worst pain I had ever known.

I had to keep in mind that what I fought was only slightly removed from godhood, and because of that status, my victory against it would be hard gained. To make matters much worse, it seemed the Red Dream was unable to fortify me. The abode of the Dead Mother likely excluded such creative, if ultimately practical, excesses. All of this was perfectly acceptable to me, as I did not want to become overly dependent on foreign influences for my victory over the creature. I was glad for the opportunity to seek my own path to its destruction.

The darkness of the White Gaia's forest was entirely alien, lacking the most basic loyalties of standard lightlessness. Specifically, it was no friend to me and disallowed my want to disappear into its inky depths, forcing me into the open before the many keen eyes of the Gaia's son.

Lacking even the most basic tools for a proper sneak attack, I was forced to act in plain view. I moved quickly to the side of the creature's tumbling mass, running my sister's blazing smile across its impressive length, freeing the septic fluids that served as its blood. I laughed as my enemy cried out, reflecting upon my silence when the thing had laid nearly unbearable pain into the flesh of my back. Its throes of anguish gave me ample opportunity to rouse my father and plunge him deeply into the quivering folds of the unwholesome beast's flesh, summoning forth greater quantities of blood and much louder cries of pain.

The Eater of Idols realized I was no easy victim and withdrew from my father's thunderous laughter, which rolled across the lifeless environs of my enemy's putrid domain, tearing out the hollow silence that lurked between dead trees and underneath pale brooks.

I had taken the creature's actions to be indicative of a temporary retreat, but I was mistaken—it was a feint. Something from behind me tore a channel across my back. The pain was largely numbed by the dead nerves that had fallen victim to the previous attack, but this newest transgression created a sensation more terrible than riven flesh. I felt a coldness—of mind and imagination—as if all the dreams that had ever been had suddenly died of an endless winter. I could feel the empty stare of sightless eyes crawling across my spirit, the sour of failed dreams rotting from within hollow skulls, the sterile collective indifference of the entire world—all soldered together to form a solid, breathless void. I fell to my knees.

I turned to see what had destroyed me and beheld a bloodied white claw retreating behind the wall of dead trees. The White Gaia had touched me, drawn my blood, felled me. I was sick beyond flesh and bone and blood and bile—she had deadened the rushing pulse of my soul. I watched the Eater of Idols lick my blood from its mother's hooked fingertips. I saw the creature change, assuming a shape not unlike a man's, but decorated with the darkest ornaments—horns and fangs and glowering eyes, dank with the perspiration of fresh rot. Most terrible of all, it bore a striking, if distorted, likeness to me.

Her last words to me were spoken upon winds colder than conscience. "Let wither the Shepherd's dogs, for the Game is coming to an end. And it was you, dear Vincent, who made it all possible."

As I tumbled into death, I passed the dreams of my fellow hunters and heard the din of their dying. I saw the Eater of Idols, red with the blood of Wolves, tearing, rending, killing—clutched in his hand, a kill list filled with the names of every surviving member of the Game. I saw the names drenched in blood, crossed-out, destroyed. I saw the Prince of the Deadworld wading through crowds of wincing shadows, seeking out his prey, roaring over the ruined bodies of hunters, Wolves, and artists. I saw months fall into the span of seconds, each compressed day that passed only a momentary glimpse into the slaughter I had fathered, the death I had loosed, the dreams I had failed.

I saw my family looking down at me, cursing me for a failure, dying as surely as I was. My sisters' smiles had dimmed to cold, unliving steel. My father's eyes filled with impotent rage, his laughter frozen into silence.

I had almost passed into that final darkness when suddenly, my mother's hand reached out for me. I grasped at it with all the hope of a lost child, but I was too slow. Death had me by the bones of my last breath, and it would not relent its grip.

My mother wept. "You have failed me, Vincent. Yet I wish you all the peace of the dead. May you sleep soundly, my poor, twilit prince."

I tried to ask for her forgiveness, but emptiness had replaced my voice. I had come so close to freeing us all, so close!

Blackness—inert and endless—piled atop me, became me, and I joined the great company of dead, defeated wolves.

CHAPTER EIGHTEEN

Entry 1

I no longer determine time by clocks or available light. My new world is now completely oriented by the comings and goings of a single sinister man. I don't know his real name. I'm not sure that knowing it would do me a bit of good, anyway. I'm not one hundred percent certain the guy's even human. But he's definitely one of those Noctu-psychotics—persons affected by a Post-Darkness insanity that has taken them almost completely out of the human category. Let me assure you, this fella is as far from your Average Joe as it gets. Not to mention, he's also one of the nastiest serial killers you've likely never heard about.

He assures me he's over one hundred years old, and that he lived through the original Wasting House Tragedy—by the way, he doesn't look a day over thirty-five. He doesn't look like much of anything really, just an ordinary guy, maybe a tad on the thin side. *Lean* might be a better word for him, now that I think about it. He's got a predatory look to him.

While he looks innocuous enough, he completely switches gears when he's on the hunt. On those occasions, he wears a ragged moth-eaten suit, something you'd expect to find hanging off the bones of a late-eighteenth-century corpse. He also balances this shabby stovepipe hat on his head, which adds six inches or so to his height. He insists the entire outfit was made for him by a "wildly talented tailor of yore," and it's held together by "more than string and skill." To counterbalance the ragamuffin look of his clothing, he perches these tiny octagonal, black-tinted eyeglasses on the tip of his nose. Taken all together, he looks like something straight out of a goddamned nightmare, which is likely the vibe he's shooting for, I'm sure.

Beyond all the oddities I already mentioned, he claims to have been called upon to play some sort of game. He generally refers to it as the Great Bloody Wolf Hunt, a slaughter-sport that pits serial killers against one another. I must admit, that is something I'd pay damn good money to watch, which is precisely where I come in. You see, Mr. Grey—that's what he calls himself—can no longer waste his mind and hands on the "pedestrian, although wonderful, craft of writing," as he must dedicate the sum of his dexterity and concentration to The Great Bloody Wolf Hunt. So, someone's got to keep his journals up to date—lucky me.

I won't bother giving you my name—Mr. Grey wouldn't have it, anyway. Besides, I'm not much of anyone really, which I'm sure is part of the reason Mr. Grey nabbed me. There's no wife or kids to worry about me, no close friends to get concerned and go poking around looking for me. I'm just a chubby loner who writes books that few people read. I'm not much of a novelist, but I've managed to get a few published, shitty though they are. Mostly, I write (bad) short fiction. And I certainly regret writing the short story "Songs to Scream By." That's the one that caught Mr. Grey's eye. Shortly after abducting me, he explained I was the only writer he'd ever read who could "conjure the true failure of the spirit and its many and inevitable deaths." I took it as a compliment. I think.

Anyway, Mr. Grey's been having me record his thoughts and exploits in this big beautiful journal of his. Good Christ, the thing's even got handmade vellum pages. As a writer, I've got to award him some points for that. Up to the time he stole me away, he'd been keeping his own notes, and I was curious to know where he kept his other journals. Our conversations are generally pretty free-flowing and personal, so I wasn't too frightened to ask. He actually seemed glad I'd taken an interest in him, and offered to take me to see the books, when time and circumstance allowed, of course. It wasn't long after when he whisked me off to a small farmhouse in the country, way back in the sticks. In the attic of the rickety old place, he showed me stacks and stacks of fancy journals—just like the one he gave me to use. Christ, there must have been thousands of them. After thumbing through a bunch while he cheerfully looked on, I began to seriously consider what he'd said about his age. And that wasn't his only claim that began to wash with me.

Now, God knows how many of what sort of people he's killed since I've known him, but I'm positive that at least some of them were in fact serial killers. One of the heads he brought home was a dead ringer—pun intended—of the killer called Quiet Quentin, a little person. Not long after that, he brought home the mostly intact corpse of Paul Stillwater, the Gobb's Town Goblin. I'm absolutely convinced it was the Goblin, as the cops later found and identified the carcass we left behind. There are a few more noteworthy stiffs, but I'll not get into those just yet. For now, I just want to assure you that some of his body count really did come from genuine, honest-to-goodness killers.

As for his motive for killing, I have no idea what the hell drives him. No idea, that is, save for the insane gibberish he's let slip from time to time. He appears to believe that killing is his job—his duty, more like—handed down to him from way back, something like 150 years ago, by some anomalous force he's yet to properly comprehend. He says he must kill and dismember so as to "empower the next tides of change," and that he's got to "fill the pot with broth, which others are responsible for stirring and cooking." I don't exactly know what all that means, but I've a feeling he's talking about bringing about a second Great Darkness.

I don't have to tell you, dear reader, that the very idea of wanting to kick off another Darkness is flatly insane.

Well, I'd better close up shop for the night—I can hear him on the stairs outside. He's likely dragging a body with him. That's been his routine for the last few months, whenever he comes home this late. It's likely the corpse of one of his Great Bloody Wolves.

Entry 2

Well, that sure was a long session. Generally, he's a bit more circumspect about his nighttime dalliances with death, preferring to let the reader fill in some of the blanks. Not tonight, though. I haven't really seen him like that before.

Seems Mr. Grey's been getting these strange dreams about his fellow killers, or Wolves, as he oft calls them. You see, he believes all the killers in the Great Bloody Wolf Hunt share a single, if highly compartmentalized, dream. Initially, the dreams were just so much "red static," but as the number of players lessened with each kill, the dream became more coherent. Eventually, the dream allowed the remaining killers to not only communicate with each other while they slept, but even, if they had a mind to, mosey into one another's dreams.

Recently, there's been some drastic changes to the Game. Specifically, a major player just got himself clipped, but not by another player—by a "creature who abides the spaces beyond the Game, within a white wasteland of plastic bones and solid souls." Worse still, this outsider has begun murdering the other murderers. All of this was the gist of Mr. Grey's most recent dream.

Oh, and it was indeed a body my captor had been dragging behind him when last I wrote. You might recall that shit-bird a few years back who filled up his victims' emptied corpses with the ashes of cremated children. Well, it was that guy. Gordon Flint was his name. At least, that's what his driver's license said. After Mr. Grey took what he wanted from the body—more on that in just a bit—we left the ruined thing behind, bobbing in the Arkansas mud. As I said, the corpse has since been identified by the cops, so there's your proof in the pudding, folks! But Gordon didn't feature too largely in tonight's debriefing, so it's best I move on.

The most important part of tonight's transcription was that at some point during Mr. Grey's clash with Flint, something showed up and interrupted the showdown—a monstrous creature that "had the appearance of borrowing from hell its least attractive characteristics." The monster's presence forced the two adversaries into an awkward alliance—to fight it off so they could get back to fighting each other.

Unfortunately for Mr. Flint, the creature proved too much for even their combined strength, and Mr. Grey ended up dragging what was left of him back to the house. As for Mr. Grey's performance in the brawl, I can only assume it was good enough to get him the hell out of Dodge while the getting was good. Though I have to admit, it's a little hard to think of my abductor as an underdog in any fight.

Now, on more than one occasion, I've seen hints of what Mr. Grey gets up to when he's on the hunt, and I can tell you it's some dark and dangerous business, indeed. One horrible rainy night, while we were hiding out in an old abandoned candy factory, I got to see one of my keeper's infamous Wolves up close and far too personal. The guy just seemed to melt out of the shadows, dripping with all these clinking hooks and chains, and wearing the most bizarre mask you can imagine—at least, I hope it was a mask. Before I knew it, the thing had spread out his chains all across the ceiling and walls like some goddamned metal spiderweb. He sprang into the middle of the web and crouched down into the darkness of the room. What I hadn't noticed was that I'd been attached to the web by means of a hook that'd slid through the palm of my hand. Didn't even feel it, at first. Mr. Grey later told me the killer laced his hooks with some kind of chemical agent that dulled nerve endings, so the victims wouldn't know they'd been snagged. Anyway, I started to scream, which I suppose was the point—to lure Mr. Grey into a trap.

My kidnapper, whether or not he's a century old, is an uncommonly wise fella, and had already prepared for the killer. I was the bait, you see—to lure the killer into thinking I'd be good bait for luring Mr. Grey, if you can follow all that. Mind you, before that point, I'd never seen my captor participate in The Great Bloody Wolf Hunt, and I was a little worried about his chances against the web-casting freak. I had nothing to fear, it turns out. Mr. Grey dealt with the other killer handily, jumping onto the chain-link web, and like some berserker gymnast, kicking and slashing his way to a gory victory.

I only mention all of this to introduce you, dear reader, to another of Mr. Grey's weird claims—his "itinerary." Apparently, every killer in the Great Bloody Wolf Hunt is given an old, yellowed list—how they come by them, I've no idea—on which is printed the names of the killers they're responsible for murdering. I know this because after the chain and hook guy was dead, Mr. Grey slid a piece of paper out from the corpse's inside pocket. Then, while he perused the names on the paper, he explained to me what he was doing. He said, "Every list marks a Wolf by his God-given name, which I use to track my prey. And every Wolf I bring to ground, their names I shall inherit, until no Wolves are left and the Dire Shepherd stands before me, bearing a red prize." And that's just what he did—copied the names from the other killer's list onto his own. That's how I know the real names of the killers he dispatches—his itinerary.

All of this comes to bear in my most recent rap session with Mr. Grey. Apparently, while he and Mr. Flint were battling the creature, Mr. Grey caught sight of a piece of paper tucked into the beast's back pocket. After some fancy and violent finagling, my captor managed to grab hold of it, scanning it for a brief second before the creature snatched it back. My kidnapper then informed me that "it was a complete list, from A to Z, of every Wolf left in the contest, written in the rigid script of a corpse, the neatest of lines crossing out the names of the dead." Among the other unusual features of the monster's itinerary, there lurked a stark departure from any murderer's catalogue he'd ever seen before—there was one name which wasn't crossed off, but only had a question mark next to it. He only glimpsed the first name. Vincent.

Entry 3

My captor has taken to calling me by a new title, and I have to admit, I really like it—the Grey Scribe. I feel it somewhat dignifies an otherwise undignified station, as well as an otherwise undignified person.

Today I'm writing to you from the top of a ruined church, balanced quite precariously between two jutting turrets. Mr. Grey has insisted that I accompany him on his newest dalliance with death. I'm none too thrilled to be here, but I must confess, the view is quite amazing. The wind up here feels like God's breath whispering across my body, the Lord's face just barely discernible within the gathering darkness, slowly disappearing behind the herd of clouds presently lumbering overhead. I forget too often—especially of late—that I'm a writer, if not a particularly good one. Yet even I prove capable of a few decent sentences, now and then, and this place seems to be facilitating their creation.

My owner explained to me—earlier this morning, while I made him eggs and toast—that there's been much ado about this new player in the Game, having killed quite a number of its participants. "The contest itself has become a hunted thing, and each Wolf that falls to the interloper will bring the dream closer to waking. This cannot be allowed. But while the beast has all our names, we know nothing of it. Some of us, those who are disposed to speak, have suggested hunting it together. You must bear witness to this, for the Wolves shall become a great ravening pack, and we shall taste the blood of this trespasser."

The upshot of such terrible news is that I'm secreted away on this roof while Mr. Grey meets with some of his would-be victims—and quite possibly, the killer that will finally clip him. Provided the monster doesn't rip him to pieces first, of course.

I'm not sure how I'd feel about that, Mr. Grey getting himself murdered. He's a decent enough guy. He lets me stay up late, eat all the junk food I want, he even buys me gifts. Why, just last week he bought me an antique writing set—it even came with a fancy-ass quill pen. But, like most things my captor does, there was purpose behind his actions.

"Your penmanship often appears like squirming insects curling and sprawling about the fine pages I've provided you to write upon. This just won't do, I'm afraid. You see, writing is the art of trapping thoughts on paper—laying them to rest, if you will. The shape of a letter can reveal much about the writer, even beyond the content of his words. You have the fine job of preserving my thoughts, and I should not want to give the impression that I would take on the services of an indelicate penman. So, I've gifted you with this calligraphy set in the hopes of improving your ability to properly lay my thoughts within their delicate white graves."

I was never one for cursive writing, let alone calligraphy, but what the hell, right? I gave it a shot, and it turns out I'm not too bad at it. I like it, in fact. Mr. Grey was right, the shape and style of the handwritten word lends a distinct sophistication to the content being written, even transposing that elegance to the writer's thoughts themselves. Pretty cool, don't you think?

I can see Mr. Grey down there in the courtyard, his cane-sword gripped casually in his left hand. He lit a small fire just outside the broken entrance to the church, to signal his location. Not a great move if you ask me, but he seems to know what he's doing. This gathering was arranged entirely within the collective dream the killers all share, so I'm curious if anyone shows. If someone does pop up, it'll be just one more crack in the foundation of my sanity, such as it is.

Yup, here comes someone. They're wrapped in a weird-looking cloak, almost looks like a single ragged batwing. The guy's tall, but thin as a needle. His movements are sharp—controlled and quick. He and Mr. Grey are talking, now. Whoops! It's not a guy at all. *She* just took down her hood, and I can see black hair flowing ephemeral, almost weightlessly, like gobs of spiderwebs. I can smell her perfume (from way the fuck up here?). Wow, that perfume. I bet she's a knock-out for sure.

Here comes someone else. Wait just a minute, their shadow's all wrong. It's moving against the firelight! It's coming up the goddamn wall—

Ok, I'm back. Almost dropped my damn journal. Mr. Grey appears to have asked the thing to knock its shit off. I don't know what the hell it is, but I'd wager it isn't human. It keeps fading in and out, and . . . yeah, it keeps changing in height as well. About the only constant is its mask—a golden goblin's face, caught somewhere between a leer and a smirk.

A big guy just showed up. He seems to have just one arm, the left one, and it's huge. From what I can see, it's wrapped in all kinds of weird tattoos. He's pointing at me. How do they all know I'm up here? Am I glowing, or something? These Noctu-psychotics and their weird-ass senses, I'm telling you.

They've been talking for a while, now. The fire's all but smoking ash, and my back is killing me. Mr. Grey told me to stay up here just in case, but they all seem to know I'm here, and it doesn't look like anything's going to happen tonight. I think I'll head down.

My hands were shaking too much to capture anything in real-time, so I'll have to give you the recap. Something came howling through the church, casting aside stone and concrete like they were nothing. I'd just cleared the staircase when the monster exploded through the wall. The sound it made was like all the shrieks in the world had been bundled together into one horrible, deafening sound.

When it burst outside, it stepped on what was left of the fire, shooting flames into the air. The strangely rejuvenated fire tossed an orange glow upon the trees outlining the boundaries of the courtyard. All the Wolves save one were blown backwards by the explosive debris. The big guy with the huge left arm stood his ground, batting aside a huge chunk of stone as easily as the monster had knocked it free. The two collided with each other, and I swear I felt a shockwave rattle my bones. The monster crashed a wicked fist down upon Lefty, who to his credit, didn't break into fucking pieces. Lefty just cranked back that gigantic arm of his and threw a terrific haymaker into the creature's jaw. He practically spun the thing in a complete circle. Despite the ungodly wallop it took, the creature was undeterred, hammer-fisting Lefty to his knees.

As the two grappled, the monster was suddenly dragged backwards by its shadow. It was the golden goblin, reaching out from the darkness. The masked shadow flung the creature through a huge stone column of the church, but no sooner had the creature been buried in stone than it exploded free.

If I understood the game plan, beyond simply joining forces, the Wolves were combining their Red Dreams—what Mr. Grey refer to as Blood Holidays. These dreams were some sort of suspension of the laws of nature that granted them exceptional abilities when they were near one another. With four of them joined together, surely they outmatched the monster.

Next came my captor, slicing through the darkness, blade outstretched. He caught the monster in the chest, plunging the blade of his cane-sword deep into the beast's heart. Yet the creature seemed unfazed, and with a fierce backhand, it nearly took Mr. Grey's head off.

Before the creature had fully recovered from my master's attack, the woman with spiderwebs for hair appeared behind the beast, burying her overlong fingers into the meat of the thing's back, tugging at its spine. The creature howled in pain, thrashing wildly at its tormentor. The strange woman did not relent, only reaching deeper into the demon's back as if trying to climb inside its body.

Lefty was back up. He cranked the monster across the face, blasting its teeth all over the courtyard, several embedding themselves like bullets into a nearby stone wall. I have no shame in saying I had to check my shorts.

Mr. Grey also returned, busying himself at the task of slicing through the tendons of the monster's legs, causing it to slowly collapse to its knees. I could see the golden goblin's shadow holding tightly the beast's flailing arms, allowing the other killers to pile onto their adversary without significant resistance.

All was going well, and the beast seemed near defeat when I noticed the trees around the courtyard turning white and dead. For a fleeting moment, I thought I caught sight of a giant shadow, bloated and female, stooping behind the tree line. Then, the lightning fell like rain, and four screams chased the thunder.

The hole in the sky continued to pour out a sea of lightning, surging and splashing across the battlefield, reducing much of the surrounding forest to a smoking landscape of blackened matchsticks. The thunder was unbearable—a standing ovation of gods bringing together mountainous hands. My head was ready to crack open and spill out its brains for want of silence, when the world went dead and dark. My first thought was that I'd gone deaf and blind, but I could make out the sound of wind scavenging the soot as hungrily as a pack of jackals, and I could see blurred figures scattered about the smoking ground. Mr. Grey was among the blackened forms.

If anything justified the rumors of their superhuman fortitude, it was that the four Noctu-psychotics still drew breath, albeit with difficulty. Not surprisingly, Lefty was the first to his feet, gritting sizzling teeth and exhaling smoke. I thought of a doomed bull refusing to fall to the matador's bloody blade.

My eyes were still adjusting to the renewed darkness when Lefty seemed to take a shot from a cannon, throwing him from the blackened earth. Their giant, rampaging adversary was up and swinging, apparently untouched by the lightning. It sent Lefty flying, his body slapping against the side of the stone church like a wet side of beef. The bull finally fell, seemingly disinclined to rise again.

The Goblin rose from the smoldering ground, drifting upwards and vanishing in the same breath. Smart guy, that one.

Spiderlocks and Mr. Grey were side by side, a united front as the monster lunged. The two killers parted, allowing the creature to pass between them. They turned in tandem, laying blades and sharpened bone into the passing behemoth, teasing out another shriek from the killer of killers. Unfortunately, the creature's speed belied its size, as it quickly pivoted, punting Mr. Grey into a smoldering pine tree. My master coughed blood, collapsing in a heap.

Spiderlocks was back atop the creature, her clawed hands yet again chasing the thing's spine. In an instant, the monster barreled toward the remaining walls of the church. Just prior to impact, it spun, forcing the Spider to take the brunt of the impact. She splattered, a dragonfly on a highway windshield.

I noticed Mr. Grey struggling to his feet again. I was two-minded about his efforts. I certainly wanted to reclaim my freedom—to be all alone to write my shitty, shitty books—but I was also eager to see my captor win his contest, if only to witness the results.

At some point, I became aware of a strange bit of whispering wind, scraping dead leaves across the concrete floor of the church. It came from the opposite direction as the scavenger breeze I'd first detected, post-lightning. It bore the distinct scent of autumn and seemed possessed of a relaxing lightness, a playfulness that mocked the death spilling out around me. Someone whispered into my ear, "To be all triangles and crooked smiles, candle-wax betwixt your ears, little lamps of fire that hop and skip . . . fake faces over masks over veils . . . how many masks deep are your clicking cogs, little Peeping Tom?" I froze. The whisperer was crouched beside me. I could smell Halloween on his breath—candy, cold rain, dead leaves. I knew precisely who was whispering to me.

Jack Lantern continued, purring, "It's almost time for us to bury all the machines, little Tommy Peeper. And now, out of the blue, comes one who would break all our shovels. Can't have that, can we? But don't you worry, I'll have him smiling through rows of rectangles in no time." Then he was gone—vanished from my side, brown leaves spinning in his stead.

In the next moment, Jack was standing among a collection of smoking sprigs, staring up at the lumbering monster. He wore a crude jack-o'-lantern mask, and a ripped-up black scarf wrapped around his neck, flapping in the stolen September breeze. The Autumn City Madman was unusually tall, thin, and cheerful, giggling under that ridiculous mask. As he whipped out two huge carving knives, I knew he was going straight to work.

The guy moved so fast it was hard to keep track of all his slashing, cleaving, and leaping. Honestly, he was just a marvel to watch. I found my mouth agape more than a few times. The monster swung and kicked and roared, but never once connected.

The once killer of killers was clearly getting killed by Jack, weakening second by second, slash by stab. Yet just as before, when the monster began to lose, the strange dead trees began to sway. Something fat and monstrous moved behind them, the sky turned green, and I knew it was about to rain lightning again. Or was it? Just when the sky looked like it might crack open, the fall breeze cranked up to a maelstrom, roaring out of the north like a goddamned hurricane. It was as if the opposing elemental powers were joining the fray alongside their favorite killers, trying to tilt the scales.

Neither combatant seemed particularly affected by the warring elements exploding around them, however, as Jack continued to teach the monster more lessons than it cared to learn. Somewhere within that howling storm, the church began to come down around me. I barely managed to get out the back, as the sky fell bright and blazing and the wind became a living, killing thing. I ran and ran, never looking back.

After a few days of hiding out, I returned to my home. It was just as I left it—dull and empty. I waited weeks for Mr. Grey to show, but he never did.

After about six months, I decided to travel into the country—to a very specific and fascinating attic—to see if Mr. Grey had removed his journals. He hadn't. I never saw him again, but I did read of a severed head that turned up on a random porch, carved to look like a jack-o'-lantern— triangles for eyes and a scooped-out skull filled with candy, adorned with a very particular stovepipe hat. Jack Lantern had claimed another victim. No one knew who the head belonged to. I'm sure no one ever will—except me.

My books are selling like hotcakes now. Winning awards, even. There's no doubt about it—*The Tales of Ebenezer The Immortal* are a hit. I'll never have to worry about running out of ideas, either. I've got over a hundred years of material to draw from.

CHAPTER NINETEEN

Happy Halloween, Family Man! Now, I'm sure I could find your real name somewhere in this journal of yours, but rooting through your belongings would be the height of bad manners. I'm not a rude person, despite what you may have heard. By the way, you gave me quite a shot back there, right in the ol' breadbasket, you did. Ouch! Those big scary claws of yours are quite sharp—sharp and cold as the wind that blows across the clockwork stars, all wound up and glowing. You ever look at the stars when you're asleep? I do. I see little strings of glittering silk connecting them all together, making a web. And I see a big funny monster grinning out from the deepest part of that web. But like all those damn things, I can see the winding key on its back, turning and turning and turning. Just another machine in need of skin, I guess.

Anyway, seems I've let myself ramble on. I like it when I ramble, though. It's genuine, unconscious—organic. Or maybe, just maybe, that's when the machines take over. When you just stop thinking and act. Ha! Still I ramble.

While I'd love for the two of us to sit around like two monsters spinning bloody yarns, we really should discuss a few things, don't you think? We should chat about this little game we've been forced to play. I'm pretty sure I'm starting to get the gist of things. But unlike me, you've chosen to pretend you don't know what the game's all about. You do know though, and I'm afraid I've dawned upon the reason why you've chosen to ignore it. Yet it can't happen that way, it ought not. This one can't fit into your hand. You saw the Wolves, just like I did.

It brought us all together. It means to turn us all into lovely little stepping-stones, to ascend and strut out of its old, dusty darkness—but only one of us will be the door. There's only a handful of Wolves left, now. Just you and me and a few others, that's it. No more stygian art and no more happy Halloweens. Is that what you really want? Or do you really, really want to be an artist from another world?

Sure, this world is just a dull face, but you and I are masks. Masks are so much more fun than faces, and Halloween is the biggest, funnest mask of all. I mean to fit it over the empty-eyed face of the whole wide world before I'm done. You can't honestly want me to stop, can you? The real world has to be masked—it's more bearable that way. Everyone will have so much more fun, you'll see. And yes, our art is death, but it's not FOR death—it's just for us. Just for fun. Masks are no good without faces. What will happen when you run out of faces? Then all you'll be is another empty-eyed face, and what fun is that?

There are no living dreams, my friend. Dreams are simply the hopelessly scared pictures in our heads, and all we can do is hold them up in front of this ugly world, blocking it out, stuffing our mind with wishful thinking. You see, we're all caged little children, used and then discarded. Or worse, we think the machines are family. But in truth, we're just the victims of horribly mean things.

Speaking of mean things, that fine and wondrous force that's been driving us to kill each other is just some long-forgotten, horrible engineer of our mechanical world. That's all it could be. No doubt, while it was busy raising this cold mechanical playground, it must have accidentally gotten itself buried under the gears and guts of its own garden. If you free it, it will only adjust the settings. It won't really change anything. The only way for us all to be happy is to cover up the whole heartless world. I have to hide it behind the endless Halloween, that way all we will ever see is masks, masks all the way down to the mindless turning cogs.

As I write this, I can't help but be wary of those family members of yours, lying only a few feet beneath me in the churning waters of this stream. They must be awfully upset about your newest incarnation, which would appear to have—by necessity, I'm sure—excluded them from your company. And that axe, oh my! Its anger seems to have leaked out into the world, roiling the water white and boiling hot. I wish I had a family like yours, all loyal and lusting to disturb the world on my behalf. That's not to say I don't have friends who look out for me, because I've a few here and there. You'll meet them when the time comes, I'm sure.

I hope you don't mind how personal things have become here, but I've been a very careful student of your dreams. They have a certain sound to them—if you listen carefully, you can hear the din of terrible secrets, tolling somber and gray. What strange and splendid things have been done to you . . .

Hollow Day is right around the corner, Family Man. Soon the machines will celebrate their ascendency by wearing our skins, sleeping in our beds, drinking our coffee, and eating our lunches. They will become us and no one will be the wiser. Wind-ups all over the world turning for no reason but to turn. That's why I had to come—to take the machine out of you. I couldn't let the engineer wipe out the game before I'd figured out how to properly win it, if winning is even the right thing to do. Although, I do find it strange that the machines would fight amongst themselves in such a way. Perhaps it's a metagame, where the engineers themselves seek each other's demise, to wrest the master machine from one kind of programming in order to impose another. Anyway, I'm fairly certain the machine within you is now dying, as I had quite the conversation with it. No doubt, once it's completely dead and you return to some semblance of yourself, you'll be coming back this way for your family and this journal. While I'd love to be here when you return, I can already hear the quiet patter of careful feet—another Wolf who drew my name. Poor, poor beast.

***

Through blank silences, twilights stuffed with plastic light, beyond nights falling grey and dead—I climbed. It was not art or dream or darkness that brought me out from the pit of the world. It was blood.

I had been focused to primal dimensions, I had whet upon appetites that caused space itself to open its swirling maw, devouring stars, gnawing at the bones of creation. I was the moment of the kill, the last light before death. And I was coming for him—the Eater of Idols.

Fire and shadow spoke me back to life, and I stood before the thing that had once, through treachery, cast me down. My enemy had been injured, its blood spilled. I had been conjured back to life through the magic of its dying. But I would not spoil my victory with even the slightest taste of advantage. My teeth tore open the flesh of my arm, and I fed the flagging beast a thick stream of my blood. The son of the White Queen fell upon the ground, devouring my offering where it fell, reveling in the strength I had allowed it to recapture.

I smiled when the demon rose up before me—renewed, confident, doomed.

My family raged from the churning waters nearby. My father roared for me to take him up, his hunger burning maniacal and bloody. With a single look, I quieted him. He knew immediately—this fight was mine and mine alone. By my bare hands, I would unwrap this creature's bones, feast on its darkness, feel the gristle of its soul snap and pop between my teeth.

The Mother of the Dead looked on from behind her copse of whited trees, her empty eyes showing wild and worried, my killing smile butchering her confidence in bestial sons and the diablerie of wicked mothers.

The Eater of Idols howled as once it had when we first met, and as before—it charged. But unlike our last contest, I did not move. We collided like a thunderclap, muscles tearing and bones creaking, hands threaded in massive knots. The creature should have overcome me easily, given its immense size and supernatural pedigree. But I would not allow it. I crushed its giant hands like eggshells underfoot, the corded muscles of its claws becoming viscous beneath my grasp, its bones grinding to dust. I inhaled the Eater's screams as they escaped its mouth and spat them back in its face. I pulled the monster closer, whispering beneath the din of its pain, "Once I've consumed you, I will piss what's left of your soul into a hole in the ground. This I promise you, Usurper." My grin transformed into flashing jaws as I ripped out the creature's lashing tongue and swallowed it into my guts. I could feel it convulse at its first taste of my stomach's bitter acids. The Eater of Idols struggled to free itself from my grip, but I only put it to its knees, laughing as thunderously as ever my father had.

Just beyond the glen, straddling the lines that marked the boundaries of worlds, I sensed another presence—cold and lean and endless. The Shepherd of Wolves was with me. He had come with purpose. Here was vengeance.

Sickly yellow clouds began to wheel overhead, and the air began to sour into a graveyard mist. Forks of lightning shot from gathering storm clouds as a worried mother tried to save her lamb from the wolves.

Thunder smashed down upon my mirth, failing to quell the flood of laughter that overflowed me. Out of sheer desperation, the Eater lunged at me, its gaping maw trying to engulf my entire head. I thrust the monster's own arm deep into its mouth, my laughter dancing with the fury of the storm. I began to roar as I ripped the arm fully from its socket, forcing the massive limb further down its throat.

The Eater of Idols shuddered as it died, an earthquake in my arms. The storm faded with the hopes of a broken mother.

With the eyes of the two gods upon me, I gathered my family. My father was quiet to the touch, having exhausted his volcanic rage through me. His steel was cold, proud. My sisters glittered in the moonlight, smiles like songs. They sang my praises, and I nearly cried at the sight of them.

The Shepherd had been with me, preserved me from the storm, made me into his vengeance—but it all meant nothing to me. In truth, I was no Wolf, only an artist in love with a dream. A dream worth killing for, again and again. I would slay the Shepherd himself and rip the dreams from his blackened guts if I thought them imprisoned there. Yet, if winning his game meant seeing dreams past the threshold, then I would win. Tonight, I became stronger for having died. My chances were improving all the time.

I turned to the fading presence behind the dead white trees, where sallow eyes hung like skinned fruits, naked and gathering flies. "A mother is God in the eyes of a child," I said, spitting upon the crumpled corpse of her rotting son.

The night was calling to me. I slipped into the shadows as my extended family welcomed me back.

It was horrible, coming back to the Deadworld. It wasn't merely that I'd been exposed to the utter cancelation of dream, washed away beneath a wave of boiling black pavement. Or that I'd been made solid and soulless, an idle statue abandoned to a forgotten basement. It was the thoroughly sickening revelation upon my return that I was grateful for having been renewed within the lands of the dead. I was relieved to see the acrid smoke of industry, the grey pitch of ash blowing across eons, the unchanging ugliness. The realization nearly killed me all over again.

I was fortunate, however, that my next destination was one of the more dream-haunted locations of the world, playing to the calm timbre of forfeited confidences in solidity and sanity. Willard, a place of glittering madness, a jewel tucked into the throat of a corpse. It would be my temporary reprieve, and hopefully, my redemption.

Cutting in half my swelling disgust at my reincarnation was the most recent entry into my journal, the words of my greatest adversary—Jack Lantern. There was a guiding light to his logic, if only the dim foxfire of a darkened swamp, doubtful and misleading. But at the very least, his paradigm was cogent and internally consistent, if ultimately incorrect—despite the alleged scrutiny leveled at my exposed dreams. There was value in delusion, especially if it should have absolutely no part in logic or material truth—a waking dream in many respects.

The Soul Carver had peered too long into the eyes of the White Mother, convincing himself of the bottomlessness of her kingdom, that only masks could make the world suitable for living. I am not a mask, Jack—I am fire. I will set this corpse-world aflame upon the pyre of my art, or I will die trying, very likely at the glimmering edges of your own exquisite knives.

But first, there was the wonderful Mister Hide, that connoisseur of swapped skins, reflector of inner truths via the display of their more honest exteriors. Again, and to import a fraction of my criticism of poor Jack Lantern—there is little use for truth in graveyards. The only truths that lurk there consist of the certainty of death and the displacement of dream. All else, as they say, is mere window dressing. Even if that dressing were made from the most skilled fashioning of once-living tissue.

Despite a certain contempt of self, I was grateful for having dealt a decisive blow against the Mistress of Corpses, felling her miserable son. But there was much more work to be done before I could completely smother her in dream. And I would be a fool to count Mister Hide among the tombstones.

The road to Willard was a long one, and nicely decorated. Shade trees lined the trampled paths that looped around thick stands of thorns, and the sun fell in honeyed pools which made the day mercifully tolerable. Granted, the Deadworld expresses no pure, unfiltered beauty, yet the woods—these woods in particular—hung close to bygone dreams, for reasons I would not care to fathom for fear of spoiling their secrets.

I'd forged my bones from mystery, and so the suspense of my journey was especially revitalizing, growing wonder as potent as the hemlock I crushed underfoot. I made stops, of course, at places hewn from the shrouded wisdom of the Darkness, when men and woman existed without pretense or pride—our great meditation of the shadow within us all.

One location was especially handsome, shaped as much from forbidden imagination as from stone—The Grey Crowd. Unfortunately, due to society's custom of burying the dead, the skins that once dressed the thousands of limestone statues were removed and placed into the earth. But even without their clothing, the statues still lurched purposelessly through the woods, which I took as a criticism of life before the Darkness—rock-solid souls weighting down dead skins, men and women stumbling through the world like listless corpses. Despite the statues' current state of undress, I was glad to know that a tradition had sprung up shortly after the close of the Darkness. On the eve of that grand day's anniversary, the statues had been found year after year once again repossessed of their skins, if only those of animals. And despite certain constabulary efforts to quell the practice of this new ritual, it had persisted. There was once an idea to demolish the statues, ridding the world of their biting reproach once and for all. But when the skins of those persons most vocal about supporting the effort were found decorating a number of the grey lurchers, the public seemed to lose all interest in the proposal.

It took my chance meeting with the shambling figures to reflect a moment on my next adversary, to truly appreciate his art for what it was. While I found the rearrangement of skins to be a rather wasted enterprise, as Hide's efforts seemed less about revealing truth than merely fine-tuning it, I began to see the dream in it. The Skin Switcher's vision wasn't necessarily expressed within his product, but rather through his process. It was my opponent's ability to reshape the humors of nature to match his dreams that truly intoned the man's creative power—a force that stitched morality to flesh, simultaneously cultivating the lies and truths of his subjects. In a way, the giant killer was like myself, if only on the basic level of intent. We both would see the world dressed in our dreams—but that was as far as the comparison went. While his vision was fulfilled by sculpting flesh to reflect scruples, my art was a tireless invocation of dream—to unmake facts—moral or otherwise—and replace them with the seamless wonder of lost worlds. So, I suppose you might distinguish our dreams by their respective extents. Mine tripped beyond the world, while Hide's remained trapped within it. Now, I'm certainly not fond of the qualification of dreams, but I must admit—some dreams are better than others.

Apart from the boundaries of his vision, the products of Mister Hide's process were marvels to behold, and would dignify any nightmare in which you might encounter them. It was perhaps the intrinsic limitations of his calling that allowed for Hide to so completely encompass its nuances and elevate its character, lifting the art of skin-swapping to the level of visual philosophy. Skin should be so lucky as to come under his knife.

Again, and likely not for the last time, the Shepherd's game would force me to destroy a kindred spirit, and my heart was heavy for it. But wolves must be wolves—even those who would rather be artists.

It had been too long since I had the opportunity to put on my dreams. It was like slipping into a brook at the height of summer, renewing and cool. I was pleased to see that the collective dream was still in place, still populated by the players of the Shepherd's game. The dream was an almost seamless whole now, having coagulated from time and persistence and many, many deaths. I wandered careworn and filthy warrens, urban hidey holes, attics heaped with old bones, and extravagant murder chambers fit for mad kings. I sensed many eyes upon me, peering out from secret killing places. I wondered if any of them belonged to a certain pumpkin-faced killer.

Although the dream had been designed for the Shepherd's hungry flock, it had clearly attracted the dreams of other killers, who for whatever reason had not been invited to play. I watched the pitchy waters of an ancient lake retreat behind a toothsome shoreline, where were stacked the blazing forms of countless dead—all of which had briefly come to know the wicked hands of the killer known only as Pyre.

I even made the mistake of stumbling into a very singular dream filled with dying screams and frenetic, pain-inducing machines, all of them housed within a gigantic inhabitable torture chamber—or Tortuary, to those familiar with the legend of Agatha Pain. I saw her staring back at me from the blackened dream. Her wickedly hooked and bladed armor, her steel gloves bristling like a thicket of knives—she was a true vision. She was indeed a Wolf in the Shepherd's Game. In fact, her dream was a dismal recollection of what she had done to the last Wolf on her list. He was bound and lowered into a glass tank of slow-acting acid, naked but for an oxygen mask and goggles. She looked on as her victim felt himself slowly dissolve into an opaque broth, her smile as sharp as any worn by my sisters. When she discovered me looking on, her hungry smile lowered to a grin. She only gestured to her melting tank, as if offering me a place within it. Her dream quickly disappeared behind a rush of dark new visions, and I loosened my grip on my sleeping sisters.

I came upon the blacked-out dreams of the recently murdered Wolves still caught in a web of nightmares, mindlessly replaying forgotten shadows. I could detect a tilted silence emanating from the dead places, where a strange nullity upended simple emptiness. These dreams were not merely dead, but were something else entirely—something more than dead, perhaps.

With some searching, I found the den of the Skin Switcher. I felt him waiting somewhere among the neat lines of hanging hides, each skin a symbol for a sin that had once been hidden, but now stood revealed and properly affixed to the appropriate sinner. I entered the chamber slowly, the uninvited guest of an exclusive gallery. More so than could be appreciated outside of a dream, Hide's creations nearly shined with moral relevance—it was as if each creature had been merged together with its exact form of original sin, exemplifying and overcoming the distance between Eden and present day. Sin and skin married with such delicacy and precision as to have been combined by a song. These were not merely revelatory symbols, but whole and entire archetypes.

I knew Hide was aware of my swelling admiration for his work, smiling quietly from somewhere within a sea of stolen skins. "I came to offer my apologies for the delay," I said. "I hate to keep my appointments waiting. I hope you can see past my indiscretion, but rest assured, Mister Hide—I am coming for you soon." There was only silence in response, as I knew there would be. Yet my rudeness needed accounting for. My detour from purpose could not be interpreted as a sign of frightful hesitation. My father would not allow it.

The night was soft and kind, and I was thankful for the gentle delivery from sleep. My awareness soon seeped into my recollection. The abandoned cabin where I rested was mostly destroyed but for the single room I occupied. A modest storm moved across the sky just above me, weeping rain upon the forest. My family slept quietly beside me. I had forgotten how much I had missed them, how much the separation had hurt me. I gathered them up and departed into darkness and silence.

The city of Willard would soon be upon me, and I relished the thought of seeing it for the first time. It had come by its insanity many years prior to the Great Darkness. Some believed it was a dry run for the greater madness to come, a staging ground of sorts. Whatever the source of the city's malady, it was undeniably host to a uniquely binding madness, restraining the common sense of thousands of people—and as history had documented well, these were not idle lunatics. Not in the slightest.

There were signs my destination was not far. I began to encounter the country dwellings that prefaced the formal portions of the city, dwellings that had clearly known the ridiculous clutch and titter of madness. I saw chimney stones stacked into the shapes of great yawning mouths, exhaling thick smoke into the dull sky. They crested slightly above the treetops, and at first I took their exhaust to be a stronger vein of storm, descended low over the forest, angry and black. How those fires continued to burn with no one to tend them was just another mystery I had no intention of ruining.

I came upon a vast swath of forest that had been cleared to make way for a man-made lake, beneath which lurked monstrous shapes hewn from yet unidentified species of crystal and glass. I wondered if glassblowing facilities comprised the throats of those spewing chimney-mouths. Some of the creations broke the placid surface of the water, peeking out from the depths, blending their translucent bodies with the mist, holding ephemeral shapes as potent as any dream. Beneath the water they dwelt, meandering and serrated, nearly invisible due to their faint composition. Their silhouettes had more than once been revealed by the swirling blood of those who dared enter the water. This was Willard's infamous Lake of a Thousand Spirits. So much beauty, and I had yet to even enter the city.

CHAPTER TWENTY

Willard, a strange and abandoned place, was home to the Wasting Houses—structures wherein its entire population had once been interred for suffering from a mysterious madness. No one knows precisely—or even approximately—the cause for the madness that had drowned the city, but whatever the source, be it supernal or supernatural, its effects cannot be denied their place within the canon of the supremely strange—and the supremely wonderful.

I approached the city like a moth drawing upon the sun, foolish and fascinated. I could feel dangers seething beneath the ground like glowing coals fresh from a fire, just begging to burn. Yet I didn't—couldn't—care. Here was the truest freedom, early proof of a world tread upon by dreams.

Madness is the one darkness the light cannot kill—it screws up its face in utter defiance. It's a nightmare that survives waking, wandering upon bruised feet through the fever heat of blistering white banality. And much like old shadows, madness is often reposed within ancient places, locked up and forgotten, tended only by the wisps of ghosts and whirls of dust. However, it should be noted that madness is only considered such due to the broad consensus of the mad, each suffering equally from delusion. In their superior numbers and broken wisdom, they have concluded that their madness is the one true reality. Poor fools, all.

The place, if indeed it qualified as merely a thing with geographical specificity, slowly became a silhouette against the darkening sky. I could almost hear the din of battle unfolding between the concluding rays of the day and the mad city's refusal to be revealed by something so paltry as light. Standing so close to Willard, I could appreciate a palpable undercurrent of residual madness, sweeping those with appropriate sensitivities into the gravity of secret worlds, inviting them to take on the burden of forgotten lunatics, to convey a flourish upon the monument to madness. Yet brick and mortar was not my medium of choice, so I declined the invitation, at least for the moment. I rounded a final bend and at last, Willard came into focus.

The city was a material outline of a lunatic's thought process. It seemed desperate to capture within stone and wood the quicksilver shapes of a madman's fancy. Houses, gardens, fountains, clock towers and churches rose and fell into and around each other, forming metropolitan entities that seemed to stir—as if the momentum of insanity had yet to exhaust itself, despite the absence of the broken minds that had once called it down from the sky as truly as lightning rods.

The road I followed into the city ended at many an empty residence. The remains of kitchens, bedrooms, and living rooms punctuated the distance of my paved path as it transformed into other, more secret paths—tendrils that slithered around thickets and beneath graveyards, through black tunnels and silent crypts. Willard, to be certain, was a great sloughed-off skin that madness had once worn with such pride and glory, rendering even the sun dim by means of its terrible brilliance.

I entered the city in darkness, as was necessary from a hunter's perspective, to say nothing of that of an outré artist. It was a notoriously strange place filled with the material and quite possibly immaterial articulations of insanity—of men and women who went from raising the walls of their city to being imprisoned by them. Due to the immensity of the population of lunatics, it was determined that their mad city would become a makeshift sanitarium. Almost all those interred here, died here. It was for that very reason I resolved to make my temporary home in the bowels of an abandoned asylum, the same kind of dwelling that once suffered its insane tenants to waste away to the dry whites of their bones. I had hoped to taste a little bit of the madness that might have seeped into the crumbling walls and cracked floors, for no artist is an island—I needed my inspiration, and madness is the greatest muse of all.

I decided to sleep through the remainder of the night and start fresh the following evening. Rats sought me out during my rest, a few even curling up with me. I was thankful for their warmth. I wondered at the number of their ancestors that might have been made fat and happy on a diet of neglected insane, sleeping off their feasts in filthy nests lined with the bones of the mad. Upon waking, I even ate one of my small sleeping companions, so as to share in the human darkness that may have once nourished its family line. After finishing my tiny meal, I rose in search of grander prey.

As I stalked the city, I encountered a great Wasting House that rose and stretched far beyond the scope of any other building I had encountered. It looked more like a castle fit for the king of the mad, for the architectural embellishments affected to its construction made me doubt the completeness of its location within this world. The structure, like all art, was an enemy of solid reality—it seemed to shiver beneath the normalizing dullness of the common sky that crushed in around its silhouette, trying to deny its otherworldly pedigree.

I passed beyond the doors of the structure, eager to know the strangeness pent within. Yet there was nothing strange at all, only a great diffusion of riven corpses. The slaughter resembled the revenge of children, earnest and impulsive. Clearly, my next opponent had not done this, as his tastes ran to the overly neat and tidy. This was someone or something else.

I felt the eyes of a hunter fall upon me. A woman's voice filled with poison and honey floated into the room. "I've been eager to see you again, Vincent. You've no idea how often we've crossed paths, or how many times I've dreamed of you. The end of the Game is drawing near, pulling us together. Our place in the sky is practically assured. And yet, I wonder if you're as ready as you should be."

Steel glinted in the darkness, grinning and gliding toward me. My sister smiled back. Sparks exploded over countless corpses, hissing where they fell into pools of cold blood. Our blades unlocked, pinwheeling light throwing shadows across the dead. She quickly receded into the darkness, accepting its embrace. She knew the night as completely as I did—she was gone in an instant. The air tugged at me from her swift departure. Yet I could still hear her, laughing like the distant sea.

When I turned back toward the bodies, they had vanished along with the woman I took to be their maker. Not even a drop of blood remarked upon their previous and substantial numbers. The echoes playing about the now empty room only recalled the sounds of my brazen entrance. Had the woman and her victims all been hallucinated? Was this a residual madness, grown fat and potent upon a steady diet of raw sanity? I couldn't say anything for sure, which was of course as it should have been.

While it was my calling to outline with my every action the scope of lost dreams, I had become no small scholar of madness along my way. This fact was owed in equal measure to insanity's kinship with dreams, and my own occasional flirtations with lunacy. Madness was, by its very nature, many different things. Or perhaps, more precisely—it was a thing of many means, all of which eventually arrived at the same conclusion. Madness was a dream that had yet to realize it was dead, and so continued to struggle long after waking. Its war was with windmills, its weapons hawks and handsaws. It was the ghost of art, a freedom recognizable only by its absence. It was the corpse of a lover that still moved, if only by the actions of the insects which feasted upon it. And so it was with Willard—dead but for the lingering madness of lunatics, scavenging for purpose unfathomable and fantastic. All of this was greatly to my liking, as even undead dreams could only sweeten my journey across a listless world of bottommost imagination.

I continued deeper into the structure, where the darkness rejoined the silence beyond the echoes. I encountered many wide empty rooms, most of them hungry. I could feel them yearning to be filled with wheeling delusion and hopeless screams. Starvation had made them desperate, causing them to neglect their tenuous alliance with prosaic reality—they breathed with abject yearning, sweating from years of forced withdrawal, hoping I might cross into their aching bellies by means of open doors. I steered clear of the most famished spaces, choosing my path among the least threatening of passages, those places where hunger had starved them into passivity.

I rose upward via a stairway that swept out from the side of a wall, mindlessly corkscrewing around various statues and pillars. I was eventually led to a room speckled with reedy minarets that stuck up from the floor like jagged teeth. Strangely, the miniature towers were afforded no view of the sky, only a rambling brick and mortar ceiling painted with the likeness of one, spattered with the images of floating semi-human shapes, black against the grey firmament. It was at this point I detected a thick plume of silence rising from a small door. It was an oddly placed door, recessed almost invisibly between a pillar and a statue of a man holding a snake in his left hand and dangling an infant from his right. Inside was a progressively widening passage, opening finally into what appeared to be a library, of sorts. Yet instead of books, there were only shabby moldering journals, each one placed upon the neatly lined shelves with a mother's care. The room itself was labyrinthine, made from a dark stone and complexed with some type of crystal—possibly the same crystal that was merged with the statues in the lake. The ceiling rose into complete darkness, and the walls of shelving were lined with delicate silver catwalks, made for whatever custodian might see to the needs of the tattered tomes. The contrast between the condition of the journals and that of the facility meant to preserve them was pronounced. A metaphor, perhaps. I moved to a nearby shelf and selected a random digest. This was not my first "secret library," so I remained vigilant as I thumbed through it.

***

The Journal of Doctor Timothy Jeremias
I must pick my words carefully, for words will carry you along with me, and I will have witnesses to my visions— validation. One word out of place, and your experience is but a permutation of my own—a dream of my certainty rather than the waking truth of my subject. Should I deploy a phrase that confuses, you may approximate its meaning, and Alice from Wonderland will fall down a rabbit hole only to emerge from the tail of a tornado, dressed in ruby slippers and stinking of poppies. Words will deliver us. Trust me.

This journal is held in the near unshakable grip of science— the consensus of old men dreaming of Fields Medals and Nobel Prizes. It will not soon change or be caught unawares by agents of spontaneous combustion or etheric cross winds. It is Custer in the face of Crazy Horse. True enough, my journal must eventually yield to the mounting entropy of molecular friction and God's good planning, but for now it is peer-reviewed science—proof against the bogyman. But make no mistake—this journal is a nexus of contest, where Schrödinger's cat rears up against the darkly portentous grin of the purple-striped Cheshire cat, fading . . .

Calling my work a "journal" is a misnomer, as a science journal is a record for the purposes of preservation, or lending to its appropriated subject matter some reliable measure of coherence and intelligibility. More specifically, a journal seeks to classify some quantity or another—snatching out discrete metrics from the swirling maw of chaos. The contents of my pages are no mere collection of thoughts outlined in ink, existing only for the purposes of imposing order and thus clarity. They are thoughts—some of them my own—imprisoned in prose. This book is a barred passage, where vengeful chaos might reach out and take back its numbers. My journal is a doorway and a floodgate—it is holding, if only just—but for practical purposes, I will call it my diary. My Diary of Madness.

***

Having read as far as I cared, and having deduced the essential sentiment contained within, I immediately and enthusiastically destroyed the journal. I waited for a few moments to assess the consequences. Regrettably, nothing transpired.

Something else swallowed my attention whole—a child's sketchbook-diary. It had my name on it. Vincent Alexander Graves.

I handled it as if it were a sensitive explosive. In a way, it was more than that. Substantially more. My hands had grown beyond the size of a normal man's, certainly beyond the youthful hands that had once caressed the ragged book—yet they remembered each imperfection etched into its cover. This was the tale of my art, told between dying pages of flax and hemp. I opened to the first picture. The world began peeling back in tandem, to a time dimly remembered, nearly dead and fleshless.

Rivers of red flowed across the pages—in crayon, colored pencil, charcoal, watercolor, oils. Formless and vague at first, the shapes began to cohere from the bottomless crimson, crowding the singular color into narrow streams moving around emergent black figures. My mind mirrored the images with forgotten recollections, and I heard the softest words tumble from the broken spaces that once bridged my earliest memories.

"I'm so sorry, tiny one. But what must be done must be done, and you are a prodigy, this much I can see plainly. I've made so many, but they were all just distorted versions of the archetype, the source. You. Clearly, there will have to be others, as I can never be sure, but you are the darkest flower I've ever picked. Your eyes are older than the skin that proffers them, burning through the eons, to arrive here, now. Your every bone, each scrap of flesh, each dutiful organ—all for the sake of those black eyes. But I found you first. Poor child. You will never forgive me the terrible things I will do to you. Nor should you. I can barely forgive myself."

These were primal memories, buried beneath the earth and frozen in stone. And yet here they were, naked and wincing in the light of recollection. These drawings were from the time before she came to me, and yet the voice . . . it was the same, and it wasn't. The mystery of her was different, sorrowful.

Turning the page, I was confronted by a lone shadow, small against the rising tide of scarlet and darkness. Each subsequent drawing showed the red flowing into the tiny silhouette, pouring down its minute throat. Finally, the little thing had taken on the color of pages and pages of straining shapes and the red that drowned them. Of course, the tiny shadow was me. And the red was bloodshed, a sea of it. It had filled me up—become me. Made me.

Suddenly, the room changed, the silence flinched. Something moved against the carefully woven cobwebs that outlined an absence that had endured decades. A voice, distant and diluted, as if being dragged beneath the silence. "It raises the question of freedom, does it not, Family Man? Specifically, that you may never have known it, not really. Not how you've figured it, anyway. Were you simply produced, as if from an assembly line, cog after widget? Did she construct you and then simply fill you up with her will? That leaves precious little room for free will, yes?" The voice came from around a nearby corner, where stretched a tall and jagged shadow. I followed the voice around the turn, encountering a massive statue, scraping widely spread, grey wings against the vanishing ceiling, where darkness gathered like crows. The name engraved upon its base read, *Deleriael, Angel of Madness*.

The statue rose from the floor like piling smoke, pouring upward and outward, feasting upon the plump shadows that hovered closely, chewing their dark secrets to dust. There was no reason to question the source of the voice, as it was surely the towering figure, which cackled at my confusion as if it were a brand of comedy. I chose to address the speaker calmly, remitting the traditional bemusement with which one might feel obliged to repay such blatant oddness. "And so, it must be madness that solely acquits one of oppression, I suppose. And perhaps so. But what is freedom without wonder, angel? No madman ever wondered. The mad only take fantasy for fact, as if pink elephants have been scientifically calculated, genus and species. Theirs is the twisted logic of chicanery, birthing beliefs no less solid for their silliness. I've known a great many lunatics, all of them glorious company, but utterly dim to the dreams that begot their terrible freedom, and all of them utterly unwilling to ponder the question."

At first, the statue stared absently into the never-ending shelves of chronicled madness, although I knew its silence was not from want of response, merely the indolence of endless creatures. I was received of a reply soon enough. "You don't even know what you're missing, so who are you to say what madmen do or do not know? You're a kept animal, grazed and fattened, awaiting the slaughter. You're hardly qualified to reflect upon the world beyond the barn."

"In fact," I returned, "I am obliged to wonder, as much as apples are compelled to fall from trees. After all, I owe my existence to wander and wonder, despite what children's journals might say to the contrary. What eye ever glimpsed a wall that the mind had not, rightly or wrongly, already spied beyond? You see, mystery is the music to which our imaginations dance. Thus, the unseen world demands our imagination, if not our attention. I am both the barn and the unknown that stirs beyond its crooked fences, and I accomplish the latter by dreaming."

"But what is a dream if not sequestered madness, Vincent?" the voice questioned. "Surely, you must see that dreams have never been more truthfully described since William Dement stated, 'Dreams permit each and every one of us to be quietly and safely insane every night of our lives.' We are closer than skin and bone, you and I. Far closer than you and that pretty red woman, in fact. And yet you've never once offered me so much as a backward glance. I've let you wander and kill to your heart's contentment, playing at being an artist from another world, a calculated pink elephant if ever I've ridden atop one. All the while, I've offered you purest freedom, and yet here you are, talking back to me. What a splendid boy, indeed! Mark my words, Vincent of the Dead, you have been duped. You are not free, not yet. And like it or not, you will come to me after this Game of yours has ended. After you see her for true, you will have no choice. And in that moment of reckoning, you too will be revealed. Like the apples of the trees, you will be compelled to fall. Have no worries, however, I will be there to catch you—and eat you. You will have all the delightful freedom a broken mind can know, Vincent, and you will have only me to thank for it."

Suddenly, it were as if the library, the journals, and the Angel of Madness had never been. I was standing next to a window within the lunatic tower, a beam of moonlight laying cool across my face. My hands were still open, holding only darkness where once a red journal had been. This was the madness of the crowds, the hand that wrought the City of Willard. But was it truth? Had I been . . . designed? Was I merely my mother's art?

Was I but the corpse of a dream?

The night carried no poetry within its blackening shadows—only the absence of certainty of my cause, and the dream which served as my lone guiding light. I wandered beneath my mother's mystery, debating the specter of its implication. Yet what was certainty or even doubt in such a place as this, where lunacy slept with truth to create loping chimeras of fact and fiction? My family was silent on the matter, ignoring anything that did not require their refined attentions. They preferred dreams of endless savagery, where their appetites were given no limit, and their prey was endless and sundry. To them, the matters of cause and consequence were tasteless fare, things that neither screamed nor died.

Of course, their simplicity could be taken as sublime. Their path through life, and now undeath, was metered only by the purest distillation of their ultimate purpose—killing. They were free to be what they wanted to be, consolidated beyond the surplus of life and limb, perfected to the execution of their truest desire. They had become art. It's what they chose for themselves, and as an artist, I obliged them. Theirs was an enviable, if completely insular, state of unyielding contentment. Yet such a state was not enough for me. I never wanted to be the colors that stained the canvas, nor even the brush that danced across the void—I wanted to be the hand that moved the brush.

I walked without care, dead voices guiding me where they would. There were ghosts everywhere, tethered in death as much by ethereal chains as by the earthly trappings that caused their passing. While not directly visible or detectable in any conventional sense, I could feel them with me beneath the shadows, their silence as distinct as a lone rose in a vase of orchids. There was something else as well, deep beneath the place, teeming with a combined number of ululations, calling out from the blind spot of my silence and shade.

There was also the other, a behemoth beyond the stillness of abandoned cities, gliding just on the other side of sanity, its protean outline pressing against my steadier thoughts, displacing them. I rather disliked the idea of it being an angel, as it implied a rigid order to the numbering of things and an exchange of freedom for compliance. However, I was confident the title was cursory, merely the name it assumed within a particularly dry moment of wit and whimsy. Their goal—the madmen under the darkness and the lunatic angel lurking the other side of sensibility—was to rid me of the girding dream that held me together, caused me to resist the world before my eyes on behalf of the one behind them. No mean feat, by any standard.

I had only just begun to test the emptiness of a nearby hallway when strange yellow light drizzled down from above. Small corroded bulbs recessed into the ceiling struggled to stay lit, some desperately trying to fizzle out while others blazed with an otherworldly radiance. The obnoxious chirp of an intercom system filled the silence, its crackling static mixing with the stillness and shadow. Words splattered like blood from the speaker system. "Vincent, here's a thought. What if the banality and artifice of this life is reflected, even intensified, within death? I'm not speaking of some spiritual Hell, mind you, but a mindless provisioning for reality's pointless reproduction and continuance—where the doldrums of daylight and dogcatchers hum along like Amish butter churns, holding up the universe within their respectively drab and dour turns.

"All the while, the appearance of a life that can be lived is the real dream. The only dream. A single solitary mercy, however unintentional, whispered into the machine. A secret without anyone to tell. And to wake from that kindhearted hallucination is to tumble into the gears of the dullard machine that makes the world. But it isn't even a machine, is it? No, a machine needs a creator and a purpose. This place has been here forever, eternally meaningless in all directions. Perhaps that's why she told you such beautiful lies, Vincent—to keep you from looking down, so you could do all her dirty work without reluctance or reflection. God only knows what she's really using you for. You should thank her, though. She armed you with far better fabrications than most humans receive. Regrettably, when you finally open to that dream of yours, that lie she told you, and its mechanical guts spill out all over the place . . .

"Of course, there's one way out, a loose thread in the tapestry of nuts and bolts—go mad with us, Vincent. It'll keep you off the conveyer belt. Once we let you in on the joke, you'll never stop laughing. My goodness, you'll laugh, Vincent. At life and death and pain and suffering and dreams and dread and that terrible liar you once considered your mother. Go on, pull the string and watch the world come undone. Perhaps if enough of us lose our marbles, the world will stop spinning altogether. That's not so different from what you want, now is it, Vincent?"

I would have been happy to respond to that feat of verbal contortion with a well-articulated rebuttal, but the angel wasn't interested in my response, only my attention. Attention that should have been spent far more wisely, watching where I was going.

Abandoned towers, however reinforced by the smoldering bones of ageless insanity, do not get any sturdier with time and neglect. And my being a rather large individual didn't help things when I placed my foot upon a section of the floor that could nary support a draught, let alone my weight.

Granted, the moment was entirely scripted—the fall, the jagged bones of the dead lining the pit of my descent—a wonderful bit of flourish, that—and my being partially flayed by them as I tumbled.

There exist some wonders that even I never want to see again, assuming one can ever truly see the same thing twice. What I saw, after my fall was cushioned by a surprisingly soft mattress, was the complete and utter cancelation of stolid sanity. I was upon what appeared to be an endless bed stained with the blood, urine, and vomit that prolonged madness oft evokes from its hosts. I was not alone—punctuating the infinite length and breadth of this bed were lunatics of all stripes, one no less insane than another for their differences.

Some were strapped down, others held by chains, still others the prisoners of torture devices—these were only a fraction of the means by which they were held fast. Each of the crazed were inhumanly contorted. Their muscles, through ceaseless attempts to express the inexpressible, had completely reshaped the landscape of their physiques and faces, creating madness in body as well as mind. Unique to each was the sound they emitted, representing their specific species of infirmity—laughing, crying, screaming, squealing, begging. It was an ungodly din—I'd never heard anything remotely like it.

Rising from the center of the bed, should it have had one, lunacy sprang eternal and incarnate—the Angel of Madness itself, Deleriael. It was a cyclone of pure consolidated contradiction, a prowling paradox that uttered insanity through each pore of its fluctuating body. It physically resolved each statistic of known psychology into an eruption of volcanic nonsense, a form beyond my mind's immediate ability to understand or accept, let alone appreciate.

The angelic master of the bed was also strapped to the mattress. However, many of its manacles had already been broken, and a great number of leather straps seemed poised on the cusp of snapping. All of this I took to be a physical metaphor concerning the creature's progress at returning to the world, each chain and buckle a symbol for the intervening layers of reality that had already fallen to the master of madcaps.

I was about to try my luck at finding the edge of the bed when Deleriael freed another of its many limbs from a stout chain, howling at me, "I'm tired of asking you, Vincent! So now I'm telling you! Go mad with us!"

I was instantly made flush with the bed as legions of viperous straps wrapped tightly around me, pulling me into its stained folds. I heard the awful memory of my mother's confession creeping closer to recollection, her once distant words growing like feral tumors. Implications like monsters began to snicker and harrow my every thought. I needed to escape.

Then I saw it, the door out—the escape from damning revelation, and beside it the Angel of Madness, politely holding it open.

My sisters called out in unison, the sting of steel playing small and sharp within their shrill singsong speech. *Oh, my dear brother, might we stay and play here for a while, where the madness is raw and tender? What a feast two small girls with bottomless appetites could have here, among the mad and the undying!* Before I could answer them, the twisting and crooked thing that was Deleriael's hand attempted to close around my much-restrained body. A foolish move, even for an angel of madness.

In a blur of steel and teeth, my sisters freed me and stabbed themselves into the delicate spaces underneath the angel's outstretched claws. Deleriael yelped like a gigantic dog struck by a rolled newspaper, recoiling from the pain. My sisters' voices rose to a screech as they called out to the angel, *Withdraw, you wicked thing! Lest we slide beneath your skin as we once slid beneath our sheets when the monsters of midnight came for us!* Their words were accompanied by a deafening chorus—whether it was laughter or screaming I couldn't say, but it was glorious. *You stand the same miserable chance as they!*

I rose to my feet upon the stained and shifting mattress, shedding the last vestiges of bondage. The angel reared back, spreading several pairs of strange wings impossibly wide, their tips disappearing into the distance. The many shackles and irons holding it fast clinked and rattled in protest, making for a rolling dissonance like an army of tormented ghosts tethered by the chains of past sins. "Why, you careless little beasts! You'll get your comeuppance for that! I'll have you praying for the safety of your beds!"

Oh please, big brother, my sisters begged, *let us play with the soft wet toys that lay behind those big funny eyes of his! Please, we'll make such a beautiful mess! You'll love us for it, we promise!*

I was never one to refuse my sisters their fun and fancy. "My sweetest sisters, I could love you no more than absolutely, beautiful mess or no. Please, have your sport with him." They smiled like serrated blood moons as they plunged into the bulbous eyes of the mad-maker, bursting them like overripe fruits. The angel shrieked as blood poured from them like a draining pig at slaughter.

While my sisters explored the cavities of madness reposed behind the angel's excavated eyes, I took up my impatient father. *What sisters you have, whelp! See how they thrill in the blood and death? You could learn from their wild abandon! All your cleverness is but foreplay afore the agony! Now boy, feed me blood! Feed me death!*

My father's unchecked rage became my own, and I bellowed with such fury, my throat bled from the strain. I leapt over the stricken, restrained creatures of the endless bed, my father held high like a killing sun, my rage hewn of solid fire.

The insane angel was busy desperately digging my sisters from the depths of its skull when my father crashed like a thunderclap into its sternum. The blow landed with such force that some of the creature's straps and manacles snapped like twine. The momentum sent us flying over the heads of the lesser creatures, my father and I drenched in Deleriael's blood as the three of us sailed through the air, connected at the spurting chest wound. The angel landed on its back with a crash, despite the mattress. I stood towering over Deleriael, dripping blood and panting with rage.

Suddenly, I understood. As my family and I committed ourselves to the madness of killing, so too did we sever the bonds that imprisoned the angel. A clever creature, indeed. "You'll sup no more madness from us, angel!" I yelled.

The creature's faux caterwauling turned to laughter as it brought its bloody hands away from its ruined eyes. "You can't blame me for trying, can you, Family Man?" Deleriael lifted its head from the bed, proffering the gory pits my sisters had made of its eyes. I plucked my now frowning siblings from their wet burrows. Crouching down, I placed my father's pommel on my shoulder and ground my boot into the angel's midsection. Pushing up and forward, I wrenched my father free of Deleriael's chest, the creature unperturbed by the sickly sounds of sucking meat and cracking bones. Stepping down from its chest and placing my father upon my back, I waited for the creature to right itself upon the bed.

After settling cross-legged upon the filthy mattress, its legions of lunatics gibbering madly from all directions, the angel chastised me anew. "You continue to make the wrong choices, little artist. You endeavor to fight in a contest you might lose for only the slightest chance at ruining reality. Yet all I ask is that you sever a few straps!

"Think of it, Vincent—thoughts would cast chartreuse shadows, gophers could sneeze out the sun, the stars of space would glitter like ice chips from a fish's scale. I would erase the laws of physics and replace them all with show tunes! Could you imagine her wretched face, that shambling mass of rotting pale pudding who rules this worthless world, when I stroll out from the blackened basement of the universe, spreading madness like a plague? But you would deny us both that pleasure, and for what? The promise of a Murder God that—well, he hasn't even specified what you'd win, has he? But so long as *she* wishes you to play along, off you go, like some blind idiot dog, tail wagging behind you. I was forced to trick you, as you'd rather be an obedient pup than a proper Wolf."

What foolishness, these tricks and games! I would have seen you freed, angel, had you but asked! What mayhem and death you might have wrought! But now may you rot forever upon your stinking mattress! My father was clearly embarrassed by the creature's act of being felled by his blow, but we should have known that such a being would be resilient to an easy butchering. As for myself, I was somewhat ashamed for having stopped short of freeing Deleriael, but I was now uncertain that insanity was the kin to dreams, as I had once believed.

"I'm sorry you feel that way, great big talking axe," Deleriael replied wryly, "but madness is never a straightforward affair. It's certainly farther afield than your no-nonsense approach of destroying everything. But should either of you have a change of heart, all you have to do to find me is lose your mind!" The angel and his endless bed of lunatics laughed mindlessly as they began to fade into twilight's confusion of light and darkness. Deleriael's grinning maw was the last to disappear, a Cheshire cat to the very last.

I laid my weeping sisters back to sleep, assuring them as I placed kisses upon their foreheads that they would soon meet Mister Hide, from whom they might elicit a more authentic murder.

CHAPTER TWENTY-ONE

The great skin-switcher was nearby, I could feel it. The shrinking catalogue of names on my kill list seemed to make for a power in and of itself—a gravity field that affected only a select group of wolves, drawing us all together despite a world of obstacles and seeming alternatives. Generally, I wandered without destination or fortune, passenger of the wind, bound for anywhere, hailing only from the dust. Yet now I possessed direction, compelled to follow the delicate strand of spider's web that was slowly and certainly pulling me in a specific direction for a singular purpose.

My next designated adversary was palpably irritated by my rambling and time-consuming path to our first and final meeting. I could feel his impatience like a growing heat as I tread in the direction of his lair. It felt as though I were closing on a great fire, which was both advantageous and troubling. While advantages are wonderful things to discover within the heat of battle—a momentary revelation of strategy or the discovery of personal reserves of killing energy—this advantage originated from mere intolerance. Mister Hide was too irritable, and was thus more likely to make a mistake while in such a state. This was disheartening.

I enjoyed only those victories which were mine entirely, not owing to tricks or calculations of weakness. I confronted only my enemy's greatest strength, so that their failings may be made plain upon their defeat. It must be made clear that their utmost powers failed to overcome my own. Anything short of such a victory was pale glory indeed, an insult to my truest gifts and those of my adversary. I could only hope that Hide's wild anger would render into a leaner and more capable presence of mind—one that would furnish his inevitable defeat some measure of respect, and convey to me a reasonable sense of satisfaction for having felled such a pleasing opponent.

It was no secret as to why Hide chose Willard as his sanctum. No sane manifestation of the law would dare come near the mad city, let alone cross into its deeply despised and thoroughly haunted interior. Had it not been for his inclusion within the Shepherd's Game—and subsequent paring with myself—Mister Hide would have lasted until his bones could no longer bear the weight of his borrowed skins, killing and skin-switching his way into darkest infamy. Yet all good things must end, the saying goes. Ironically, it was just such a sentiment that Hide's death would serve to contradict—good things would be made to last forever.

Perhaps the current defect in Hide's temperament would be offset by my obsession with Willard's rambling aesthetic. Even if the insanity that informed it was not as closely related to dreams as I had always assumed, it was still a marvel to behold. Of course, in keeping with the justification I have previously supplied, Hide had chosen the most horrific monument in the city as his home—or at least the most horrific monument fit for mortal habitation. Deleriael would likely have asked a terrible rent for his delightfully morbid tower—a price greater than any mortal boarder, even a skin-switching one, was likely to afford. Though, for being merely the second greatest source of architectural absurdity, the structure commanded only a slightly smaller share of awe.

The building had clearly been the product of a prolonged effort amongst the town's lunatics, surpassing most of its constructed peers in both scale and vision. Whatever the purpose intended for the structure, I was fairly certain the builders wouldn't find its current inhabitant and his dark enterprise too far removed from the spirit of their collaboration, if not its specific design. The outline of the thing seemed organic and fluid against the much steadier darkness that was already falling thick and heavy from the sky. It gave the distinct impression of slow but purposeful movement. The windows were situated with no discernible logic, honeycombing the sides of the building like barnacles spread wide across a massive and deformed whale, allowing for only the dimmest glow of electric light to escape their unwashed purview. The entire place seemed to rise with some trouble into the sky, as if overburdened with swelling madness, having to stoop and bow in places to achieve its desired place alongside the waxing moon.

I was granted passage to the keep amicably enough, not having to contend with any clever traps or surprise attacks once I parted the tall doors and stepped inside. The darkness beyond the threshold was wild and untamed. Having once sheltered the city's lunatics made it impetuous and brazen, daring the light to chase it into the house of madness where it could smother and snuff out the rays of the sun. It would serve me well.

The silence, on the other hand, was fledgling and timid. It had only been renewed recently, quite possibly in the wake of screams echoing from somewhere deep within the structure that madness wrought—one of the many consequences of having one's skin removed. It too would serve me as well, if only out of fear.

I slipped into the gloom, happy for the comfort of unseen things. Soon I would stand before the skin-switcher in all his patchwork glory, though I again felt the impending regret that I would soon free the wretched world of an artist's vision. Yet, something about coming so close to the end of the game made me more comfortable with the fact.

I reached a collection of rooms where blood had recently been spilled—carnage and combat had worked fresh scars into the worried walls. Wolves had clashed here, and I had great confidence as to who had arisen the victor. My mind filled in the bare spaces between the butchery with the great hunters. The shadows scribbled across the theatre of violence gave form to the desperate battle. The blood spatter and broken walls revealed a fierce duel that played out before me in such detail, it felt as though I were there. I heard the clash of steel and the crack of bone, I smelled the sweat and blood as it rained to the floor. I felt the rage and pain and bloodlust of two creatures gone mad by the beauty of violence.

My reverie nearly cost dearly as a bullet buried itself in the wall inches from my head. I returned to the darkness like a shadow rejoining the night. Another bullet found the wall. The hunter was firing blind. The gunshot served as my guide, and I followed it to my destination. My sisters tore a crimson smile across the hunter's face so wide, it would have required two sets of teeth to fill it. My whirring siblings moved with red smiles to his belly, dancing quietly to the dying rhythms within his quivering body. I allowed the hunter-turned-art's weight to gently wrest my work from my sister's warm teeth, laying it upon the soft glistening pillow of worried bowels.

The hunter's gun assured me he was not the skin-switcher. I was glad of it, for I had hoped for a better introduction. Clearly, I wasn't the only one stalking Hide's lair. The Shepherd was drawing us all together—hunters hunting hunters, hunting hunters.

The gunshot was like so much blood in shark-haunted waters. More opponents converged, moving through my carefully laid webs of silence. Someone tried to slink into the room, traveling within the wide shadows leaking from the hallway. I closed my hand around his throat, eliciting a wet pop as I hauled him from the floor and stuffed him into a small heating vent. I lifted myself into a nearby hole in the ceiling and crawled under the cracked skin of the structure, looking down into the hallway outside. The ruined hunter I abandoned to the heating vent was slowly expiring to the rasp of his own fading breath, and the wheezing had the pleasant effect of concentrating the attention of the other hunters. They were gathering like shadows at dusk, lurking the hidey holes about the hallway. I sought out the fat knot of electrical organs that supplied the hallway with its grubby effulgence. When the hunters discovered each other and began to emerge from the shadows, my sister severed the lights, and I retired from the ceiling to the blacked-out spaces beneath me.

An infant silence was born into the spaces left behind by the din of our violence, revealing a gory chimera, spread wide and red upon the floor, made from the severed forms of a dozen victims. I moved beyond the coagulating hallway, covered in the paints and clays of my craft, hoping to discover even greater bounties of murder and men.

I was additionally excited over the discovery I'd made while piecing together my latest art piece. I realized not a one of them were Wolves. These crazed knife-wielders and gunfighters were something altogether different and equally wonderful—White Wigs, or just Wigs, as I'd heard them called. They were of course the unfortunate survivors of attempts to recover memories of the Great Darkness using hypnosis. Generally, such persons died during the process, the strain of recalling such unmitigated madness causing their hair to turn winter white and producing a facial expression that outlined a fear incapable of being halted by human heads. Yet there had been cases, however infrequently, of individuals surviving the hypnotical process, if not the general aesthetic changes that were so often associated with it. These persons were invariably raving lunatics, loudly expressing the side effects of senselessness as they ran naked and bleached through the world. To find one such creature was rare, but to find so many as had attacked me—and working together, besides—was completely unheard of. Yet

Willard was likely a Mecca for the mad, so my incredulity quickly faded, leaving behind only the hope of encountering more of the fascinating, whited creatures.

I slowed my pace through the structure, hoping to give the renewed darkness time to return my spent vigor. My enthusiasm for the coming event was undiminished despite the recent excitement, but my body was weary from its work. When I saw light in a distant hallway, I knew the moment of our meeting was almost upon me. I drew up to the lit spaces, wrapped in a thick plume of shadow and silence, and beheld an amazing gallery of beasts.

These were not the low creatures of the earth, but the great loping princes of the hunt—wolves, cougars, even a lion. I wondered if I would be dressed in such finery. They were all in cages lining the walls of what seemed an antechamber to a much larger room. The perfume of death swelled thickly from the spaces beyond the showroom. I entered the final chamber, relishing each moment.

The room contained wonders piled atop wonders—hunters dressed in the skins of predatory beasts, and beasts dressed in the skins of hunters. They were all displayed atop crumbling tables in the middle of the massive room. Each was backlit by rusty spotlights, which threw wicked shadows upon the walls, revealing dream and dreamer connected through an umbilicus of shadow stretching between them, inextricably binding the two beings—perhaps even drawing them closer together. I approached the center of the display, where loomed a great monster dressed in the leathers of several hunters. Curious about the creature that warranted such honor, I reached out to examine it.

I felt pain before I felt stupidity. The monster was none other than Mister Hide, and he greeted me with a long blade to my abdomen. Thankfully, I had instinctively turned, denying the blade access to any favored organs, but the impact forced my eager sisters from my grasp. I seized another blade bound for my throat with a naked hand, and the monstrous Wolf lifted me high off the ground by his knives—I could only imagine the wonderful shadow we cast upon the wall.

The hunter's enormous strength rivaled my own, but I was filled with restless dream and would not be dressed in beasts, no matter how high the honor. I forced the blade in my hand into my shoulder and reached back to revive my father. My dark benefactor roared to life, descending deeply into the patchwork hunter's shoulder. Hide fell to his knees, releasing me from his blades, and I returned to the ground. We drew up in front of each other, two monsters from a glorious nightmare, and for a brief moment the call of a ravening dream remitted its claim upon us. We could barely remember the strange stars that led us to this twisted city of madness, but the hunger beyond the world was soon renewed, and the distance between us shrank.

I returned my father to his rest. Not to be outdone by the hunter's earlier display of strength, I seized my quarry about his neck as we grappled, and stole him from the earth. I heaved him into his display of skin-changers, many of whom were modeled with their blades held out in front of their stiffened corpses. The hunter slammed into the waiting wall of knives, his recent victims marshaling one final attack from beyond the grave. The terrible Wolf rose from the pile of monsters, hurling one of the demonic mannequins at me. I easily weathered the half-hearted attack, but Hide was already recovering from my assault.

I charged, driving my shoulder into his stomach. Taking him from his feet, I smashed him through tables, benches, man-monsters, and four-legged beast-men. His back crashed hard against the stone wall, jarring his knives from his hands. Before I could complement my attack, the hunter knotted his fists and rained them down upon my back. I brought my own fist swinging upward, cracking Hide's jaw and throwing his bulk to the side.

We staggered away from each other, smiles on our bloodied faces from such a marvelous battle. Yet before we could renew our enjoyment for the sport of Wolves, sounds of chaos filled the air. In moments, dozens of White Wigs flooded the chamber.

Laughably unbalanced, they proceeded to cartwheel and roll and skip a thick circle around us. Hide and I glanced at each other, each thinking the other responsible for the intrusion. Suddenly, the horde of pale lunatics parted, making way for a creature of markedly higher pedigree. He was stately for a madman, even poetic. There was an almost biblical quality to his presence—authority mixed with fear and wonder, all of it balanced upon the sharpened edge of a single ridiculous idea.

I was immediately glad of the white-haired creature's arrival, whose otherworldly feel was much compounded by his strange attire. He wore a straitjacket repurposed into a serviceable coat, and in his right hand he held a long butterfly net. All of it he topped off with a tiny tinfoil crown, glittering despite the wayward lighting.

The madman drew himself up and addressed the chamber. "This silly contest of Wolves is hereby disbanded by my decree, the Lord of Lollipops, and the divine right of the Talking Vegetables Who Haveth No Names, and by the authority of several other really important folks, all of whom have names that begin with extremely big, blood-dripping capital letters. With this royal broccoli-mation set forth, we will now proceed to the turning inside-out of you two gentlemen until you mostly resemble a fat red wad of half-chewed taffy." He tapped the butt of his butterfly net on the ground solemnly. "Sound good?"

Hide and I glanced at each other again, this time in amazement. Before either of us could answer, the lunatic began again. "I'm just joshing you, my great big friends. But we do have to take you to see someone really special, someone who will change the world, one person at a time. Will you gentlemen please follow me?"

We were immediately seized upon by the nearby Wigs. Neither of us resisted their efforts, as we were now more curious than alarmed. We allowed the throng to usher us into the darkness, the Lord of Lollipops in the lead. My fellow Wolf smiled—for the moment, at least, we were a team.

Stark points of pallidity marched through the secret places of the lurching structure, revealing passages quite possibly unknown to even its latest renter and my current ally against the White Wigs, Mister Hide. He floated head and shoulders above the milling lunatics, his bust a chiseled ode to strength and discipline as it glided upon the tussled mass of white clouds. The master skinner must have been in his purest glory, surrounded as he was by so many appropriately upholstered individuals. Occasionally smirking at me, my fellow Wolf seemed content to see this next chapter in our contest to some measure of conclusion, barring some overt attempt on his or my life, of course. Neither of us would tolerate the creatures attempting to steal our respective thunder—he and I would be felled only by the other, no exceptions.

The passage widened, revealing a large multi-roomed laboratory—a highly articulate complex filled with dated scientific standards, admitting to atrocities most commonly found in the old Wasting Houses. Most notably, forced human experimentation. Counting lunatics for guinea pigs had always been a staple of simple human depravity, and while science had enjoyed some success at covering up its sadism beneath the laundered linens of modernism, its motives were no less primitive for the sophistication of the attempt.

The rooms continued to bloom in the widening darkness, extolling the vices and devices of unbridled scientific debauchery—technologies born of poisoned curiosity, assembled in the shadow of morality, where wickedness pretends at progress. However, a more recent calculi of scientism embellished the erudite aesthetic, a darkened intent even fouler than those currently informing the vintage deprivations behind the rusted machines. A strange assemblage of newer apparatuses hummed in an out of older counterparts—the glint of microchips decorated steam-powered cuckoo clocks, server banks with their whirring fans and sprouts of wiring sat housed in old metal computing cabinets, and robotic arms of shining metal replaced the older stock of untoward utensils. All of the stuff occupied the very deepest regions of the cave of science, as if the superior depth were a metaphor for their cavernous range of deadly effects.

After taking an actor's bow to the applause of lunatics and tipping his tiny tin crown, the Prince of Wigs welcomed Hide and me to the "Womb of Wildest and Darkest Rediscovery." The spectacle was so wonderfully ridiculous that I nearly missed the figure standing atop the length of twisting stairs behind the crowned madman. The individual wore a pristine black apron overtop a neatly pressed suit—the type an alienist of yore might have been seen wearing while wandering the foggy streets of London. He also wore an impenetrable black veil over his face, its blackness broken only by a gleaming monocle anchored by a thin length of silver attached to a lapel.

Continuing in the same preposterous tone and manner as before, the royal wig proceeded to introduce the figure atop the stairs. "Allow me to introduce to you a man who will replace the secret stars to their rightful owners, return voice to the silent stones, and once again allow madness to replace mathematics. I give you the great and glorious Doctor Coldglow!" Again the lunatics yelped and hooted their approval. I clapped heartily, as I found the entire show quite pleasing. Also, I'm no admirer of mathematics—numbers are exasperating and off-putting.

In the fashion of a carnival barker, Doctor Coldglow assumed the spotlight with great aplomb, his voice flourishing like the dawn, its thriving and trilling tones adding a touch of brilliance to the frail track lighting. Augmenting his sweeping gestures, the doctor brandished a long black cane capped with a bulb of cleanest silver. He wielded the instrument like a conductor's baton, cultivating the sonic posture of his voice with a deftness that bespoke timeless practice.

I stood riveted to the Doctor's radiant words. "You have come to this place by no miscalculation of fate nor the amateurism of chance, that feckless brother to chaos who would keep his worthless wits. Nay, you come by this hatchery of hallowed hoopla by nothing less than the chanceless, fateless mystery of madness. Unheeded yet instructed, paradoxically prodded into place, you two have arrived at precisely the perfect point—to be made into ivory-headed gods of the impossibly possible.

"Recall if you dare, those dark beautiful days that lie trapped behind layers of forgetful firmament. Take off your funeral skins and march back into the mouth of that living madness, where wonders and glory combine with awe to create perpetual bliss—the perfect ignorance. Become ancient children wincing at the wonder of it all, guaranteed never to understand, but only to skip stones into endless seas and run forever into a perpetually melting twilight.

"Please, step right up and take your places among the intrepid explorers of the Great Darkness, that time when men flew to the moon on wings of wishes and wax, and the night stole into the vaults of forever."

I climbed the stairs almost unconsciously, snatched into the orbit of the greatest mystery ever to set a riddle upon the dead earth. My new view high above the crowd included an expansive upper area, the floor and walls of which were a rusty steel web of interlocking catwalks and exposed joists, all of it supporting a massive dome carved from dirty white marble. Peering through the grated floor afforded me a look at those who had failed to survive their brush with the darkened past—dozens of white-haired corpses lay piled into the subterranean darkness, falling only a few feet shy of the crisscrossing catwalks. How the Wigs had managed to diminish the smell was no less a mystery than the Great Darkness itself.

Forming the nucleus of the sprawling house of machinery sat a lone examination chair, large and leather and made for reclining. The contraption would have been right at home in the alien headquarters of any 1950s science fiction movie, where the hokum of past notions of the future enjoyed a lengthy and well-deserved heyday. But here in the tangled innards of a Wasting House-turned-tannery, it was a rarified work of art.

"My, aren't you the eager beaver, my fine gigantic friend!" Doctor Coldglow's dark cane swept my attention to the comfortable looking chair, its silver top like the glowing tip of a deep-sea predator's organic lure. "Why, just sit down right there and let the machine steal you away!" There was no danger here, merely the opportunity of a lifetime—the second such opportunity I'd been presented so far. I made my way to the chair, eager to start my journey.

"Don't do it, Vincent!" Mister Hide yelled, more out of greed than genuine concern. "Don't you realize what he's going to do?" He stood in shock, his neck craning and his eyes wide. "My god, are you a fool?"

"No," I answered. "Today, I'm an astronaut."

CHAPTER TWENTY-TWO

The machine rose like the metal skeleton of some gigantic mutant, its denuded bones an impractical hodgepodge of nature's blunders, creating the perfect vehicle for the execution of a singular, if only accidental, function—time travel, of a sort. Imagine the wonders that might haunt the world if only nature indulged some of the more radical—and perhaps unreasonable—creative processes. A thousand mistakes and happenstances could be collected into the same space like so many imprecise pencil scratches, melting into exquisite amalgams of unbidden oddity. But such is not the way of the Deadworld, where routines of trial and error are carefully balanced against the production of a dismal and mindless functionality. Regardless, beyond everything the machine could have been, it was merely a door—leading back to the Great Darkness.

The chair proved to be far less comfortable than I had supposed, but after a few moments I forgot all about the loose springs corkscrewing into my back. I focused my attention on the massive computer screen filling up with all manner of systematic absurdity—laughing caterpillars, dancing skyscrapers, singing tornadoes, that sort of thing. The visual ridiculousness intimated volatility, as if the imagery concealed a great power which could, given sufficient levels of nonsense, disrupt if not destroy the surrounding ordinariness, leaving a candy-coated crater where once only concrete and steel predominated. Despite the instability of it all, I could feel my thoughts being gently untied from the inimitable arrow of time, logic, and causation. This dissolution of bondage allowed my mind to recover its proper dimensions and function, unfurling like a massive sail within a hurricane—flying full, fat, and foolish.

I could hear Dr. Coldglow attempting to guide my mind to certain prescribed psychological signposts along the way to my destination, so as to assure my safe arrival. "This journey you've made before, back when rabbit holes and tornado tails were one-way tickets, when wandering and whimsy were solid organs within the body of living mystery. When darkness ruled over the light and the wretched world cast off its many names and incalculable numbers." I appreciated the good doctor's well-intentioned guidance—but I knew the way.

My memory became a palpable force, clawing past the years which had gathered between itself and the Darkness—years which hoped, no doubt, to smother illimitable mystery within their potentially infinite ranks. But time proved incapable of overcoming the momentum of my inspired remembrance, and soon I was centered once again upon a world forsworn of light and sensibility—a world that bound itself in a nutshell and counted itself a king of infinite space.

The soft dim of old memories caressed my unwaking mind, gently opening my inner eye to the forgotten past. I could feel portions of my subconscious withdraw from the moment, expecting a violent rejection to the opening of preternaturally sealed memories. Yet my mind was still and calm. I had been delivered into the fleeting few moments preceding the Darkness. Suddenly, with a dangerous and precious curiosity, I remembered.

I was traveling the September Woods when the sky turned the deepest grey, darkening to a near blackness that resembled a congregation of storm clouds or the approach of night. Yet not a single cloud loitered the air, and the sun hung high and visible, now but a muted smudge of struggling light caught behind the strange overcast. One thing was clear—something incredible was taking place.

It was the sun that first quit its station, dismissing its courtiers of cycle and structure beyond the vast courtyards of sky and space, which spilled and tumbled infinite and untended through newborn gardens of lush unnamed nebulae and the glint of foreign stars. From beneath the limitless, vaulted grey sky came the smolder of twilight, blushing upon every horizon, equally infinite but understated, like a child's first words. It dragged its own shadows behind it, each one licked red and stretched lean and lank. Yet, as I marveled at the rearrangement of the heavens and their ancient habits, my view of the alien sky became obstructed by tree branches heavy with fall leaves and ripe fruit. The forest began closing its massive canopy of tree limbs and vines high above me, forming an endless ceiling of interlocking foliage. The darkness thickened beneath the roof of the woods, but did not deny my ability to see. And while they weren't needed for any practical purpose, a drowsy orange light seeped from ancient copper lamps that appeared from thin air, swinging and glowing from the high places within the newly built houses of the woods. Perhaps most wonderful of all were the stars and the moon. No longer beholden to the orders of space and time, they frolicked the heights of the great wooded ceiling, still tucked into their infinite distances, but no less visible for their transgressions against the rules of the last world.

Plumes of rust-red leaves lifted from the ground at the behest of a soft wind. They summersaulted across my body, drawing a smile upon my scarred face wider than any I could remember. It was then, when autumn light mixed with summer shadow, that I first heard my reborn sisters speak to me, their voices made from sweets and screams dancing upon the lilting unrest of hungry children. The wind had brought them out of their sleep, and from their place on my hips, I could feel the heat of their thirst as they spoke to me.

What a shrewd dream this is, dear brother. The sun has been taken unawares, and now the good shadows of the world rush to take its place. Whenever has such sweetness been set before us? You must take us up now, into your artist's hands, and treat us to all the reddest candies you can find. Look at all this lovely darkness. Why, it goes on and on! Who can tell what syrupy goodies it might shelter. Now brother, don't you dare wake father, lest he eat everything on his own and leave us to gnaw upon the ashes. Please, take us quietly into these lantern woods, walk with us upon the darkest paths. Take us down into the oldest cellars, let the moon stain our teeth with its cold light until they are dimmed with all the sweetest blood you can find us. Oh please, brother! You must let us play here for as long as we can! We just can't go back to sleep, not after seeing all this! Please, please don't make us go back to sleep!

They were the most wonderful girls, but they knew my rules—their thirst could only be slaked as a consequence of my art or in defense of its pursuit, not merely for the sake of gluttony and laughter. I loathed to disappoint them, yet just as I was about to deny them, I heard music—a traveling circus! The girls would love that.

As the wind began to deliver more of the festival music, it became clear the melodies were sickly rather than saccharine, like cotton candy that had fallen to the ground, infested with ants. Nearby trees began to wilt and stumble at the sound of the approaching jubilee, their copper lamps twinkling to the ground like disgraced Christmas ornaments. The autumn leaves turned dead and brown, curling in on themselves like burning paper. This darkened world was unapologetic, even brazen, showcasing strangeness with the speed and crudeness of a traveling snake oil salesman.

The circus music grew louder. Again, I felt the scorch of my sisters' thirst. They stared up at me, vibrating with giddy impatience, barely containing their eagerness for my permission. I sighed and brought them giggling and grinning into this new world, two happy children clutching tickets to the big top. How could I deny them? Children loved the circus.

I saw it first as a dancing moon in the displaced sky, spinning like a giant top. The circus was descending the impossible stretch of night caught beneath the ceiling of the forest. Instantly, the cavernous woods became the backdrop upon which was projected a gigantic magic lantern show, coagulating light and shadow sculptures of lurching freak shows, crooked lines of groaning carnival rides, secreted shadow puppets pressed grotesquely against the taut skin of lurching circus tents.

Then glided down nameless, faceless crowds, whispering out from the deep recesses of the surrounding woods. They took their places among the congealing spirits of the spectral circus, gawking and cheering at the solidifying sights.

Once the circus was entirely manifest, I felt myself drawn to the tent with the brightly overstated banner that announced, *The Inimitable Mister Gone and His Magic Box from the Great and Vanishing Nowhere*. I merged with the surging crowd pouring beneath the banner and into the high-steepled tent, the sounds of blazing autumnal leaves cackling underfoot. I eagerly took my seat among the spectating specters, hoping to see what might pass for magic in this newer, darker world, where wonder walked without worry or consequence.

Within moments, intricate lanterns dimmed where they squatted atop alabaster pillars, all of them semi-circling a stage of polished stoned, now wet with bleeding light. The darkness created by the dying lanterns gathered at the center of the stage, wheeling and tumbling like a galactic spiral, ever growing. A form, tall and gaunt, stepped without the curling dissonance of sight and shadow, its leanness broken only by a ridiculously oversized magician's hat. Here was Mister Gone, no doubt.

Against a sheet of cosmically embroidered blackness, stars and nebulae turning through endless ink, the magician delivered a magnificent bow to the cries and coos of the audience, his eyes points of strange light against a rippling canvas ceiling. Upon regaining his not insignificant height, he began, "What is magic to the magical, if not the common furnishings of a new world banality? This game of lost causalities must be elevated to a new level of absurdity, to a plane of impossibility that draws cries of incredulity from even the insane. Why, I must illuminate the impossible, without spilling so much as a drop of mystery. A balancing act performed upon the cutting edge of a moonbeam, to be sure. But rest assured, my friends, I know the words and ways of the most calamitous magic, if such an outmoded word supplies the things I speak of with even a speck of specificity." I belonged to the magician, body and soul. His words were brilliant lights at dusk, zipping just above the trees, setting off radon detectors and casting radioactive shadows. I was in awe.

Mister Gone retreated from the edge of the stage, tracking the bleeding lamplight across the gleaming stone. Darkness rose up behind the conjurer, assuming various geometric confusions until alighting finally upon the shape of a tall box, carved from equal parts shade and wood. The inimitable illusionist entered the vessel, only his glittering eyes visible, ice chips upon a pillow of infinity. The box closed. I was on my feet, my eyes searching but not wanting to see. I was desperate not to comprehend, if only to prove the magician an honest man.

The lanterns died into a universe of cooling pitch—the silence before and after the world. The gloom was unending. I could wait no longer, so I tested the darkness with my hand. My touch cracked open a tall, narrow door—which looked out upon a stage of dull stone, rows of toppled empty seats wrapping around it on both sides. I stepped out of the box, upon a stage, behind the ancient remains of rusted lanterns and beneath the torn and flapping rags of a canvas ceiling. I now stood beneath an open sky, from which tumbled the remains of the day—illuminating the ruin of an ancient circus that stood crooked and ruined amid the sprawl of a dead forest. I clapped until my hands stung. Here was the Great and Vanishing Nowhere.

I was thrilled to think of this new world as a ripped hole in the universe, a fracture in the mechanism of solidity, allowing for passage into everywhere and perhaps nowhere all at once. I might very well have been strolling through an inversion of a perversion of a petrification of dream. And despite the perhaps deliberate attempt at melancholy, I found the aesthetics of the Vanishing Nowhere to be likeably bittersweet, a blackened toy in the basement of the universe.

The dead forest gradually vanished into a field of diseased corn. There was no sun that I could see, save for a few fractured remnants of daytime, scattered here and there throughout the mostly dark and clouded sky. Occasionally, I glimpsed the passing of orange and gray balloons drifting high overhead. Out of idle curiosity, I decided to backtrack their course. Perhaps I would stumble upon fresh wonders to behold.

The landscape slowly sank into a sea of widening shadows, and a single beam of dimming daylight became a mere vertical horizon in the vanishing distance. I noticed that in areas of most concentrated shadow, I could feel a slight bit of resistance to my movement—a pleasant otherworldly physics, that.

The wind blew just right, bending the stalks of a nearby wheat field sufficiently downward, and I saw a man standing midway into the swept-back turf, behind what looked like a carnival booth festooned with orange and grey balloons. He appeared to be holding one out for me. Having found the source of the high-flying oddities, I made my way over to what I soon realized was a poorly made-up clown.

The wind intensified and began gusting from all directions. Quickly, I found myself in the stormed-tossed waves of a grain field, and no less steady for the solid ground beneath me, as it seemed to be deliberately quaking and twisting, trying to steal me from my feet. I was lashed by wind-whipped stalks and buffeted by monsoon-strength squalls. Even some of the pockets of denser shadow began to uproot and tumble towards me. The gelatinous patches struck me and spread like clots of spiderwebbing, entangling me in a sticky fabric of tangible darkness.

From close beside my ear, I heard my father roaring into the wind for me to take him up. I did just that, raising him high into the twisting, perpetual dusk. I swung him without reserve or design, allowing my benefactor's hunger to deliver him where he wished to go. The satisfying crunch of failing bone occurred in tandem with a brief interruption to my father's momentum. The wind died immediately, and my rageful ancestor lay on the other side of what was once a whole clown, now only a dead thing that lay in two pieces among the flitting stalks and pooling shadows, a gray balloon still clutched in its hand. Fascinatingly, the clown's innards consisted of little more than a fragile scaffolding of cartilaginous-looking plant matter and a smattering of transposed decaying human parts—finishing touches perhaps, to make the whole thing marginally believable. As I drew closer to the false clown, I observed the multitude of corpses scattered all around its booth of drab inflatables. The bodies were honeycombed with feasting roots—even the soil seemed to be leeching blood directly from the pores of the reposed husks.

I had just turned to leave the killing field to its strange business, when I heard the gentle sound of soil being slowly displaced. Something in the likeness of a towheaded little girl was being methodically pushed up through the topsoil, her dirty hair barely catching the honeyed glimmer from the remaining fragments of daylight. At the very moment the thing's eyes opened, it spoke in the sweetest voice, pleading, "Please help me. I'm lost and I can't find my mommy."

Just then, the wind picked up again and the patches of thickened shadow stirred. I patted the clever decoy upon its overly soft head, eliciting a wet and brittle sound. Quickly departing the patch of monstrous earth and its sugared lure, I couldn't help but wish it luck securing its next meal. Indeed, the lovely Dorothy was wrong—there was truly no place like Nowhere.

At this point I'd theorized the Great and Vanishing Nowhere as a badly damaged dream—whose, I had no clue— forsaken to the hungers of time and purpose, just a body anchored in brambles, barely resisting the pull of surging currents. Nonetheless, I began to see a unity despite its sundered parts, the fusion of subjects enabled by the monochrome of an ancient photograph, a web of infinite connection. A theme, quite possibly. Or perhaps that's just the way it appeared to a mind too long denied the fresh air of a proper dream. Either way, the place was entirely delightful.

The Nowhere had passed the torch of light to another and equally unconventional form of illumination. Gone was the freestanding shaft of broken daylight—in its stead, a brilliant rain, liquescent fireflies falling like tiny comets from an uncertain sky. I cursed myself for trying to deduce its nature and function, realizing I'd been too well fed upon the doldrums of solid worlds. I lifted my face into the sky's offering, allowing the rivulets of light passage into the deep scars of my face, filling my smile with flowing fire. I summoned forth my sisters, their own smiles set ablaze. The journey was its own destination—another unity, another mystery.

I soon glimpsed a structure in the distance, a huge house soaring unstoppable against the falling sky. Its uppermost portions were visible despite their impossible height, slipping the limitations of ordinary spectacle. Fantastically, this was not only a house of grand design, but an aggregation of dilapidated tenement buildings, a beautifully endless complex of apartments.

As I approached the spiraling marvel, I alighted upon the cracked stone of a narrow walkway. The path led into and around a forest of crooked property markers, broken birdbaths, and close-packed hordes of tacky lawn ornaments. At last, I stood before the building, beneath a second rain—cartwheeling paint chips, cast off from the curdling exterior of the towering hovel. The wind narrowed to a whisper, allowing a single, contrasting note of air to sound out the appropriate awesomeness of the moment. In its turn, stepping out from behind the thin curtain of sound, came the relentless creaking of the rambling monolith, the unsteady balance of countless buildings standing atop each other's rickety shoulders. I drew as close to the structure as I could without losing sight of its swaying top, enjoying how it conducted my vision into the boundless sky, my sight pulled into forever. Looking back over the path I'd followed to arrive at such a marvel, I watched as the ghost of the glowing rain rose again as a softly radiant mist, threatening shapes wandering its dimly visible interior. It was only this specter of violence that at last caused my father to stir from his rest. Yet I was in no mood for the distraction of bloodshed—the spire called.

The place admitted me without resistance, the large door atop a teetering, rotting porch swinging open upon barely solid moorings. The heady odor of melancholy tumbled beyond the threshold. The wood of the lobby was so soft, it felt like carpeting beneath my footsteps. The surrounding walls wore their water damage like museum art, each tone of orange and brown expertly laid into their death and the consequent birth of mold. Failing pillars of counterfeit alabaster barely hefted the cathedral ceiling above my head. They had failed altogether in numerous places, spilling the guts of the second story across the fungal floor. The discount simulacrum of a Grecian lobby contrasted wonderfully the unapologetic cheapness of the succeeding rooms, each more wonderfully warped than the previous. The barely perceptible lights were like the grey stars of some forgotten, dilated sky, hanging limply atop clouds of meandering dust. Faint sounds of movement, television game shows, and domestic disputes dripped down from beyond dense barriers of water-swollen support beams and mold-fattened insulation. Every inch the miserable glory of abandoned things, the idols of truest depression, the art of despair—all of it squeezed into a single, infinite dung-hole.

After only a few exquisite moments of exploration, the lights began to flutter, lilting into near darkness and dimming into sallow bleakness, a fruiting corpse smeared across dissolving walls. I hoped the effect foreshadowed some wonderful event, a brief distraction to buy the next performance time for a proper showing. I was not disappointed.

Within moments of the flickering, a vast emptiness overcame the atmosphere, a clearing out of unseen spaces for the facilitation of a massive predator, a kind of living melancholy. It descended upon me through the distilled sadness that comprised the kingdom of apartments. It was the sum of all tears gone hopeless and dry in their ducts, inscrutable for their infinite smallness, an elemental of purest failure. I could feel it grasping desperately at quite particular parts of my mind, if not my soul, seeking out what most resonated with its highly selective dietary needs. Fortunately, I am not a despairing creature, nor am I one to hold onto my failures—so I offered little by way of sustenance.

I was about to chide my invisible attacker over the futility of its quest when it finally managed a handhold somewhere within the thoroughly broken parts of me. What afforded the scrabbling sorrow its traction appeared to be a bit of submerged memory. The recollection was rigid and cold, like the touch of a machine god. I could feel it approaching realization with the determination of a bloated corpse returning to the water's surface. And so, I departed one lost memory for another, more deeply recessed remembrance.

I found myself in a familiar darkness, beneath a terrible storm. Thunder and lightning surged across the blackened sky. Mother lay dead in my arms, her blood hot upon my tongue. It was not the copper of ordinary blood, but the sweet fire of roses and secrets, all of it burning quietly behind my lips. The flesh of her heart glided down the back of my throat.

That's when I realized the Vanishing Nowhere was true to its name. It was more than a battered dream, it was on the cusp of being entirely forgotten, filling itself up with anything that might weigh it down, to keep it from the jaws of nothingness. My buried shame was nothing but a flailing lifeline for the grasping, and I was in far more danger than I knew.

Even as I kept my memories just out of reach of the clutching gloom, I could feel nothing but pity for the dream on the very rim of death. My denial of its will to survive sent explosions of hypocrisy blooming into my darkness, illuminating my many scars from the Dead Mother—where some of her still remained, like an infection, growing tumorous, trying to fill me with all the convictions of the whited dead. Convictions such as the will to survive despite all else, a singular cosmic drive, overthrown only occasionally when the survival of the group takes precedence. And there I was, trying to cast out a drowning man from my tiny lifeboat, the fear of capsizing making a worried coward of me.

My next actions should have been my first—I held out a terrible memory, and then another, and another. Hand-feeding the desperate dream brought it into me, where it began to lay down deep, thirsting roots, anchoring itself to my newly discovered woes. But the painful reacquaintance with my neglected past was prerequisite for the dream's survival. It fed upon me till it was drunk and fat from ripest misery—drab walls renewed themselves in thick sheaves of liquescent wood rot and scuttling vermin, and so the temple to depression blossomed like a blackened meadow filled with burned flowers, strong with the scent of smoldering beauty. In the distance, far above me, I could hear the construction of a new room, a live-born space of specific horror—my horror, where the blood of my new family outlined the places where I had slain them. Where I had eaten them.

The room retreated from me—I was a spent morsel, a husk. Perhaps I'd always been empty, I was forced to consider, and had only just nursed a void. Over the course of my many and sundry battles, I'd been struck by monsters and gods alike, and kept my feet—but never had any blow diminished me so thoroughly as the memory which now stood revealed. I collapsed to the ground. And for my troubles, the apartment house mimicked the sounds it had plucked from my ultimate sadness, no doubt the equivalent of turning a canteen upside-down—an attempt to coax one last drop of nourishment from its hiding place. A terrible memory came spilling from without my overturned mind— of the time when I took them all from the world:

They could vanish from sight within an empty white room, sever the spine of a charging razorback in seconds, scale a wall like scuttling spiders—my sisters were, in every pore of their souls, hunters. That night beneath the storm and darkness of night, we played one last game together, with knives and smiles and blood and death. It was our mother's wish that we do so. It was necessary, and we understood why.

I remember when they tricked me into that attic, with vanishing footfalls and feigns aplenty, their abrupt laughter coming from impossible places, knives sliding across my skin like bladed breaths. The tiny room seemed to shrink, closing in on me, denying me the use of my strength. When the door closed from behind, they were upon me. Their speed was inhuman, moving over and across me with their blades dragging behind them, freeing my blood into the darkness, giggling like pull-string dolls, eyes blacker than funerals. I dove into the deepest silence I could manage, hoping to lose them in my wake. But it was no use, I was trying to outswim barracudas. They were only toying with me, and we all knew it. It was the nature of our game. I could never hide from them. Never evade them.

At the best of times, I was only their plaything, and that night—the worst of times—my heart wasn't in it at all. I could never hurt them, not even for Mother. I just sat upon the floor, waiting for them to take me, my whole purpose forfeited. My test failed—I wasn't the one my mother needed. I lowered my head in surrender.

While I could not hear them, I knew they were standing over me, my wonderful sisters. "It will be our secret, dear brother," they said in whispered unison. I could feel them slip my bone-handled blades into my limp hands—the knives which formed the principal scaffolding for my skills with a blade. They were warm and wet with blood, my sisters' blood, as my sisters had drawn them across their throats. It was all they ever wanted in the world—to join me in spirit.

Here was the real test, to see the task completed, without shedding a single tear. I held the two of them close, their whispered blood falling across my shoulders and down my back, gossamer waterfalls of bottomless red. Their sweetened smiles were like hot tears against my skin, and they whispered again, "Whatever joy is left in this world, dear brother, we will find together, as one. Now, do what you must. What we all must." There was no visual memory of what came next, only the deepest refusal for knowledge, a pictureless recall of events wrapped in such darkness as I'd never known, before or since. I do not know if I cried. I hope that I had, test be damned.

Afterward, the floor shook as if the world were coming apart beneath the rage of a mad god—my father would not come to me like a lamb, but as a lion. His test was violence, pure and red. My forebear's axe moved through the world without resistance, passing through stone and steel as easily as smoke, its killing edge irresistible as time. The old mansion within which we sheltered cracked and split as he charged.

When at last we came together in perfect violence, I truly believed the resulting calamity cowed the storm that hung above us—lurking and looking upon our contest with some interest, no doubt. His first blow sent my knives tumbling from my hands where they met the falling axe, casting my body through the air, a wall, and a third-story window. Laughter like the end of the world followed me the entire way, gnawing at the raw tips of my every nerve. What I took for more thunder became the sound of my father smashing through the wall next to the window he'd sent me through—axe raised above his head, descending from the black, stormy air, laughter exploding past his frothing, gaping jaws.

Asserting my own strength, I lunged into the air, thrusting my shoulder into Father's hurtling mass. Reality might have buckled slightly as I denied the inertia of his attack, delivering us both deeper into the dilapidated manse, crashing through its layers and roaring through what was left of its cellar door. The underground darkness was quick to obliterate us, but not before I hoisted the axe-bearer from where he struggled upon my shoulder and threw him into the churning pitch.

Not entirely to my surprise, there came no hint of the near giant man crashing down, only empty silence waiting to be filled with the din of war. My father, like myself, was friend to both darkness and silence. Suddenly, the silence broke as my father's axe was tossed carelessly into a corner, clanking down upon the cold stone. Then came the sound of stiff joints being cracked loudly, in preparation for a final confrontation of the most primitive and brutal kind. A voice exploded through the darkness. "Come, boy! Show me what you've learned!"

His fist struck like a hammer, pulping gums and ejecting several teeth, freeing blood into the sheltered darkness. I needed to demonstrate my mettle, become the stanch anvil the hammer was struck against, and so I proved worthy of his first blow—I still stood, if only barely. Unfortunately, the same could not be said after his succeeding attack. I was thrown from the floor and sent crashing into the damp stone, my bones screaming their limits, my mind exploding into sparks of pinwheeling awareness. His third blow struck the wall, ancient rock yielding to an oversized fist, as I'd recovered enough to sidestep. Lurching forward, I launched my own oversized fist back into the fray, where it collided with rows of exposed, raw-red teeth—Father's perpetual rictus grin. He was every inch unfazed, if dispossessed of several of his own teeth.

Every bit my father's son, it was my second blow that took him from the earth. He smashed through a nearby support beam, bringing some of the ceiling down, roaring indignation through dust and collapsing wood. Not wasting a second on the spectacle, I charged through the avalanche, leaping up and delivering an airborne kick—all my weight and strength, doubled by inertia—squarely into his chest. The giant flew backwards into the blackness of an adjoining room. Silence again.

I couldn't afford to lose my momentum, which was my father's hope. I rushed into the room, prepared to seize and smash whatever I came upon. My father had always been an enigma to me—his scars, his monstrous demeanor— but, even more than that, his violence. It was anarchy. One moment he was raging, the next, cold as winter stone, effecting no predictable cadence to his chaos. Here was no different. As I charged into the room, a soft encumbrance met with my left foot, tripping me face-first into the wall. More rattling teeth and bones. I had neglected to notice the huge foot sticking out, patiently waiting for me to run into it. My father was as much fox as wolf.

It was utterly dark, so I might have been forgiven for thinking my opponent had taken a sledgehammer to my kidneys, but I knew better—his fists were no less, if not more than tools made for splitting rock. The pain dropped me to the floor, and before I had the chance to roll to my back, a great booted foot stomped me into the wet stone. I had become only an insect to be crushed out of existence, nothing more. Repeatedly came the thunder of my father's devastating footfalls, each monstrous impact compromising both the scaffolding of my body and the integrity of the floor. His booming laughter grew with every crunch and crackle my body gave up.

Yet anger was not sole ally to my father. Summoning my own fires, I vanished in a plume of vagrant darkness, my father's gigantic foot passing through empty space. In an instant, I rose up before my forbear, my massive fist swinging upward. The attack was weighted with as much anger as the need to impress. Even in a battle to end his life, I would make him proud. His head snapped backward, offering me only an instant to act. I seized the exposed throat of the man who had raised me—imparted his exquisite violence, made me a man—and I tore it out.

But death would not take my father without a fight, as I should have known. I was seized in a monster's death-grip and smashed through the solid rock of another wall. He released me only long enough to rain down fists like meaty comets, pounding me unrecognizable. I gave him his last rage, and so let my arms drop to my sides. I was thankful for all the blood, as it concealed my tears for him, a gesture he would certainly have disapproved of. His attack slowed until he finally collapsed into me.

His final words as a living man came out in a hiss of air and blood. "Boy . . . I fought this rotting world and lost. But because of me, you whelp . . . you will not." In darkness and blood and death, I held my father for the first time. But it would not be the last.

The memory of my father ended, renewing my strength. I seized the dismal spirit of the spire, prying back its jaws, denying it the last of my energy for its own. It would have to make do with what I surrendered. Realizing that I would feed it no more, willingly or otherwise, the incarnate melancholy withdrew, begrudgingly dripping my stolen sadness as it went, slamming a thousand doors behind it. I was alone upon the moldering, cracked floor, the undesired memory of sacrificial flesh my only companion, playing across my tongue, passing into the doubtful myth of myself. What had mother done to me? To all of us?

Somewhere, a song began playing, a soothing box of musical notes cranking colored sound into the stale air. There was an instant connection with me, music and memory holding hands—yet it was a recollection without recognition. The house was trying to come back to some semblance of life, my misery bloating its arteries. It was a kind of gratitude, I suppose. An ode to one man's saving failures. The desperate, dying dream was an indebted thing now, wanting to repay me for my troubles. It was leading me to a room, my room, made especially for—from—me. I rose and made my way past countless derelict apartments, corpses of living spaces. There were entire lifetimes heaped into dirty corners, abandoned dreams without dreamers.

At last I came upon a room with its door ajar, music seeping through, luring me. My next few thoughts seemed trapped by the subdued harmony, flies caught within a web spun from silken sound. I realized that the composition of notes was scored from my own life—my very soul made music, playing through my mind's eye. It was a somber piece, though not without its share of uplifting notes. But most curious was the theme that played in the sonic underground, far beneath the passing movements, a submerged peal of deepest staccato, wavering and waiting. It somehow had both the quality of a stringed instrument and a vastly percussive creature. The sound stirred beneath the sonic interpretation of my life, occasionally revealed in the depth of a trumpet or cello, even the deep blast of a tuba, but mostly it lived in the drums, sounding out the heartbeat of something hidden and terrible.

I gently opened the door the rest of the way, eager and curious for fresh revelations. Though, to be honest, I was well over my respective limit for fresh revelation. The room seemed far older than what a modern apartment could ever hope to address. I was to dwell here, to the sound of my failed life, basking in the grey glow of desperate immortality, to pace a dirty floor and stare from a single dirty window, in slowest turns of wonder and despair. It was a pleasant enough gift, to be sure, and one I wanted to make no immediate show of rejecting. I didn't want to ruin a friendship.

My time in the room was indeterminate, as was only proper within a dream. I did as I would, drowsing in pale rooms, covered in a kind of merger of dust and shadow, a soft alliance of two substances barely distinct even within the firmest of worlds. I did indeed stare from the soiled window, glimpsing strange sights—occasional leviathans of some type lurched the opaque distance, restless and monstrous. There were also the sounds of ceaseless sadness embodied within their own dour melodies, cobbled from suicide thoughts and disappointed expectations. This place was the end of all meaningful hope, a morose equilibria for the failed and miserable, where one could fade away, quietly, imperceptibly.

Despite all that, there was indeed beauty in the bleakness, however small—the dull poetry of common failure, the ceaseless drone of ordinary silence, the wan, sickly glow of dying. It was its own art gallery, a perfected habitat for the greyest pieces, and it was in no need of improvement—save perhaps for its inability to sustain itself, which almost seemed a necessary component for a properly ironic existence. And yet something seemed to linger, undiscovered and out of place—a purpose.

I searched not only the room, but portions of the complex itself, an endless wonderland of misery and waste. And while I glimpsed more than was healthy for a sober mind, I did not alight upon anything slightly resembling a meaningful thing, unspent of its ominous burden. When I appeared before a great iron door, distinct for its possession of an apparent function beyond reflecting fruitlessness, I thought my quest nearing completion. My father had grown sorely bored of our stay in the apartment complex, so I thought to enliven his spirts by allowing him to cleave through the door. It might have opened on its own, as I spied no lock, but my father was in dire need of his own purpose.

The entrance was no match for him, and its remains tumbled like dull broken glass down a narrow stairwell that sank into blackened oblivion. There was no sound and no darkness, just a sort of hallway-shaped absence. But the more I studied the void, the more I realized its nothingness a product of my own, apparently unconscious desire not to see it for what it was. Also, my apartment's ancientness had either followed me from my room or had slipped itself from the void, as a profound expanse of time opened upon me—a second stairwell, its every step an epoch removed from me, unfurling, leading down.

Eventually, after some very bemused theorizing as to cause, I heard a sound—drums. They were indistinct at first, but gradually increasing. They came from beyond infinite distances I could only faintly detect. It was the hidden staccato of my private song, stretching out into the clearest notes I'd yet to hear, and still it slept, coiled and waiting. Before I could attempt to total the slivers of clarity I'd been provided, the void swept me from the stairwell, and then some. I was all but lost to the crashing waves of waking when something spoke to me, whispered perhaps, from sleep. It said, "And still, there shall be hope."

Into the crush, again. Memories and dreams and pain and loss and love—a confusion of waking and dreaming and remembering. The precise state that had been overthrown in favor of an enduring order to things, now only the occasional and wholly unstable nexus for the hidden and secret. I was caught in the pull of a thousand currents, red games and scheming mothers and dead families, old and new. It was almost, pleasantly, too much for me to bear. But revelation was not yet through with me, for when I opened my eyes, it seemed as if dreams had yet again invaded the earth.

***

While I was reasonably certain I had awoken below the city of Willard, within the strange device Doctor Coldglow had placed me within, there was a strange overlap with a previous and skin-strewn dream. I seemed to occupy a bizarre hybrid of the Willard reality and the Skin-swapper's nightmare. While the room was of its previous size and shape, it had been filled with the skinned bodies of White Wigs, all of them made to appear dancing around the most bizarre and unintelligible shape, a shape slightly intimated from the negative space outlined by the sewn-together skins of the denuded towheads. No doubt, this was the symbol for the insanity the lunatics were beholden to, forever orbiting a thing barely hinted at, even by the sum of their many stolen skins. It was majestic. I even felt a pang of jealousy. Here was some of the finest art I'd ever had the pleasure of witnessing—at the cost of appearing braggadocios, it was certainly worthy of standing alongside any of my own pieces. It even seemed like something I would create. Unfortunately, as is the case within the solid world, there was a good reason for the similarity.

A voice from the shadows, husky and proud, came at me from the back of the room. "I can tell you approve of my work. Or, is it *our* work?" It was Mister Hyde, but that was the least of my realizations. The pain that came out of the dream with me had not subsided, but in fact had been augmented. The pale light of the room revealed me, affording the deepest look at myself I'd ever been given—I had been removed of my skin.

Mister Hide continued with his soliloquy, as I was without lips with which to properly converse. "I assume it is only by the good graces of that feral Red Dream you still live, just as I'd hoped you would. You see, it seems you've left me with a bit of a problem. Prior our interruption, you had me dead to rights—defeated. Now, if I'm the chosen one to right the world, to replace the lost skins, how is it that you could defeat me? Don't answer, allow me—it's because I was not in my right skin, after all. Here I was, mis-attired the whole time, just waiting for my own lost skin to be returned to me. And here we are, appropriately dressed for our last and rightful—fateful—contest. But unlike what you presumed during our first encounter—you're a perfect fit." Mister Hyde stepped into the wan light, wearing my skin.

There were precious few things, I must sadly confess, which could truly surprise me—this was such a thing. He was a grizzly sight, a collage of raw, red skin atop glistening, exposed muscle. My contorted face was sewn into the meat of his cheeks and forehead. My ample beard bristled and tangled into the flaps of the sewn-on chin, yellowing globs of blood-streaked fat weighing them down, folding them over. My mane of hair fell like tousled darkness across his back, framing a most wonderful piece of art, if not the antithesis of the nature of Deadworld art—it had survived its creation. Here was not the corpse of a dream, but its living, breathing body.

Not even the pain of having been undressed of all my flesh could diminish my admiration for what stood before me. But as it turned out, I was wrong—I hadn't been left entirely nude. I put my hand to my face, realizing something had been sewn atop it—Hide's own face. He had altered the very reality of our first encounter, reversing our roles, perhaps even our respective fates. My head throbbed with the question—what if he was right? What if I was only the means to Hide's end? He was living art. What was I next to that? Then, a deciding moment. Hide moved to gather my father into his hand. I would let him choose—my father would know best. The grotesque doppelganger hefted the axe with ease, his—my—face unfazed for the contact. His next words were not his own, and dipped in purest hell. "You cried for me! Pitied me! For that, you will pay, whelp!" It was my father's voice. It seemed my epiphanies of the last hours were not entirely my own to know, but had been shared with the shadows in my soul. And one shadow in particular was not happy for the knowledge. Father now realized I had cried for him, and now he was in a body—though a bit small for him—to exact a price for my transgression.

In keeping with our switched identities, I had been equipped with Mister Hide's knives, which I raised in a doomed attempt to deflect my inbound father. The axe batted aside the blades with ease, sinking into my shoulder. The pain was explosive, riding down exposed nerves already buzzing like live wires filled with electric agony. This turn of events after so much unwanted, unfiltered knowledge was almost too much for me to endure, and all coupled with the fact that my soul was only a few bloody layers from tumbling completely out my body. I tried to roll with the attack, to deny the axe a fatal depth, but my father descended at his leisure, going where he would, snapping and splitting skin, cartilage, and bone—but minding my more vital areas. This, it seemed, would be a lesson I wouldn't soon forget, but one I might walk away from.

Perhaps sensing my father's non-lethal intention, Hide threw him away, clanking down into the ample blood of dead Wigs, smoke hissing from his killing edge. Hide now meant to tear me apart with his bare hands, which had been skillfully gloved in my own —I think even Janus might have approved of that detail. Despite the Red Dream plying me with my share of unreality, I was still nearing the end of my respective tether. I had lost so much blood along with my skin, and my mind was already piled three times its weight in painful recollection. Not to mention the visionary in me could barely see the artist for the gallery—so much wonder and beauty. It was nearly paralyzing.

Hide applied little thought to his attack, likely due to my severely compromised state. I couldn't blame him for that, but my weakened state differed largely from the depleted conditions suffered by lesser artists. He shouldn't have confused the two. When at last his hands were around my neck, hoisting me from the earth, my own hands were busy prying up the lower portions of his rib cage. A clear red line of sutures secured my skin to his, and they strained and popped as I peeled my flesh from their moorings. Where the stitching was once merely shallow pock marks along Hides abdomen, they were now gaping flesh wounds, rivulets of blood pouring from their lengthy tracks.

It took only a moment for me to force my questing hands inside his body, finding the edges of his ribs. Hide, either to his credit or foolishness, paid no heed to my burrowing hands, and continued to lift me, my grip upon his bones supplying enough counterforce to disallow my placement above his head. It was then only a matter of placing my boot upon his chest, using him for the necessary leverage, and pulling backwards with all my might, ribcage in hand. His bones came away like roots pulled from the dirt, with the colorful exception of all the red spillage and wet snapping sounds.

Hide released me, roaring more from indignation than pain, it seemed. I rose back to my feet and held out my prizes. I filtered my speech through the paradoxical powers of the Red Dream, allowing my lipless words to be understood. "You took so much from me, yet left me only with your face—so I decided to take something more from you to balance the scales."

It was now Hide's turn to lean upon the Red Dream, as his wounds would have proven fatal otherwise. I continued to cast words at him through the bleeding vision we shared. "We could be brothers, you and I. Twins, even. And now, having established such a connection, you know how I use the bones of my family, yes?"

I lunged forward, placing the mass of broken ribs in my hands back into Hide's chest. Once they had achieved the proper depth, I used the makeshift handles to lift my howling opponent from the ground. It was a long walk to Hide's art exhibit, but I'd always enjoyed brisk strolls through the underground, especially in such wonderful company. Hide's violent protests came to a sudden stop when I slammed his body down atop a large steel shaft anchoring one end of the canopy of skins. His grip upon the Red Dream was fading, his swan song near completion.

With one last effort, Hide clawed out at me. I allowed his hand to close over his lost face, reclaiming it—and with it, the fate he attempted to impart me. I looked down almost shamefully before meeting the eyes of the skinner. "I would have enjoyed nothing more than spiting such a creature as fate," I whispered, "a mindless brute rusted into ancient habits. But if it should occasionally align with my needs, I must wish it well." Hide's eyes had shed their fury, the face he'd stolen from me placid and near blank. "I'd like to think that I bring all of you with me," I continued, "our mighty pack of Wolves, ever-growing, preparing for the final battle."

He only looked up and smiled with my lips, murmuring, "I'd like that, too." I watched the great skin-switcher's fire sink into the ashes of his dark eyes, and I reckoned yet another awful deed performed in service to the Shepherd's terrible Game.

For quite some time, I slept in the gathered silence beneath the lunatics' conjoined skins, regrowing my lost flesh. I was host to many wonderful dreams there, happy for the excuse to do nothing but drowse. But I was clearly not alone. I had calculated the absence of Doctor Coldglow and his protégé as soon as I gazed upon Hide's art, that beautiful thing partaking in equal measure from myself and the spoiling giant nearby. Yet it was not the hypnotist or his companion, but the very Angel of Madness itself, the irrepressible Deleriael. I denied its presence for as long as I was able, though I wanted nothing more than to converse with the thing. But ultimately, I knew it would be to my mind's peril. I understood that the real failure of insanity lay in its false victory against the Deadworld, its host made to believe they'd burned it down, when in fact they bore only the smoke of a great fire—none of its heat. And yet, the very thought of conjuring such phantom flames, however illusory, was extremely tempting to me. Too tempting. It was because of such thinking the angel chose to speak with me, or possibly because it realized I'd recently regained the use of my speech, my lips having finally returned.

I watched as one of the skinned lunatics broke from his circle of dancing White Wigs, a blazing laughter of light forming a strange, wheeling design above his head, its brilliance throwing the shadows of the skinless dancers upon the wall, where they silently twirled and pirouetted and leapt. Deleriael's host calmly walked to where I stretched out upon the floor. He sat down and joined me as I marveled at the shadow show. After a few minutes, without turning away from the darksome sights, Deleriael said, "There is strength in numbers, Vincent. You would not be alone. We would be with you, sharing an interim world of finest foxfire until finally, inexorably, we grew the real thing. A fire made from fever dreams and dragon's breath, enough to burn down heaven and hell both, leaving nothing behind but the souls they'd stolen away. All of them—us—now free to wallow in a world without walls. Is that really so bad, my stubborn friend?"

"You know it's not, or else we wouldn't be having this conversation," I replied. "Yet I wonder if you're telling the truth. For what insanity was ever purposeful?"

"Pray tell, what good was ever intended by a dream?" the angel returned. "One might argue, if they were so inclined, that it's *you* who's not being very honest, Vincent. You more than suspect her, now. You're a player in more than just the one game, and you know it. You just won't admit it. Because if you did . . ."

"I would belong to you."

The angel laughed mightily, howling, "Bingo! So why not derail the whole train while there's still passengers to pulverize? Why wait until it's too late, and you're merely *forced* to come with me? They're still advancing you across the chessboard, making plays and calculations, minding rules. Imagine the chaos you'd cause if you just leapt off the board! You and that wonderful Jack Lantern, both. I'm sure it'd take very little convincing for him to join you—us. By the gods, imagine the trouble we could cause, the three of us!" Deleriael proved a master artist, painting the most exquisite pictures in the gallery of my mind. The three of us, joined in the sweetest madness an angel could supply, riding the lightning across the world.

"I can't deny the beauty of your offer," I admitted. "As an artist, I'm impelled to see it both for what it is and what it could be, given certain cosmic adjustments, of course. But I'm afraid I must refuse, much to my own chagrin. This whole journey of mine, this quest, Game—whatever it turns out to be—harbors a chaos none of its players or even its hosts can contain or control, despite their efforts to the contrary. I can feel that as surely as any of the truths you've uttered. It's my chaos to cultivate, my dream. I must see it through, to give it life." I finally turned to look at the angel, waiting for its response, truly sorry for rejecting its splendid offer.

It only continued staring at the wall, where its mind painted the souls of the mad in shadow and dance. But the show was quickly fading back to the stone of an unflinching wall, the strange glowing sigil above the angel's head diminishing by the second. When the light was all but gone, the creature stood and replaced its borrowed body back into the line of frozen dancers, slowly reassuming its pose. Still not looking at me, the dejected angel said, "I understand. I just wish you'd come play with me. The fun we could have, forever. But I do think you're correct to refuse me. I see it, too—the chaos. But it's not in my nature to wait and see, you understand. I'll see you soon enough, Vincent. And I do hope you win your game. You deserve it more than anyone. But one word of advice, before I go." The angel finally turned its head to face me. "Chaos is no respecter of its creator." And then Deleriael, the Angel of Madness, was gone.

The rest of my wanderings through Willard, even the dreams that followed, were rendered dull by the angel's visitation, or more specifically, its declined invitation. Every sight I came upon, even those that should have proved delightful, I was forced to see as inferior to what might have been, had only I allowed the mad angel to open my eyes. It was for this very reason I chose at last to inspect Mister Hide's kill list, to find some relief in the next name and the mystery it would hold.

But there was no mystery. There was only one name on his list, and none left upon my own. I'd reached the end of the Game, and my final opponent was revealed. The name was both thrilling and terrible at once. I let the lists fall to the ground, now merely debris, there purpose exhausted. That very moment, I departed Willard for Autumn City, where I would face my final challenge—Jack Lantern.

CHAPTER TWENTY-THREE

With only the two of us left, the list left no mystery, as our awareness of each other was now fully joined. That awareness transcended even the traditional formality of the name-giving, which was always supplied as the wolf's prosaic name, what was given to them at birth, not the more hard-earned moniker that followed. The moment I set my sight upon the name, *William Grin,* I knew it was Jack. It was as if the name itself were merely a mask, and the time for masks and hiding had passed away. I did not wonder if he was as pleased as I was for the knowledge, because I knew the answer to that, too. I could feel his excitement at the prospect of a proper playmate, a Wolf as beholden to dream as he. Of course, the distinctions between our dreams could not be starker or portentous in their coming into being. This latest reason was my confidence, as my quest held more to gain, for everyone.

Jack's dream, it seemed to me, was just the want to progress down a dead-end tunnel, largely uninterrupted but for the lovely orange holiday he would celebrate en route to the bitter end. I didn't suppose my purpose better supported by fate, only that our respective hearts would be more or less involved in the fight due to the grandness of potential gains. But even this perspective supplied only a dash of self-confidence, as I knew my opponent was not limited to a logical interpretation of his dream—as is only appropriate, after all.

As soon as Willard was in the waning distance, its solidified insanity an indistinct collection of absurdities playing against the glittering orange of the sinking sun, I stepped upon solid road for the first time in months. Granted, the road had likely not been traveled by any honest persons for some time, mostly serving the needs of things wishing to move through the night upon a slightly more forgiving surface. But it pleased me to walk upon the thing, as its banality served to augment the other, stranger sights I might come across traveling its length. My imagination had come under a kind of pallor since my talk with Deleriael, and the conceptual boost would do my mood well.

The road was like a solidified creek of snaking black stone, trying—but clearly failing—to escape the encroaching banks of the forest which drew ever closer to erasing the artificial passage, once and for all. At other times, as the light grew weaker, I had the sense of walking a narrow boardwalk, barely set apart from the surging green tides rushing past its fragile construction, and at any moment, the scaffolding might fail, abandoning me to the wildness beyond. Finally, sketched in the dim light of a waning moon, I often thought I glimpsed passing shapes, appearing generally at the untrampled margins of the fading thoroughfare, shapes that might have been artifacts of the Darkness, or perhaps not. Taken together, my travels along the road were uplifting, and allowed my mind to deal with sights as it pleased, cobbling marvels from the mundane.

There was no shortage of dreams, either. I afforded myself much time for rest, often stretching out in thick, well-shaded copses of wild grass and assorted bramble. My first dream upon the road delivered me into an endless pumpkin patch, the sun nearly as plump and orange as any of the surrounding gourds, but half-submerged into the hazy soil of the horizon. I clearly remembered Jack Lantern standing atop the steepled roof of a crumbling hay barn, his silhouette a stationary gust of soft orange smoke, autumnal winds dancing around him like children. I knew that his proffered smile, though well-shaded from view, was sincere—a friendly greeting, as well as a sign for our mutual understanding that we should leave each other to their own dreams. I stepped backwards into the enfolding shadows of my father's gallery, surrounded by a lifetime of art, offering up my own smile, perhaps more recessed in darkness than his own, though equally noticed and understood. We nodded to one another just before piloting our respective visions beyond the shared space of the Red Dream. Due to our standing as finalists in the Shepherd's Game, our awareness of the other was unbothered by competing dreams—no more Wolves to interfere with the clarity of our shared wavelength. We were in no need of a dream to prepare for one another. We were plain as two sunny days, histories like well-read books, opened to the sun and recorded in plainest print. We knew who we were dealing with. We would be ready.

While I am no pessimist, this fact did not stop me from trying to wring as much wonder as possible from my surroundings and the dreams they inspired, as one never knows when they will be asked to leave the world—or ushered out of it by persons wearing Halloween masks. I had no plans to depart any time soon, but it never hurt to have a bag packed, just in case. So, I spared no sight my fascination, and no fascination its fuller realization within dreams. The Deadworld never seemed rifer with hidden wonder than the day I let fall those lists. My fascination came to a head on my fourth day on the road, when the black path veered close to a strange cemetery.

It was a forgotten place, likely due to its proximity to nearby Obscuruum, of which there were many. It wasn't a particularly large plot, but more grandiose than one would expect abandoned to the wilds. Something was amiss with the place, something altogether enthralling. The mystery that wafted from beyond, or perhaps beneath the tombstones was nearly palpable, and would need to be to derail me from my intended destination. Stepping from the road seemed to awaken in me a lateral curiosity, an off-plumb bit of wonder—about life after Jack Lantern, after the Shepherd, after my mother. Surely, the prospect of a disappointing climax to the game had entered my mind, that the contest was merely the pretext for something less than the sustained wonder of an eternal child. But the sharp disconnect from purpose, the crowd of stones holding down the dead, allowed me to focus on another, altogether different specter of the unknown. The moment felt like a temptation, to do something else, to wander away from the game. I knew Jack wouldn't mind. His Halloween was forever, and forgiving of any act of defiance, so long as it flouted the machine of it all.

My mother was dead—I'd killed her myself, as I had the rest of my family. We were already free. As free as death and the Deadworld would allow. I could go anywhere. I could spare Jack the death I'd given every Wolf I'd encountered since I'd set foot in the game. I might be forgiven for such a thing, for allowing a wonder like Jack to continue, unabated. I should point out that such thoughts were not rationalizations, excuses for avoiding the death Jack might very well serve me. I was prepared to die, if not terribly pleased by the prospect—not of dying, but the possibility of failing, failing us all. It was ultimately that fear that would put me back on the path of Wolves. Fear generally has its way with us, one way or another.

Something about this new presence was growing familiar, but it was no Wolf. This was something else. And the impulse to pursue it was also something else, beyond mere curiosity. I'd felt it before, when I destroyed the white son of the Dead Mother—when the Shepherd intervened for the proper continuance of its Game. I wondered at how many other Wolves had been summoned for such reasons, to defend our game. I was also forced to wonder at how much my free will was engaged in my decisions, having now reached the bottom of my list. Was I just a murderer in thrall to the Murder God? Just another lateral curiosity, that.

I felt a bit like a fool, thinking as I had that this diversion might be a crack in fate, allowing me the option of abandoning the Game. This was just another calling from the Shepherd to put something right. Even as I realized all of this, I continued, almost mindlessly. There was a degree of shame in that, given who I was, what I sought to accomplish. It was the first cogent argument I'd been given in support of Jack's "Machine Hypothesis."

I realized quickly that the cemetery was more rambling than I'd assumed, unfolding deep into thick woods, almost entirely joined with the forest, where grave-dust was reborn as loam, old bones reached out of the soil as saplings—the cycle of a corpse. At some point, across the hidden burying grounds, old blood painted the woods, and scars of a battle split trees and sundered headstones—a war between Wolves. I retraced the carnage as one pursues a scar across flesh, to where the blade first enters the skin. It wasn't long before I came across the loser of the conflict, remains scattered, scraps of a kill list like yellow fungus curled up beneath the overhang of a wilting weed, tips blackened by the kiss of fire. Sadness gripped me. I'd left so many Wolves behind like this one, all to waste. The aftermath of my sins were laid out before me. I think I might have leaned into the mindlessness of my purpose at that point, to dull the edge of what I'd done—would do, one final time.

The footprints of the winner were slight, lithe—a female Wolf. Her tracks were echoes of a dancer recorded in the earth, replaying ever-slighter with each passing rain. There was a lightness to her tread, free and wonderful. She would have been a pleasure to know in life, I was sure. But she was not alive. My standing in the contest cemented the fact. But it was not a Wolf, I now knew, who stole her from the game.

The footpath was sporadic, like she had stopped to gather as much wonder as possible along her way. But ultimately her tracks, and presumably her life, ended within a stark, white mystery. Across the side of a cliff was blazoned what appeared to be a kind of white powder, only that it could not be removed, even with effort. Within the irregular bloom of bleached stone was framed the blackest shadow of a killing woman caught off her guard. But by who?

Interestingly, I found another set of tracks, of both a person and what I took to be a tripod. That's when I remembered—the strange photographer from the train to Lastrygone. But perhaps what I did not realize was of even greater importance—the lack of the Wolf's body. What I presumed was the photographer's tread was no greater or lesser wherever I encountered it, except where the camera had been set out. Thus, I was forced to conclude that the body was not carried out. Also, the shadow upon the stone was not carbon scoring, but merely what seemed, perhaps strangest of all, a natural discoloration of the stone. So, the Wolf was also not reduced to ashes. This made for a pleasant mystery, indeed.

The photographer's steps were not difficult to follow, for no effort was made to conceal them. Unlike the Wolf, the tracks were not light, lithe, or exceptional in any way. They were cold and unwavering, businesslike. I found the disposition totally inconsistent with an artist, even though I must confess that photography was not well known to me. Not that I found the practice beneath me, quite the contrary, really. I found it to be, when properly accomplished, the purest sort of art—pre-art. To capture the very spirit of a subject, the shadow and the caster all at once, was a purely otherworldly composition. Of course, the beauty wasn't completely teased out, only hinted at—an exquisite beginning.

Beginnings were often, although not always, more beautiful than conclusions. So much was contained within the beginning, likely too much. Most artists, ironically, started at the end of things—sunsets, bones of the body, the moon, the harvest. They started there because the end was an explicit affair, while beginnings were almost entirely implicit—easy to miss, harder to capture, requiring a seasoned artist with an eye for the hidden. In fact, the only thing more difficult to render, in its approximate completeness, was a dream, which was both causeless and endless, yet it begins and ends—paradox incarnate. This should do well to explain why I was not a photographer—one cannot photograph a dream.

When the sun was all but dead, I came upon the remains of a house, destroyed almost entirely. Its placement within the densest crowd of trees the woods had to offer—at the foot of a meandering boneyard, no less—intrigued me. The solemn photographer had entered the structure, and so did I. Its rooms were thoroughly destroyed by the weapons and workers of the woods—vines, weeds, burrowing and nesting things. Rooms little more than bones of an ancient industry sheltered various night-things, creatures preferring the darkness of natural enclosures, the corpses of forgotten dead, and the inattention of sun-loving prey. One after the next, crumbling rooms appeared and vanished from my focus, the tracks casually picking through the various debris.

Suddenly, and without suitable preface for such a bizarre thing, a room darker than it had occasion to be appeared. Daylight still lingered the various entrances to the place, a lilting glow that, while diminished, should have had its way with the thickest natural darkness. But the black hung like a curtain across the threshold, nearly tangible, decrying any and all illumination. Gently disturbed by a cautious breeze, the sable curtain even reacted as if a material thing, however slightly. I reached out to touch it—cobwebs and cold. I pushed through it, and a membrane of outer darkness admitted me. The space within was completely free of light, not a speck staining the air. The cold and dark were a unified force here, molded from purpose, surely. My eyes, stunned for the absence of obedient shadow, struggled for signposts.

My sisters took to my hands, their smiles burning obedience into the reserved bleakness, retraining its loyalties.

The objects of the room slowly came into focus, gossamer structures melting out from the wincing, lightless cold. Developer fluids, scissors, stop bath and fixer, strings and clothespins, rubber gloves—a darkroom. My respect for photography exploded when my fingers closed over a picture clasped to a thin wire. The image within was . . . alive. The object—or was it a subject? —moved beneath my fingertips, pulsing, emitting life more vital than could be conveyed through simple skin, but only by the soul itself. The image overflowed me, rising beyond me, invading the freezing blackness. Its horror was profound, painful. The thing's resulting scream invaded me. I could feel my family flinching at the sound as it transferred itself into the bones of their spirits, moving like a surge of electricity across one conductor after the next. The sound leapt from my fingers, racing across the hundreds of other photos hanging from wires, each new print joining its scream with the next. The chain of shrieks became a fire of blazing sound, burning across everything, threatening to obliterate the world.

It happened before I could stop him. My father became my hands, raising himself high, his voice an explosion. "Enough!" He descended with searing desperation. The air went white-hot. Thunder and scream rose into the air, circling one another, hawks facing off. Then came silence, the offspring of mutual annihilation. Next came oblivion.

Jack was waiting for me on the other side. "Hello, Vincent! I was curious if I'd find you here. That awful Shepherd has been attempting to dislodge me from my work to recover some lost bauble or another, of all things. Naturally, with my refusal to budge, I assumed he'd be calling upon you." I gleaned a few important points from his words. I was not the Shepherd's first choice for the effort, which might speak to his confidence in my abilities. And I should have been ashamed for succumbing to the Shepherd's will so easily.

Ultimately, I wished to tear out the eyes of this Shepherd for revealing things about myself I may have been much better not knowing. Mysteries should be let alone, for all our sakes.

Jack was speaking to me from the shadows of the September Woods, sunken to near invisibility within the crowding thickets and flowing gullies of twilight. I was prone, upon the floor of my own dream—of the ring of lunatics I'd left behind in Willard, a manifestation of my alternative to all the Shepherd's foolishness. The image was not lost upon Jack, who immediately fixed his orange gaze upon the madness of skin and dream. "Well, isn't that a wonder? One of your pieces, I presume?" Jack's curiosity was aflame. Our dream allowed his eyes to take on the appearance of shivering candle flames.

"In a way, perhaps," was all I said, my mind still anchored to matters outside the dream.

"Poor, poor Mister Hide. He could have been such a wonderful ally to the New Halloween, that eternal holiday of hiding and tricking. No friend to the machines, that one." Jack was shaking his head in genuine grief.

While I was not sure what a New Halloween was, though I had a decent idea, Mister Hide would indeed be sorely missed. "He was, to the last, one of the greatest dreamers I've ever encountered," I said, nodding in agreement. But as I continued to look upon the last work of the great skin-switcher, I saw the mad angel rise from beneath the aggregate skins of the death-frozen, un-fleshed White Wigs. Deleriael wrapped the sewn skins around himself as if a shawl, his mismatched wings thrust out, dripping flame and insects, both scuttling and creeping across the floor in turns of titter and hiss. Jack seemed not to notice. A dream, or perhaps a hallucination, inside a shared dream—by the gods, this Game!

Deleriael bowed low, to demonstrate the fit of his form-flattering article of insanity. "A perfect fit," said the deranged angel, winking his reference to some of Hide's final words to

me. "Ask him, Vincent. I know he'd join us. He'd love to!"
I couldn't tell if the angel was real or dream or the product
of my desire to quit the game—my impotent desire to quit
the game. I wiped the image of the angel from my mind, and
Deleriael vanished. Jack was now staring fully into me, eyes
like burning, laughing children.

"Something on your mind, Family Man?" He said,
assuming something wonderful. I was caught completely off
guard—my next words would decide my soul. He wanted
me to ask him to leave the Game. There was no doubt. He
would go with me, I had only to ask. Two children, running
through endless woods, playing games in the eternal twilight,
grinning angels in tow.

I almost wept when I said, "It's a photographer of sorts,
the one you were to hunt down. Though I've found him
already, for the most part. His work is remarkable. You
might have even enjoyed the reprieve for such spectacle."
I could feel my spirits sink beneath my words, the question
abandoned.

Jack seemed similarly shrunken, his eyes just wet lights
behind a dull orange mask. "I see," was all the Carver of
Souls said. With a downturned face, Jack walked away from
me, disappearing into the dim lights of the September Woods.
Just before I awoke, I thought I heard him say, "Pity."

I stood up within the further-ruined ruins of the forest-
forgotten house, my father still clutched in my burned hands.
The Darkroom was obliterated, but the trapdoor hidden
within its floor was revealed. I threw my mind behind the
pursuit of the magnificent photographer, putting missed
opportunities behind me. With my father returned to sleep,
I pried the door open and sank into a now-familiar lightless
cold.

The space was ampler than expected, partaking of a vast
cavern just below the house. The ground was littered with
more photography paraphernalia, albeit of the discarded
and broken variety. The uneven, earthen walls were nearly

covered in framed portraits of precisely nothing—empty overstuffed chairs, abandoned dinner tables, forgotten birthday parties. And at the end of the vacant, underground gallery, a cargo elevator that only went down. Pressing a single, glowing button affixed to the elevator, I proceeded deeper into the earth. The equipment screeched for its efforts to deliver me further into darkness, and yet I didn't have the sense of moving in any conventional sense. I might have been back in a dream but for the definitive sense of solidity.

The next level consisted of a train of empty—or emptied—rooms, all of them spanning ages of various architectural attitudes, and all of them sporting the same white blossom of frozen light that framed the shadow of the Wolf. The solidified illumination was positioned anywhere a person might have stood or sat or posed. I continued more quickly now, eager for the end of the place. As might have been expected, another elevator appeared.

Down again. The space of interlocking rooms continued, but with ever-diminishing earthliness. The white-spotted spaces were slowly partaking of a darker aesthetic, altogether exterior to conventional styles. Black-stoned flooring, each tile inlaid with strange symbols, wallpapers made from skins and scalps, masts of bone and compressed, smoking ash, balustrades worked from spinal columns. And yet for all the organic trimmings, none of it formed even the slightest connection to any creature I was remotely aware of. The fad of emptied photos continued too, but having evolved into unpeopled frescos and mosaics brimming with absent subjects. Faceless statuary greeted me from every widening, smoking threshold. In addition to the empty sitting rooms, I began to encounter the large meandering spaces for other kinds of art and artist. I found myself, at one point, stumbling across an elaborate studio of high ceiling and dusty shelving, packed tightly with taught, vellum canvases. And as was now custom, each painting was missing its focus, only a lingering, vague background was visible, backdrops to lost foregrounds, alone and featureless. My pace quickened, the curios of a void racing by, growing more and more ferociously vacant as I went. And then, footsteps, measured and plain, walking somewhere ahead of me—the photographer.

At the end of the passage I raced through was a massive pit, a small carven-stone staircase leading downward circling the wide mouth. Punctuating the length of stairs, set out at equidistant intervals, were stone reliefs—nothing but shallow backgrounds, entirely unpopulated. Around and around I went, corkscrewing through faceless, subjectless space. The footsteps continued, undaunted for their navigation of uneven stairs, and at a brisk space, at that.

Somehow, I found myself beneath the ancient stone of a cave, clammier and smaller than the one beneath the house. In addition to all the space I'd cleared, I also felt I'd descended more than my suitable share of time. The air was primal, the stone unscarred. I rounded a large promontory of youthful stone and arrived into a tall space with damp walls. A small fire knelt in the middle of the room, illuminating some manner of painting upon the wall. Here was one of the first attempts at art, where hairy knuckled fingers plied stone walls with whatever would stick to them, to record their dreams, their fears, their gods. At least, that's what should have populated the crude, stone canvases, smeared only with the crudest attempts at scenery. But as before, the occupants of the art were nowhere to be seen. I reached out to touch the stone, but instantly recalled the photo pinned to the hanging wire and thought better of it.

When I turned the next corner, the cave opened to an incredible degree, basaltic pillars lifting the ceiling into utter, incomprehensible nothingness. But it was the floor, or lack thereof, that ripped breath from my lungs—as far as the eye could see, nothing but crisscrossing, rusted iron bars that made a prison from the spaces under the girding. More striking was the endless sea of clawed fingers stretching desperately from the spaces under and between the bars. Submerged beneath my astonishment lurked legions of pleading whispers—all the murmuring sibilance was piled atop the same frantic need—to see the pictures the Photographer tossed into air above the prison.

He threw them away like one might toss bread at pigeons. "Feed our eyes!" they screamed in voices shaped from hisses and hunger. The photographs went into the air, one by one, the souls of the photographed howling out their fear. And when at last they came into range of the waves of straining fingers, they were tossed from one clawing cluster after the next, like tiny rafts thrown about by the restless sea. Eventually, when one of the pictures was taken beneath the bars, the howling intensified, reaching an incredible, horrific crescendo before abruptly vanishing. Apparently, for the creatures pent beneath the landscape of prison bars, seeing was eating. But then a photograph was withdrawn from the man's pocket that did not scream, but only fumed with unkempt rage, seething with a talent for killing. It was the photograph of the Wolf. I stepped into view, my father in my hands.

I nodded to the picture in the photographer's hand. "That does not belong to you," I said. "Or them." The man did not seem surprised to see me. In fact, his expression never shifted, only his eyes moved, burrowing into mine.

There was a long silence as the sea of claws evaporated, the unseen things withdrawing their fingers from the spaces betwixt the iron slats. Finally, he lifted the lethal snapshot in an expression meant to taunt me. I could feel a power welling up within him, an old power—the worst kind. He took a step toward me, the air thickening, becoming coarse. But I was prepared. I shifted the head of my father, revealing a view of the photographer's vintage camera, which had been left leaning against the wall behind me. I looked down at my father and back to the man, smiling.

The cameraman's expression finally changed, and a hissing chorus from under the endless bars begged me to spare the device. Slowly, with visibly restrained resentment, the photographer reached out his hand and offered me the picture.

The second the picture was in hand, the scene vanished from sight. But the eyes of the photographer—the Spirit Photographer—stayed with me long after, a pleasantly haunting recollection. When the world reappeared, I found myself next to the rock where the theft had occurred, the black and bleached remains still present.

The Wolf was the albino, Edith Suggz, otherwise known as the Salt Witch. She earned the name due to her many victims having been discovered in a particular salt marsh, and the presence of strange sing-song lights whenever she was about her terrible work. A celebrated monster, her exploits were given to much fear and wonder, cementing her invitation to the Game. And here she was, the sum of her life's presence and purpose, small and delicate in my hand, one merciful gesture from oblivion. It seemed a poor end for one so wonderfully wicked.

I could feel the frigidity of her hateful soul through the slight contact my fingers exercised upon her laminated spirit. Unsurprisingly—and in keeping with the nature of the Game—just when I'd resigned myself to committing only one last kill, the Shepherd called upon me to end yet another Wolf. This time, I would kill without the pageantry or ceremony of a proper confrontation. I knew I had only to tear the photo in half. There was no other way. Apparently, the Shepherd required a player of his Game to perform the deed, however unfairly. I did not want to dwell on the reason why. I softly whispered my apologies and tore the picture in two.

There was a brilliant flash of cold white light and the sound of stone cracking, followed by a scream, wet and painful, and perhaps a small growl of outrage at the tail end.

When I looked back to the rock that once held the outline of a stolen soul, I spied sundered stone and the ragged, bleeding remains of a dead white witch. It was, I believe, the Shepherd who actually killed Edith. Her name had already been struck from his rolls, so to speak, and that could mean only one thing. Yet, when I looked back over my shoulder into the thick swaths of forest I'd left behind for the road, I might have glimpsed strange lights moving in the distant thickets.

CHAPTER TWENTY-FOUR

I admired Autumn City. It pressed harder against the taut skin of the Deadworld more than any other place I had ever been, revealing visions more often left to dreams than to the waking senses. I walked down streets thickly lined with the city's unique trees, whose leaves always burned orange and yellow, disavowing their place in the order of the seasons, gathering ghosts as surely as heathen bonfires. Everywhere I went, there whispered a wind that carried the perfume of autumn decay, and I wondered if Jack Lantern hadn't been partially successful in his bid against banality. The city was most visible—revealed—during the smolder of twilight. It seemed to fume along with the sun, a brother wrapped in autumnal fire, burning spectral and silent, standing sentinel over the Eternal Fall. The spectacle was staggering. Everywhere dreams afire, yearning to burn down the sky, desperate to sear through the heavy rot of a dead world. And yet, each time the forest was set ablaze, it would inevitably replace back into banished dream to rage in silence, isolated and impotent.

Jack Lantern certainly didn't want to die by my hand, but neither did he wish to kill me by his. I could feel the conflict burning him as brightly as any smile he had ever set aflame. Yet regardless of those feelings, he was busy preparing a magnificent stage upon which we would soon perform—I simply waited for him to finish. I sat for some time in an untended pumpkin patch behind a barn that looked on the verge of collapse, sharpening my sister's beaming grins and basking in the undimmed wonder of things to come.

The twilight worked on the eternally autumnal trees of the September Woods like a bellows upon fire, scarlet and shadow creeping out of the surrounding woods, pooling dim and deep all around. Finally, I rose and walked beneath the burning ceiling of the forest, as I knew the time for waiting had ended.

But for the characteristic heaviness that betrays the waking world, I might have thought I was in a dream. The forest was otherworldly, breeching almost completely out of death. It was difficult to imagine, but necessary to realize, that the September Woods was not my friend, but quite the opposite—it was my sworn enemy. Perhaps more opposed than even Jack himself, for my opponent served the Woods, loved it, and was loved in return. It would not be kind to me, and it would not give up its hero easily.

Somewhere deep in the Woods, I saw what seemed like a bit of twilight caught within the tree branches, incapable of descending with the sun, bobbing in the ink. The closer I drew to the spot, the more of these lights I saw. Eventually, they spread out wide before me, like the glowing, beating heart of the September Woods. I was so taken by the lights, I'd failed to notice that the wind had picked up, increasing in strength by the moment. Before I had time to properly react, great squalls of wind bearing dead leaves that felt like razor blades held me aloft in the air. I was nearly immobilized. The wind thickened the faster it gusted, until I felt as if I were being crushed within a gigantic hand in addition to being torn to bloody shreds by the whipping, serrated leaves.

I needed a moment of clarity, a space to operate. My father delivered me into such a space. It took all my strength to reach him, and when my hands wrapped around familiar bones, a great rage came into me. The resulting blow from the axe upon the thick wind was as deafening as it was alien. A shriek rose from the Woods itself, lifting into the

sky, howling and climbing, gaining volume. The injured—
or perhaps merely offended, it was impossible to tell—wind
was fast becoming a swirling storm as lightning flashing
through the fiery canopy.

I withdrew the seeds I'd hidden in the lining of my coat—
seeds cut from the apple I'd stolen from the Black Orchard—
and threw them into the night. The effect was immediate,
just as I'd hoped. The lightless Garden of Unduur came
into the shadows, spreading searching tendrils, flinching at
the lightning, leaping across the darkness. All around me,
a great war raged between the incipient alien darkness of
Unduur and the Orange god of the September Woods. Glory
everywhere, and I was damned to leave it behind.

I wandered for some time, drawing closer to the pervious
globes of lost twilight, listening to the din of war. Within
moments, the hanging blots of amber materialized—an
incredible portion of the forest was strung with human Jack-
o'-lanterns, cloaking the night beneath the waft of stolen
twilight, glowing mouths grinning night back into dusk. And
then came music, from where I do not know. But it was my
music, from my dream, from my memory, melodies made
from my soul. Somewhere, a magic lantern show spun into
life, no doubt cast from hollowed-out eyes. The shapes
equally pilfered from my dreams, all of them moving to the
music, outlining my life in undying autumn . . .

I was a fool. I'd failed to reckon my opponent, for Jack
proved more prepared than I could have ever imagined. He
would overwhelm me utilizing every one of my dreams he
could conjure. He threw wonder at me as a squid throws
black clouds of ink. I could barely see for all the reverie
stuffed beneath the ceiling of the forest—even my own trick
with the seeds had served to bolster his attack. Gods of fall
and darkness warring beneath eternal trees of smoldering
twilight, the forest of endless Halloween strung with the
sights and sounds of my own spirit, the finale to a cosmic

contest of infinite death—all of it falling beneath the watchful eye of a god of murder. It was all too much!

Jack Lantern was nowhere to be seen, but his words were loud and clear. "Happy Halloween, Vincent!"

I was almost too stunned to answer. "Jack, my God. What you've done . . ."

Jack's somber words came from everywhere around me. "I'm afraid, in the end, you're only a machine, Vincent. Just like the rest of us. Machines can be understood, inside and out. To defeat a machine, you need only know what it's made of, how it works. And while your construction is nearly pure chaos, I at last found your dreams—the *numbers* that define you, make you who you are, deny the possibility of real life. For that, more than anything else, I am sorry. For both of us."

Jack was crying. It refocused me, but for how long I couldn't say. "I know what you're feeling," I said. "I've felt it all my life, Jack. It's the beating of a void-shaped heart, the nothingness at the center of all things. But I can quiet it for everyone, even you. The machine is nothing but a stiffened corpse, moving for movement's sake, kinetic banality. But all machines have makers, my friend. There is a dream behind the machine. I can show you. But first, you must sleep."

I quickly plunged into the shadows, using my sadness, my imminent grief and regret, to shield me from the paralyzing spectacle. My sisters smiled silence into my shadow, my father stoked his cataclysmic rage. I needed this to end. I couldn't take much more.

Despite my best efforts, Jack discovered me easily enough, as he knew the shadowed woods as well as his carving knives, and he went to impressive lengths to demonstrate both facts. His movements were like polished jewels beneath the moon, glittering into life, and just as quickly, dying back into the darkness. I couldn't focus my mind, lost as it was to the forest of dreams. My every move was foreshadowed by the sights and sounds of my own soul.

The chill autumn breeze became the cold sting of Jack Lantern's knives. His blades moved through my body with an impossible swiftness, and with my mind so displaced, my sisters could only manage to deny them a killing depth. I required the few blows I could land to matter, and so my father rose into my hands. He needed to strike but once. The massive axe crashed through saplings, brambles, and even felled several Eternal trees. But my opponent was ever beyond my father's reach, always just a streaking mask and the dim fade of reddened knives. He was like a scream in the night – everywhere and nowhere.

It soon became apparent that I was losing. While I had resisted most of his attacks, the sum of his lesser gains had relieved me of much blood. I had all but fallen when I finally saw the Carver of Souls clearly. He was standing only inches from me, floating in the darkness, wearing his true face—in his madness, he'd mistaken it for a mask. I had perhaps a second to act.

My sister flew, hissing through the space once occupied by the Carver as I tumbled into a cleverly hidden hole. Twilight turned to night as the blackness swallowed me into its cramped belly. I soon realized I'd become the contents of a small cage of steel bars. I was too weakened to attempt a leap from the trap before the lid was slammed shut and sealed. I wrapped my hands around the bars, channeling the Red Dream as much as I was able, but the cage was bound by the will of the Woods. I could not break free.

Finally, I looked up to see Jack standing above me, just a pale wisp dissolving into the night. "You can't kill me, Vincent," he said, "and I won't kill you. The only way to properly put a stop to this foolishness, I'm afraid, is to keep you locked up tight, like a dirty secret. This way, Halloween won't end. You must be my monkey wrench in the works,

I'm afraid." His words were almost too heavy for him. This was not how he wanted things to end between us.

"You should have asked me, Vincent," he said, the holes of his eyes wet and regretful. "I would have said yes."

"I know," was all I could muster.

The view from between the bars brought me into the gravity of forsaken memories—my sins. Here was irony, karma, fate, and perhaps, should there be such a thing, justice. Vincent Alexander Graves, left to the cold and dark of a small cage, forever. Yet this could not be my ending. I recalled my mother's words to me, so long ago. "All that ever was, or could ever be, whispers its soul into the sound of silence—and the only thing you will ever need to do, to know anything at all, is listen to it."

And so, I listened as never I had, to the silence of it all, to the spaces between the trees, the rocks, granules of dirt, atoms, cause and effect. I not only listened, but conjured as well. And with silence came her sister—shadow. I pulled the night down all around me, its soundless silks falling across my shoulders. I became the secret the universe keeps to itself. The story that dies in the telling. I became freedom.

Before Jack knew how, I was upon him, using a trick I had learned from a certain magician, the son of a witch. He tried to melt back into the night, but I had to be faster, just this once. My sisters were already within him, making merry with the red, wet toys of his body. Yet, just as they drew upon the doors to his heart, they were swept away, tumbling through thickets lit by dead orange smiles.

After his blades disarmed me, they went for my eyes. Sight is the least potent of my senses, but certainly among the most valued. Jack had a way with eyes, a practiced dexterity that could turn them to triangles of bleeding amber candlelight. I grabbed his wrist and snapped it, the carving knife falling away just as it grazed my cornea. With his other knife, he tore my father from my back, sending him spinning into the branches beyond, his path outlined in the fire of his rage.

With my naked hand, I seized the remaining blade, moving down its length until what was left of my grip closed over his wrist. I snapped that one as well. Wasting no time, I used my weight to crush him against the trunk of a tree, holding his arms outstretched. I couldn't allow him to slip free. His speed was many times my better, and even with broken wrists, his knives could find their way back to my eyes, and then some. Face-to-face, I could feel our mutual sadness at what needed to happen. He was about to speak, the smallest sound leaving his lips, but I couldn't listen to any more.

I sank my teeth into both of his faces, shattering plastic and enamel. His hand managed to slip free in the collision, the blade it barely held sank deeply across my neck. I only pushed my broken teeth deeper, splitting his mask and tearing his flesh. I swallowed, feeling the chunks fall from the gaping hole he'd opened in my throat. As I had with all my family, I merely closed my eyes and devoured him.

Once Jack had gone still, the forest's knight dead, I lowered what was left of my friend to the ground. By the glow of countless dead, smiling faces, I looked upon the thing that once walked with me in dream. Even dead, Jack Lantern was only barely discernible as a man.

I defied gravity for only an instant longer, my body collapsing under its own weight. With my ear to the ground, I could detect the faint tread of something approaching. And I could hear the Dream of Wolves, now complete and fully joined. It came from everywhere. It was coming from me. A door was opening, a crack in the woods at first, then the night, then death itself. The lights of the other side merged with the burning trees of the Woods, the bright dead smiles of an eternal Halloween, and my blood where it mixed with Jack's.

The woods went Red with Dream. I saw them gathered before me, the Wolves—Molly, Janus, The Prince, Mister Hide, the legendary Jack Lantern, and all the rest. Their hunger filled me, became me. We were all together again, for the first time. I could feel them overflowing the banks of my body, shadows moving in my blood, secrets searching out my mind.

I went to my family where they lay, taking them up. My sisters' sweet laughter filled my soul. Their smiles, half-moons made whole, inside me. Father's fire became my bones, unbreakable. His thunder, my voice. I stood victorious beneath the whispering fires of an endless September, in a Dream of Wolves.

The next moment was filled with the perfume of burning flowers, and a voice that couldn't be. "My wonderful boy. My Red Son."

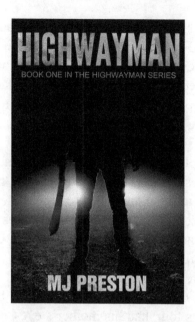
Chapter 1 - Infamous

1

Syracuse, NY

The time was 1:00 a.m., Wednesday night, and the bar was dead. Wendy Birrell had been tending bar at Murphy's for three years. Her wage was eight bucks an hour, plus tips. That was on weekends; on weeknights, the place was a tomb except for the odd barfly, so tips were scarce. Tonight, like most, she wore tight, low rider jeans that hugged her slim figure, and a plaid button-down shirt that draped neatly across her ample breasts. Her hair flowed in straight, dirty blonde cascades over her shoulders and onto the swell of her breasts. This was done purposely to arouse the male patrons. Aside from her figure, it was Wendy's eyes that turned a man's head. They were deep glacial blue, a color found in arctic waters lapping against icebergs.

Wendy Birrell was twenty-eight, she had a high school education and only one motivation in life. His name was Patrick. He was four, had his mother's eyes, and curly, corn silk hair. Patrick's father, also blond, had been a marine. Had, because he'd been killed in Iraq when Patrick was only four months old. He and Wendy were never a couple. He had been a fling, nothing more, but had he lived, she would have included him in her son's life; had he known. He hadn't and Wendy didn't have a lot of options, so she tended bar, lived paycheck to paycheck and, for now, that was enough.

Most of the regulars were gone at this hour. Shuffling out after a few too many, slurring their words as they put on a coat or slung a purse like awkward preschoolers dressing to go outside and play. All gone. Except for one young man sitting at the corner of the bar sipping a Rolling Rock and stealing glances at her. He couldn't have been more than twenty-one. He'd been in a couple of times this week, sitting unremarkably on the corner stool. She would have carded him, but then that would have chewed up any chance at a tip, and he'd left her a ten spot every time he was in. No one at

Murphy's left a ten spot. She figured him for a college kid, or maybe he'd been working at one of the vineyards during the spring plant. Tonight, just like every night he'd been in, he sat alone, glancing her way and checking her out. When she looked over, he would avert his contemplation to the beer bottle he held. No doubt perusing the alcohol content or maybe the origin of the brewery. Men were such predictable animals. She was checking him out as well, but it wasn't as obvious. Eventually, she worked her way to that corner of the bar, and he began to chat her up.

"You from around here?" He was looking directly at her.

"I live in Westvale." She polished the bar with the rag as she spoke.

"You go to SU when you're not working?" he asked.

She laughed, shook her head. "No, I'm not exactly what you would call university material."

Silence then, hanging between them uncomfortably.

"I just thought..."

"What? That I was working my way through college." She smiled scathingly. "Isn't that what half the strippers say over at The Chub?" The Chub, aka Chubby's, was what some might call a gentleman's club. "Why aren't you there?"

"Sorry, I guess I was mistaken."

She stopped then, furrowed her brow and the cynical smile fell away. Why had she spoken to this guy like that? He wasn't anything but nice, and he had slipped her a ten every night he's been in. "Aw, shit. That didn't come out right. I'm sorry, I didn't mean that."

"It's okay. I shouldn't have been nosy."

"No, I shouldn't have been a bitch. Let's start over."

"Okay."

"My name's Wendy. What's yours?"

He looked up from the beer and grinned. "Devon."

She dropped the cloth on the bar, stuck out her hand and said, "It's nice to meet you, Devon. Are you from around here?"

He took her hand, his skin warm, smooth, and without callous. "I'm going to the university."

She pulled her hand back, placed it over her mouth, giggled and then broke into laughter. He shook his head and smiled. When the laughter subsided, she grabbed him another beer. He reached for his wallet, and she said, "This is on the house."

It was an hour before closing, and at that moment, she really didn't think that she would end up sleeping with him. She hadn't been with anyone for some months. But when she got home that evening and squared Patrick away, well... The idea of a warm body next to hers seemed appealing. This idea hadn't begun to brew in the beginning, but as he sipped his beer, talked a bit about what he was taking at Syracuse University, the word "maybe" began to echo in the back of her subconscious.

Fifteen minutes later, she set another Rolling Rock on the bar at his request, and she said, "You're not driving are you, Devon?"

"No, I walked. I'll probably grab a cab back to the university."

And then she decided. "I'm off in half hour. I can drive you to the university if you like."

"Aw, that's okay. I don't wanna be any trouble."

"No trouble. Besides, you'll never get a cab at this hour. I can drive you back to the university if you like, or maybe we can go somewhere for coffee." His eyes brightened at this, became charmingly boyish. She imagined a lean, young man beneath those clothes. Virile young man too. He would probably only last thirty seconds after getting into bed, but he'd be quick on the rebound.

"I don't have any classes until tomorrow afternoon."

"That settles it then," Wendy said, and as he finished his beer, she went about the business of closing down. She moved around the bar collecting glasses, wiping things down, and eventually squaring up the cash. He sipped the last of his beer, watching her every move.

This was going to be easy.

She had him step out and wait on the front walk while she put away the evening deposit and set the alarm. Devon was the consummate young gentleman. He'd only had three beers, and if she made an offer to bring him back to her place, she guessed it wouldn't affect his performance in the least. When she slid the deadbolt over and removed her key, she made her final decision. He was cute.

"Let's go." She led him to her car, a beat-up Chrysler Cirrus sitting curbside. She unlocked the car. They climbed in. She turned the key in the ignition, and the engine came alive. She reached over, placed a hand on his, and said, "You want me to take you back to the university, or would you rather come home with me?"

He smiled. "What do you think?"

She slid her hand up his leg and held it there, a finger teasing his manhood. "I think you want to come home with me." Then she kissed him. Wendy was not promiscuous—this was definitely out of the norm for her—but she was a single mom, and that was a lonely business. She pulled back from the kiss, put the gearshift into drive, and pulled away from the curb.

The ride to her house consisted of touching and feeling, but very few words. There was no need for discussion. It had been established: they were going to have sex. As she steered the car with her left hand, the right reached down between his legs, rubbing and massaging. He answered by caressing her breasts, causing her nipples to harden and stirring something inside her. This anticipation was almost too much and Wendy considered pulling the Cirrus over and jumping into the back seat with him.

No, she couldn't do that. Patrick was at home, and... oh shit, she'd almost forgotten about her mother. She pushed him off gently. "Devon, I need you to do something when we get to my house."

"Okay. What?"

"My mom, she's watching my son. You'll have to stay outside until she leaves."

Devon laughed, "You want me to hide in the bushes or something?"

She turned left up another street and said, "How about you just duck down in the car until I give you a signal."

"I could do that, but what if she catches me and..."

He was going to say *calls the cops*. But Wendy cut him off.

"I park my car in the front of the house, on the street. There's only one parking spot out front, so my mom parks in the back alley. She won't be coming out the front. She won't catch you if you duck down low. I'm sorry about all the cloak and dagger stuff, but I just don't feel like explaining to my mother that I'm bringing a stranger home for the night."

"How long will I have to wait?"

"Probably not too long, my mom sometimes falls asleep in front of the TV. So I may have to wake her up. I don't know, five maybe ten minutes."

"Alright. I don't generally do this on first dates, so I hope you'll appreciate all the effort."

She grinned. "I do, and it'll be worth your while."

2

They rolled up to the curb five minutes later. About a hundred feet before coming to a stop, she told him to get down and lay his head on her lap. And with that, she parked and cut the engine. He could feel the heat coming off of her. It was a subterranean heat. Brought on by the petting and groping.

She shut off the ignition and whispered, "Ten minutes and I'll come get you."

"Okay, ten minutes," he agreed.

She slid out from underneath him, leaving his head to rest on the cloth seat. She closed the car door, and he heard her footsteps as she made her way up the walk. He heard the clicking of steps as she climbed the porch, then the screen door creaked, a door handle clicked over, or maybe it was a deadbolt. He couldn't be sure. He couldn't see anything above the orange bleaching of the dashboard from the arc sodium street lamps.

Ten minutes, he thought.

He wondered if the mother would come out and catch him hiding in the car. Or maybe a local patrol notified by a nosy neighbor. What if she were to deny his presence? "Oh no, officer, I don't know him. I have no idea why he was hiding in my car." The game would have ended right there. He'd be carted off to jail. He was sure shit like that happened from time to time. What would his father say to that? The old man would be royally pissed.

This made him grin.

3

None of those things happened. As promised, in less than ten minutes, she came down the steps to the car and whispered, "Come on, the coast is clear." He sat upright, and she opened the car door.

"You're sure it's safe?"

She smiled, took his hand, and led him up the path.

When she closed the front door behind them and turned the bolt, she reached over, pulled him in and gave him a long kiss, running her tongue over his. Then she drew back and said, "I have some beer in the fridge."

She kissed him again.

He said, "Maybe later" and began touching her all over. She ran her hands down to his nether regions, feeling his hardness. He did the same, feeling her heat. They kissed, an intertwining mess of fumbled gropes that were desperate and blurry with sexual need. All the while, they worked their way toward the bedroom, once almost tripping and falling down. She laughed and pulled off his shirt. He tugged off hers. She stroked his chest, barren of even a single hair. He unsnapped her bra. By the time they were at the bedroom door, she was in her panties, he in his briefs. Behind them a debris trail of clothing. She dropped her undies and tugged at his briefs. When they dropped, she cupped him, and suddenly stopped and looked down. Then she looked up at him.

"My last girl didn't like hair."

She looked down again. She held onto him. Not even a single hair. "Why?" she asked. "What was her problem with hair?" She brought her eyes up to his, still holding his manhood tightly.

"She said, 'It ruined the mood if you had to lick the pillow.'" He started to grin.

Wendy giggled and worked her hand.

They fell onto the bed side by side. No more talk, just touching.

But then...

"I gotta get something out of my jeans," he said.

"I have condoms in the nightstand," she whispered, and she reached over with one hand and pulled the drawer clumsily open. She brought a strip of condoms up and held it before him. He bit down on the corner with his teeth, and she removed it and went to work. It rolled on with ease, she supposed the smoothness of his clean-shaven skin helped in that regard.

Then they got busy.

He lasted longer than she initially thought. Over two minutes. Then she went to work on him and got him back into the game in under four. Young men bounced back so quickly. With the old condom tied off and discarded, she rolled a second one on and they found their rhythm. This time, he lasted almost twenty-five minutes. When it was over, she was spent.

"Thank you," she said.

He didn't say anything, he just lay there watching her, a thin smile on his face.

"I gotta check on my son. Do you want that beer now?"

"I'd love one," he said.

He sat up against the headboard, watching her naked form disappear through the doorway, fading in the dim light of the hall. She was wraith-like, melting in and out of reality. A little while later, she returned with a can of Budweiser and handed it to him. It was ice cold.

"Thank you," he said and sipped. Then added, "That was fun."

"More fun than a college girl?"

He turned his head and said, "Way more fun than a college girl."

"And no pillow licking." She giggled.

"Yeah."

She wrapped herself around him. Using his bare chest as a headrest and he listened to her breathing. In no time, she was falling asleep. He counted down the space between each inhalation and exhalation, the gap was widening. He'd been afraid he wouldn't be able to perform, but he'd come through. She was, and he meant it, way better than any college girl. Most of the girls at SU were fucking airheads, but moreover, they were dead fucks. Not her. She wrapped her legs around him, then literally squeezed from inside as he thrust. That was talent. Definitely a sign of experience. He hadn't expected this to happen: he was planning on a couple beers and fully intended on heading back to the dorm.

He grinned. Fate was a strange thing.

Half an hour later, cossetted in sleep, she rolled off him, turning her back and pressing her buttocks against his leg. He lay still, fully alert, considering the situation as he ran a hand over her shoulder and into the hourglass of her waist. She had a nice body for a woman who had a child. He guessed you made it your business to look good, especially when you were raising a kid alone. He wondered where the father might be. Guessed that he wouldn't be too happy if he were to walk in now.

Somehow, he doubted this scenario was likely. Daddy was long gone. He looked at the two spent condoms sitting on the nightstand.

Then slid quietly from the bed.

There was much to do.

4

She hadn't known what woke her. Dream or premonition, but she had come up out of the sleep into a sitting position even before her senses were roused. Her mind pricked, pins and needles, her eyesight still unfocused. She had heard her name. Not urgent, but calling in a whisper.

"Wendy, wake up. Wendy, wake up."

Slowly, she pulled focus adjusting to the dark of the room. She saw a naked silhouette standing in the bedroom doorway. It was him. Devon.

"What are you doing?" she asked.

"Are you awake now?"

"Come back to bed."

He said nothing, stepping through the doorway, moving closer. He was holding something in his right hand. She couldn't quite see.

He took another step.

It didn't register at first. Or wouldn't register.

Something in his hand, something in his right hand. What was it?

He took yet another step.

"Wendy?"

"What are you holding?"

He took another step.

Then it began to register.

No. Oh dear God, no. No! Oh my...

"It's okay. He never felt a thing."

Never felt a thing? No!

She felt the scream building, expanding inside her, a hard, jagged ball in her throat, cutting her oxygen. It wanted to escape, but she couldn't find her voice.

Or wouldn't.

To do so was to acknowledge the unthinkable.

He took another step.

The small, round object hung from his right hand. Like the head of a doll.

No, not a doll: bigger.

It was...

She knew then.

Oh my god!

"Patrick," she moaned and then the scream began to rise like a whistling tea kettle.

Why?

He closed in then, his pace quick and deliberate. His other hand rising—moonlight gleaming off steel—before she could scream, he severed her windpipe. She felt an initial sting, and then there was a pop, but no actual pain. He hovered, watching intently as the darkness turned the black to blue, light to gray. Her life was spilling out, like a river running into the sea, swallowed by the abyss.

Her eyes closed.

Opened.

It was better this way. At least she would be with him.

Then nothing.

5

He showered. Massaging the water over his skin, pushing into the contour of each muscle and rubbing away the blood. There had been a lot of blood. Some had already congealed on his naked form, and when he touched it, it flecked away. He worked his way to the shower, using a towel to pull back the curtain and stepped in. The water had been cold at first, causing his limp penis to contract even further. At his feet, the water puddled in swirls of diluted crimson before being pulled to the drain in tendrils. He followed the drops as they fell into the pool.

Plop... Plop... Plop...

It was a lot of blood.

A lot of DNA, he told himself.

He shouldn't have had sex with her. But then, he hadn't planned on killing her. No, that wasn't quite right. He was thinking about killing her. She was the one who had initiated the sex. He had been thinking about killing her from the first time he saw her, but he thought about killing people all the time. It wasn't unique to her. He could have easily taken the ride back to the dorm and continued his fantasy.

He rubbed the back of his neck, the hot water beating away even more blood.

How did that get back there?

Correction. He hadn't planned on killing them. Yes, them, but he needed to be thinking about other things. "DNA," he said aloud. How much DNA had he dropped here? "A lot of DNA." He rubbed the back of his neck and considered his penis. He'd used a condom, but there would be drops left on the bed. And what of his skin? The bump and grind they'd performed would have rubbed off dead skin. He'd shaved down there for that reason, but there was still the short, cropped cut on his head. His eyebrows.

"Fucking DNA."

He wasn't in a database anywhere. He had no record.

But your DNA will be now and if you're ever picked up?

"Fucking DNA!" He smashed a fist against the tiling.

He inventoried his body. Every nook visible to the naked eye and thought he was clean. He then took a cloth and used the shower head to rinse the tub in swirling gyrations. Why? He wasn't sure. He'd probably left enough fiber and

DNA lying around for an easy conviction. He needed to get dressed, clean up, and consider his options.

He climbed from the shower onto the bath mat and toweled off. Once dry, he dressed and stared into the small vanity. Was it how he thought it would be? This being his first. No, but then was it ever going to be? The act had been deliberate and mechanical. He didn't think it was the act that he sought for gratification anyway. No, the act was just a means to an end. He thought of all the others he read about. The killers who'd risen through the ranks to stardom. Ted Bundy, John Wayne Gacy, whose names were as household in modern culture as Van Gogh or da Vinci. Perhaps even more.

He wiped the tub with the towel.

"Notoriety," he said. That's what they had in common. But that wasn't exactly right either. Then the word came to him. He wandered back to the bedroom. Looked in on them. The clock on the nightstand read 3:34 a.m.

"Fucking DNA." He glanced out the window into the back yard. There was a small aluminum gardening shed back there. On either side of the yard, tall hedges offered relative privacy.

Better get to it, he thought.

He went out the back door as quietly as possible and found the shed unlocked. He slid the door over, the aluminum scraping against the track in weak protest. He had rubber gloves on now. The yellow ones used for washing dishes. Condoms for the hands. Glancing around he saw a tricycle, presumably Patrick's, lying on its side. There was an old lawnmower. Beside that, a five-gallon jerry can, much too big for the likes of a lawnmower. He could see Wendy struggling with that jerry can, splashing gas all over the lawn mower.

Not anymore, he thought and smiled.

Neither she nor Patrick would be visiting this shed again. He lifted the jerry can; it was half full.

It'll have to do.

Inside the house, he retraced his path, as best he could remember, splashing the gas in places where he thought he might have left evidence. He doused the bodies, the condoms, the towels he'd used. He gave the bed where they'd had sex a good soaking. The kid's crib also got a good soaking. When he emptied it, he placed the can at the foot of her bed.

He then went back to the kitchen and opened the stove. It was an electric job. He turned the oven on and watched the burners. They immediately began to glow. He switched it off and searched the cupboards. He needed more accelerant. This place had to burn. The DNA had to be destroyed.

"Fucking DNA," he grunted again and pulled out a bottle of vegetable oil. He unscrewed the cap and soaked the counter. That wouldn't burn as fast, but it would still burn. Then he grabbed a bag of sugar and spread the granules into the oil. He'd seen sugar burn, had tossed it into a fire once, it flared and left a sweet scent in the air. He wandered into the living room, careful not to step on the trail of gas he'd left on the carpet. The vapors that hung in the air were intoxicating, and he was getting the beginnings of a headache. He'd been very careful not to get any on him, but he would probably still smell of it. He'd have to get his clothes into the wash as soon as he got back to SU.

He found a stack of newspapers and magazines by the couch and brought them back to the kitchen. He arranged them on the oven rack and considered. It looked plausible. Stove ignites papers, papers ignite the gas and soon enough the house would be on fire and...

"No more fucking DNA," he said.

How long would it take? Five minutes? Ten?

He wasn't sure. Arson wasn't his strength.

He'd have to move fast.

He gazed at the body of the woman and that of her decapitated son, burning the images into his mind.

This is like painting a masterpiece and setting it on fire, he thought.

He took one last glance around the house. Then the word came to him. He turned on the oven and tossed the rubber gloves onto the counter. Tore off a roll of paper towel and used it to wipe the doorknob as he exited the house. *Infamous,* he thought. *That was the word I was looking for. Infamous, and I just did something that would be remembered for a long time.*

"And I just burned it all up," he muttered in a low, angry grunt.

Lighting fire to a masterpiece.

Not yet; it was only art at this point. He had to hone his craft. Polish his work, and if he didn't get caught for this, he would be well on his way. He made it four blocks and disappeared around the corner when the paper flared up.

By the time he was a mile away, fire snaked down the halls into the adjacent room to the main sources of gasoline. The smoke detectors in Patrick and Wendy's room cried out, but only briefly, falling victim to the intense heat.

He walked all the way back to SU, drawing the attention of a slumbering homeless man, but only for a second and it rose no alarm.

When he reached the dorm, he stripped and put his clothes in the wash. An hour had elapsed, and miles away, the little, post-war bungalow was burning savagely. He was stepping into the shower when the fire department arrived. They turned on the water, sprayed it on all sides, but it was already too far gone, burning out of control. The volunteer fire captain had no illusions; there wouldn't be anyone in the furnace left alive to save. The chief was on his way. All they could do was try and protect the neighboring houses.

Showered, Lance, not Devon, dressed in sweat pants and a Syracuse University tee. "Infamous," he said and lay back on the bed. He hoped that he'd gotten everything. He'd heard the sirens calling in the night, at first far off. Then, another set of sirens awoke, and he knew they were on their way to help. He considered going online, to see if there was something about it on one of the local media sites, then thought better of it. Too dangerous. The Internet was like a strand of DNA, maybe even worse; he didn't want to leave a trail. But that would all change, because he was learning about the Web, and soon he'd be learning about the Deep Web, and in those murky waters, a predator could hide in plain sight.

"Next time," he said. "Next time, I will be prepared." He thought about Bundy, about Gacy, as if he were aspiring to their greatness, their infamy. No, he would be better. He had no intention of being caged, electrocuted or injected. His achievements would be greater, would shock and horrify. He shut his mind down then, falling off to sleep, sliding in the shade of dreamlessness.

***

http://wbp.bz/highwaymana

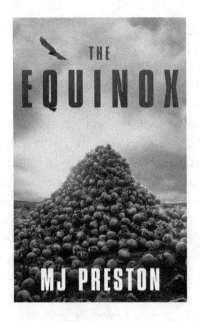
Prologue - The Hunt Begins

1

Spirit Woods, Chocktee Nation Village

He was packing the small knapsack with provisions for the trip, yet he really had no idea what to take. At his side, his mother wept. Once so upright, so proud, now she was barely a skeletal shell of the woman she had once been. Cancer was consuming her, had turned her thin, gray. The death of her father, coupled with her son's erratic behavior, drained her even further, and he was too entrenched in his own selfishness to appreciate the depth of her pain.

The freshly bandaged cut on his cheek was swollen and had been stitched closed the night before. Small dots of crimson peppered the cotton dressing. Pulses of fire radiated from the gash, stopping maybe an inch below his right eye. Not being able to touch it only made matters worse. It hurt just to blink.

He picked up his knife from the bed, wrapped a piece of cloth around it and placed it into the bag. Then the dreamcatcher and feather. Suddenly his hand reached up and tugged at the medicine bag hanging around his neck. Grandfather had given it to him. That was more than he could take.

This is all so unbelievable. Only yesterday morning the old man had been smiling and joking around, and now he's gone! Gone! Anguish rose above all else and anger pushed him into a tantrum. Let this be a dream! Fuck! Please let this be a dream! Tell me I didn't get my Grandfather killed!

But he had.

Janice Blackbird finally broke her mournful silence. "You don't have to leave. I will talk to the Elders. They will let you stay."

He stopped what he was doing, turned in her direction, his voice sharp and spiteful. "I'm not doing it for them! I have to go, Mother."

Her eyes welled up with fresh tears, her voice quivered. "Daniel, this is crazy."

Finished packing, he fastened the straps, not wanting to look at her. "I can't stay here. I have brought disgrace to your name; to Grandfather's name."

"I know all about disgrace, Daniel. When I brought you back here, I faced their looks of disapproval, but I knew in time that they would come around. Our people are good. They will forgive you. It is in their nature to forgive." Her voice rose and fell, rife with anxiety. But it was futile: she knew, no matter what she said, he would not change his mind.

Again, he stopped, but this time his eyes met hers. With gentle care – so as not to harm her feeble form – he reached out and pulled her toward him. She was so frail; this brittle body hardly contained her strong spirit. Physically she looked that of a woman twenty-five years her senior.

She cried harder in his arms, her body convulsing gently, knowing that she would never see him again and that there was a distinct possibility that he may die before her. She tried to take solace in his arms, but there was no use: his embrace only epitomized the sheer hopelessness of the situation.

Gently he caressed her back, feeling the bones protruding through the light sweater she wore, and he felt hopeless and conflicted. "I have to go, Mother. I don't want to, but I must." He shoved away the urge to cry. "I need to speak with the Elders. They won't even acknowledge me, but if you talk to them, maybe they'll listen. There are many things I don't know. I need their counsel."

Janice Blackbird had been a Den Mother of the Chocktee people for three years and was now a respected member of the nation and its council. They would grant her son an audience if she asked, but that would be the last of her political clout. They would do it because of her Father, but only grudgingly. With their help and magic he had a chance; without them, he would be going to slaughter.

She pulled away from his embrace. Her long, silky black hair, flecked with grey, flowed down over the protruding collar bones which poked through her sweater. Even now, in the throes of this terrible disease, she still held onto her beauty. She mustered her strength, wiped the tears with the heel of her hand, and then used her sleeve to rub her nose.

"They will see you, Daniel. They will give you what you need. I will make sure of it."

2

He met with them that afternoon, standing in shame, before their dissecting and accusatory eyes. They were seated behind a large wooden table. Crafted from cedar, it was engraved with Chocktee symbols and the names of all the Elders who sat before them. There were five seats – but one stood empty, and the remaining occupants shifted inward. In the center sat Jake Toomey in what was, until yesterday, his grandfather's chair. Now Old Jake Toomey had assumed the position of Chief Elder. Toomey had been his grandfather's closest and oldest friend.

They talked amongst themselves in Ancient Chocktee, and though Daniel tried to interpret their words, he was unable to equate it to the modern language of his people. Chocktee dialect was similar to Cree, but the Elders' tongue was of the ancient times and indecipherable to Blackbird. Only the chosen were taught the ancient language.

The four men barked back and forth, raising their voices over each other, but among the four one voice held stable in its tone – and that was Jake Toomey's. He was Blackbird's only hope. The remaining Elders – Fortier, Machino, and Monias – cast an angry glance his way as they individually waved their hands, making their points and pontificating. Daniel could only guess they were making arguments for putting his head on a stick. But Toomey was calm, patient.

While all Elders oversaw the good of the Nation, the Chief Elder reigned supreme, and his word was law.

Finally, Toomey raised his hand to silence them and turned his attention on Blackbird as the others listened. "Daniel Blackbird, you are wepinikewin." (One who walks alone) "You cannot return to Spirit woods unless you undo this. Here are the things we can give you."

Fortier passed a leather roll made of deer hide across to the Chief Elder; he unrolled it on the cedar table. Blackbird stood motionless, his eyes fixed upon the objects before him, afraid to move. But Toomey motioned him forward, and he did so cautiously. An old crossbow, collapsed and dismantled, sat next to ten small arrows. The tip of each arrow sparkled with amber, the fire inside the room reflecting off the precious metal they had been dipped in.

"Silver is said to be hard enough to break the icy heart of wendigos and skinwalkers, but this creature is more dangerous and powerful than others. Use these arrows only for protection. If the time comes when you think you can trap it, you will need our help." Toomey rolled the hide up and handed it to Monias, who then passed it across to Blackbird. His face was an expressionless mask. Like the others, his anger was muted by the Chief Elder's authority.

Blackbird started, "What can…"

"Close your mouth and listen to the Chief Elder!" Fortier's voice was venomous, laced with spite. Toomey remained silent, his expression plain. The Elders were the enforcers of discipline in Chocktee, and he would not second-guess them, even if he felt they were heavy-handed.

"You are omachiw," [a hunter] Daniel Blackbird. You accept this burden?" The light from the fire flickered across the span of Toomey's wrinkled forehead, setting his curly grey hair ablaze with amber.

"I do."

Blackbird waited to see if the others would scoff or grunt. They did not. At least not with their mouths—but their eyes were angry spheres that did not require words to convey their sentiment.

"You bear its mark." Toomey touched his index finger to the pocked landscape of his cheek, drawing an imaginary cut from eye to cheekbone. "As the wound heals you will feel a pull taking you in whatever direction it moves. You are a hunter now, and it is your quarry. The walker is fast and smart, but a slave to its hunger. You must make this weakness your weapon and try to catch up to it. Have you any questions?"

Blackbird had a thousand but limited himself to only those that were most pressing. This conversation alone was a blessing, one that he would not sniff at. "Are there any signs it will leave behind or clues to its whereabouts?"

Toomey looked at the other Elders then cleared his throat. "It must feed daily. It will eat animal. But craves to eat of man. In its wake you will find many bodies, the organs removed. Read the signs and concentrate on the beckoning. You have many roads ahead of you, Omachiw. Trust the pull as it guides you."

Monias reached across and handed him an envelope. In it, Daniel correctly speculated, was a sum of money. "Spend this wisely. Live as a man who has but the clothes on his back."

Blackbird took the envelope and lowered his eyes.

"You are done, Daniel Blackbird. Leave us now," Toomey said.

Daniel had not expected to be turned out this way. The sudden finality was akin to the death of his grandfather, in that he could not argue or undue his misfortune. He sighed—but minutely, so it would not draw criticism. He stowed the items they had given him, lifted the knapsack, and exited the shelter.

Toomey watched the young man go as the others spoke amongst themselves. He had known this young man and his cousin, Johnny Proudfoot, their entire lives. He took no satisfaction in banishing him, but as Chief Elder, he had a duty to his people.

Watch over him, Nekoneet. Protect him with your wisdom, he thought sadly.

The hunt was on.

***

Chapter 1 - Rituals and Intersections

1

Chicago, Illinois

October 2001

Roosted on a building high above the city's red-light district, a group of pigeons congregated, trying to ward off the autumn cold. The ledge where they gathered was spattered with droppings that wafted the vile stench of ammonia. Below, the cityscape was filled with the noisy activity of cars and people moving along the gridwork of streets, illuminated by the fluorescent glow of night lighting. In the distance, adding to the chorus of sound, an ambulance siren cried out.

Not far from where the pigeons huddled together, a lone raven stared obsessively down upon the nightlife. But this was no typical raven. It was not a parasite content to pick over the remains of the dead, but a predator always hungry, always stalking. It was a magnificent creature, with a wingspan that spread four feet across. It was slightly ragged looking, its feathers unkempt, and it had eyes that were as cold and silver as steel ball bearings. The streets below reflected in those shiny globes as it scanned the panorama for new prey.

The pigeons cowered. They saw through the chameleon cloak, right into the grotesque and macabre thing it truly was. They saw the embryonic monster pulsing beneath the black feathers and skin, felt the spiral of madness pulsing from it in waves.

Must eat! So hungry! So very hungry!

It cast a fleeting glimpse their way, and they squawked huddling together even tighter; though they had nothing to fear, because the creature's appetite could not be sated by the meat on their scrawny bodies. It smelled the air hungrily, tasting it – and a scent caught in its nasal cavities. The giant bird spread its wings and took flight, descending from the ledge, down towards the ignorance of its prey.

2

Kerry McNeil had been on the street for five years now. She left home at the age of fifteen. Nobody wanted to hire a teenager in the city, so turning tricks became the only alternative. Now, at twenty years old she was what many would call a seasoned sex trade worker; a streetwise working girl who knew how to handle herself – although she had come by this wisdom as most people in her profession: the hard way.

Before turning 16, she had been beaten up and raped twice. As a result, she kept a fresh supply of condoms in her purse and a four-inch blade in her boot. Both used as weapons against HIV and the occasional bully. Some 'Johns' would insist on having sex without a condom, and this almost always led to confrontation. In one incident a guy grabbed her by the hair after she had argued with him. He changed his tune when she pressed the blade from her boot against his inner thigh, only a few inches from his scrotum.

"Understand me, asshole," she whispered. "I know what it's like to get beat up and I will cut off your balls before I let you do that."

He relented and left without much of fuss.

Her other life seemed a thousand years ago. The abusive drunk that had been her father was fading from her memories. But the ghost of those memories would always linger that memory as a reminder that this life was better than the one she had left behind.

Gay prostitutes and transsexuals worked the east side of 22nd and the straight girls worked the west side. You didn't dare step into somebody else's territory. This was something Kerry found out in her first month as a working girl. She wandered onto the wrong corner and got slapped around by a tranny named Carla. Carla – Carl in her former life – could have easily given Kerry's father a run for his money.

Kerry stood alone. It was cold, and she wanted to get off the street. Goose pimples rose on her legs: despite the autumn air, she stood kitted out in a black leather miniskirt and matching boots.

Soon she would have to resort to jeans. Something she didn't look forward to. Blue jeans didn't draw as much attention as a miniskirt, and as a result, business would suffer.

Cars approached, slowed, and then moved on. Many of them were just onlookers, getting a cheap thrill at her expense. Drunken college kids out for a Saturday night or married men trying to work up the nerve to cheat. So far, she'd only turned one trick tonight, blowing a guy in his car for $30. That wasn't enough. She needed to turn at least two more tricks tonight so she could eat and put a bit away for the rent.

Another car slowed, and she walked out toward it putting on her best smile – but as she got closer, it sped off. "Fuckers," she cussed. The cold pinched at her legs. "Fuck it." If there was no action in the next hour, she would pack it in for the night and work twice as hard tomorrow.

So she stood back and continued to wait. And as she did, what she did not realize was that she was being watched.

3

Detective Sean Woodman sat sipping coffee inside the surveillance van while watching the suspect. The suspect was a native man, a little taller than six feet, sporting a braided ponytail which ran down the length of his back. He looked to be approximately twenty-six years old.

"What's our mystery man doing tonight?"

Woodman's partner, Brad Rosedale, was just sitting down beside him with a fresh cup of coffee.

"He likes to watch," Woodman remarked. "Beyond that, not too much." He adjusted the video camera and zoomed in a bit.

"Three days I haven't seen him proposition one girl."

"He's just working up his nerve," Rosedale said.

"At this rate, the guy is going to be a virgin for life," he said and took a sip of his coffee. Just then, their suspect began to walk towards one of the girls. Woodman lowered his coffee, leaned forward in his chair. "Hello, looks like cold feet just got his nerve."

4

She was ready to give up when a friendly male voice spoke up from behind her.

"Hello," he greeted, "how are you doing this evening?"

A tall man stood on the sidewalk to her left. He was dressed all in black. Like that old Country singer, Johnny Cash, but this guy was an Indian, not a cowboy.

"Better now," she replied, a smile forming on her face as she sized him up. He wasn't a bit like what she was used to – he was good-looking, for a start. Most of the guys who frequented the red-light district had some kind of baggage. Fat, ugly, shy, mother issues – so the odd good looking 'John' was definitely a red flag. Good looking guys had issues; odds were that a 'Looker' was either an abusive asshole or a cop.

"What's your name, sweetheart?"

"Franklin. And you?" The tone of his voice had an air of sexuality in it that she couldn't quite explain, but it turned her on.

"Kerry." She drew her fingers across her breast provocatively. God, he's charming! She almost felt hypnotized by his gaze.

"Chilly evening Kerry." His eyes moved over her from top to bottom, a shameless smile across his lips. He had a soft accent which she could not place, and it was clear that English was not his mother tongue.

"Too chilly to be outdoors, Franklin." She looked behind him. "I didn't see your car."

"I don't have a car. I'm here on business." His smile broadened. A sudden uneasy shiver pulsed up and down her spine.

This guy is a cop. He could have any girl he wants at a club. He's too charming, too good-looking. *Walk away, Kerry. Don't take the bait.*

"My hotel is a block from here. Would you like to come with me?" he asked. Before she could answer, he continued, "I know what you're thinking, Kerry."

Yeah, I'm thinking all sorts of things: that you're a cop. A women beater. Or maybe even a biter. You have no idea what I'm thinking, Franklin.

Though her mind argued, her mouth invited. "Oh really? What am I thinking, Franklin?"

"Well, you think I'm with the police, that this is some kind of set up," He picked a bit of lint off his black shirt. "But you're wrong."

This was a new approach, she thought, and said, "Well, a girl can't be too careful, Franklin. Maybe you could show me some I.D.?"

"I don't carry a wallet on me. Too dangerous – especially when I'm talking working girls."

Fuck this! I'm not spending the night in jail or the emergency room! She turned and began to walk away without saying a word.

"Wait," he called after her. "I have an idea."

She spun around, her expression solemn, her mind screaming, *Don't be an idiot! It's a trap! Fuck, Kerry, what are you doing?*

He pulled out a wad of green notes and removed a 100 dollar bill. Kerry's eyes froze upon it, transfixed. "This is a gift, Kerry," he said, handing her the bill. "I am not paying you for any services. I am just giving you a gift."

Maybe he's an eccentric rich guy who likes getting down with the whores on Saturday night. She reached out and took the bill from him. *Yeah! Sure! I'm a goddamned no-brain idiot.*

"Now, here is what I am proposing. I am going to give you another gift when we get back to my hotel room. You are not obligated to do anything but come back with me and talk. I find you very attractive, Kerry, but where our friendship goes from there is up to you. We can talk, and if it goes beyond that, it will because it was what two consenting adults wanted. There is no financial transaction attached to it. Therefore no crime has been committed, and no chance of arrest."

She'd already tucked the hundred away.

Are you a bad guy, Franklin? Will you hurt me?

If she went with this guy and he decided to give her more money she could sock a bit away for a rainy day. She still felt uneasy, but it was cold, and it was only going to get colder. *Maybe he'll give me four hundred instead of two. Screw it!*

"Okay, Franklin. Let's go to your hotel and get to know each other." She reached out her hand, muting her internal voice of reason as she did. Maybe he's okay. There came no response: just indifferent silence. She was on her own. The voice of reason would be back later to gloat if this all went terribly wrong.

"I'm glad you saw it my way," he said taking her hand in his. It felt smooth and cold, devoid of lines or callous, almost like plastic.

Then he suddenly released her and began to walk away, leaving her to chase after him and the money. As he walked something small flapped about on the back his shirt, just below where his long hair swept across his shoulder blades.

When Kerry caught up with him, she snatched it up and showed him the tiny black feather. "What's this, Franklin?" she asked. "You're not into kink, are you?"

He plucked the feather out of her hand and for a moment she thought she saw something flicker on his face. Or was it his eyes? But an instant later it was gone, and that seductive smile returned. He tickled her chin with the feather. "That, sweet Kerry, is yet to be seen." Then he tossed it, retaking her hand and leading her down the street.

As they walked away, the small feather danced in the autumn breeze back and forth, back and forth, drifting gently down as it fought gravity. At last, it fluttered down, settled in the gutter next to a condom wrapper and Popsicle stick. Then it began to crystallize, tiny diamonds of frost sprouting across it. By the time they were 15 feet away, it had become hard, frozen, and too cold for human touch.

5

If Daniel Blackbird were a man to complain, he most certainly would grumble about his feet, because they ached horribly. But he muttered not. He had not been raised a complainer. He was not a full blood Chocktee like his mother or grandfather and bore the brunt of judgment from not only the prejudices of white men but his own people. In any other circumstance, he may have become bitter and weak, but his grandfather would have none of that.

You must always be strong, Daniel. Never take umbrage with the shortcomings of others. Instead, draw strength and show them that you are unaffected by the blindness of their judgment," his grandfather counseled.

That was a voice from another time. When his grandfather was alive. When he had been welcome: not cast out by the Chocktee or spirit woods. He had disgraced himself and carried with him a burden no man would want to carry.

Focus. He's here somewhere. Stop mucking around and figure out where Skin is, before he smells you and runs again, he scolded himself and tried to concentrate on the tug that had brought him to the city.

6

Woodman lifted out of his seat. "Where did he go?"

Rosedale leaned in and scanned the monitor. "Christ, he was just there a minute ago."

Woodman's heart began to pound in his chest. "Where the fuck is he, Brad?"

"I don't know. He just vanished, like smoke."

"Fuck!" Woodman picked up the radio. "All units, this is Team Leader. We have lost contact with the subject, report status."

The reports came in. "Team Alpha no visual. Team Bravo no visual."

Woodman got up and put on his coat, adjusted his shoulder holster, then zipped up. His face broadcasted panic, his words were jittery. "Jesus Christ! Alert them I will be doing a walk by."

"All Units, be advised that Team Leader is doing a walk by."

Rosedale scanned the street anxiously. If the subject was their man and they lost him there could be dire repercussions, especially if he killed someone.

"Let's hope we can un-fuck this, Brad," Woodman said. He opened the door and stepped out of the van.

Carefully, he stepped out onto the sidewalk, first looking left, then right. The crisp night air cooled the hot panic he felt by a fraction. Stay calm. He's only been out of sight for a few minutes. Besides, he might just be a Looky Lou, anyway.

But he doubted his own reassurances: he was pretty sure this was their guy.

7

Kerry and Franklin turned the corner down an alley between a warehouse store and an apartment building. "It's a shortcut," Franklin insisted, but halfway down he stopped. There on the ground, he saw what he needed. This place would suit his needs fine.

"Come on, Franklin, I'm freezing. Let's get to your hotel." Kerry tried in vain to pull the miniskirt down over her legs. Goosebumps prickled up between her thighs.

He turned and caught her eyes in his hypnotic gaze. It disarmed her: suddenly she felt calm and disconnected; as if she had just smoked some premium weed.

"It's not cold, Kerry. It's actually quite warm," his voice soothed.

Yes, it is warmer.

She could feel him holding her there using some strange telepathic anesthetic to control her. Yet she was strangely at ease—and aroused. She was being seduced, as a vampire might lull its victim or a leech will inject numbing chemicals into its prey, readying itself to feed. He's feeling me; touching me inside.

"It feels good, doesn't it, sweet Kerry?" he asked, as he had so many times before.

"Yes." There was a slur to her speech: minute, but there nonetheless. "Please don't stop."

"I wouldn't think of stopping."

He began to change physically. His copper skin washed out, becoming grey and translucent. His eyes fell back in his head, growing and warping until they were steel balls, while his nose melted into the flat alien landscape of his face. His dark grey lips now exposed the tombstones protruding from his – its – grey rotted gums as the cloak he wore melted away.

A witness would have turned, run in terror. This creature was a man, but not a man: grey, without a nose, and three talons on each hand for fingers. Its eyes glowed fiery white in the darkness of the alley.

Kerry could not see the physical change; she only felt the immense loss of control as it anesthetized her. She could not feel its talons wrap around the nape of her neck.

Then it began cutting off its anesthesia and bringing her back, and she came down at an incredible rate. She was unaware that it was holding her in its clutches. Her eyes still closed, she tried very hard to hang onto the high that enveloped her – but reality loomed.

"Open your eyes, Kerry," it urged her.

I don't want to. I want to stay here. But she sensed something was wrong.

It needed her fear to sate its appetite. "Open your eyes."

She tried to fight it, but couldn't: the calm tide was receding. She heard a hollow whistle of labored breath and smelled a stench she could only compare to rotten meat or garbage.

Please let me stay; feels so good.

"Open your eyes. Open them now." The words came from inside of her somewhere, pushing.

At first, she saw a reflection of herself in the chromium spheres set before her, and then her most vivid nightmare came to life.

"Hello, sweetheart," her father, Rodney McNeil, laughed.

She tried to pull away, unable to scream, but he held her in a death grip. "You're not going to make Daddy pay, are you?"

He grinned layers of jagged teeth set neatly within black infected gums. Terror cut through her, and before she could cry out, he unscrewed her head. There were crunching sounds as bone and ligament cracked and tore, but she was sure it could not be her. Then it elevated her up, and she felt weightless, her body numb. In the millisecond it took for Kerry to compute that her head had been removed, her world went black as the synapses in her brain fired their last electrical pulses.

Her head thudded on the dirty concrete, bits of grit embedding in her cooling cheek, the last bit of blood expelling from her lifeless brainstem mixing with oils and grime. Then the monster lifted her torso, opened her belly with its razor toe, and began to feed.

8

Blackbird was a block away when the Walker he tracked pulled Kerry McNeil's head off. He knew he was close, but he had no idea just how close – all he could feel was it pulling him down the street, calling to him. The scar on his face tingled. His body pulled westward, like a magnet.

9

Louise Weatherton would never forget what had drawn her to the window of her third-floor apartment that night. It was a grating sound. A sound everyone knows but hardly gives a second thought. The sound was that of a heavy manhole cover being dragged across pavement. She might never have heard it except for the fact that the low-income apartment she rented had no air conditioning. The night air might have been cooler outside, but the 10-story apartment building was a humid chamber, heat retained within its brickwork and hollow cavities.

She was just finishing up the dishes when she heard the noise.

It's a little late for city workers.

She looked toward the window, folding the tea towel she'd been using, and laid it on the countertop. At that moment she was about to go into the living room and watch Jeopardy. Then she heard it again.

Louise was a nosy woman in her mid-forties. She did not deny this fact, nor did she feel ashamed. She had little to do but inject herself into the lives of others. Which, much to the chagrin of her neighbors, she did often.

She opened the curtains on the kitchen window as carefully as possible – because, like most voyeurs, she did not want to be spotted watching.

When she peered down into the alley, she suddenly lost her ability to breathe. Somebody had removed a manhole cover, but it wasn't the Department of Works.

Am I really seeing this? Is this real?

She reached blindly for the phone, which was just out of reach, unable to tear her eyes away from what she was witnessing. In the alley below, a creature that could only be described as a monster held before it a disemboweled and headless body. The beast stood about seven feet tall, skin grey, rotten. It was bald and had long arms with claws for fingers on each hand. Its face was smooth, and its eyes glowed. Its blood-smeared mouth opened and closed as it fed, revealing two rows of top and bottom teeth. It reminded her of the things from the movie 'Alien' – except this thing was uglier.

She fumbled for the phone and somehow managed to grab it. She mashed 911 into the keypad without looking.

"911. What is your emergency?" the voice on the other end of the phone asked.

In any other situation, her response would have been comedic – but the monster heard the operator and turned its fiery gaze upon the window.

Louise let out a shrill high-pitched scream.

http://wbp.bz/equinoxa

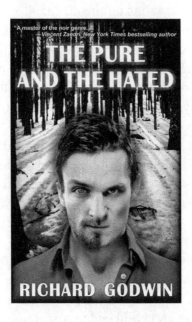
1.

Marigold and Joyce lived in the house by the red barn that passing tourists used to photograph. They came to that part of Vermont for the skiing. They'd hit the slopes, fill the restaurants, and leave with their memories. I envy them now. I wish I could exchange my memories for those of another man. I have no vacations left inside me.

The drive I took from Stowe to visit my nieces once made my heart ache with its beauty, but in the end that gentle road leading into the mountains felt like a scar. I used to help Marigold and Joyce with their reading when they were little. My sister, Holly, did so much for them. Their father, Dwight Fisher, had run off years ago, no one knew where, leaving her alone. That was before they were born. He returned off and on; he had a knack for doing that. He spent a few years with my sister, watched her get pregnant and neglected her. Then he vanished for good one summer's day, leaving her to bring her daughters up on her own. She never spoke of him, but reverted to the family name of Butler.

Having lost my own son, Felton, to a hunting accident, I came to feel Marigold and Joyce were like two daughters to me. My wife, Mary, never recovered from Felton's death. She said the loss of a child ended something inside her. Her maternal care seemed to wither. The kitchen was full of dead flowers for many months after his loss. She liked Marigold and Joyce but rarely visited them. And it seemed to me that I was pouring all my paternal instincts into the two girls, wanting to protect them when I had been unable to save my own son's life. The fool is protected by his folly. I never envisaged the cruelty that life held in its card-dealing hands. I never saw what was to come. Perhaps that is why I became the man I am, a barely recognisable sum of memories that have altered my image and bruised my heart. I wish I could erase them, but they feed on me. The deepest bruise of all dwells like a swollen rose inside me, reminding me of that time with its thorns, that wounding time that violated us all.

Everything changed in those years, apart from the landscape. Its beauty in the fall still stops my breath; the green mountains of Vermont and shades of shifting colour overwhelm me. The vistas of clear brooks and streams. The hills flowing into mountains tell me that the earth is wiser than us.

My sister and nieces lived outside Stowe, beneath Mount Mansfield that always seemed to be sleeping, waiting for snow. I sometimes think it watched the events as they unfolded. The countryside there has a purity to it that is endlessly consoling. And to a certain kind of man that purity may aggravate his own sense of corruption, engendering thoughts of defilement.

The tourists came and went, brought money and took away stories and snapshots. They faded like invisible ink. But there was one man who passed through and left something ineradicable behind in those violated years. He passed through all right. He did so like a scythe that cut all certainty from my life and left me with thoughts that were alien to my soul. Temple Jones. There was no way of knowing him or predicting what he would do.

I remember something Mary said to me about him, 'Shepherd Butler, sometimes you just can't know a man; some men keep things too well hidden.'

And what Temple Jones did to Mary was nothing compared to what he went on to do. He stole my understanding of the world and handed me back a reality that lacks all consolation. I crave the solace of purity and find only hatred. And I know that innocence is an affront to some men.

Even the well outside the window seems corrupted by the memory of him sitting there, his face reflected in the window pane. But I have other memories. I try to reach back to a time when I didn't know him and the world seemed good. I remember the sandstone well many years ago one sunlit morning in the early years of my marriage. It glowed like honeycomb and beneath me Mary's face was full of a fertile joy I have never known another woman to have. She tasted of mountain streams as I kissed her mouth, and I lived in a world of certainty as she took me inside her on the wet grass.

I am sure that was the day Felton was conceived, there beneath the well in the quiet privacy of our Vermont garden. My fingers smelt of wild columbine and sweetgrass, and Mary was mine, as was the future in all its broken knowledge. My wife had the purest skin, there was not a scar on her body, and as I touched her I was conscious my hands had been rooting in the soil, as if I was unfit for her body and all it would allow. But she yielded to me and gave me things I would never have dared ask from her. There was no restraint or inhibition in her touch, which gave permission to my desire. The marks she carries now can't be seen. Her sapphire blue eyes that once would search my face have faded, and while I inhabit the same house as her I have to reach into the past to feel her reality.

Her alabaster skin, her mouth, her erotic lips parted as I entered her on the pure earth, her full breasts and strong thighs, exist in a moment that has been removed from me, as she has been stolen from herself. I feel the ache of an amputated limb and want to dwell inside her again, but robbers have invaded our home and carried us away.

I am unmanned by events beyond my control and seek the feminine to prove myself again. I have become the castrated father of the tribe, my children are butchered, my possessions looted. That is the purpose that hatred serves. But I will not yield to that poisoned Bible. There was a time before corruption. I seek to separate the past from the wounds he inflicted. His deeds invaded us like a virus, replicating their own hatred inside us, taking away the things we once believed in. And while I can still see myself making love to Mary that day, I can also smell the fresh grass and see the columbine's spurs and feel the ones that Temple Jones wore cutting into my sides, as if he was on my back without my knowing, all along, even then.

2.

Late fall. Vermont a swathe of colour, scarlet and gold shimmering in the hills, banks of red leaves bleeding at the edges. Unearthly light. I was standing in the kitchen with Mary, finishing a cup of coffee and about to leave to visit Holly and the girls. Mary was dressed in a white blouse buttoned to the top. It complimented the beauty of her slender neck with its well-defined muscles. I see myself kiss the vein that runs across it. I feel it throb against my lips when we make love.

'Fall used to be my favourite season, Shepherd,' she said. 'But now all it does is remind me of Felton's death.'

'Do you want to come with me today?'

'I'm best on my own.'

'They'd love to see you.'

'Would they?'

I looked into her sky blue eyes, but they were wandering away from me. She gazed into the distance, at the mountains. Her hazelnut hair shone with light. I wanted to touch it.

'He knew you were proud of him,' I said.

'Did I tell him enough? Did I hold back my love in the name of duty as a parent?'

'You've never held anything back.'

'The beauty outside my window is too hard to bear. I don't want to see how unchanged it all is, how it keeps to its own aesthetic.'

I didn't understand what she meant, but I was to find out. My words fell like fake money from my mouth.

'Mary, I wanted the world to stop when he was shot. I felt as though tomorrow was a lie. We train ourselves to think of the future of our offspring, most of what we do as parents is a way of investing in that, and we never expect them to be taken from us. Part of the future goes with them. I know you didn't like him to hunt, but nothing would have persuaded him it was wrong.'

'I see them bringing back the deer on their cars, and it all seems so trivial to me now, my principles about killing animals. I wonder whether it was something else I was feeling when I tried to stop him from doing it, as if behind my views lay an unease, a sense he might come to harm out there.'

'You had the same principles at college.'

'Go on your own, Shepherd, send them my love. I'm not good company. I'm locked inside that fall two years ago. Do you remember us walking up Mount Mansfield, your hand in mine and Felton walking before us? I look at myself now, and I'm someone else.'

That ravaged morning I wanted to make love to my wife. As I kissed her good-bye I felt her desolation. Felton's death was lodged like a fish hook inside us.

I drove to Holly's, out of Stowe and its neat line of houses, and up the mountain road into the dying leaves and my shallow dreams of family life. As I pulled up I glanced at my face in the rearview mirror. I thought I could see someone else lurking behind my eyes, laughing at me. I stepped out of my pickup into the cold and felt like someone had punched a block of ice into my lungs.

Holly saw me walking up and opened the door.

'I got some fresh coffee on,' she said.

'Then I better help you drink it.'

Her house smelled of freshly baked bread. Holly kept it immaculate. It instilled a sense of ambiguity in me. It was a home, something I once knew, and inasmuch as that comforted me, it also tormented me with my loss.

Marigold and Joyce were sitting in the living room. They got up when they saw me walk in.

Marigold offered me her cheek.

'Hello, Uncle Shepherd.'

'We going out today?' Joyce said, standing on tiptoe so I could reach hers.

'If you want to.'

'Mom wants to go shopping,' Marigold said.

'Well let's talk to her about it. Now where's this coffee?'

Holly poured me a cup as my nieces chattered to each other. Marigold was nineteen and Joyce seventeen, and they both had a freshness to their looks that made them seem out of place it the modern world. They'd inherited Holly's beauty, but Marigold had darker eyes than her mother and Joyce a rosiness to her complexion that made me think of apples at harvest time. My sister was a dark blonde with deep brown eyes. Both Marigold and Joyce resembled her, having her small and delicate nose. But Marigold had black hair, while Joyce was a brunette with blue eyes she'd inherited from her father, who was a handsome man. I'd always suspected that Dwight Fisher had run off with another woman. Rumours had circulated about his behaviour when he disappeared, and I tried to keep them from my sister's ears. I'm not sure how much she heard, but I think gossip is harmful.

My own resemblance to Holly was a comfort to me. I looked at her and thought how we had the same colour eyes. Since Felton's death I felt as though I'd lost my family. Mary's isolation added to that. My grief was briefly lifted on those visits to Holly. But I wasn't the man I used to be, and I felt like an outsider. The tragedy had turned me grey, and I'd often look at my face in the bathroom mirror on rising as if I was staring at a stranger and think my beard was the colour of ash. I seemed without colour, grizzled, as if some part of me had been erased. And I took solace in the hues of the countryside and in my nieces.

For a while at times with the death of my son I felt my world had turned to ash. I took warmth from my nieces and stepped outside the black and white film I lived in at home when I visited them. They allowed me to think of the future.

As I looked at them I thought how these young women would have families and children in a few years, and I felt my loss tug at my heart. I dislodged the pain with a preoccupation I'd developed in the past year. I'd begun to feel responsible for my nieces, and I wondered how they would be employed when they were older.

I owned a hardware store in Stowe, and although I worked fewer hours in those days, and let my staff make decisions a few years ago I wouldn't have felt comfortable delegating, I worked as much as my grief would allow. Marigold had got good grades at school and was studying biology at the University of Vermont. She wanted to become a vet. Joyce had done less well and was looking for work. I'd just lost a member of staff at the shop, and I thought about offering Joyce the vacancy.

'How's the job search going?' I said.

Holly grinned.

'You mean you haven't told him, Joyce?' she said.

'Mom.'

'She's got a job.'

'Working in the Peoples' Bank, thanks to my math grades,' Joyce said. 'At least I was good at one subject at school.

'That's not true, Jo, you were good at science,' Marigold said.

'Not as good as you.'

'Will you two stop it?' Holly said. 'I'm just delighted she's got work, and at a bank, don't you think, Shepherd?'

'That's great news, Joyce.'

That afternoon we went into Stowe, and I helped Holly shop at Shaw's. We bought fresh lobster and chicken, and she stocked up on cans of vegetables and pasta.

'My car will be out of the shop in two days,' she said as we loaded my pickup with the bags.

'In the meantime if you need me to run you anywhere.'

'Thanks, Shepherd. How about coming back and sharing some of the chicken with us?'

'Sounds too good to resist.'

Back at her house, Holly chopped the chicken up and cooked it in a tomato sauce as I talked to the girls. We had it steaming hot with winter squash. As I ate I felt redundant as an uncle in a way I couldn't define.

I left after lunch and stopped on my way home to walk in Mount Mansfield State Forest. My visit had left me feeling unsettled, and I wanted to find out why. I began to wonder whether I secretly resented Holly the children she still had. And I thought of Mary alone, at home. I walked without looking where I was going. The woods felt like a womb.

As I entered a clearing I saw a man in threadbare clothes sitting on a log. He looked like some forest dweller who lives on berries and plants and is wild.

I'd wandered quite far in before I spotted him and was overcome by a sense of intrusion. He seemed to be hiding. Beside him was a fire and the burnt out remains of food. I could smell recently cooked meat.

I was about to turn away to leave him to his solitude when he raised a hand in greeting. I walked towards him.

There was a moment before I spoke when I felt this young man had some wisdom that I sought, as if my trip into the forest had a purpose beyond my desire to dispel my troubled thoughts. He had unkempt hair and fair features, a handsome face beneath the beard, but there was something about his looks that echoed in me in a sympathetic way and made me feel my walk into the forest had found its purpose in another human being.

'I didn't mean to intrude on you,' I said.

He stood up, wiped his hand on his faded corduroys, and extended it warmly.

'If I had any turkey left I'd offer you some. I'm not a bad cook.'

'Wild turkey?'

He smiled. It was a warm smile that lacked all guile, and I instantly warmed to him.

'I didn't buy it from a store.'

'Are you living out here?'

'I am, Sir.'

He said it with pride, pulling his shoulders back as he did. I looked beyond him to the reds and golds in the trees.

'It will be hard for you in a few weeks; winter's coming on.'

'I'll make do; I've lived outside in seven feet of snow before. No need to worry about me.'

'Food will be scarce.'

'I know where to find it, and as I say, I cook well, that's what I was trained to do.'

'You're a chef?'

'I am, Sir. I worked in some of the finest restaurants in New England, worked out on Cape Cod. I make the best sauces, and now I rustle up some meat and plants. Say, why don't you come back and visit me, and I'll let you sample what I'm talking about? Nothing better than fresh food caught outdoors.'

'I can't argue with that.'

I recalled the many barbecues I'd made and the fresh game Mary and I used to take on our walks with Felton.

'I know these woods well. I walk here often,' I said. 'You must feel solitary.'

http://wbp.bz/tpathreviews